HEARTMAN

HEARTMAN

M.P. Wright

BLACK & WHITE PUBLISHING

First published 2014
by Black & White Publishing Ltd
29 Ocean Drive, Edinburgh EH6 6JL

1 3 5 7 9 10 8 6 4 2   14 15 16

ISBN: 978 1 84502 775 9

CREATIVE SCOTLAND

ALBA | CHRUTHACHAIL

A CIP catalogue record for this book is available from the British Library.

Typeset by Iolaire Typesetting, Newtonmore
Printed and bound by Grafica Veneta S.p.A.

Dedicated to Jen, Enya and Neve
with all my heartfelt love and thanks

PROLOGUE

No one's as dear, as baby to me
wee little fingers, eyes wide and bright
now sound asleep, until morning light . . .

THE MUSCULAR MAN WHO stank of three-day-old sweat and stale booze led her by the hand, blindfolded and barefoot, down the twelve cold, flaking sandstone steps, which she slowly counted in her head one by one until she reached solid ground again. Her head felt light, her limbs weak, and she struggled to remain upright, fighting the overpowering drowsiness that had enveloped her body. It was only when she felt the man's large thumb lift her chin ever so slightly that she was brought back from the drug-induced limbo that had subdued her. His touch had reawakened her: back to the fear, a return to the terror.

It was earlier that evening when her introduction to the heavyset white man had been made while she stood in the crowded room amongst the many drunken party revellers. Shortly afterwards she had been escorted outside and into the back seat of a large, expensive-looking silver car. The man had got in beside her and caressed the side of her cheek with his pale, thick knuckles before tying a crimson silk scarf across her eyes. This was when the fear had taken hold of her, deep into the pit of her stomach. She had panicked and pushed herself forward, her right hand reaching out towards the car door handle, but her futile attempt to escape was suppressed by the man's strength as his forearm slammed her back and a

1

seatbelt was drawn tightly across her chest. This had been the point that mind, body and spirit had given way to the narcotic flowing through her body.

The car had pulled away slowly and she had begun to feel a strange, serene sense of calmness enter her being; the drug that had been slipped into her drink earlier that evening was now beginning to take the edge off of the unknown horror she had become immersed in and it had begun to dampen her ability to think coherently. Slumped back and cushioned by the plush leather upholstery, the man had rested her hand in the flat of his palm and he rhythmically stroked the back of it with icy fingers, which had increased the calmness inside her and her need to sleep. As the effects of the drug took a greater hold upon her, she had calmed, no longer able to resist, with no wish to fight.

It was then that the nightmare had receded from her subconscious and a gentle feeling of being rocked to sleep had falsely offered her the solace of safety and comfort as she dreamt of gently swaying to and fro in her mother's arms, just as she had done in the hospital after she had contracted rubella as a child. The high fever and inflammation around her brain had burnt through her tiny body and had ultimately taken her hearing from her. But it was her subsequent muteness, which developed during the months of distressing recovery, that had caused her the greatest agony: unable to speak, to laugh, to . . .

A violent slap from her captor across her left cheek had brought her from the warm, protective embrace of her mother back into the land of the living again. Her brain felt as if it was being knocked from side to side in her skull as bright red, blue and green spots flashed and jumped in front of her eyes behind the blindfold. Her knees began to buckle, but the muscular man gripped at her upper arm. The pressure of the tight hold he had applied to stop her falling to the floor sent a shockwave of pain throughout her upper body and reaffirmed the harsh reality of her situation.

A musty, damp odour clung to the insides of her nostrils as the man took her firmly by the wrist and guided her across the chilly floor before bringing her to a sudden halt, spinning her around on her heels and then slowly pushing her backwards until the cold burn of stone seeped through her cotton dress and chilled the skin across her buttocks. The man pushed her back, down onto a thick marble slab. He tied her wrists firmly on either side with thick rope through a pair of iron loops that had been fixed into the top of each corner of the stone plinth. The drug flowing through her bloodstream continued to subdue her natural instinct to struggle free from her enforced bondage, and she returned briefly to the heavy-eyed dream state that had previously cushioned her from the ongoing nightmarish reality that cruelly kept dragging her back to consciousness.

She wanted to call out, to scream for help . . . the unfairness of her muteness prevented that. She felt the buttons on the front of her dress fly from their stitching as the fabric was torn open, exposing her young, soft ebony skin. Her bra was cut at its straps and pulled away from her breasts. Then the man's cool hands ran up each of her outer thighs until he reached her stomach. He looped both his thumbs behind the elasticated hem at the top of her panties, drew his hands apart slightly so that they were in line with her hips and in a single vicious downward motion dragged her underwear down her legs to her ankles before yanking them off her feet.

Petrified, she lashed out with her legs into the darkness, connecting with nothing. Now alone and unable to see, hear or cry for help, she withdrew to a place deep within herself where she hoped she would be safe, protected from what was about to happen. Her tears flowed and were absorbed into the silk scarf that was still tied around her eyes and in her head she sang to herself. The same song that her mother had sung to her as a toddler all those years before, when she was frightened, when she needed to feel safe . . .

"Rock-a-bye baby, on the treetop; when the wind blows, the cradle will rock; when the bough breaks, the cradle will fall; and down will come baby, cradle and all."

The big man turned and watched as a semicircle of men walked silently out of the shadows of the cellar, all dressed in crisp black dinner suits, their faces covered by Venetian masquerade half-masks, their presence in the semi-darkness picked out by the large cream church altar candles that were housed in the small dug-out recesses of the white alabaster walls. They began to move closer towards her semi-naked body, some with arms already outstretched, their fingers eager to explore her exotically coloured flesh.

The woman's captor backed away into the shadows, returning up the sandstone steps, leaving her to an unknown fate. He tried not to think about her again, and when he got to the top, he loosened his tie and took in a deep breath of the icy night air to try to clear his head as he stood at the entrance of the cellar. He reached for the huge brass handle of the old oak door and closed it quietly, resting his forehead against one of the panels as he did so. He turned around and looked up at the clear, star-filled sky, then pulled a half-bottle of Scotch from his jacket pocket, unscrewed the cap and knocked back a hefty swig of the burning spirit before making his way across the snowy lawn towards his car, the bottle hanging from his shaking hand, which slapped against the side of his leg as he walked. An unexpected, piercing scream from the depths of the underground vault followed him and echoed out into the bitter chill of the winter night.

4

1

THERE'S ONLY SO MUCH staring through the bottom of an empty glass a man can do when he's got less than one and ten in his back pocket. Not enough to get me another pint, that was for damn sure. I tipped out the remaining copper coins from my battered brown leather wallet on to the copy of the *Bristol Evening Post* that I had spent the last hour trawling through in a desperate attempt at finding myself a job. I'd bottomed out on that and was now looking to get drunk.

I was sat in the Star and Garter pub on the corner of Brook Road, in the St Pauls area of Bristol. I'd been in the bar for the better part of three hours nursing my drink and was in need of a refill. I'd rented myself a place nearby shortly after arriving in Britain and the Star had become my local, but I was hardly a regular and the chances of me putting anything on the slate weren't happening. I was outta work and broke.

Outside, the snow was three inches deep on the pavement. It was my first experience of an English winter and my fascination with the stuff had soon worn off. I'd no interest in trudging back to my pokey terraced digs to sit and freeze my ass off in front of a two-bar electric fire that I couldn't afford to put on.

I had nothing in to eat, apart from three tins of Libby's canned fruit in the larder and a half-bottle of milk that was stinking my kitchen out. The place was as bare and unwelcoming as when I'd first moved in there.

In the March of 1964 I'd sailed from Bridgetown, Barbados. It was a ten-day journey across the Atlantic to Southampton with the promise of work at Wills' tobacco company at the end of it. My uncle Gabe had worked there for over a decade and had pulled a few strings to help me out. I'd stuck it out for ten months before buss-mout'in' the foreman, Teddy Meeks, in the face after he'd accused me of thieving cigarettes. I didn't like him and I'm pretty sure he hated me. The allegations that I was a thief were untrue. I'd sucked up all his bullshit and jibes since I'd first been introduced to him by Walter Keats, the general manager, but it was the "nicking nigger" remark that had got me mean and he'd paid for it with a broken jaw.

Why, I don't know, but I'd gotten away with the assault without any criminal charges. The fact that I had known that Teddy had been loading up boxes of two hundred cartons of Strand cigarettes onto the backs of delivery vans that would then find themselves in the social clubs and pubs all over Bristol city at knock-down prices with a nice little cut going to Meeks may have had something to do with it. Or perhaps it was because he'd heard a little of my past and my time with the police back home.

Whatever his reasons, Meeks' own illegal activities would continue and he'd still no doubt be picking on some poor bastard back at the factory while I was scratching for the price of another pint.

Now, when I could afford to, I'd drink to forget the likes of men like Meeks, and a past that I had run from, a past that still had a grip on my soul and kept me awake at nights. I didn't hold out much hope for lady luck to change things and I wasn't the praying kind.

My mama had once told me, "Child, don't you be praying too hard fo' someting God don't want you to have."

But tonight God was about to perversely answer an unspoken prayer and my late mama's words would come back to haunt me from across the ocean in a way I'd never have thought possible.

"Buy you another one of those, son?"

Alderman Earl Linney stood over me, his hulking frame blocking out the glare of the gas lamp on the opposite wall. I'd seen Linney around giving the locals his warm-handshake routine and knew of his reputation as a successful businessman. It was rumoured that he had his fingers in just about every rich man's pocket in the city, and if he was just about to stick them into his own to get me another drink, hell, I wasn't about to say no.

"I'll take a pint o' Dragon Stout, thanks, man."

Linney, silent for a moment, stared down at my paper, his eyes quickly scanning the contents of the opened pages before returning his gaze towards me.

"Dragon it is then. I'll join you, if you don't mind?"

"Makes no difference to me, brother, but you'll find me pretty poor company."

He smiled at me again, paying little attention to the remark I had just made. He took off his expensive camel-hair coat and laid it across the back of the chair next to me and sat his brown leather briefcase at the foot of it before walking to the bar.

Earl Linney's rise within the city's business community had been as meteoric as it was successful. After being demobbed from the Royal Air Force at the end of the Second World War, he'd come over from Spanish Town, Jamaica, and settled in Britain, where he then moved to Bristol. After working in a number of engineering factories he had set up in business, manufacturing aircraft parts for the Bristol Aeroplane

Company at Filton. It had made him rich. He'd not rested on his laurels, and had carved himself a place in local politics and formed the West Indian Community Council. Speaking out against discrimination and with strong ties to the unions, he was known as a man of integrity and sat with the great and the good of the city, the washed and unwashed alike. He was an honorary Bristolian, made good from the colonies, so what the hell had dragged the alderman out on a freezing-cold Sunday night and why did he feel the need to be buying a stranger a drink? He'd picked on the wrong guy to engage in a bout of deep, meaningful conversation with, and for a moment I wondered if I looked that desperate for cash that the elderly Jamaican thought I was a batty boy and up for selling my body. If that was the case, then the old boy was soon gonna be losing some of his teeth and I'd probably be spending the night in a cold police cell.

Linney returned with the two pints of stout and sat opposite me on a short backless bar stool, sliding the glass of beer across the table, nodding towards the newspaper as he did so. "Any luck?"

"Oh yeah, man, I'm just full of luck at the minute."

I reached for the pint glass and sank half of it in three solid swigs; the strong, rich, treacly ale took the edge off my thirst and started warming my insides. It reminded me of home, sitting outside Barrington's bar on the quayside at Carlisle Bay, where I would drink after coming off of duty. I started to relax, but only a little.

"You put your hand to anything?" Linney asked me dryly.

I felt that creepy politician patter coming on. I let him carry on with it. There might be another drink to be had out of him later.

"I sure do need to. My damn landlord's about to kick

8

me outta my place on Friday, so I'm not in a position to be choosey. Bristol Bus ain't hiring either," I said, with some sarcasm and a little irony thrown in for good measure.

Back in the summer of 1963 the Bristol Omnibus Company, which had a policy that coloured workers should not be employed as drivers or bus crew, had not expected a twenty-six-year-old black man, Paul Stephenson, to challenge them on a decision that had been upheld since 1951. Stevenson had changed all that after instigating a sixty-day boycott of the buses. He'd been joined by many supporters, finally seeing the overturning of the policy in the August of that same year.

It had been a gallant stand, but their victory was fleeting and I felt little had changed for men like me. It wasn't uncommon to find signs taped to the windows and doors of public houses – "No Blacks, No Irish, No Dogs" – to remind us how unwelcome we were. Britain wasn't the land of milk and honey, I was damn sure of that, but at least we got top billing on their list of undesirables.

Earl Linney now sitting opposite me was the exception to their rules. He was a man of colour made good. He glanced back down again at my newspaper and spoke without raising his head from the page.

"I may be able to offer you something, Mr Ellington."

My surname tripped off the tip of his tongue as if he'd known me from birth.

"How the hell you know my name?" I asked the alderman suspiciously.

"A man in my position is advised to know certain people; let's just say I've been asking around and I'm aware of you and your background."

"What'd you know 'bout me and my background?"

"You've been in the country for just over ten months and

you were involved in an altercation with a colleague at your previous employers, which now finds you looking through the situations vacant. Clearly a tobacco warehouse wasn't your chosen profession. Let's just say your name came up in quiet conversation. It's your previous line of work that I'm interested in, and how you may be able to assist me."

"I ain't following you; there's only a handful of people knew I was with the police force before I came over here, most of them would cross the street to avoid me, so whoever you've been talking to, they sent you to the wrong guy."

"I'd be correct in thinking discretion was a quality much sought after in a police officer? It's discretion I'm looking for, Mr Ellington, discretion and the ability to ask questions in our own community without arousing the suspicions of the people you're asking."

I could see why Linney made a good politician: he smiled in all the right places and when you asked him a difficult question he gave you the answer you wanted to hear. Whether he was speaking the truth was another matter, but hell, that could've been said of all politicians, in my opinion.

"A man in my position needs people he can trust; those kinds of people are few and far between, so naturally I value my trusted staff greatly. It is a member of my personal staff who I have concerns over. Her name is Stella Hopkins. She's missing. We have not seen her at work nor has she returned home for the last ten days."

"Well, I'm truly sorry 'bout that, Mr Linney, but I don't see how I can help you or why you're telling me any of this. But hey man, I'm grateful fo' the beer; I sure as hell don't have the money to buy you one back."

"I don't want another drink, thank you, but I may be able to address your financial difficulties, should you wish to consider my proposal. I'd like you to look into Miss Hopkins' disappearance and to locate her current whereabouts. I'm sure a man with your talents, a discreet man such as yourself, could be useful when making inquiries for a third party."

"What if she don't want finding? Maybe your Stella's found some guy and is shacked up with him somewhere. Maybe she's happy an' in love and she ain't coming back. It happens."

Linney appeared to be visibly shocked by my remarks, as if I'd touched a raw nerve.

"Stella is . . ." Linney hesitated, searching for the right word. "Stella is vulnerable, Mr Ellington; she is a simple soul with a pure, God-fearing heart. If she had met a man I would have known of it; she was not comfortable around strangers, especially men."

"In what way is she vulnerable?" Despite my reservations, I thought I'd let him tell his tale a little longer.

"Some would say that Stella Hopkins is more child than woman. She is a mute and can barely read or write. She sees the world differently to you and me."

"Differently? How does Stella see tings differently?" I was starting to become intrigued by the Jamaican's description of this Hopkins girl.

"She sees the world in a very simple way, trusts very few. Mr Ellington, she's naive, gentle. It's those qualities that make me fear for her well-being. She's a young woman who could easily be taken advantage of."

"Why ain't I heard any of this in here?" My finger tapped down on the open pages of the *Bristol Evening Post* in front of me.

Linney reached over to the chair where he'd left his raincoat and fumbled in the inside pocket, pulling out a small newspaper cutting.

"This appeared on the bottom of page twelve of the *Post*, some four days ago. I contacted the editor, whom I know personally, and asked that he have his staff report on the matter. It should not surprise you to see that such a meagre amount of column space was allocated. Stella's disappearance, as you can see, does not make for interesting print."

I read the eleven lines of simple, factual prose.

> Police are investigating the disappearance of Miss Stella Hopkins, a 22-year-old Black Female, of Number 45 Thomas Street, Montpelier, Bristol, who has been missing since Thursday January 8th at around 5pm after leaving her employers at Bristol City Council. Miss Hopkins is of slim build and approximately 5 ft 4 in. in height with short dark hair. If anyone has any information regarding her whereabouts could they please contact Detective Inspector William Fletcher at Bridewell station on Bristol 4362.

"Did Stella live on her own, Mr Linney?"

Linney hesitated before answering. "Yes, she has done since the passing of her mother. I knew Stella's mother, Victoria, well; she died three years ago, cancer of the throat, quite tragic. Despite some obvious limitations, Stella coped admirably well living alone. We, that is, myself and my wife, Alice, provided the things that she was unable to do herself."

"What kinda tings?" I asked him bluntly, wanting to get him to cut to the chase.

"Well, our help, of course. Stella doesn't understand the value of money, so I pay the rent on her flat, we handle her bills. She's paid a salary, Mr Ellington, but she knows little of what to do with it. Alice will cook and she takes hot meals to Stella's flat every other day; otherwise, she's quite self-sufficient."

"You say she worked at the council offices fo' you: doing what exactly?"

"There was always something for Stella to do. She had certain duties, let's say, things that only she could do."

"Are you talking about her making tea and tidying your desk?"

"Absolutely not. I told you, she is a valued and trusted member of my staff."

I wasn't sold on what I'd been hearing. Something about it stank, and my guts told me to drink up and get the hell out. If Linney thought that his lost Little Orphan Annie tale was gonna tug at my heart strings for the price of a pint, he was mistaken. I knew I wasn't that cheap. Thing is, so did Earl Linney.

"I'm willing to pay for your discretion, Mr Ellington; I'm willing to pay you to ask the kind of questions a man in my position can't, without people . . ."

Again, he carefully considered his words before continuing.

"Without people wanting to know why I'm asking, shall we say."

"When you say people, by that you mean the police?"

Linney's round-the-houses way of answering my questions was beginning to grate on me, and my mentioning the police had unsettled him. He sat with a sour expression on his face, like a cat had just took a shit under his nose.

"All the usual methods of inquiry into the matter that concerns me have been unsuccessful; I have many contacts within Bristol City Constabulary, Mr Ellington, and they continue to question and search for Stella. All their conventional investigations appear to have failed. I could consult a private agency, but if the police cannot get people to come forward and talk, I doubt if a white detective could

13

either. It is the unconventional I'm seeking, hence the reason we are talking tonight."

Linney took a sip of his beer: he was weighing me up like a prizefighter before landing the knock-out blow, saving his best till last.

"I'd be willing to pay you five pounds a day, plus expenses, for your services."

He put his hand into the inside pocket of his jacket and pulled out a brown, wage-packet-sized envelope and dropped it onto the newspaper.

"That should get you started," he said with all the arrogant self-assurance of a man used to getting what he wanted.

I picked up the envelope and peeled it open. Inside, neatly folded, were ten crisp five-pound notes and a small black and white photograph of Stella Hopkins.

Linney got up from the stool and reached for his raincoat, pulling it over his large arms and tugging at the lapels to bring it into shape across his chest, then buttoning it. He picked his briefcase up from the floor, and then looked back down at me, waiting for my reply.

I downed the remainder of my pint and looked at the alderman.

"So where can I contact you?"

2

I LAY STARING FROM MY bed at the brown envelope that I'd left on my dressing table after I'd got in from the pub the night before. There was more than enough money in there to pay the arrears on my rent and put food inside of me, that was for sure.

It was Sunday morning, just after 6.30 a.m. I'd slept very little, and Earl Linney's proposition that I find the missing girl had been rolling around in my head for most of the night. I was still unsure if I'd done the right thing in taking the man's money. Was Stella Hopkins alive? If she was, she was obviously lying low and didn't want to be found. If the police were struggling to find her, what difference would it make if I was chasing her tail?

Feeling the worse for lack of sleep, I knew I had to drag my ass off of the mattress or I'd not be getting up for the rest of the day. I pulled on my pants and opened the small cupboard door that was home to the immersion heater. I flicked the switch on, hearing the tank fire up, then went into the kitchen. Filling my old tin kettle with water, I lit the gas and put it on the hob to boil. There was about half a teaspoon of Nescafé Blend 37 in the almost empty jar, and I made a note in my head to add it to the milk I needed to buy.

After making myself a drink, I sat on a high-legged stool at the tatty breakfast bar and took a sip of the liquid masquerading as black coffee. It was a world away from what I used to drink back in Carrington Village, but so was I.

It was hard, but I tried not to think of St Philip parish and the family I had lost. I missed that old life, my job, the white sands and azure sea of home, and I sure as hell missed fresh coffee. It's strange how the simplest of things brought back memories best forgotten. I rubbed at the two-day-old growth of salt-and-pepper stubble on my chin and decided I needed to clean up; I was starting to stink as bad as my kitchen. I pushed myself up, dropped my mug into the sink and let the excuse for coffee drain away down the plughole.

I went into my tiny damp bathroom and ran hot water into the sink. Staring at my reflection in the bathroom mirror, I looked every one of my forty-two years. I'd a little grey hair around my temples, and the small half-inch scar that ran along the left side of my brow had faded little since my sister, Bernie, had thrown a broken conch shell at me when we were playing catch as kids.

Opening the medicine cabinet, I took out my cut-throat razor, shaving brush and soap and sank the brush into the water before lathering it. I painted my jowls in the lightly scented suds, took my blade and let it glide across my face. It took me all of three or so minutes to shave.

I threw the now lukewarm water over my face and took a bar of soap from the edge of the sink and rubbed under my arms and chest with it, using the remaining water to rinse before drying myself off with a navy-blue hand towel.

Returning to my bedroom, I took from the wardrobe my grey herringbone tweed jacket, a white cotton shirt, charcoal tapered cuffed trousers and a pair of black leather plain-toe derby brogues, and quickly got myself dressed. The only items of luxury clothing I possessed were an Aquascutum overcoat and a black felt trilby hat, both hung in the hall and which had been invaluable these last few days in keeping me dry.

16

Walking over to the window, I wiped away some of the condensation with the flat of my hand and looked out down onto the snow-filled street below, which was unsurprisingly quiet. My thoughts turned to breakfast, my guts churning. I didn't have anything in to eat, but I knew exactly where I could get my fill of the best food in St Pauls even this early on a Sunday. Picking up the brown envelope, I pulled out Stella Hopkins' photograph and placed it on my dressing table, then took the two fivers out, unfolded the bills and put them into my wallet, before putting it into the breast pocket of my jacket. I went into the hall, picked my keys off the hook, and grabbed my hat and overcoat from the stand before heading straight out of the door to pay a visit to my uncle Gabe and aunt Pearl.

Gabe and his wife, Pearl, lived on Banner Road, just three streets away from my place. Their rented Victorian-built double-bay home was the bolthole I'd run to when I found myself short of a few pounds or if I needed the taste of some home cooking. They'd lived in the house since Gabe had left the army, renting it from the same miserly landlord who owned my digs. Along with my sister Bernie back home, my cousin Victor and his parents were the only family I had. Gabe was my father's brother and they looked a helluva lot like each other. My own papa had been dead for over twenty years, but Gabe and Pearl treated me like one of their own. Their front door was never locked, and I made my way up the three granite steps, which my aunt Pearl scrubbed every other day, and went inside without knocking.

"Hey Gabe, Pearl, where you both at?" I shouted down the hallway.

"Joseph, is that you, boss man?" Gabe called from his kitchen.

"Sure is. Man, it is freezing out there." I beat at my arms with my hands, the watery snowflakes falling from my coat onto the hard wood floor in my aunt Pearl's hallway. I kicked off my shoes, the soles sodden from the sleet and ice, and I took off my hat and coat and hung them on the top of the banister at the foot of their stairs before finding the two of them sitting at their dining table.

The old black Aga was thankfully throwing out some heat; a pot of cornmeal porridge bubbled gently away on the back. I pulled up a chair and drew it in towards the table, directing my wet feet at the warmth of the metal range. I patted at my stomach with the flat of my palm and stared over at my aunt's breakfast pans. My hunger settled over the room like a shroud on a corpse.

"There ain't no need axing why you here at this time in the marning, I suppose you'll be wantin' me to cook you up some eggs?" my aunt Pearl asked me as she rose from her chair, already knowing what my reply would be.

Her accent was deep, rich Bajan. Our language, to those not familiar with it, could sound stern and authoritarian, but to me its lilting tones were a gentle reminder of happier times from my childhood. My years with the Barbadian police force had clipped my own use of our mother tongue, the service preferring its men to replicate the speech of its British Metropolitan counterparts here in the UK.

"You know I ain't gonna say no to you, Pearl. Eggs sound good to me. How about you bringing me some of that fine cornmeal pap." I rubbed my hands together in eager anticipation. I felt like a child again, eleven years old, sat around my mama's table waiting to get fed. I forgot the cold and smelt the exotic aromas of the Caribbean rising from my aunt's old metal cooking pan.

Pearl dished me up a bowl of the steaming hot cereal, which she had sprinkled on top with cinnamon, and brought it over to me along with a spoon. Back home we called it "pap" because of its thick consistency. It looked like baby food, but thankfully didn't taste like it. Pearl returned to her stove and cracked two hen's eggs into a black iron skillet and gently began to fry them while I filled my face.

"So what you gotta tell us, Joseph? You dressed real sharp, brother," Gabe said, lifting his head outta his newspaper as he spoke to me. He was one of the few people who used my given name; Pearl, what was left of my family, and the few friends I had always called me JT.

"I've been offered work, but I'm not sure if it's fo' me, Gabe. That's why I came over; I wanted to run it by you."

"You did? When did you need me tell you to take a job? You sure as hell need the money, that's fo' damn sure."

"I'd be working fo' a guy named Earl Linney." I waited for Gabe's reaction, unsure of how he'd take the news. Historically, Jamaicans looked upon the other, smaller Caribbean islands with disdain, calling our home in Barbados one of the "little" islands. It was fair to say there was no love lost between the two peoples when it came to the hierarchy of our individual atolls.

My uncle Gabe was distrusting by nature and I could tell that he was not impressed by the possibility of me being employed by the wealthy Jamaican politician. I watched the old man sit back in his old armchair and prepared myself for a grilling.

"The alderman, what the hell kinda work a man like Earl Linney got fo' you? You ain't an airplane engineer and you know nuttin' 'bout pol'tics," Gabe snapped at me sharply.

I didn't reply and quickly skirted over my uncle's aggressive questioning, changing tack a little and perhaps digging a

19

bigger hole for myself at the same time as I offered up a little more information to him as to the real nature of my new job offer.

"Gabe, you read 'bout a young woman from Montpelier go missing a short while back? Name's Stella Hopkins?" I asked him gingerly, then wished that I hadn't.

"We heard," Aunt Pearl interrupted. "Pastor at our church, he got us pray'in fo' her. You axe me, that poor ting she in the ground."

"Nobody knows that, Pearl; just cus she not been around, don't mean she dead," Gabe growled back at his wife.

"Well, you tell me where that girl walking 'bout then?" Pearl was having none of her husband's bullishness. Nevertheless, my uncle Gabe continued to make his point.

"Woman, it ain't fo' lack a tongue that a horse can't talk. Ain't no good sayin' that she's dead when you don't know a damn ting."

"Well, I read 'bout that poor child in that paper you go poking through every night. She ain't been seen fo' over a week, where she be then, you tell me?"

Gabe sat in silence, knowing better than to continue the argument with Aunt Pearl, a battle of words in which he would not be finally victorious.

Pearl picked up my empty bowl with one hand and placed a plate of fried eggs in front of me with her other. She had sliced some bread that she had recently baked and put it onto another, smaller tea plate along with the butter dish.

"Help yourself, I'll bring you some coffee," she said, her finger pointing at the bread and butter as she spoke.

"Thanks, Aunt Pearl, my belly sure is grateful to you." I soft-soaped the old lady and began to tuck into my breakfast.

20

Pearl walked back to the kitchen sink, shaking her head and mumbling to herself 'bout how my uncle Gabe had "hard ears", that he didn't listen to her. I could see her point of view, but Gabe's sixty-three years had made him wise. He was a thinker, calm, reflective. Everything his dead brother, my papa, wasn't.

"He wants me to ask around this area, but kinda on the sly, Gabe, if you know what I mean?"

"Oh, I know what you mean. But you needs to be axing yo'self, why's the man need you to do his donkey work on the sly, Joseph? He's a big enough fella, he should be doing his own sniffing around if you axe me. Someting stinks to high heaven 'bout the whole story."

Gabe was on a roll, there was no way I was going to get him off of his soapbox. I was regretting that I'd ever opened my big mouth.

"An' another ting. If Linney wants this Hopkins girl finding, then you tell me why he not gone to the police?"

My uncle Gabe was fishing for the truth. But I had none to give him; I could only offer up what the shady councillor had already told me. As I retold the alderman's tale to my uncle, I felt his words were already making a liar out of me.

"Linney said that he'd been to the local law, Gabe, says they've come up with nothing. The man knew I'd been on the force back home on Barbados, thought I may be able to help. Poke around without upsetting folk. He said he was prepared to pay me well fo' that kinda help."

"Yeah, is that so . . . You know that's the first ting I'd be worrying 'bout if I was you. When a man offers you big money fo' work he don't wanna touch himself, that either means he's damn lazy or he's lying 'bout what kinda job you're gonna end up doin' fo' him. Just remember: man needs money, but he

21

also needs to be able to sleep at night once he's earned it. You be sure you can do that, Joseph, just be sure."

It was the kind of good advice I knew was worth taking, but sometimes, the advice from those who love us dearly is also the most difficult to accept. And in not heeding their words of warning and making those fateful mistakes, our fall from grace in their eyes is so much harder to bear.

Today I was again about to ignore the words of the wise. My own previous fall from grace, which until now had been a well-kept secret, was to return to haunt me as I looked into the eyes of my elderly relation. It was a darkly clandestine past that my uncle and I never spoke of.

3

I DIDN'T SPEAK OF THE missing girl or my involvement with
Earl Linney to Gabe and Pearl again while we sat finishing our
coffees. I felt I'd disturbed the calm of their Sunday morning
with my talk of Stella Hopkins and the up-front easy money
Linney had paid me to find her.

Gabe saw the world and those who lived in it simply. You
were either good or bad, and I got the feeling he thought that
the Jamaican politician didn't fit into either of those categories.
Gabe had said his piece and in doing so had heightened my
distrust of Earl Linney's motives and made me question
whether he'd been straight with me.

I'd promised Pearl that I'd drop by on Wednesday evening,
her invite to supper too good to miss. I thanked her for
breakfast, grabbed my coat and hat, and kissed her cheek
before turning to Gabe, who had returned to reading his
newspaper. He'd just lit up a cigar and was drawing on it
before blowing out plumes of grey smoke around the kitchen.
I could tell he wasn't happy about my involvement with the
alderman and the flash up-front cash he'd handed over. He
sat with a face like an angry old goat that was ready to butt his
way out of a farmyard pen. I approached my curmudgeonly
relation cautiously before speaking.

"Hey Gabe, you have any idea where Vic is?"

"That boy was up with the lark, said he was going to meet
Carnell Harris at Perry's gym down on Grosvenor Street, they
shifting someting or other down there."

He sucked some more on his stogie and shuffled uncomfortably in his chair, aggressively shaking the opened pages of his newspaper out in front of him in frustration at my continuing probing as to the whereabouts of his nefariously felonious child.

"So you ain't expecting him back any time soon?" The overeagerness of my questioning had started to provoke my uncle to become suspicious of my motives in wanting to meet up with his son. Gabe was guarded in his reply and was in his own way protecting me as much as he was his own boy. The old man knew that when Vic and I got together we had a habit of finding trouble for ourselves.

"Vic makes up the rules as he goes along. He could be back tonight or it could be tomorrow night. Vic's never lived by God's time." Gabe shook his head at me, a look of weary resignation on his face as he considered for a moment what criminal activity his wayward offspring may be up to.

He knew Vic was as cunning as a fox, handy with his fists and could take care of himself, and yet he worried constantly for his child's well-being. He was the kind of father I wished I'd had, and after my own old man's untimely death he'd done his very best for me. The thought of worrying about both Vic and myself was clearly a great strain upon my uncle and it showed in his manner. He deserved better from the two of us, and a wave of shame crashed over me, dragging at my heart like a lead weight.

"OK, thanks, both. I'm going to try and catch up with Vic at Perry's."

I could see that Gabe was getting increasingly agitated. I'd spooked him by bringing into his home the prospect of misfortune and possibly implicating Vic in it. As I turned to leave, he called out to me, his voice now sombre and full of troubled concern. He stared up at me, his watery eyes piercing into my own.

"Joseph, you know that Vic dodges round the darker sides o' life without you pushin' him further toward it. Think about that real hard befo' you start on someting with him you may end up regretting."

The old goat was way ahead of me.

"I just wanted to git together with my cousin, Gabe. Maybe git a drink in the Jamaica Inn at lunchtime. This family gotta stay tight. You know that."

But the old man wasn't sold on my upbeat patter. He saw through the lie I'd just told him and was still suspicious of my true intent as to why I wanted to find my kin so urgently.

I left my uncle feeling lower than Judas Iscariot in the garden at Gethsemane. And like that ancient traitor who had hidden in the darkness while he betrayed those he professed to love, the shadow of my deception followed me as I left the room and cruelly clung at my heels as I said goodbye to my upright, vexed relations.

"Git together my ass!" Gabe shouted back to me from his armchair, his angry words ringing in my ears after I walked out the door.

Back on the street, snow had started to fall again and was settling on top of what had already fallen. Large flakes floated from the thick grey sky and fell onto the back of my neck, the icy droplets melting as they hit the warmth of my skin. I drew my collar up around me and headed for Perry's gym, the chill of the day making me shudder.

My cousin Vic spent much of his time in parts of the city that other people would steer well clear of. Most like to deny the existence of such areas. And while respectable folk entertained their families and dinner party guests in the chic

25

three-storey townhouses of Clifton and Kingsdown, men like Vic felt at home in the run-down terraced streets, clip joints and whorehouses of those less inviting suburbs. If I had been stealing cigarettes from Wills, then Vic would've been the man to take 'em off me and get 'em distributed. Vic dealt in most contraband and just about anything else if there was a favourable end profit in it for him. He was a couple of years younger than me, and we had been close as kids. Vic had never distanced himself from me when I joined the police service. He didn't like it, but we were family and our mutual respect for each other was undiminished.

When Gabe had told me that Vic had left early for Perry's gymnasium, I knew he had a score going down, something good enough to get him outta his bed at the crack of dawn. Vic was well known and liked in the community and had a reputation as a hard fighter and the sort of guy you kept on the right side of. Despite his illegal activities, he never brought trouble to Gabe and Pearl's door. They both knew their son sailed pretty close to the wind, but he was too clever to bring trouble to anybody's door, especially his own.

Perry's gym was only a short walk from Gabe and Pearl's. At such an early time on a Sunday morning there'd be nobody training in the place, and the only way in was via the iron fire escape at the rear of the three-storey building. I climbed up the old metal stairs three steps at a time, knowing Vic would've gone in the same way and that the gym's owner, "Cut Man" Perry, would keep the door unlocked for his break-of-day, cockcrow guests to get in. I walked through a series of unlit corridors that led to the shower room, which stank of testosterone and three-day-old sweat.

I found Cut Man in his tatty office, staring at a huge pair of white breasts in the centre pages of a dirty magazine. He had not realised that I was watching him. He was sitting in an off-white grubby string vest and wide red braces that held up a pair of creased pinstripe trousers. His feet lay across his desk, and he was smoking one of his usual stinky Woodbines, which hung out of the corner of his mouth, held tight by huge purple-tinged lips. Hung on the walls were yellowing boxing posters and an array of old photographs, mainly of Cut Man standing at gala events or ringside with local dignitaries and the odd rare contender out of the aging gym who had done good. Cut Man, originally from Jamaica, was around sixty-five years old, balding, and at least twenty-two stone in weight. Over the years he'd made quite a lot of cash in various shady businesses and was known as being a real penny-pincher. Apart from the gym, he owned a number of letting properties, betting shops and off-licences, and a shuttered-up backstreet clip joint that rolled out over-the-hill strippers. He was a bad-tempered, greedy, untrustworthy bastard who treated those who worked for him like something that he'd scraped off the bottom of his shoe, but in typical two-faced Cut Man fashion, he sucked up to money and power and was often to be found in the presence of the criminal underclass of the city. He truly believed he was the epitome of entrepreneurial black style and most hadn't the courage to tell him different.

But Cut Man's notoriety was all bluff and bluster, and he was nothing without the protection of the thugs who frequented his establishment.

I wasn't fazed by his gangland associations and neither was Vic. My cousin was equally, if not better, connected to every villain and shylock around. His dealings with Cut Man were kept on a strictly professional level. Cut Man feared Vic and he didn't trust me, and that's just how I liked it.

I stood at his open office door, watching him leer over the pale naked flesh of the centrefold. A thin trickle of saliva dribbled from his mouth, slid down his chin and plopped onto the saucy nude picture below.

"Am I interrupting you?"

Cut Man, startled, dragged his legs off of his desk and, as quickly as his massive bulk would allow, drew his chair underneath it. Closing the titty magazine, he attempted to hide the cover with his fat hairy arms. He then tried to give himself an air of businesslike respectability. He failed.

"What the fuck you doin', man? Scaring the shit outta me like that."

"So how's tings, Cut Man?" I tried not to laugh as I asked the question.

"I was fine till you showed up," Cut Man snapped back at me. "How the hell did you git in here?" Cut Man was acting like his usual cagey self. He was naturally distrustful of most people, and especially those who'd just caught him ogling naked women in a top-shelf dirty skin rag.

"How'd you think, Cut Man? I ain't crawled through your nasty bathroom window. Your back door's off the latch."

"That muthafucka Vic. I told him to lock it when he came in. I could git turned over, him leaving doors wide open at this time o' the morning."

"Who's gonna steal from you, Cut Man? You too cheap to keep anyting in this rathole that's worth pinching. So where's my cousin at?"

"He been doin' some bidness with Carnell out back."

Cut Man was trying to be casual with his answer. But the sweat running off his head and down his brow and the stink coming from under his arms gave him away. Cut Man was the only black man I knew who could sweat like a pig in the ice cold of winter.

"You know, Cut Man, I never have understood why you're always on edge when I'm around you. I ain't the law, you know, brother."

"No, no you ain't. But I hear you used be." His reply to me had the wary intonation as a condemned man on the gallows being told he was free to go while he still had the noose tight round his neck.

"Hey, Cut Man, where's my cousin? I ain't got all day, brother," I asked impatiently. I was getting queasy at the cheesy pong coming off of Cut Man's hide and wanted out of his rank office.

"He's in the locker room; bottom left as you head on down the hall. Been real good seeing you, man."

He sneered back at me with an insincere gesture of farewell.

"Thanks, Cut Man. Good to see you too," I lied. "Say, anybody tell you you're looking real sharp in that vest, brother?"

"Fuck you, Ellington!" Cut Man shouted as I began to close his office door, sealing him into his smelly workplace with his rancid personal-hygiene problem and grubby skin publication.

I found Vic standing over around sixty boxes of stolen imported Mount Gay rum, a pencil behind his ear. He was pointing at each box while he counted them out loud. He was shirtless, his powerfully built body covered in beads of sweat from shifting the heavy cargo from Carnell's van to Cut Man's locker room. He was darker skinned than I, with short-cropped tightly curled hair, and he was well over six feet tall. His voice was deep, and as smooth as the knock-off rum at his feet.

29

"You send all that booze off to the Salvation Army, Vic?"

My cousin turned quickly, surprised that I had crept up on him.

"Jesus, JT, you scared the shit outta me creeping up like that. How the hell you know to find me here?"

"I just had breakfast with Gabe an' Pearl. Your old man told me you'd be here. I think he was hoping that you might be putting in some time on punching those bags out there," I said, nodding towards the gym. "I just left Cut Man's office. I was getting real high from the scent of his foul perspiration. It ain't much better in here, brother. Damn!"

"Hey, that's pure hard work you're smelling there, my man, and I keep it tight in the ring, you know that, JT." He laughed as he clenched his enormous hands into fists and punched the air with a series of skilled uppercuts and jabs.

"So this is what Cut Man meant by some bidness?" I said as I slid my hand across the top of the dusty liquor boxes.

"Man's gotta make a livin', JT. I'm just working my way in the world. You know how it is?"

"I sure do, a man's gonna be living pretty well after a couple o' bottles of this inside his belly."

"Taste o' home, JT, it's a taste o' home." Vic smiled as he took a pearl-handled penknife from his back pocket, sliced open the tape securing the box and pulled out a couple of bottles of the amber-coloured spirit and passed them to me.

"Here, these gonna keep you warm at night, my man." He grinned at me as he handed them over. I thanked him and stood the bottles on the table behind me.

"Where's Carnell, Vic?"

I didn't want to start up a conversation about Stella Hopkins and the councillor's job offer only to have to cut it short if we were interrupted. Carnell was a good guy, but I needed to

30

keep a lid on what I was up to for now. Vic was a lot of things, but a blabbermouth he was not.

"He been gone around twenty minutes or so: that bitch of a wife, Loretta, gonna want his ass on a church pew this morning. I paid him his cut fo' the use of his van and fo' his help to lug this lot up here."

"Vic, you hear anyting on the street 'bout that missing girl from round here, name's Hopkins, Stella Hopkins?"

"The mute? Yeah, I heard she's missin', but I'm only hearing the same shit you probably have: that she's simple, can't talk and she's gonna be found wanderin' 'bout on the pier at Clevedon. Either that or her ass gets washed up on the beach. Why you bothered 'bout some piece of skirt like her anyhow?" Vic returned to box counting, irritated at having to start over again.

"I've been asked to see if I can try to find her. Do a little digging around in the neighbourhood, but nuttin' heavy." My answer was evasive. I was beginning to sound a lot like Cut Man.

"Tell me, who's been askin' you to find some stupid-minded skank, JT?"

Vic looked up from tallying the rum cases. His distrustful nature had started to kick in and I could tell he was already dubious about the person who had requested I undertake such dirty work on his behalf.

"It don't matter who's asking me, Vic. Look, I need you to keep this under your hat fo' now, so don't be spreading the word I'm lookin' fo' her. It ain't gonna help me none. I need to take it easy fo' now. I gotta be discreet."

"Discreet? That's cool, JT, it's cool. I just got my cousin's best interests at heart. Now you know I got your back if any shit goes down, brother?"

As he spoke, Vic gave the same look that he would give anybody fool enough to take him on when we were kids. It was the kind of look that said he wasn't for messing with.

"Thanks, man. I appreciate it. You still own a set of lock picks, Vic?"

My question had surprised Vic: something I normally wasn't able to achieve. He had one eyebrow raised and was staring over at me, his brain ticking over the unlawful implications of my request and no doubt thinking to himself, "What the hell am I about to git myself into?" I should have known better than to wander into Vic's world of criminality and not arouse his suspicions of my own larcenous intentions.

"Yeah, I got 'em. You want me to come along and open a place up fo' you?"

"Not this time, brother. I ain't dragging you into trouble you got no place being." I put my hand on his bulky shoulder, thinking about Uncle Gabe as I did so, and smiled. "But you know I'm real grateful fo' the offer."

"Yeah I know ... Tell me, you ever been in the Hatchet Inn?" Vic quizzed me.

"You mean that old honky pub on Frogmore Street? I know it, but I've never put a foot inside of the place."

"I'll see you in there at nine thirty. And JT, when you git inside ... you just try an' be discreet fo' me, brother; they know they ain't too keen on black dudes hanging out in their pub, sets their teeth on edge."

"So why the hell you wanna meet up in there?"

I wasn't happy about Vic's choice of venue. Most of the pubs in Bristol city centre didn't welcome black men into them. You had to fight to get into most and while I wasn't scared of a scrap I didn't see the point in making life any harder for myself than it already was.

"Cos my man, no honky's stopping me from drinking anywhere I wanna drink. And there's a hot piece o' skirt they've got working behind the bar that has a real ting fo' me."

Vic burst out laughing, and I could still hear his laughter as my feet hit the street.

4

I'D SPENT THE BEST PART of Sunday afternoon lying on my bed drinking a half-bottle of Vic's stolen rum and wondering what the hell I was doin' with my life. Later I'd made a corned beef sandwich, drunk a mug of coffee, then stuck my head into a sink full of cold water to shake the alcohol from inside of me. I changed into a light-blue shirt, brushed the creases out of my trousers, pushed my feet into damp brogues and splashed on a palmful of English Leather aftershave. I grabbed a small torch from my bedside table and put it into the inside pocket of my coat before leaving to meet Vic.

There was a real chill in the air as I walked out from my digs, and I started to wish I'd stayed on my bed and finished the other half of the bottle. I was still unsure if Linney had been straight with me and whether he had given me the whole story on Stella Hopkins and her vanishing into thin air like a conjurer's assistant. Had I become so desperate to know I had cash in my hip pocket that I was prepared to take on what looked to be a fool's errand? Like a knight errant, it appeared that I was.

"There ain't no fool like an old fool," my mama would say. I could be walking into a whole world of mess and all for five pounds a day. Was it worth it? Hell no, but I needed the money.

The snow had stopped falling earlier that afternoon, and after what little sun we'd had dropped out of the sky, the temperature fell and it had started to freeze, making the pavements icy and difficult to walk on. I arrived at the Hatchet Inn just after nine o'clock. It was quiet, thankfully, and the few customers sitting inside were more interested in their booze than in some black guy needing a drink on a cold Sunday evening. I went to the bar and bought a pint of Guinness and a double shot of Lamb's Navy rum from the blousy barmaid that Vic had his eye on, then went and found a secluded table at the back of the pub, took my raincoat and hat off, and threw them on to chair next to me. I drank a third of my pint before pouring the rum into the rest of the beer, then took another swig of the ale–spirit mixture before sitting down.

My lack of sleep the previous night was starting to take its toll upon me. I yawned as I ran my hands down my face from forehead to chin. The liquor I'd been drinking earlier in the day had left me feeling ill-tempered and restless. I wasn't in the best frame of mind to be jemmying into a house I had no place being in. With no idea what I was looking for, I knew I had to start earning the money that Linney had coughed up and Hopkins' house seem as good a place to start as any.

Something was niggling at me about Stella's disappearance that I couldn't put my finger on. The alderman had left me some basic details, which included her home address, physical appearance and a couple of contact numbers where I could reach him, but I knew little else. She had no real friends or family, and didn't socialise with colleagues or have any romantic associations with the opposite sex. She did odd-job work at the council chambers, which from what I could gather added up to nothing more than counting paperclips; she was capable of using public transport, which she used to get from her home to work and back but went nowhere else unaccompanied; and it appeared that Mr and Mrs Linney did everything else for the girl from cooking her meals to wiping her ass. She'd walked out of the offices on to College Green in the centre of Bristol city on Thursday, January 8th and hadn't been seen since. From what I understood, the police had put up missing posters, dragged the local rivers and had gone door to door around the streets near her home in St Pauls, but they had come up with nothing.

I took another hard draught of my beer and slumped back into the crimson velour chair, turning my pint glass in my hands before raising it to my mouth and finishing the ale in two more hefty gulps. I leant forward and placed the empty pint onto a beer mat on the brass-covered circular table in front of me.

The pub was practically empty. "Who in their right mind would wanna be out on a lousy night like this?" I asked myself.

Two men sat at either end of the bar, both worse for wear because of too much Scotch, their lifeless, alcohol-flushed faces peering into their drinks, their sins staring back at them from the amber malt, each seeking an absolution they'd never find while they kept sipping on the hooch. I closed my eyes and pinched my nose with my fingers and stayed like that for what seemed like an age before being brought back to the land of the living by the sound of glass touching metal.

"Here, looks like you could use this."

I opened my eyes, which at first struggled with the low lighting before refocusing on the replacement pint of stout in front of me. On the opposite side of the table stood Vic. He was wearing a long black leather coat, a black polo neck jumper, and trousers. His hands covered in a pair of tight-fitting black leather gloves, his face hard like stone, staring down at me. He looked like the Grim Reaper, only with a helluva lot more style.

"Ever since I can remember, you gits a face on you just like the one you got now when you been drinkin' rum."

"You're the one handed the damn stuff out to me," I said sourly.

"Maybe I did, but you didn't have to drink so much of it, fool. Anyhow, this should put a smile back on that sorry-assed-lookin' face of yours."

He quietly laughed to himself as he took out a small black hip flask from his pocket, unscrewed the silver cap and poured a nip of rum into the beer he'd just bought me. Vic put the flask to his lips and drank from it slowly, savouring the aged flavours of the stolen rum before wiping the back of his huge gloved hand across his mouth. I watched as he drank, and then glanced over to the bar to see if the barmaid or landlord had caught sight of what he'd been doing. Thankfully they hadn't. The last thing I needed was for Vic to be getting into a brawl over drinking his own illicit booze in another man's joint. I looked at my wayward cousin and shook my head.

"What? Hell, I ain't buying any o' that shit from the bar when I got my own. I look stupid to you?" he asked me, as he stuffed the hip flask back inside his coat, his voice full of boyish playfulness.

Before I could answer him he leant forward, firing off another question, only this time his voice was a whisper, the playfulness gone.

"So you still thinking of creeping in through that gate-door?" His eyes bore into mine as he waited for my reply. I knew he wouldn't be happy with the answer.

"Course I am, it's someting I gotta . . ."

Vic interrupted me, still whispering, still holding my eyes with his own.

"You ain't gotta do shit. JT, this ain't your way, man, you a thief-taker, not some damn cat burglar. What the hell you think you gonna find in that house anyway?"

I didn't have an answer for him and Vic knew it.

"Whatever you got yourself mixed up in, snooping round that bitch's house ain't gonna help you any. Now you let me go straighten tings out with whoever got you mixed up in this bullshit, you hearing me?"

"I hear you, Vic . . . I ain't mixed up in nuttin'. Like I said, I'm just doing a little digging around."

I was struggling to convince him.

"Digging around, shit, who the hell you think you are, Perry Mason?"

I stared at my cousin, and in the language of a lesser man I offered him nothing but my silence. Despite the fierceness of his demeanour, he had only my best interests at heart, his concerns both valid and heartfelt. He deserved better from me, but at that moment silence was all I had to give him.

We sat for a couple of minutes, our faces staring out across the room, neither one speaking to the other, our mutual hard-headedness preventing further dialogue between the two of us. It was I who finally broke the stillness of our self-imposed taciturnity.

"You brought me those picks?"

Vic reached into the inside of his coat and drew out a small dark-brown chamois wrap, tied tight with a single piece of nylon cord. He slid his hand from his chest underneath the table in one smooth motion and gently dropped the tools into my lap before standing up and pulling his gloves off, finger by finger, then slapping them onto the table in front of me.

"You gonna need these, unless you wanna leave your name all over every part o' that house," he said sternly as he walked out of the pub and into the night.

5

A SHARP FROST HAD BEGUN to set in by the time I left the Hatchet Inn. It was just before ten thirty and the city was practically emptied of human life. I made my way across town into the Montpelier district, taking as many of the back lanes and smaller roads as possible. There was no moon to illuminate the evening sky, and I tried to stay clear of the amber street lights that picked out my shadow as I walked. At this time of night a black guy out alone would definitely attract the suspicions of the local law working the graveyard shift. The last thing I needed was to be pulled over by the police and found to be in possession of a set of lock picks and a pocket torch.

By the time I reached Thomas Street and the missing girl's house it was just after eleven. Her home sat at the end of the road facing St Agnes' church. It was a flat-roofed two-storey building that looked the same as every other in the row. The front door was set back off the pavement and the property was shielded by a two-foot-high red-brick wall. I opened up the waist-high iron gate, then checked behind me to make sure nobody was about.

The front door was fitted with a brass cylinder pin lock. Picking it wouldn't be easy: it required patience and a sureness of touch. Vic was a specialist in the art; he could open one up in a heartbeat. But I wasn't as skilled as my cousin and it would take me a little longer.

I took the chamois pick bag out of my coat pocket along with the torch. I switched it on, then stuck it in my mouth, holding the blue plastic torch between my teeth. With both hands free, I removed a tiny tension bar and a snake rake from the bag. I placed the lip of the bar into the lock, applying a little weight to it, and then gently inserted the rake until I felt the mechanism; I rapidly began sliding the pick past the series of pins repeatedly until the lock released. It had taken less than a couple of minutes and I was in.

Now I'd walked into houses where a rotting corpse had lain undiscovered for weeks. You don't forget that kinda stink in a hurry. But this was different. The first thing that hit me when I walked through the door was the smell of disinfectant: the scent of heavy pine permeated the house, its chemical stench hitting the back of my throat, making me gag. With my back against the front door, I ran the beam of my torch up the length of the hallway towards what looked like the kitchen at the rear of the house, and then shone the light across the walls, locating the stairs and a closed interior door to the right of me. The place felt colder than outside. My breath caught in the torch's beam.

I went into the kitchen and quietly opened drawers, which contained very little. The cupboards had no tinned foods or dry goods. The work surfaces had nothing on them. An unopened box of sugar puff cereal stood by the electric cooker.

The fridge was empty, scrubbed to within an inch of its life and pristine white. Next to the back door was a small larder, the light from my torch hitting the shelves, which were all strangely bare. On the floor, arranged in neat rows, were dozens of tins of Jeyes Fluid, bottles of bleach and other cleaning materials.

I made my way back along the hall, opened the door and went into what appeared to be the living room. Like the rest of

40

the house, it stank of antiseptic. I suppressed a series of coughs by covering my arm with the sleeve of my coat before shining the torch across the room: there were no pictures on the walls and no photographs of friends or family. A single armchair was positioned next to a tiled fireplace, its grate prepared with fresh kindling, and above it, resting on the mantelpiece, was a wooden crucifix. There were no letters, books, magazines or newspapers.

I closed the door of the living room and carefully made my way up the stairs. At the top of them, directly in front of me, was the bathroom. Even with the slight beam of my torch I could tell it was pristine clean. There was no mirror, and sat on a shelf mounted on the wall over the bath was a single bottle of shampoo. A tube of toothpaste and a brush stood next to each other in a glass perched on the edge of the sink, and next to the toilet were more bleach bottles.

Making my way along the landing, I entered the open door of the first of two bedrooms. A single bed, its sterile white sheets crisp and clean, was positioned against the far wall. The curtains were drawn. There was no other furniture in the room, and its floor was covered in the same dark carpet as the stairs. It reminded me of my place, only cleaner.

The last room's door was closed. I took hold of the Bakelite handle, turned it and went inside. Again, the curtains were drawn. Inside, it reeked of a heavy, caustic odour. I began to heave as the acrid vapours filled my nose and mouth, my eyes watered from the overpowering chemicals. I swallowed hard to fight off the desire to be sick.

Taking centre stage was a large double bed, which was raised high off the floor by large brass legs. Its frame glinted back at me as it was caught by the strafing beam of my torch. It was neatly made up with a heavy red quilt on top. Another small crucifix was nailed to the wall above the bed, which gave the room a peculiar aura. I had the feeling that I was standing in a place of holy orders, where monastic vows had once been taken. Unlike the other bedroom, this one contained some pieces of furniture. There was a dark wood dressing table at one end of the room and a wardrobe on the far wall.

An opened Bible sat on a small table next to the bed. In the corner of the room stood a galvanised bucket. I approached it cautiously and found it filled to the brim with what appeared to be a mixture of water and more bleach.

I went through each of the drawers and found underwear, stockings, socks and assorted cardigans and tops. It felt wrong to be going through her belongings, and I closed the bottom drawer sullied by the task and no wiser as to what I was looking for. In her wardrobe, dresses and skirts hung alongside a winter coat, and numerous pairs of shoes were lined in a uniform row below. I closed the door and stepped back a few paces. I turned back to the bed, ran my arms around the base of the frame and lifted the mattress with one hand – nothing.

Getting onto my knees, I shone the torch under the bed, which had been brushed clean, and as I was about to get up my eyes were drawn to the legs of the wardrobe and the four-inch gap beneath its door. I moved around the bed on all fours and sank to my stomach to get a look underneath. I lit up the floor with my torch only to find bare, scrubbed floorboards. Sticking my arm into the gap, I felt around and touched the skirting board with my hand. As I drew my arm out, the cuff of the back of my glove clipped something attached to the base of the wardrobe. Turning on my side, I used my fingers to trace what felt like a thin book that had been securely taped at each of its edges. I grabbed hold of the spine and pulled hard.

I sat up, my back resting on the bed, the book in my lap. I

shone the beam of my torch on to the cover, which had the words "News Cuttings and Scrapbook" printed on it. I took off one of my gloves and opened it up, flicking through the pages, which were all empty.

From the looks of things there had once been photographs carefully stuck inside, but they were now all gone. Each one had been attached at the corners with a small clear triangular mount. It wasn't until I reached the inside of the back cover that I found glued to it, face down, a brown Manila envelope. Inside that was a small back and white photograph. It was hard to see who was in it. I held it closer to my face, but still struggled to make out what I was looking at. I'd had enough of crawling around in the dark and retching my guts out. I picked myself off the floor and slipped the photograph into my back trouser pocket, then stuffed the scrapbook inside my coat and put my glove back on. I quietly closed the bedroom door before making my way down the stairs and out of Stella Hopkins' home.

Outside in the street, I took deep breaths of cold, fresh air to purge the taste and smell of the house from inside of me. As I walked away, the image of the opened Bible on the girl's bedside table crept back into my mind and lingered like an unwelcome companion in my thoughts as I made my way back to my digs.

6

IN MY NIGHTMARE, I watch as the chattel house burns. Two big men hold my arms and shoulders while a third grabs my waist as they drag me to the ground. I frantically fight to free myself from their powerful grip, my legs flying out in all directions until they too are pinned down on the concrete road. My face contorts with anger and fear. Smoke and flames billow from the windows, the glass blown out by the extreme heat. Shouting out her name, my cries are lost in the roar of the blaze. I watch helplessly as she runs through rooms on fire, her hair alight and the skin on her body blistering in the white heat of the inferno.

It was her screams that wrenched me back to consciousness. I sat bolt upright in bed, perspiration covering my face, neck and chest. The stale taste of alcohol clung to the inside of my mouth as the reoccurring nocturnal horror withdrew back into the hidden recesses of my memory. With my back against the headboard, I smelt the warm, pungent scent of my sweat, which alerted me that I needed to take a bath, badly. I drew my legs over to the edge of the bed, my head in my hands before looking up at the clock on the wall: it was eleven thirty and I still felt tired.

I forced myself up and slowly made my way into the bathroom. The bath, a big white enamel tub, took a good ten minutes to fill from the slow-running hot water tap. I left it to do its thing and walked naked into the kitchen to make myself a cup of coffee, hoping that a caffeine hit would knock some of the fatigue out of my body.

I shaved, then grabbed a towel from the airing cupboard, wrapped it around my waist and lent against the bathroom wall, sipping at the boiling-hot liquid, my eyes closed, listening to the flowing stream of water. I got in and slid underneath the water, the warmth soothing my tired muscles and calming the edginess out of me. I ran a bar of soap across my body and hair, then lay there for a good twenty minutes before getting out and drying myself.

Winter sunshine rays illuminated the bedroom as I pulled open the curtains. The street below was still covered in thick snow with no sign of the start of a thaw.

I opened my chest of drawers, pulled out clean underwear and fresh socks, and flung them on the bed, then chose an olive-green plaid shirt, dark Levi's and a thick knitted cardigan from my wardrobe. On the inside of the door a full-length mirror caught my reflection and I stared at myself for a moment. I'd gained a little weight around my waist, but was still in good shape, and the excess I'd easily lose with some rope work at Perry's gym. At over six feet, I was broad and muscular across the shoulders, like my father. My eyes carried the same hazel colouring inherited from my Mama, but, sadly, I did not have the kindness of her smile. I dressed slowly, strapped my old watch to my wrist, rubbed Bay Rum through my hair and took the newspaper out of my shoes, which had soaked up the damp in the soles overnight, and put them on, tying the laces tight.

My digs were on the second floor of a two-storey Victorian red-brick corner house on Gwyn Street, with the living room situated at the rear of building. It had none of the comforts of a real home, but, in truth, I didn't know what a real home was like any more. A beaten up armchair and a rectangular coffee table, both left when the previous owner had done a runner after not paying the rent, were the only pieces of furniture in the room. Sat on an old tea chest was a Dansette record player. A stack of LPs stood against the side of the chest. I turned on the player and searched through the record sleeves until I found my favourite album. I carefully placed it on the turntable, gently dropped the needle onto the revolving black disc, then turned up the volume and let Etta James do her thing.

The scrapbook and Manila envelope I'd taken from Stella Hopkins' house stared back at me from the coffee table, where I had dropped them when I'd got in last night. I picked up the envelope and took out the black and white photograph. It was creased down its centre and dog-eared, with no writing on the back of it. There was no developer's stamp either.

In the picture, taken in what looked like a garden or perhaps a park, was a child, a little black girl, no more than six or seven years old, hair tied in braids and pinned across the top of her head. She wore a candy-striped dress, little white socks and patent-leather shoes. She smiled happily while sitting on the knee of a well-dressed black man. In one hand she held a small cloth toy rabbit while the other clasped his palm. He was in his early forties and well built, with strong features. He had a real presence to him, something I couldn't put my finger on at first. Perhaps it was the dark, hard eyes that unsettled me, or the awkwardness in his unsmiling face. He was a man who looked uncomfortable having his photograph taken. He was a man who looked a lot like a young Earl Linney.

★

It was just after one thirty on Monday afternoon and I was sitting in the Star and Garter in a booth at the furthest end of the pub. My pint of Dragon Stout was already half drunk. Lunchtime drinkers stood at the bar laughing and chatting while The Kinks' 'Tired of Waiting for You' played on the jukebox. The events of the previous night while checking out Stella's home had dragged up more questions than answers for me. If the police had searched the house, they hadn't gone over the place very thoroughly. There were things that didn't sit right in there. Surely alarm bells were gonna ring when the whole place stank like a washed-down morgue.

But I had found something other than the photograph and empty scrapbook. Something I hadn't seen in a long time. It was the one thing the law would not have picked up on, even in the most disciplined and determined of searches. Not unless, like me, you knew what a duppy was and its connection to an open Bible by a bed.

My mama had been a dignified and proud woman with strong religious beliefs and a determination to teach her son about the customs and traditions of our people. Juju stories were part of that tradition, as was the legacy of our servitude and bondage. The slave routes from West Africa brought my ancestors to the island of Barbados in the mid 1600s. They brought with them a vast cultural history, and their strength and skills put to use in the hard labour that the rich Dutch settlers demanded of them on the sugar plantations on the island.

Through locust plague and hurricanes, famine and bloodshed, my forefathers, many of whom died before reaching their destination, continued to suffer the deprivations of cruel slavery until its abolishment in 1834. Those who survived and found freedom continued to work and live hard, oppressive lives. The struggles faced in their pasts long ago had created the resilient Bajans who now populate the island today. But my people also brought something to those islands unheard of before.

Travelling with them was our folklore, and with it an altogether darker side to our lineage. They brought with them the duppy.

A duppy is the manifestation of the soul of a dead person. It is a malevolent spirit that can appear in either human or animal form. It is said that a duppy can be heard in the dog howling in the night or be found in the buttress roots of silk cotton trees, patiently waiting for the moment that its evil intent can be released upon the innocent. It is believed that babies and children are susceptible to these ghouls. An open Bible is often placed in a newborn's crib or bed to protect it and ward off evil. The Bible is usually left open at a Psalm. Just like the one I'd found next to Stella Hopkins' bed.

My cousin Vic, even as a child, had referred to the supernatural superstitions of our descendants and elders as a "pile of mule shit".

"Why you worryin' 'bout some claptrap? It means nuttin' except to some stupid old fool who tellin' you tales at the foot o' your bed at night," he would say to me.

As kids, Vic and I would sit and talk at night in the ruins of the old sugar mill close to our homes. Our conversations were often dictated by my fascination for the stories that would be told to me by my grandmother.

Her yarns of ghosts, or duppies, as she called them, would frighten my sister and me before going to bed, keeping us awake long into the night. My need to recite those old wives' tales to my cousin would always fall on deaf ears.

Then, as now, Vic feared very little other than the back of

48

my uncle Gabe's hand. His attitude to such things remained undiminished as he grew older. I, on the other hand, was not so sure. Perhaps the incubus I feared as a child still held me in its grip all these years later.

Something told me that Stella had left her Bible open for a good reason. But I didn't know what that was. What kind of duppy had she feared so much that it made her clean down that house as if it were a hospital ward and then finally run out on the place and not be seen again?

I took the last few sips of my pint before getting up to the bar and ordering another. The landlord, Eric Coles, was a bad-tempered bastard at the best of times. He allowed "coloured people", as he called us, to drink in his establishment not out of any sense of moral responsibility but because St Pauls was becoming something of a black ghetto and he knew we liked a drink. Coles took advantage of that, knowing that our money was as good as any white fellow's. You'd just never hear Eric say that. He tipped my glass slightly to the side in his huge blue-veined hand and poured the bottle of stout into it, a caramel-coloured head forming as it filled, then stood it with some force onto a beer-soaked mat close to where I stood.

"That'll be one and ten," he said in a deep Somerset accent, holding out his palm towards me.

I leant over for the drink and pulled it towards me, reached into my wallet, picked out the change and handed it to him.

"You got a phone I could pay to make a call on, Eric?"

Coles stared at me for a moment, his head tilted to one side, the look on his face a mixture of dismay and curiosity as to why I would need to use his phone. I watched him as he thought for a moment before he turned around and picked up a green table telephone on a large lead from behind the counter and dropped it down in front of me.

"Leave the bleedin' money on the bar when you're done," he mumbled gruffly as he walked away.

I took a small piece of paper out of my jacket pocket. On it was written the number I needed to call. Lifting the receiver, I dialled and waited. After it rang a couple of times, a woman with a voice that sounded as if the entire British Empire's integrity rested upon it, answered.

"Bristol City Council, how can I help you?" she asked.

"Can I have Alderman Linney's office, please?"

The line went quiet as I waited to be connected.

7

By the time Linney had picked up his phone I'd been hangin' on the end of the damn line for the better part of five minutes. When he finally answered, he greeted me with all the disdain of an elderly schoolmaster who was about to give one of his pupils several sharp belts of his cane.

"Mr Ellington. You have something to tell me, I trust?"

Even though I couldn't see him, I got the feeling he was looking down his nose at me, like some rich uncle having to put up with an unwanted nephew who had snot on his sleeve.

"We need to talk. I got some more questions fo' you."

I heard him take a deep breath before he spoke again.

"Questions . . . What kind of questions, Mr Ellington?" His speech was calculated and precise.

"Like why Stella Hopkins' house smelt like an abattoir after a spring clean."

There was silence for a moment before he spoke again.

"Meet me at the old observatory on Clifton Down at 4 p.m.; don't keep me waiting, Mr Ellington."

I didn't get the chance to reply. The burring tone in my ear was Linney's parting gift to me.

It was getting dark by the time Earl Linney arrived. I stood watching him get out of his car on the road below. He made his way up the pathway to the observatory that looked out across the well-heeled community of Clifton and the Avon

Gorge. He was dressed for the cold weather in a heavy winter wool coat, navy silk scarf and a felt trilby hat that was pulled down low over his face. An icy wind blew across the down as I waited for him, stamping my feet on the snowy ground, my toes turning to ice in my shoes.

"You sure do know how to pick a meeting place."

Linney gave no reply to my sardonic remark; he was maintaining his appearance of superiority. The straightness of his spine and the determination of his gait left me in no doubt of his mood. He looked me up and down, drawing the lapels of his coat across his chest before speaking.

"Let's walk, Mr Ellington, keep the blood flowing. You look cold." He smiled at me. It was the kind of smile that makes me want to smack somebody in the mouth. "You have questions for me? Let's have them."

He'd caught me off guard with his abruptness and he knew it. He was clearly unhappy with me after finding out that I'd broken into Stella's home. I steadied myself for a moment, mentally, before coming back at him.

"Did the law search the girl's house?" I asked, my tone now as point-blank as his own.

"They did."

"So, did they speak to you 'bout her house when they searched it?"

"Briefly, yes."

He was giving nothing away. It was like playing a game of verbal chess with the man. Perhaps it was his own sense of self-importance that made him so guarded, or perhaps he just didn't like the way I spoke to him. I pressed on and was unable to disguise the irritation in my voice.

"Police officers go into a house like that, they're gonna have someting to say."

52

"What was there to say? I explained to the police about Stella's somewhat unusual lifestyle, and that she had her own ways of coping. They were happy that nothing was unduly amiss in there. The girl simply liked the house to be clean." His retorts were both clinical and concise.

"Brother, there is clean, and then there's that kinda clean. That shack had been through one big shakedown: the walls were scrubbed and floors I coulda eaten food off of. It was sterile. There was hardly a scrap of furniture in the house, no food, not even a picture of her dead mama."

I'd touched a raw nerve. He stopped walking and turned to face me square on. His eyes bore into me, the anger in them barely held back by a hard-pressed self-control. They were very similar to those that I had viewed earlier that day. Only this time they weren't in some old picture and no child was holding his hand to keep him on the level.

"What the hell does it matter to you if the child owned few belongings, or that she was neat, orderly? Tell me, what did you actually achieve or find by illegally forcing your way into the house? I asked you to tactfully make a number of enquiries for me. Not to commit an act of breaking and entering."

It was at the moment when he said the word "find" that I chose not to inform him about the photograph or the scrapbook that I had found in Stella's bedroom. It was a decision that I was going to regret.

"Where is this line of questioning taking you, Mr Ellington?" he asked.

He was calm again and his composed demeanour had returned, but inside of the man, I knew something was stirring him up.

"Well, I ain't too sure, Mr Linney. But you got a missing girl you got me looking fo', and the way I see it, it don't look like she wants finding. Now from what I can tell, there was only a handful o' people who knew her; they've been questioned by the police, who have come up with nuttin'. So maybe I'm thinking I ain't getting the whole picture here?"

I stood, my arms folded across my chest, shivering, waiting for him to answer me.

"You don't often come up to this part of town do you, Mr Ellington?" His question was loaded and he took some pleasure in asking me it.

"Ain't much reason fo' a man like me to be wandering round Clifton in the cold."

"On the contrary, it's exactly the sort of place you should be wandering around, as you say. In fact I would wholeheartedly encourage it. Do you believe that the colour of your skin prevents you from living where you wish or from achieving what others, such as our white brothers and sisters, perhaps take for granted?"

"Let's just say I didn't feel too welcome when I last walked through the doors of the Berkeley Square Hotel. You know what I mean?"

Linney gave a wry smile at my remark.

"Oh, I know just what you mean. But I believe that I belong anywhere I choose to go. I also believe that the future prosperity for black people is this country is restricted by that same narrow-minded Uncle Tom thinking that you currently possess, and there's no room for that kind of thinking any more. We need to be looking towards the future, Mr Ellington, and how we mould that future to our own good. Now, as far as I am concerned, you have the whole picture regarding Miss Hopkins. You didn't think your five pounds a day would be such easy money, did you? Now, just keep searching for the girl and apprise me of your findings, and promptly, please."

He turned and began to walk away from me before stopping in his tracks and returning to where I still stood.

"I'm sure this will be of some use to you? Goodnight, Mr Ellington."

He held his hand out to me and casually waved in front of my face the same kind of envelope he had given to me before. I took what he offered and opened it up. Inside, there was money: a lot more money.

Out on the downs, the winter evening twilight had an almost mystical feel to it. I looked out towards the city, then across to the suspension bridge, before I began to make my way back towards Clifton village. The lights of the houses flickered, their collective illumination casting an air of prosperity and security around them. It was only then that the alderman's words of achieving greater things and wanting more out of my life suddenly resonated within me, and in that moment I felt cheap and foolish for what I had said to him in defence of my status and colour.

I walked back down into St Pauls as if I'd achieved nothing. But that couldn't be said for the guy who'd been following me since I'd left my meeting with Linney.

8

AT FIRST I THOUGHT the guy following me was hired muscle, perhaps somebody to watch Linney's back while we were having our little chat out on the downs. But I was wrong. He'd stood in what he thought was good cover, obscured by the trees, but I'd spotted him soon after the alderman had turned up. He kept a healthy distance between us as he shadowed me on the opposite side of Cotham Road as I headed back towards my digs.

After about a mile and a half, my new buddy was still with me, and he didn't appear to be bothered that I knew it. I turned to get a better look at him, and from the orange glare of a street light could see he was white, powerfully built and over six feet tall, with his dark hair kept neat in a military-style crew cut. There was a confidence in his swagger that told me this guy could handle himself.

Anyone who was prepared to follow me this far either wanted to know what I was up to or where I lived. But I didn't want him knowing either. I wasn't going to lose the guy unless I tried to outrun him. But I got the feeling the bastard behind me was gonna be real persistent. I needed to put some more distance between the two of us while I thought through the best thing to do. Adrenaline pumped through my body as I quickened my pace.

Heavy sleet had begun to fall as I entered the Kingsdown district, closer to my home turf. I began to walk a little quicker, and when I got the chance took myself off into a side street and kept moving, increasing my speed as I turned into each new road before reaching the steep incline of Marlborough Hill, my tail still hanging in there behind me. I began to climb the slippery cobbled road. I pulled my hat further down over my brow to protect my face from the freezing rain.

Reaching the top, I took a left and pushed myself as close as I could against the red-brick wall of a Georgian house and waited for the guy to catch up. The sleet bounced off of the pavement as I listened for his heavy footsteps, giving me an idea of how close he was. With my heart pounding in my chest, my muscles tightened and I slowed my breathing while I steeled myself for what was to come.

He turned into me with real force as he reached the top of the hill: he had already pre-empted my attack. I lunged from the wall to grab him with my outstretched left arm, my right fist clenched tight, but he was already a couple of steps ahead of me. I felt a sharp, burning pain across my shoulder blade as his first blow made contact, but it wasn't flesh and bone that had struck me. I caught sight of a slapjack in his hand. I raised my left arm low and tried to connect a solid punch to his ribs, but failed as the big man followed with two more vicious blows to my body.

I fell onto my ass and immediately began to push myself backwards across the slushy ground and towards the kerbside, trying to create some distance between myself and my assailant.

Despite his bulk he moved quickly, his weighty arms swiping the cosh towards me as I fought to get up. He was almost on top of me and about to rain down another hefty swipe of the lead club when I lifted my leg and slammed the flat of my foot with all the strength I had into his kneecap, bringing him down hard onto the pavement in front of me. I brought my foot down again twice more, smashing my heel into the back of his head as he writhed in agony.

There was no siren, only the familiar blue flashing beam of a police car that caught my eye as I struggled to my feet. I turned with relief toward the oncoming vehicle, fighting hard to stay upright as it drove towards me.

Rather than slowing down as it approached, the car began to accelerate.

As it drew along side me, the passenger side door was flung open, hitting me square in the chest, spinning me around and knocking every bit of air out of my body as I was flung across the street and into the gutter. Motionless and sprawled out in the street, I faintly heard a man's voice call out "check the spade" before I lost grip of my conscious world and darkness welcomed me with open arms.

★

The unwelcoming rank smell of the sewers woke me with a jolt: face up, my head on the iron grating of a drain. Sleet still fell from the night sky; I was soaked through to the skin, the cold ground numbing my limbs where I lay. I pulled myself up and sat on the kerb, hands on my knees, my scuffed knuckles stinging and head pounding. Not a soul passed as I sat for what seemed like an age, freezing water running over my sodden shoes, the blood from my nose dripping into its heavy flow and washing it down the road.

After picking my hat out of the snow, I slowly walked the mile back to my digs with every step sending a sharp jolt of pain through my beaten frame. When I finally reached my front door I fumbled with the keys, fingers frozen, hands shaking with cold as I let myself in, taking each step of the stairs one at a time and falling through the door into my bedsit. I wanted to sleep, just hit my bed and forget everything. But that was foolish thinking. I needed to check myself out first. I took off my sodden clothing and left it in a drenched pile in the hall. In the bathroom, naked and on my knees, my head over the toilet bowl, I threw up until my guts had no more to give.

Straining to get myself up, I leant against the sink and looked at the mess that greeted me in the mirror. My face had got off lucky, a cut across my cheekbone and a badly bruised nose was the sum of it, but I had a nasty gash at the back of my head. I ran the tap and rinsed a towel under it, placing it over the wound for a moment. I felt my scalp and winced as I caught the quarter-inch opening with my prying fingertips. The rest of me was a mixture of grazes and developing bruises that would show their true colours by morning.

I got into bed, pulling the sheet and blankets over my perished body. There I lay in the dark shivering, hoping that sleep would soon be with me. I closed my eyes and began whispering her name over and over again to myself until the phoenix rose out of the ashes of my heart and took me by the hand to the place where she always waited for me.

"Hey, hun, you rest now. Ellie gonna take good care o' you," she whispered.

I smelt the scent of the poinciana flowers in her hair, then felt Ellie's warm body move in close against my back as she softly caressed my face with her hand. I felt the child in her belly, its soothing heartbeat pulsating in time to the rising of my sleeping breaths.

★

I was awakened from the deepest of sleep by a heavy thumping at my door. Bright sunlight shone through the curtains, which gave the room a false sense of warmth. I looked at my watch, which was still strapped to my wrist. It was just after three thirty in the afternoon. I hauled myself into an upright position, my head throbbing, and threw the stained bedclothes off of me.

It wasn't a surprise to find that my upper torso was covered in a series of emerging, and painful, black and blue bruises where I had been beaten with the slapjack. I pulled a sheet around me and wrenched myself outta bed and down the hall to where my door was about to be took off of its damn hinges by whoever was banging on it. I opened it with a look on my face that the devil would have shied away from.

"Git your sorry, lazy ass out—" His sentence abruptly halted, a shocked and now silent Vic stood before me, his gaze focussing on my knocked-about face.

I swung open the door to let him in. I felt weak and leaned against the wall to keep myself from falling over. Vic closed the door and, with his back against the stained-glass panels, flicked on the hall light to get a better look at me.

"Muthafucka . . ." I heard him mutter deeply under his breath. I looked up and watched his face harden and his eyes close, thoughts of revenge burning within every inch of his being, while he desperately tried to hold at bay the brutal retaliation I knew he wanted to inflict on those who had done me harm. I took a step towards him to calm his anger, arm outstretched in a pacifying but futile gesture as my head began to spin and my legs gave away from under me.

9

VIC HAD CARRIED ME back to my bed, where I'd slept for another six hours.

During that time I dreamt that Stella Hopkins had found me in the street where I had been beaten. She'd picked me up and tended to my injuries with a lace handkerchief that had the same sanitised odour of her home. She folded the bloody cloth tissue and pushed it into my hand before walking away into the wintry dimness while I kept calling out her name, pleading for her to return to me.

When I woke, it was after nine in the evening and Vic was standing over me, the light of my bedside lamp casting his shadow on the wall. His arms were folded across his massive chest as he smiled down at me.

"'Bout time, too. We got to thinkin' you might be dead, you been laid in that bed so long."

I heard a familiar laugh, and I lifted myself up on my elbows to take a look and found Carnell Harris on the other side of the room. He was sitting on my kitchen chair, its back reversed so that he could rest his big arms and chin on the arch.

"Hey, JT, you look like crap."

"Thanks, Carnell, you're all heart."

I dropped back onto the bed. A feeling of nausea rose from my stomach into my mouth as the strong smell of the fiery jack ointment hit me. Someone had smothered it over my torso, and its unfriendly aroma wafted from underneath my bedclothes. Vic bent over me and slid his arm under my back; I flinched in pain as he pulled me forward, propping me up with my pillows.

"I got Carnell to bring Loretta over; she cleaned you up and rubbed that nasty shit all o' your body."

I heard the tapping of a pair of stiletto heels as they walked on the wood floor in the hallway outside. Carnell's wife, Loretta, appeared at my bedroom door, her curvaceous figure leaning on the frame. She wore a tight-fitting scarlet satin dress cut with a deep V in the chest that flatteringly showed off her amply proportioned breasts. Her long jet-black hair was pinned back tight across her head and tied with a red ribbon in a bun. From where I was sitting, she looked too damn good to be playing at night nurse.

"He awake? How's he doing?"

"Boy gonna be just fine, except for the horse cack you gone and smeared all over him," Vic said.

"That horse cack gonna save his pretty face and take the sting outta his messed-up hide," Loretta replied, quick as a whip.

Loretta gave me a sultry wink before walking over to my bedside. She stood for a moment, looking at me, her heady perfume going head to head against the overwhelming medicinal scent of the fiery jack before dropping a familiar-looking brown envelope in my lap.

"I found this in your coat pocket. I'm taking your wet clothes back with me to wash. I'll drop 'em off fo' you in the morning. You sleep on some more now and take no notice o' these two fools, you hear me."

She picked up her fake-fur coat from the edge of my bed and turned to her husband, jabbing at his foot with the toe of her high heel.

"Carnell, git your fat ass outta that chair and take me home, you been sat on that ting fo' hours like you got your butt glued to it!"

Vic let out a roar of laughter at Loretta's damning gibe as Carnell sluggishly got up, rubbing the top of his balding head.

"OK, cherub, you got everyting?" Carnell asked Loretta, barely masking his indolence.

"Oh yeah, I got everyting I need, including a big lazy-assed fuckin' excuse fo' a husband!"

"Loretta, girl, you got the body and looks of a goddess and the mout' of a whore, you know that?" Vic was desperately trying to keep his face straight as he spoke.

"Yeah, is that so? Well, from what I been hearing the only whore been in this pit is the one he been calling out fo' while he been sleeping all this time."

Her words echoed around in my head as I watched her saunter out of my bedroom with Carnell in tow like a medieval serf holding the trailing robes of his magisterial sovereign.

★

I was dead to the world for the rest of Tuesday night and woke the next morning just before eight thirty to the sound of Vic clanking about in my kitchen, where he was cooking eggs and bacon. He had pulled the armchair from out of my lounge and into the bedroom, then slept by my side through the night, using his overcoat as a blanket.

He'd heard me as I was getting out of bed and stuck his head around the opened door. He looked as rough as I felt.

"Sit your ass down, man. You know you need to git yourself some decent fuckin' furniture in this dump. My back feels like I had Carnell's big ass sitting on it all night."

As he spoke, he waved around in his hand a rusty metal spatula, the grease flying off of the end of it, hitting the walls and leaving a series of small oil stains across them.

"You ain't got a damn ting a bit o' use in that kitchen out there. Chipped plates, nasty old cups, knives and forks that are all bent outta shape, and you got fuck all in that fridge o' yours too. I even had to drag my butt down the street in the snow to buy you fuckin' breakfast this marnin'."

"I've been limited on funds lately." It was all I could manage in reply.

"Shit, man, that's seriously limited out there. You need to git your ass down to a soup kitchen an' git fed, if tings are that bad."

"Well, I might not need the soup kitchen fo' a while. Take a look in there."

I grabbed up the brown Manila envelope that Earl Linney had given to me on Monday evening from off of the bed and threw it over towards Vic. It landed at his feet. He bent down, picked it up, opened it and pulled out the folded five-pound notes and began counting them.

"You got yourself fifty pounds in here, man. Where'd you git it? You been selling ganja?" Vic asked suspiciously.

While we ate breakfast, I told Vic about my meeting with Linney on Monday evening, the money, and being followed by the guy I got into the fight with. I sat with a mug of strong coffee, warming my hands while my cousin listened in silence to the details I recanted.

"So, let me git this straight. Some big honky follows your ass from Clifton then beats you with a sap. Then you're kicked across the street by a police car, and the fifty notes in your pocket they don't touch. Someting stinks 'bout it all, brother."

Vic was on a roll and he had a point.

64

"JT, the ting you need to be asking yourself is why the Babylon are interested in you meeting up with that old Jamaican bastard. You think on 'bout that befo' you start worrying 'bout anyting else."

Vic ran me a hot bath and I soaked my aching body before shaving myself with an unsteady hand. I stretched out in the tub and enjoyed the soothing heat of the water on my limbs. Getting cleaned up had made me feel a little more human again. I put my towel round my waist and returned to my bedroom with Loretta Harris's comment last night about Stella Hopkins being a whore rolling round in my head.

After slowly changing into a fresh shirt and jeans, I sat in my armchair in the bedroom and struggled to bend over to put on my socks, my beat-up body smarting with each movement I made. Loretta arrived just after eleven with my clothes from last night washed and ironed. Carnell had taken my shoes with him, dried them out and polished them within an inch of their life, buffing away the white tidemarks that the snow had created and leaving a shining gleam on them.

Loretta kissed Vic on the cheek before coming in and sitting down next to me on the edge of the bed, running her red-nailed fingers across my scalp and rubbing my neck before speaking.

"How you feelin', JT? You sure looking better than you did, lover."

"I'm good, Loretta, good. Thanks fo' cleaning up my stuff."

The humility in my voice caused her cheeks to flush.

"You needn't thank me, JT. I know you'd do it fo' me an' Carnell."

She smiled and took my hand in hers as she spoke. I looked up towards her and lightly squeezed her fingers. It was a simple gesture of gratitude, which was all I could muster at that moment.

"Loretta, what you said last night 'bout that missing girl, Stella Hopkins, being a whore. What you mean by it?"

"What's to mean, JT? Last weekend I was with Jocelyn Charles in the Prince o' Wales. She's one of Papa Anansi's girls." Loretta grimaced as she spoke the pimp's name. "Anyhow, we git to talking 'bout how that Stella girl had gone missing and that Jocelyn had seen her at a party she was working at."

"You happen to know where I can find Jocelyn?" I asked.

"Baby, if you wanting somebody to hook up with to keep you warm at night, I can think o' somebody a little more righteous than Jocelyn."

"I'm sure you can, Mrs Harris, but I kinda need to speak to her urgently."

"You can try the Speed Bird club, she normally in there most nights filling herself with rum when she ain't selling her pokey."

She got up to leave and turned towards me. The sensual beauty was gone from her face, replaced by worry and fear. Her eyes were telling me what her lips could not. If she had spoken, she'd have told me to stay well clear of Papa Anansi and his girls.

I sat and listened as Loretta spoke to Vic in hushed tones out in the kitchen.

After a short while she called out her farewell to me from the hallway and said that Carnell would be coming around later to collect my bloodied sheets and bedding so that she could launder them. I felt I had given a good friend the unnecessary burden of having to worry about me and that my decision to enter a nocturnal domain where only iniquity resided had been the most unwise of choices.

Vic returned to my room. I had my head in my hands and was lost in my thoughts.

"Hey man, you OK? Look, I'm gonna split, git myself a shave and a few hours' sleep. I overheard from Pearl you had a dinner date with 'em tonight. I'll let her and Gabe know you been on the hooch and you ain't well enough to head over fo' supper later. You don't want either of 'em seeing you all busted up like that."

"Thanks, man, you—"

Vic butted in, not giving me chance to thank him for all that he had done for me these past twenty-four hours.

"Now Loretta says to tell you that if you're going looking fo' that cock-rat Jocelyn Charles, that you'll recognise her by the mangy old fox-fur stole she wears round her neck. So we gonna pay us a visit to the Speed Bird later tonight then?" he asked enthusiastically.

The playful look on his face gave me little chance to reject his enthusiastic proposition.

10

OTIS GREY WAS THE stuff of nightmares. He was the kind of man we know exists but we'd rather not think about. At over six feet tall, the powerfully built Jamaican possessed a pockmarked and scarred face that resembled the kind of gothic creatures you would normally find hanging off the inside pillars of a church. Otis inhabited a world of prostitution, drugs and violence, the last brutally meted out to those stupid enough to cross him. The street girls he controlled lived in fear of his cruel wrath and his tendency to inflict physical pain with a large butcher's knife that he kept hidden in a sheath sewn into the long black leather greatcoat he always wore. Only his mother had ever called him Otis; to everyone else he was simply known as Papa Anansi.

I had grown up around men like Papa Anansi all my life. As a child I had witnessed the violence and the fear these men elicited when they applied unwanted protection to local store-owners and publicans, and in later life as a police officer I'd see at first hand their rancorous acts of savagery as they waged gang war against each other. They built wealthy empires on misery and then one day would lose all they had to other monsters with equally, if not more, inhuman criminal behaviour than their predecessors had.

I needed to talk to Jocelyn Charles without Papa knowing. But that was easier said than done. Papa had a never-ending string of lackeys who were prepared to offer up the most meagre information for the price of a ropey joint. On top of that, if Jocelyn was found to be talking to me about his business affairs or the other girls in his pox-ridden harem, she would most probably say goodbye to a couple of fingers, or worse.

The Speed Bird club was on Grosvenor Road and only a short walk from Cut Man's gym. I'd arranged to meet Vic in the Prince of Wales pub at ten that evening, hang around till last orders, then move on to the Speed Bird. I took the only suit I owned from my wardrobe. The navy-blue worsted fabric was wearing thin, but I still looked pretty sharp in it. I picked out a light-blue shirt and a dark knitted tie. I smarted from pain every now and then as I dressed. Loretta had made a fine job of cleaning down my overcoat and hat. I put 'em on, took a couple of aspirin to hold the stinging in my shoulder at bay, then headed out.

I opened my front door and the cold air hit my face, taking my breath away. Coal-fire smoke ran up the chimneys and billowed out into the night, mixing with the freezing fog that was dropping down in the streets as I walked carefully over the frozen, compacted snow and ice on the pavement.

It was just before ten by the time I pulled open the door to the Prince of Wales pub to meet Vic. A heavy mist of cigarette smoke floated across the lounge, where my cousin stood at the polished oak bar talking to the barmaid, his eyes staring downwards towards the low-cut top she was wearing and the ample cleavage on display. The juke box was playing the Rolling Stones' "Little Red Rooster" to a small, unappreciative audience of mainly elderly men whose only interest was the liquor that sloshed around in their beer glasses.

Vic was clean-shaven and dressed in a black velvet jacket with a purple paisley shirt, its top three buttons opened, and

69

around his neck he wore a thin silk scarf held by a gold hoop. His tight dark-grey flares were held up by a wide black leather belt, its diamanté buckle hanging suggestively above his crotch. I called out to him and he turned and walked towards me, a massive grin on his face. He greeted me with all the exuberance of a man who permanently lived his life to the full.

"Brother, you see the titties on her?" he asked. He gave a gentle nod backwards with his head towards the heavyset barmaid. "She carrying more milk in there than on the back o' a Unigate float." He gave out a loud belly laugh at his own remark. "What you drinking? No, wait. I'll git you a rum, you looks like you freezing ya ass off!" He rubbed his hands together excitedly as he returned to the bar.

We found a table that over looked the entrance to the pub and drank in silence. I knew that Vic wasn't happy with my decision to keep searching for Stella, but he'd go along with me, right or wrong. The way he saw it, you didn't run out on your family when they needed you the most – it was as simple as that. He looked around the room before knocking back the rest of his rum. He slammed the glass down hard on the table, breathing in deeply through his nose before he spoke.

"Man, this place is giving me the shits. It's like some nasty honky morgue. Let's git the hell outta here."

The Speed Bird club was a brothers and sisters kind of place. That's not to say that white folk weren't welcome. It's just that they chose to stay away. It was run by Elrod Haddon, a one-time heavyweight boxer and now small-time gambler who'd bought a stake in the bar. He'd earned the nickname "Hurps" during the Second World War on account of how many times he had caught the clap off of the hookers that he'd bedded as he made his way across bombed-out France.

"I had me a rifle in one hand and a tube o' medicated dick cream in the other," he would joke to those who enquired after his moniker. His character was as large as his ego. Hurps was well known in St Pauls. He was a no-nonsense kind of guy who didn't take any shit from his customers and expected none back. I liked him.

The Speed Bird was a cellar club that rarely required a doorman. You went in to drink, smoke and dance. You took a fight out in the street, and if you pushed your luck at the bar you'd end up with your ass kicked out on the road. Vic would feel right at home. The effects of the aspirin were wearing off and I just wanted to find out what Jocelyn knew and head back to my bed.

The place reeked of patchouli oil and three-day-old reefer, and like the Prince of Wales, it was practically empty. On the far wall overlooking a small dance floor was a series of American-diner-style booths, each with leather seating on either side of grey Formica-topped tables. We chose the last booth, and Vic slid across the seat and rested his back in the corner, one leg propped up on the cracked leather cushion. He took his hip flask out of his jacket pocket, unscrewing the cap.

"I got no need to ask what you drinking," I said sarcastically.

He took a heavy glug of rum from the flask before answering me.

"Hell, you don't buy ice and fry it, fool. I got a shitload o' this stashed. You know what Hurps can do with his old piss water over there," he scoffed, waving the back of his big hand towards the bar dismissively.

I crossed the dance floor over to where Hurps was sitting. He was perched on top of a high-backed chrome stool, with a pair of half-framed gold spectacles perched on the tip of his nose while he read a copy of the *Bristol Evening Post*. Bobby Bland's "Stormy Monday Blues" was playing on the sound system as I stood beside him.

"How's tings, Hurps?"

He looked up from his newspaper, lifting his line of sight over his glasses to get a better look at who was speaking to him in his dimly lit, cavernous bar. He took a moment to recognise me.

"Hey, JT, everyting's good, real good. You ain't looking too bright at the minute. What you been doing to git a cracked-up face like you got?"

"Fell like a fool on that damn ice out in the street, Hurps. It hurt my pride more than my head," I lied.

"What you drinking, brother?" Hurps asked me.

"A shot o' that Red Heart rum would go down real nice, Hurps. Thanks, man."

Hurps called across the dark teak counter to a skinny white barmaid. Her dyed blonde hair was cut short into her neck and she wore too much eyeliner, which made her look like a circus clown.

"Shirley, git this man a double Red Heart on me," he snapped at the clown.

She fetched over the bottle and poured a large measure of rum into a small glass with all the finesse of a bricklayer mixing wet concrete. It overflowed and spilt onto the bar.

"Jesus, girl. Why don't you give the floor a fuckin' drink while you at it!"

She took a rag from underneath the bar and wiped up the overspill, then pushed the glass across the bar towards me. She looked at Hurps and flashed him an insincere smirk as an apology for the mess she'd caused.

Hurps shook his big head from side to side in dismay. "Fuckin' woman. She makes my ass itch. More damn trouble than she's worth. I only keep the skanky bitch on cos I been screwing her mama." He laughed to himself. "You here on your own, JT?" he asked.

"No. I'm with Vic. He's sat over there in one o' your booths."

"Goddamn, no. Not that big muthafuckin' cousin o' yours. You tell him to keep his fists in his fuckin' pockets while he's in here. I don't need him treading pig shit all over my club. Last time he came in, he t'rew some poor bastard over this bar. I can do without his kinda crap at my age. You hear me?"

"He's cool, Hurps. I'll keep my eye on him. You got my word."

Hurps stared back at me with a look on his face that didn't express a great deal of confidence in my assurances to him. Vic had enjoyed watching Hurps getting irate at me and got up from where he was sitting and swaggered over to the two of us, laughing as he walked.

"Hey, Hurps . . . You lookin' good, man. Where you been stuffin' that worthless old prick o' yours this week, brother? That damn ting ought to a dropped off by now and crawled up your ass to git a rest from all that pumping you been doin'."

Hurps ignored Vic. He slid off his stool and turned to me, pointing his finger at my face as he began to walk away towards a door behind the bar with a sign on it that read "Staff Only". As he walked, he shouted over the music, "Just tell him he needs keep his gorilla fists off of my customers, you hear?"

Vic and I watched Hurps mumbling to himself as he strode around the bar and left through the staff exit out to his office. The sharp pain across my shoulder intensified as we both burst out laughing.

I picked my drink off of the bar and called over to clown girl, who was half-heartedly polishing the bar with her dirty rag.

"Hey, Shirley. You know a working woman by the name o' Jocelyn Charles?"

"Nearly everybody who comes in here knows Jocelyn. I suggest you stay well clear of her unless you want your cock to drop off."

"I'll sure bear that in mind. So you expecting her in tonight?" I pried.

"If she can't find somebody to pay for her cunny, I'd say she'll be in before midnight."

"Can you drop me a nod if she comes in?" I pushed a one-pound note across the bar to her. She covered it with the palm of her hand and slipped it into her apron pocket.

"Yeah, I can do that." She smiled at me and continued listlessly rubbing away at the teak surface that was Hurps' pride and joy.

We sat back at the booth. I folded four one-pound notes into small squares while Vic tapped his foot to the music as he watched the comings and goings in the bar. He was biting at a hard piece of skin at the edge of his thumb. He pulled at the calloused flesh, breaking it off with his teeth and spitting it out onto the floor before speaking. Clown girl had just caught Vic's attention and signalled the hooker's arrival.

"Say, brother . . . looks like your cock-rat's arrived." Vic leant forward from his seat and gave a hard stare at the Speed Bird club's new arrival. "Shit . . . Man, she's looking plain nasty. You need to keep your dick well clear of her, JT, I'm telling you straight!"

Jocelyn Charles stood at the bar. She was wearing a multicoloured mini-dress and black high-heeled platform knee-high boots. Three large, fake golden sovereign rings adorned her small fingers, which had poorly manicured nails. She had no coat on despite the freezing temperature outside.

The hideous fox-fur stole hung around her neck like a grisly trophy. She bought herself a large glass of Navy rum and strutted over to a secluded snug on the edge of the room. I got up and winked at Vic. He grinned at me and went on biting at his thumb as I walked back over to the bar.

I bought myself another shot of Red Heart and took myself over to where Jocelyn was sitting. I guessed she was around thirty-five, and she had way too much make up on her dark black skin, which piled the years on her, giving her face a real lived-in feel. She and clown girl made a good pair. I put my drink down on the table and smiled at her.

"What the fuck you lookin' at, mister? If you wantin' pussy, you shit outta luck cos I'm off the clock."

I moved around the circular table and sat down next to her, squeezing myself in closer towards her and making the fabric of her dress ride up over her crossed leg, exposing her stocking top. I picked up my drink, took a sip of the spicy spirit and looked into her tired, rum-soaked eyes.

"Git your fuckin' face outta mine befo' I stick my glass in it!"

"Hey, be cool, sugar. I just want ask you a couple o' questions, that's all."

"Questions? What do I look like to you, monkey ass, some kinda public-info'mation service?"

The rum running round her blood was starting to get her mean. I cut to the chase.

"You know of a girl called Stella Hopkins?" I asked.

"Never heard of the bitch. Now fuck off!"

I dropped a folded pound note into her lap and waited. She looked down at the money, returned her gaze to me and sneered a look of disapproval. I put another note on top of the one I'd already dropped. She lost the sneer and replaced it with a scowl.

75

"You talkin' 'bout that dummy from round here that's gone missing?" she asked as she snatched up the cash and stuffed it into her purse.

"Yeah ... That's the girl. Let's just say I heard you saw Stella at a party not so long back. Where was it you seen her?"

"It's over in Montpelier, a big white place on the corner o' Richmond Road. They used it as a shebeen."

She clammed up again and looked out vacantly across the dance floor towards Vic. I dropped another pound note on to her rainbow-coloured dress to get her attention again, and then fired another question at her.

"Who was she there with, Jocelyn? A girlfriend perhaps, some guy?"

I pressed away at her, but she remained silent again. I watched her as she bit at her waxy red-painted bottom lip, her brain ticking over the risks of telling me more.

I let my last note fall, hoping she'd go for it. Jocelyn hesitated, looking down at the money, weighing up in her head how bad business had been lately. She was unsure whether to continue blabbermouthing to me. Thankfully, she did.

"Papa Anansi brought her with him one night 'bout a two month ago. He had her stuck to his side like she was made o' gold. The only time he let her outta his sight was when some white guy who looked like he had a silver spoon stuck up his ass came in and took her away with him. I never saw the girl again."

She went back to her rum and I got up without thanking her and walked back to the booth feeling liked I just escaped from some kind of witch's lair, her curses clinging to my back as a reminder of the price I'd just paid for my liberty.

Jocelyn Charles hid the rest of her easy-earned thirty pieces of silver at the bottom of her purse and sank the rest of her rum in a single swallow, then watched me and Vic leaving before getting up to go to the bar to order another double rum. She caught her reflection in the large mirror that ran across the length of the back wall of the bar and smiled to herself as she thought of how she'd spend her newly gained wealth. The clown brought her drink over. Neither of them spoke as she paid. Jocelyn picked up her drink to toast herself in the mirror for a job well done.

The scarred, unmoving face of Papa Anansi stared back at her as she raised her glass.

11

THE FOG HADN'T LIFTED as Vic and I walked along the Grosvenor Road. I told him what Jocelyn Charles had said about Stella Hopkins and how she had seen her with Papa Anansi at the illicit drinking den in Montpelier and the mysterious white dude who she had left with. He took in every word without comment or interruption until I had finished speaking. Then he hit me with the million-dollar question.

"How the hell did a simple bitch like Stella Hopkins end up in some knocking shop speakeasy with Papa? It don't make a damn bit o' sense."

Vic was right: it didn't make sense. My body ached like hell and I was too tired to think about it any more. I arranged to meet up with my cousin for a drink later in the week. We said goodnight to each other and he left me a short distance from my digs. He'd told me earlier in the evening that he was going to hook up with one of the many female companions that he knew and take it easy for the rest of the night. He walked away, his collar turned up on his velvet jacket, kicking chunks of snow out into the road, his arm outstretched into the air, a white piece of paper held in his hand.

"What the hell you got there?" I shouted out after him.

"It's that barmaid's phone number an' address from the Prince Of Wales. I gotta git me a taste o' some o' that milk, brother."

He hollered with laughter as he vanished into the mist, his hearty guffaws reminding me of the childhood we could never return to.

It was just after one thirty in the morning by the time I got in. I hung up my suit, popped a couple more aspirin, knocking them back with a swig of rum from the bottle, and crawled into bed.

While I slept, an act of unimaginable cruelty was being committed as punishment for an act of indiscretion that did not merit its severity, unaware in my slumber of the unintentional part I'd played in the fatal downfall of another soul.

*

I stirred just after 9 a.m. My body was aching less and the bruising across my chest had blossomed overnight to leave a blue and yellow mottling on my skin. I made coffee and ate a couple of rounds of toast at the kitchen table before having a strip wash. Looking in the bathroom mirror as I shaved, I noted that the swelling on my nose and cheekbone had gone down a little.

I applied some more of the fiery jack to my tender bruises and then made my bed before putting on some fresh underwear and dressing in a pair of brown straight-leg cords and a beige polo neck jumper. As I was about to close my wardrobe door, my eyes were drawn towards the old shoebox that sat on the shelf on the right-hand side of where my clothes hung. I had put it there when I first moved in and had not touched it since.

I sat on the edge of my bed, placing the white box at my side, staring at the lid for a moment before lifting it off. Inside, carefully wrapped in scrappy pieces of old newspaper, were the only surviving memories of a distant and happier life. I picked up the sepia photograph of my parents on their wedding day and the look of happiness on my mama's face. At the moment that it was taken she had been unaware of the miserable life she, my sister and I would endure at the hands of my father's violent temper. I tossed it onto the bed and picked out the other precious keepsakes. A small gold oval locket, the only piece of jewellery my grandmother had ever owned. Threaded through its chain were mine and Ellie's wedding rings. There were some hand-made fishing hooks and a bone-handled penknife I'd used as a boy and my Barbadian police force silver cap badge with a pair of bronze sergeant's stripes that I had worn on my uniform shirtsleeves.

Lastly, at the very bottom, a small, leather-bound Bible that had belonged to my dead wife, Eleanor. I carefully lifted it out and opened it up. Inside were the only three photographs of Ellie that I possessed. They were taken outside of a photographer's store in Bridgetown on a sunny August afternoon. She was dressed in a pure-white linen frock, her jet-black hair tied back in a ponytail, the smile on her beautiful face beaming back at me. In my head I heard her calling out my name softly. I snapped the Bible shut and dropped it back into the shoebox, quickly covering it with the other items I had already taken out. I closed the lid back onto the box, ignoring the tiny silver key taped to the inside, a harsh reminder of the kind of man I used to be.

I needed to shake off the ghosts of the past that had sprung up in my head after sifting through old memories and get to work on what I'd learnt last night. So after paying off my rent arrears and giving a little up-front cash to my landlord, I walked the short distance into Montpelier to take a look at the house on Richmond Street where Jocelyn Charles claimed she'd seen Stella.

Finding the place hadn't been a problem; getting in to have a look around or ask a few questions wasn't going to be as easy. I stood across the road in the doorway of a tobacconist, looking over the two-storey property with street-level stairs that led to a basement flat. I turned and looked behind me at the shopkeeper standing at the counter; he peered through his shop window at me, wondering what I was up to. A worried expression on his face suggested that he thought I was about to come in and rob the place blind.

As I stood in the cold, I went over in my head the little I knew. How had Stella Hopkins met a nasty piece of work like Papa Anansi and what were her reasons for being at an all-night drinking den and brothel in the first place? The two of them were from different worlds. Neither individual's paths should have ever crossed. Thing was, they had, and more importantly, if Earl Linney supposedly had Stella's best interests at heart, then why the hell hadn't he know about her visiting the place? Either Stella was not the simple or naive woman I'd been led to believe she was or old man Linney was lying to me. I was damned if I knew which it was.

I'd already taken one beating from somebody who didn't want me snooping around into Stella Hopkins' disappearance. Whatever she had been up to, it was a helluva lot more suspect than the perfect picture of a sweet little mute girl that Earl Linney had made her out to be. I'd come this far in my search and had little to show for my efforts. Linney was happy to hand out his cash to me, but all I had come up with in the last few days to earn any of it was the word of a rummie hooker who claimed she seen Stella at the illegal drinking den that I was now standing across the road from, and a good kicking to my ribs.

But something in my gut told me to stick with it, rather than tell the alderman to stick his money and get out while the going

81

was good. I was never any great at taking advice, especially my own. So I thought I may as well poke my battered nose a little further into the trough and ask around some more. The scared shopkeeper whose fretful gaze was burning into my back seemed like as good a place to start as any.

I walked in. The bell on the door rang. It announced my arrival to the old fellow, putting him even more on edge than before. He'd have preferred it if I'd stayed out on the street in the snow. He was white, in his late sixties, bald with red-flushed cheeks and a port-soaked bulbous nose. The shop smelt of oak-aged fortified wine barrels, spilt brown ale and cigars. I felt right at home.

"Can I help you, mister?" He asked the question with all the warmth and friendliness of a female alley cat spitting at a horny tom.

"Yes. You got a two-ounce tin of Wills' Golden Cut tobacco?"

The old fellow pulled a circular black tin off the shelf without turning away and placed it on the counter in front of me. "That'll be five shillings eleven."

I gave him the money and put the tobacco into my jacket pocket while he rang up the amount on his till, dropping the coins into the cash register individually as if he need to check that they were real by the sound they made when they hit the metal tray in the opened drawer. I was half-expecting to see him bite into one of them, just to make sure I wasn't trying to fiddle him. Instead, he handed me my change.

"Thanks. I'm looking to find a place to rent," I lied. "What's it like round here, man?"

"Well, it's not how it used to be since ..." He stopped speaking, suddenly realising that he was about to state how the area had gone downhill since the arrival of anybody who

82

had black skin. He looked me up and down nervously and thought better of continuing, which was a good job, as I was about to kick his honky ass through the store-front window. After reconsideration, he began to speak again, his Bristol accent becoming heavier as he spoke.

"Anyways, it depends on what you looking for, don't it, and how much you wants to pay? Most of the 'ouses round these parts are moonlight flit holes. One minute they're filled to the brim, next they've all pissed off cos they can't afford the bloody rent. You won't have much trouble finding a place round 'ere, son."

He'd given me his best answer and smiled, waiting for me to get the hell out of his shop.

"I'd heard from a fella in a pub last night that the place on the corner over there has rooms to rent." I pointed to the corner property on Richmond Road. The old fellow burst out laughing at me.

"You can find yourself a room in there if you want, son. But I don't think you'll be getting much sleep if you does." He continued to laugh to himself.

"Why's that?"

I'd got him on a roll. "Keep talking, brother," I thought to myself.

"On account that they got more shenanigans going on in that place than you can shake a stick at. Strange bloody sorts come and go. There are whores going in, plying their bloody trade after dark. Loud music that's playing all hours of the night and day. No consideration for anybody else in the street." The old man suddenly leaned forward towards me across his cracked Formica counter. "What amazes me is that considering the police always seems to be knocking on that bloody door they never brings anybody out in handcuffs."

"Police?" I asked, the tone in my voice implying a sense of innocence I did not possess.

"Yes, the bloody police. They think I don't see it all going on. But I bleedin' well know different. Thing is, when they do turn up, it's not your bobbies in a panda car types. These blokes are in plain clothes. I see 'em turn up, go in and come out again half an hour later laughing and joking. So you tell me, they in there checking the place for overcrowding? I don't bloody well think so."

Somehow, I thought the mean-spirited old bastard might have a point.

12

JOCELYN CHARLES' BODY was found dumped in undergrowth on the Arches bridge that crosses the Cheltenham Road in Montpelier, not far from the area that she worked at, around six thirty on Thursday evening by a British Rail signalman who had stopped to take a pee in the sidings at the edge of the track. As he relieved himself, his urgent stream of urine had caught her bloodied, grey, lifeless face where she'd lain hidden in between the blackberry briars and nettles. She had been beaten and had her throat slit, and stuffed inside her mouth were four neatly folded one-pound notes.

Jocelyn was quickly identified by one of the local beat coppers who had arrested her in the past for soliciting on the streets. Her demise hadn't come as any great shock to the police. If you were on the game, ending up dead in a ditch was par for the course, as far as they were concerned. But the money left ceremoniously in her mouth was an altogether different matter. A whore carved up and flung down a railway embankment was one thing. A call girl killed by one of her punters generally had her belongings taken, especially any cash. But this was different.

The banknotes discovered were a cruel warning and a message that had spread across the city like wildfire, but nobody, including the police, understood what it meant. Nobody, that is, except me.

It was Friday evening, just after six, and I was sitting in the open snug room of the Star and Garter, my body still aching, waiting for Vic to arrive. Even from the back end of the pub, I could hear the morbid chattering, the rumour and hearsay from the locals at the bar discussing the discovery of the dead call girl Jocelyn Charles.

I took a hefty swig of my beer from the jug-handled tankard before returning back to the copy of the *Bristol Evening Post*, whose headline featured the prostitute's murder across its front page in bold, black aggressive print. There was no mention of the folded money in her mouth in the paper. That sordid piece of information had filtered its way through the pubs, clubs, fish and chip shops, off-licences and street corners across the St Pauls and Montpelier areas overnight, its origins no doubt derived from the tongue of a slack-mouthed member of the Bristol constabulary. Bad news travels fast. The news of a violent death gets around even quicker.

But where I was born, we believe in the bogeyman. The harbinger of such dark news of death is often fearful that their demise may follow hard on the heels of such bleak tidings. So we don't speak ill of the dead. We leave death well alone.

Just less than a week ago, I had been sitting in the same pub, minding my own damn business, reading a newspaper, broke and jobless. Now I had money in my pocket and a job I didn't want, and I was one of the last people to see Jocelyn Charles still alive and possibly about to be linked to her murder enquiry. I'd a helluva lot to thank Alderman Earl Linney for.

I watched Vic breeze through the pub, dressed in a long dark leather coat and blue jeans, his body loose and heading towards the bar. I called over to let him know where I was sitting and he acknowledged me by raising his cupped hand to his mouth to ask if I wanted another pint. I nodded my reply over to him. I made it a habit never to refuse a pint of beer, something my cousin knew only too well.

"How's it going?"

Vic brought over two double rums and pint stout chasers, carefully holding the four glasses in his huge splayed-out fingers. He placed the drinks onto the table and sat in the chair opposite, staring at me.

"Brother, you got a face on you like you just stepped in dog shit and you had to scrape it off your heel with your damn hand."

He cracked up laughing before slugging his rum back in a single gulp, setting the empty glass down in front of him. He then started on his ale, downing a half of it before he spoke again.

"So let's git this straight. That miserable look you got on your face is all down to that frowsy, dead cock-rat they gone an' found up on the Arches last night?"

Vic was the exception to the rule when speaking ill of the dead. He wouldn't be checking over his shoulder for the bogeyman. He'd made a deal with that duppy along time ago. Vic *was* the bogeyman.

I leant across to Vic, folding my arms and lying across the table, my voice at a quiet pitch.

"Look, man, somebody snuffed out Jocelyn Charles because she spoke to me in the Speed Bird club on Wednesday night, and whoever did it left the cash I'd given to her inside that poor woman's mouth to make a point."

"Yeah, what point them trying to make then?"

Vic didn't bother to be quiet.

"Well, whoever killed Jocelyn would have beaten it outta her befo' she died to find out what she'd said to me. Then they stuffed the four pounds that I gave her into her mouth. She'd have told whoever was knocking five strips of crap off her hide how some guy had been asking about Stella Hopkins going

87

missing. And about the shebeen on Richmond Road and the white guy that Hopkins left with that night. Somebody don't want that information going any further, Vic."

"You give that whoring bitch your name the other night?" Vic asked.

"No. But that don't make a damn bit of difference: my prints are on the money the police found in her mouth," I snapped back.

"Keep cool, brother. Hell, everybody's prints are on goddamn money, you fool. Just cos she got four notes rammed in her mout' with your fingerprints on don't mean they can put you in the frame fo' killing the bitch. Git your head straight on this."

Vic was right. I'd spent the better part of the day worrying about how I could go down for Jocelyn's murder rather than thinking why she'd been killed in the first place for the information she had given me.

Stella Hopkins' disappearance was clearly a secret worth killing for. I got me to thinking if Stella was even alive. Perhaps her dead body was also in a ditch somewhere? I told Vic about my conversation yesterday afternoon with the old shopkeeper in Montpelier and his various sighting of the plain-clothes coppers who he'd watched going in and out of the shebeen on Richmond Road.

"They most probably on the take. You know how those bastards work, JT. They know there's shit going down in there. They just wanna piece of it."

"Maybe so, but how many white folks you know go inside a shebeen, Vic? Damn, most wouldn't even know what the hell one was. Yet Jocelyn Charles sees some white guy walk out with Stella Hopkins one night and you possibly got honky police cutting in on a piece of the action from the booze and whores." I looked at my cousin hard before continuing. "I gotta decide, man: I either say fuck it and git out now or I stick with it and try and find the girl. If I stay on this, I need to git into that shebeen to find out what the hell's going on, cos if this shit gets any deeper, my ass is gonna be heading fo' a prison cell."

Vic smiled at me, shaking his head from side to side, his criminal mind weighing up the pros and cons of my situation. He chose his next words of wisdom carefully before enlightening me with them. When he finally spoke, his words were as profound as ever and came in the form of a question.

"JT, firstly, when have you ever said 'fuck it'? And there's another ting 'bout all this that's putting a bug up my ass," he said, his tone contemplative and serious.

"Yeah, what's that?" I asked him suspiciously.

"Earlier this week you told me that you didn't wanna be dragging me into any trouble I had no place being in . . . right?"

"Yeah, that's right, and I meant it." I looked at him, searching inside for the right words of apology, my shame at dragging my kin into possible danger surely evident by the look on my face.

"Well, ever since you've been searching fo' this dummy Stella Hopkins, all you've given me is muthafuckin' trouble, just like you did when we were kids. Shit . . ." He laughed at me before picking up his pint and leaning over across the table, getting real close to the side of my face. "Anyhow, you fool," he whispered into my ear, "You don't need to go into no hooker's shebeen when you got yourself a Clarence Mayfield on the gate door o' one o' those damn places."

He leisurely sat back into his chair and winked at me.

13

CLARENCE MAYNARD WAS one big, mean brother. But he had not always been like that. He was born in a rat-infested back alley in Basseterre on the island of St Kitts. His birth was not welcomed by a devoted mother and father who would love and care for his every infantile need. Instead, he was callously dumped outside the Catholic sister's mission on Cayon Street by the drunken old harpy who had given birth to him in the hope that he would fare better in life in the hands of those of a more devout Christian nature. His deluded, rum-soaked mama was wrong. Clarence endured the harsh discipline of the nuns at the local orphanage, where he grew to understand the meaning of cruelty and how, if applied with the right menace, it got you the results you required. The godly women in black taught him that. It was a heartless lesson he never forgot.

One night, tired of the endless abuse and beatings he'd received from a leather strap, Clarence threw his bedding from the second-storey window of the orphanage and followed it out. He hit the ground running, not daring to look back. The sisters never reported him missing and nobody cared if he was alive or dead. His speedy flight from the ruthlessness of the religious order saw him return to the place of his birth and there, at the tender age of ten years old, on the streets of the island's capital, he found a different kind of family, and they would care for him in their own way, rearing him up as one of their own and educating his mind in the harsh ways of the street. He spent the rest of his childhood and youth among the whores, pickpockets and lawless lowlives that inhabited the city's dark underworld. By the time he left St Kitts at the age of eighteen, for a new life in England, he had become a very different kind of human being from the skinny, scared and frightened kid who had run from his pious, punishing carers.

Now, at the age of twenty-eight, his extreme stature and a powerfully built frame had made him infamous within the Caribbean community in the St Pauls area. It had been developed through hours of pushing weights at Cut Man's gym, going head to head with tough young boxers eager to prove themselves in the ring, and eating huge steaming plates of rice and peas, which he heartily consumed with his beloved fried chicken. If Clarence wasn't working or fighting, you'd find him stuffing his gargantuan face with soul food.

The hard years on the streets and lack of formal schooling had made Clarence a violent-tempered and dimwitted man who stood side by side with the pimps and the criminal underclass, always on hand to do their dirty work for them. He'd muscle in on punters who were stupid enough to try to run out on paying up for the services of the local prostitutes. He collected bad debts from degenerate gamblers on behalf of greedy bookies and applied strong-arm tactics for money-hungry loan sharks. He also worked at minding the doors of local pubs, clubs and shebeens.

Everybody knew of his connections to the local criminal fraternity, and unless you moved in those circles, hung out with hookers or crossed one of the big men who used his bulk to enforce their bidding, it was unlikely you'd ever make contact with him. Clarence simply kept himself to himself.

This was no bad thing. Clarence Maynard was in the employ of Papa Anansi, and like all men who live their lives in the heart of crime and violence, he had to keep secrets, and Clarence guarded the secrets of others – and his own – very well, or so he thought.

It was just after eleven thirty on Friday evening, and Vic and I were sitting, parked up around five doors from the shebeen on Richmond Road in a 1963 Mark One black Ford Cortina that Vic had borrowed from Carnell Harris. It was in pristine condition both outside and in. The comforting smell of leather had come off the red upholstery when I first got in, but that hadn't lasted for long. Vic had insisted on lighting up and smoking a joint as we patiently waited and watched Clarence Maynard's formidable figure open and close the front door of the illegal hooch house to his bosses' many nefarious guests. The radio was tuned in to a late-night local station and was playing Sam Cooke's "Twisting the Night Away". Vic tapped his fingers on the steering wheel in time to the beat as he blew out another mouthful of cloudy marijuana smoke into the already smoky interior.

"Jesus! Do you have to do that in here?" I coughed as I wound down the window.

"Hey man, this is some o' Carnell's finest shit. You can't git better. I gotta sit in this hearse with you, freezing my ass off; I sure as hell need someting inside of me to keep me mellow."

"Where the hell did Carnell git this motor from, Vic?"

I recognised something about the car. I just couldn't put my finger on it.

"You know Errol 'Sure Ting' Toleman?" Vic asked me without turning his head away from watching Clarence's activities on the door of the shebeen.

"Errol, the bookies' runner, this is his car?"

Now I remembered seeing Sure Ting's ugly mug driving about in it.

"Well, these wheels were Sure Ting's." Vic smiled.

Errol 'Sure Ting' Toleman was the kind of man who my mama would say "needed a good leaving alone". He was a weasel-featured Barbadian who stank of bad luck and was as stupid as he was greedy. He made a cut out of anyone who favoured frittering away their money on the horses, dogs and anything else you cared to bet on. You could find him skittering in and out of anywhere that housed a card game and he parasitically attached himself like a leech to those poor creatures intent on losing either all the money they had in their hip pockets or the shirt off of their backs. On a Friday, if you had just received a wage packet and you liked to gamble, Sure Ting would be hanging over your shoulder like a vulture ready to tear the flesh off a rotting carcass. He was far from your nine-to-five kinda guy.

"Now ole Sure Ting, he thought he got a better hand o' poker at the table than Carnell, tinks he's got him on the ropes. Fair hand, the man's got. There's two hundred notes on the table and Sure Ting offers up his motor, cos he shit outta cash and those cards he's holding, well he knows they're a sure ting, or he tinks they are. You know what I mean? Carnell, well he takes the bet offa the man. Only Sure Ting forgot one real important ting."

"Yeah, what he forget?"

Vic had me hooked. He stared over at me with a knowing twinkle in his eye.

"Carnell cheats like a real muthafucka!"

Vic shrugged his heavyset shoulders and began to chuckle to himself as he returned to watching the door of the shebeen.

We sat and I continued to listen to Vic laughing to himself as he relived the tale he'd just told me in his head. On the radio, Ken Dodd began to sing "Happiness" and Vic hurriedly snapped the wireless off, scratching the back of his head furiously with his fingers, the white-hot-tipped joint hanging from the corner of his mouth, a tiny trail of smoke rising up and gently bouncing off of the inside of the roof and soaking its pungent scent into the back seat and passenger shelf of the car. He looked over at me, his face full of bemusement at the music he'd just turned off.

"There ain't no way I'm listening to that ugly-assed, buck-toothed honky Scouser. Not now, not ever."

He shook his head in disgust, then returned to watching out for his chance to move.

Earlier in the evening, Vic had gone into minute detail as to what was going to go down later that night when we were face to face with the hulking doorman. My cousin had left me in no doubt of the kind of damage and pain that Clarence could inflict if he was of a mind to. I was trusting Vic to keep the giant's mind on other things.

"OK, JT, now you clear on what we gotta do, brother?"

I nodded sharply, as Vic continued to go over his plan of action again.

"Let me do the talking, it'll be cool, man. We git the information you want real quick and we git outta there an' drinking my rum back at your digs in twenty minutes instead o' sitting in here like a couple o' cold stiff dicks waiting to git laid." Vic swung open the passenger door, readying himself to leave. "Now c'mon, let's git this shit over and done with." He nudged me in the ribs with his elbow and I yelped in pain. "Sorry, man, I forgot 'bout your tenderness down there." He laughed at me as we got out of the car.

Some light flakes of snow had begun to fall as we walked over to the shebeen. We climbed the large granite steps and

Vic gave a hefty knock at the dark wood-panelled front door as I stood by his side. Behind us, the only light was the orange glare of the street lamps. Clarence opened the door, with a slight look of surprise on his face when he saw the two of us standing in front of him.

"Hey, Vic. What you doin' here, man? The pumped-up doorman frowned at us. "I don't normally see your mean ass outside o' here."

Clarence spoke with all the grace of a man who had a house brick tied to the end of his tongue. He came out onto the step, closing the door behind him.

The man's huge bulk was now blocking our further advancement towards the entrance of the shebeen, but we had no interest in going inside.

"You sure right 'bout that, Clarence. I don't normally find myself needing to buy pussy or cheap rum from one o' Otis's joints. But my man here is looking to find himself a special kind o' lady an' I thought you might just be the fella able to help him out."

Vic was keeping his patter nice and light, but underneath the froth he was ready for Clarence to turn on the pair of us. He started to push the doorman's patience a little further.

"Only you see JT here, well, he's kinda reserved, shy even, and he was hoping to git himself an introduction of a more personal nature. He's looking fo' someting with a little more class than him ending up knocking his ting up one o' Otis's cock-rats in those nasty back rooms you got going on there." Vic pointed over the bouncer's large shoulder towards the shebeen's closed door. "You know what I mean, brother?"

Clarence, clearly irritated by our presence and Vic's banter, moved towards us and we took a step back down the icy steps.

"Hey, Vic, Papa wouldn't want you using his other name like you keep doing."

Vic's plan was starting to successfully unfurl, and with the cunning of a black widow spider had begun to draw the big fellow towards his web, readying himself to strike.

Clarence looked directly at me, sizing me up before speaking again.

"If the brother here wants to meet a special kinda lady then he either needs to step inside o' here with a full wallet or git himself to church and find himself a wholesome piece o' tail there."

Another step backwards, closer to the pavement and Vic's web.

"Well, like I said, Clarence, JT's kind o' unsure if he wants to be wiping his ting on one o' Otis's skanky bed sheets with the sort o' bitch that's gonna leave more than a lastin' impression on his cock in a week's time. You can see my point, brother?"

"Look, I ain't got time fo' any more stupid questions 'bout finding your boy there a clean whore. If he wants some o' what we got, he pays the lady and he gets a piece o' ass. If not, take a hike."

"Hey, we don't wanna spoil your night, Clarence, my man here's willing to make it worth your while."

Vic held up two fingers and his thumb and rubbed them together hypnotically. Clarence wasn't the kind of guy to be hypnotised, but, if we were lucky, he could still be bitten by my cousin's careful scheming.

"I ain't interested in that nigger's money, now git the fuck off my steps."

Clarence outstretched the palms of his large hands in front of him and, still without touching either of us, used them to back us down the remainder of his precious steps away from

96

the entrance – just as Vic had told me he would. He'd bait him one more time to get Clarence where he wanted him.

"Hey now, there ain't no need fo' you to be blowing no blood vessels. You need all the red stuff you got to keep it rushing to that big ole head o' yours an' stop you falling on that fat ass that's hanging out the back o' those baggy trousers you wearing, Clarence."

That did it. The big man flipped.

"Git your muthafuckin' asses off o' my gate door, who you think you're talking to?"

Vic had pushed all of Clarence Maynard's buttons and it had nearly paid off for us.

We retreated backwards one more time, and I caught Vic darting his eyes quickly from left to right to check that the street was clear of passers-by or punters. When our feet hit the pavement, I moved quickly to my left as Vic came in close towards Clarence's body and shot his knee hard into his balls, immediately making the big man double over in pain and grasp with both hands at his testicles. Vic then tore down with his fist across the incapacitated bouncer's nose, blood spraying onto the path in front of our feet. He quickly forced his left hand under Clarence's thick neck, pinching at his throat with his thumb and forefinger and gripping tightly at his windpipe, crushing his ability to breathe. I took hold of the doorman's enormous left arm at the wrist and bent it around fiercely behind his back, pushing him forward, as Vic quickly led the incapacitated Clarence by the throat down the next set of steps into the basement area, pushing him violently against the wall and slamming his fist into his nose again.

I then heard the mechanical sound of a blade disengaging from its metal and bone handle and in a split second Vic's flick knife was held firmly against Clarence's jugular, the razor-sharp edge drawing blood as it sliced a thin cut into the bouncer's skin.

"Let's be cool now, real cool." Vic pushed the blade a little harder into Clarence's neck before he spoke again. "Now I know I got your attention, brother? You just smile back at me, no need to try and nod that hunk-o'-lead head of yours. I don't wanna have to slice it off with my pen knife – you git me?"

Clarence stared at Vic, eyes watering, his anger abated by the razor-sharp cutting edge at his craw. He pulled more of a grimace than a smile as he obeyed my hot-tempered cousin's request, showing the whites of his gritted teeth, which were stained with his own blood. Vic calmly continued with his instructions to the big man.

"Now, my man here has a couple o' questions fo' you, an I don't wanna be holding this chopper at you ugly-assed head fo' too long, cos your breath's starting to fuck up my sense o' smell. We on the same wavelength here, Clarence?" Vic twisted the knife into the big man's neck to make his point. "You need to be smiling, brother."

The doorman smiled again, the severity of his predicament now fully realised. I moved in closer towards the bloodied doorman, who stared back at me like a roped-down bull desperate to break free of its secured bonds.

When I began to speak, Clarence immediately started to suck air in between his crimson-tinted teeth as a precursor to our conversation, which simply stated in street parlance that he had nothing to say to me. Vic thought differently on the matter, and like a cobra striking at a mongoose's unprotected hind he struck out at the giant's shin with the toe of his shoe, dropping the huge man to the floor, then pushed down hard with the flat of his foot onto the hulk's face, pressing his cheek and jaw into the slushy concrete. Now Vic was pissed off.

"OK, enough of this fuckin' around. You wanna hiss through your teeth like some old bitch on the hump, that's fine, brother. But you gonna have to do it with that thick throat o' yours cut wide open, you hearing me?"

"What the fuck you want with me?" The goliath had finally got the message that Vic meant business.

I bent down in the wet ice so that I could make myself understood more easily. He was going have a hard time hearing what I had to say with Vic's sole across one ear and the other pinned down into the wet ground.

"Few weeks ago, a white dude, could've been a cop, walked through that door above us. Then a short while later he walks out again with a lady on his arm. Now I know that upstairs ain't the kind place that honky coppers frequent without a good reason. They either come fo' cash or a piece of ass. That's right, ain't it, Clarence?"

Vic pushed down hard again onto the decked man's thick skull, prompting Clarence to speak.

"Yeah, that's right . . . They coming fo' both, most times."

"So how often do they come and where they taking those girls who walk out with 'em?"

I stayed calm, keeping my questioning relaxed. Vic was doing all the hard work, and he looked like he was enjoying himself.

"I don't know where they take 'em. Papa got a couple o' pigs in his pocket. He keeps 'em sweet with a little cream off o' the top and a choice of some cunny, that's all I know."

Before I got chance to press him a little harder, Vic took his foot off of Clarence's face and quickly knelt down next to the big man, his knife in hand, its pointed tip placed firmly inside Clarence's ear.

"Let me tell you what I know 'bout you, dirty bullaman." Vic spat out his forthcoming threat with real menace. "I know you like pushing that nasty cock o' yours in places it don't belong and that you like to be around schoolboys in your spare time." Vic gave Clarence the chance for a moment's reflection. "Now I know that's someting you don't want getting round, cos it's gonna fuck up your reputation as a stand-up kinda brother. You getting me, you ass'ole? Now unless you start giving my man here some answers to the questions he's asking, you gonna find yourself walking round this neighbourhood with everybody knowing you is a one-eared, kiddie-fuckin' nigger."

The beaten colossus didn't need further persuasion to continue to spill his guts.

"There's two of 'em, both on the take outta Bridewell police station. They come any time they wanting some action fo' themselves. But only one of 'em comes every other Saturday night to collect a special piece o' ass that Papa brings fo' him. The pig's an action-man-lookin' type o' dude, with a crew cut. I don't know names or where that honky takes the bitches, and I don't care, I swear, man."

"When you expecting him to pick up his next girl?"

"Keep him talking while he's still scared," I thought to myself.

"He should be over tomorrow night, after eleven."

Vic kept the pointed end of his blade firmly in Clarence's ear. He looked over at me to make sure I'd got all I needed out of the fearful child molester. I nodded that I had, then Vic got to his feet, took a screwed-up piece of paper out of his back trouser pocket and flung it onto the downed man's head. It bounced off onto the wet asphalt in front of him before Vic gave him a series of simple instructions.

"There's t'ree numbers on that paper in front o' you. Somebody who's gonna answer any one o' those numbers can git a message to me within five minutes o' you calling. When that honky cop turns up tomorrow night, you git yo' ass to a phone and you make that call to me, brother. Cos if you don't, an' I have to come looking fo' your ass again with this cutlass, I promise you I'm gonna off cut that scabby prick o' yours and feed it to my dog."

Vic gave Clarence a hard, swift kick in his back before then jabbing his thumb in the air towards the direction of the steps, informing me our time was up and telling me to exit back up the steps and onto the pavement.

We left Clarence Maynard laying in the basement doorway, wet, scared and cold. After what Vic had said about his wicked predilection for young boys I would not have given a damn if the demons of a hell-fired underworld had risen up from out of the frozen earth in front of me to grab his worthless soul and drag him to the torture of eternal torment that he rightly deserved.

Snow was now falling out of the night sky in larger flakes, covering the road with a fresh layer of the godawful white stuff that I was quickly growing to despise. I looked at Vic as we walked back to the car and laughed as he was opening the driver's side door of the Cortina.

"What?" he said, irritated by my unexpected laughter. I watched him about to get into the car; a single snowflake fell onto his face, catching his eyelash, which he quickly wiped away with his hand before turning back to me. "You got someting to ask me, man?"

"Yeah . . . You ain't got no dog, Vic."

"I know that, fool, but next door sure as hell have, and that poor ting, it always looks damn hungry to me."

And at that moment I had absolutely no doubt in my mind of my cousin's cruel ability to make good on the threat he'd just made to the petrified doorman.

14

THE SOUND OF SNOWBALLS being repeatedly pelted at my bedroom window finally woke me from a deep, dreamless sleep on Saturday morning. I pulled the blankets across my naked shoulders and walked over to the single-paned window, which was patterned top to bottom with a spider's-web effect of frozen ice. Taking the cold brass loops in both hands, I drew the up the sash frame, poked my head out into the cold air and peered sleepily into the street, which was coated in a deep covering of freshly fallen snow. Looking up at me, framed in all the blinding whiteness around him, stood Carnell Harris. He was dressed in a pair of brown carpenter's overalls and a black donkey jacket buttoned up to his collar with a thick blue and red scarf around his neck. Hiding the top of his bald, shiny head was a dark-green woollen bobble hat, which initially made me think that I was staring down at an oversized black dwarf who belonged next to Santa in a fancy department-store grotto at Christmas.

"What the hell time is it, Carnell?"

An unpleasantly chilly wind blew through my blankets, making my skin rise up in large goose bumps and setting my teeth on edge.

"Marnin', JT, it's just after eight o'clock. Vic asked me to come round to yours early. We picked up some furniture fo' your digs a couple o' days ago." Carnell pointed to the back doors of his rusted-up old Bedford van, which he had pulled up onto the pavement directly underneath me. "He told me he didn't want any of that shit I got in the back o' there cluttering his lock-up fo' more than a day or so and that I was to git it loaded up and to help you shift it."

"Are you kidding me? At eight o'clock in the fuckin' morning, on a day like today? Are you plain shit stupid, Carnell?"

The big lummox just stood there and took my thoughtless insult on the chin. I regretted almost immediately my ungrateful rebuke to my friend and I shot a half-cocked smile down to him by way of apology for my short-tempered remark and he returned it with a goofy grin that made me question what the hell Loretta ever saw in her witless, lethargic, but good-natured spouse.

"Just gimme a minute . . . OK?" I drowsily called down to him.

"You take your time, JT. I like the snow."

It was a witless remark like that made me realise it was gonna be one of those kinda days. I wondered for a moment if I could just leave the dense bastard out in the street while I made myself a hot cup of coffee, but I thought the better of such a cruel idea and reluctantly made my way outta my digs and down the stairs to the front door to let the brains o' Barbados in.

Carnell entered into the hallway with all the grace of a bull elephant that had accidently caught its nuts on a wire fence. His big feet dragged in half a streetful of snow onto the floor. He stopped and stood in the doorway for a second, taking a moment to undo his coat before stamping the rest of the wet crap that had accumulated on his hefty size nines onto the hessian mat. As I waited for him to haul himself a little further into the hallway, another gust of cold air howled around my bare feet and legs, the icy draught blowing up inside the blankets I'd covered my nude body in, sending a chill up my ass that increased my temper tenfold.

"Fo' Christ's sakes, Carnell, why don't I just stand here with this damn gate door open fo' the rest of the day? Maybe if you hang round long enough, some more of that white shit out on the sidewalk can blow in here and you can make yourself a goddamn snowman."

By the time I'd finally got him inside and closed the door, my frozen heels had stuck to the tatty linoleum flooring and I couldn't feel my toes any more. Not only was my patience wearing thin but so was the skin on the soles of my feet.

"Go on up, man." I impatiently put my hand out in front of me as a polite gesture that my my sloth-like buddy should go on ahead of me and that I would follow him. Every step on the cold lino felt like I was walking across a frozen glacier and my efforts to get quickly back upstairs and return to the now-dying warmth of my bed were hindered by the weighty trudging of Carnell's fat ass in front of me.

"Carnell, you ain't climbing the north face o' the fuckin' Eiger, man. Git a goddamn move on befo' I freeze to death out here on the landing."

"Sorry, JT, I ain't as fit as I used to be. Loretta says I need to git myself a set o' weights and a skipping rope to knock some of these pounds off o' me."

He undid his coat as we finally reached my room. His chubby hands held a length of his fat stomach, which he wobbled up and down in his thick fingers to emphasise his obvious weight problem. I looked at him playing with his fatty flesh and at first didn't know quite what to say to him, but not for long.

"Carnell, man, if you use a skipping rope to jump around with a big-assed gut like you got going on there, you gonna do yourself and anybody stand' within twelve feet of you some serious fuckin' injury, you know that, don't you?"

I couldn't help but see the funny side of my large friend trying to skip and burst out laughing, while Carnell just looked on at me in bewilderment.

After I'd dressed, the two of us made our way back downstairs and out into the street. Carnell opened up the double rear doors of the Bedford and inside was a large ruby-red-coloured settee and four wooden kitchen chairs. Balanced on top of the sofa were a small oak writing desk and a cardboard box that contained cooking utensils pans and a set of six drinking glasses, which Carnell cheerfully informed me Loretta had sent "special" for me.

It took us around half an hour to lug the heavy couch and the rest of my newly acquired furnishings up the stairs and into the various rooms. When we'd finished, I filled the kettle at the kitchen sink, lit the gas hob and sat opposite Carnell at the table on one of the dining chairs he had carried up.

"Carnell, where the hell did Vic git all that stuff we just dragged in?"

As soon as I'd asked the question, I wished I hadn't.

"You remember old girl Walker, JT: that sweet lady who lived opposite Loretta and me in one of those run-down tenements?"

"No. Should I?"

I didn't like where any of this was going.

"Well, she passed on t'ree weeks back. See Vic and me, we did the house clearance as a favour fo' her sister on account the deceased was a good friend o' your aunt Pearl's."

"So all this shit we just dragged through the snow and up them stairs used to belong to an old dead woman? Tell me she didn't croak it on that lounger that's sitting in my front room."

"Hell, no, JT. She died in bed. Now, I asked Vic if we should bring that along, and the mattress fo' you too. But he didn't think that you'd want it. Said it was shagged out and he knew you got tings sorted in the eiderdown department."

The well-meaning oaf nodded his woolly-hat-covered dense head in the general direction of my bedroom and grinned at me again.

"Well, thanks, Carnell. I'll rest easier knowing I got friends who know me well enough to realise that I ain't too keen on sleeping on some poor old stiff's night-time chaise longue. That's sweet, man, real sweet."

"Oh, you're welcome, JT. Any time, man."

I made coffee for the two of us and we chatted for a while 'bout anything and nothing, and the latest news of the cricket back home, both subjects Carnell specialised in. As he prattled on about everything under the sun, my thoughts became lost again in the mystery that was Stella Hopkins' disappearance and how I needed to speak again to Earl Linney at some point before the end of the day. I watched as Carnell drained the last dregs of coffee from his mug and then raised his bulk up from off of the chair before sticking his hand in his donkey-jacket pocket, pulling out a set of keys and throwing them across the table to me, then buttoning up his coat as he spoke.

"They're fo' the Cortina you and Vic were sitting in last night. He said you may need a set o' wheels fo' a while, and befo' you say anyting, it's only gonna sit outside my place rusting up just like my damn van does. You'll be doing me a favour taking it off my hands fo' a while. You'll find it still parked up outside o' Gabe's. I'll be seeing you around, JT."

He gave me a final gormless smile as I sat and watched him aimlessly wander out of my kitchen. I heard him fumble with

106

the catch on the front door as he was leaving, finally closing it behind him with a loud, ham-fisted slam. I was speechless and humbled by my lumbering friend's act of generosity and kindness.

A cloak of shame dropped over me for the unkind comments that I had made to him earlier. The cruel ignominy I had meted out to Carnell was not deserved, and I felt a lesser man for it.

It was after midday by the time I had had a shave and cleaned myself up. The bruises on my body had started to lose their aggressively dark hue and were not as painful as they had been. I dressed for the bitterly cold weather outside, putting on a pair of jeans, a powder-blue herringbone shirt and then a thick crew neck Arran jumper before slipping on my shoes and double-knotting the laces. I took my hat and coat from off of the hanger in the hall and picked up my wallet and the car keys, which were sitting on top of the writing desk that had been placed against the back wall of my bedroom. As I was about to walk out, I turned and stared back at the dusty piece of antique furniture that old Mrs Walker had unknowingly bequeathed to me. It suited the room, and for the first time my inhospitable abode started to feel, just a little bit, like a possible home.

I picked up the Cortina from outside of Pearl and Gabe's, reminding myself as I started up the engine that I needed to pay them a visit real soon after not turning up for dinner last Wednesday evening. I drove the two miles out of St Pauls into the centre of Bristol, parking up close to the city's cathedral on Deanery Road, and found a phone box to make my call to the alderman.

The red iron and glass-framed phone box stank of piss and lord knows what else as I dialled the second of the two numbers on the slip of paper that Linney had given me. It rang six or seven times, before the pips sounded in my ear to tell me that my call was being answered. I pressed a coin into the slot to pay and was then greeted by a woman's voice.

"Hello, Bristol 8424." A warm, richly lilting Caribbean voice, which was akin to my own deceased mama's, threw me off kilter for a moment and I stood silent for a moment. "Bristol 8424, can I help you?" the woman repeated.

"Can I speak to Mr Linney please?"

This time it was my turn to hear silence on the other end of the line. She finally replied, but had lost the warmth in her lyrical expression.

"Who's calling, please?" Her tone had become more cautious, suspicious even.

"My name's Ellington." I kept it short and sweet. She didn't sound like the kind of woman who wanted to get into a deep and meaningful conversation with me.

"I'll just get him for you. One moment please." I heard her put down the phone and walk away in heels onto a hard wood floor while I continued to stand in the cold with the smell of urine wafting up my nostrils. A few seconds later I heard a door close in the background before the alderman finally came to the phone and greeted my call with a disposition that was as chilly as the weather outside.

"Mr Ellington. I had expected to hear from you a little sooner." Linney was his usual brusque self. It was good to hear that he'd missed me.

"Is that so? Well, I'm sorry 'bout that. I took a day's bed rest after we last met and I've been chasing my tail in the snow doing what you asked me to," I replied sourly.

"And you have reliable information for me?"

He was still keeping it to the point and his blunt manner towards me was really starting to wind me up.

"Yeah, and this job has brought me nuttin' but grief up to now. We need to meet, today."

"We do?" he asked, then fell silent again.

I wasn't in the mood for any more of the councillor's taciturnity. Thankfully, my growing ill-temper with the man was fortuitously held back when Linney finally spoke, giving me another of his to-the-point commands. I played along.

"Do you know Dundry Hill? I'll meet you on Downs Road as you leave the village at four thirty sharp."

He was about to do his favourite trick and have the last word, but I interrupted him, speaking back down the telephone before he had a chance to cut me off.

"Why in the name o' hell you wanna meet up there I don't know. But I'll be there, Downs Road, four thirty on the dot, and Mr Linney . . ."

"Yes?" He snapped back at my audacity, surprised to be outmanoeuvred by such a hasty retort. I could hear his impatience on the other end of the line. I held off a moment longer, giving him a taste of his own medicine before I finished my sentence.

"Just make sure nobody knows you're coming to meet me, and bring your wallet with you!"

I dropped the receiver into the cradle, smiled to myself and pushed open the door, taking in a noseful of clean air as I got out.

15

I NEEDED TO KILL A little time before meeting Earl Linney later
that afternoon, and my brief, uneasy telephone conversation
with the man had left me feeling irritated and in need of a
pint. It was a short distance up to the Hatchet Inn, which was
busy with Saturday lunchtime trade. A group of men were
crowded around the bar in a semicircle, each of them wearing
a red and white scarf displaying their proud allegiance to
Bristol City football club.

I pushed my way through them and waited patiently for the
overworked barmaid to catch my eye and finally serve me.
I ordered a pint of stout and the last cheese and onion cob,
which sat on a covered plate next to a tired piece of pork pie
on the back of the bar. A sign above the food read "Freshly
Made", though I wasn't convinced and it didn't give me a lot
of confidence in my forthcoming lunch. But I was hungry, so
I took my chances.

I paid up and found myself a seat in the snug area, took off
my hat and coat, and quaffed over half of my drink before
sitting down. I took a bite of the roll and wished I hadn't.
I dropped the stale sandwich onto the plate and pushed it
across the table away from me, then washed the fusty taste
out of my mouth with my ale. While I drank, I went over in
my mind all that had happened in the last few days and the
things I would tell Linney and, more importantly, what I was
going to keep to myself. He knew more than he was letting on

about Stella, so I had to play the wily old fox at his own game, gain some ground and try to come out of our next meeting knowing more than when I went into it. But it wasn't going to be easy.

Alderman Linney had depicted Stella as a mild-mannered mute with little family and few friends, and who was rarely ever seen out, except to attend work or church, and she never ventured far from home. But then the last time she had been seen anywhere other than her usual haunts was by local hooker Jocelyn Charles in an illegal drinking dive with one of the nastiest pieces of work in the area, and she had left on the arm of a suspected crooked copper. So far I'd had the crap beaten out of me and nearly been run down by a police car, and Jocelyn had been found dead in a ditch less than twenty-four hours after giving me the information. I could now end up as a key suspect in her murder and I still didn't know what the hell was going on.

I sat, thinking how I could play things with Linney, my drink in my hand, swilling the last inch of beer around the bottom of the pint tankard. I lifted it to my mouth and sank the last of the dark, toffee-tasting liquid and then stared down into the bottom of the empty glass. The memory of my first meeting with the well-connected politician came back to mind and I wished I'd never set eyes on the man or taken a penny of his lousy money.

The escarpment of Dundry Hill rises to over seven hundred feet and normally forms a green backcloth for the whole of the south of Bristol. Today those emerald downs were covered in a white blanket of snow, and my journey to meet Linney was hampered by the icy roads and my inexperience at driving in such treacherous conditions. Back home, we call Barbados Bim, and we don't see too much snowfall on Bim. I shook all thoughts of my place of birth out of my head and concentrated on my driving. By the time I reached Dundry village and our meeting point, dusk was falling and the alderman was already waiting for me. He was sitting behind the wheel of his Austin Cambridge, which was parked on the side of the road with the car bonnet facing an impressive view that looked out across towards the city in the dimming light. I reluctantly got out of my car, pulled my coat collar up around my face and trudged through the snow towards Linney's vehicle. As I got a little closer he flung open the passenger side door and impatiently called out to me.

"Come on, man. I'm losing all the heat in here with this damn door open for you."

It was the kind of friendly greeting that really had me warming to him. I didn't rush to get in, and when I finally did, I sat opposite him, rubbing my chilled hands vigorously before cupping them together and blowing warm air through them. Linney was dressed in a thick plaid winter coat, with a beige felt fedora hat neatly positioned on his head, so the peak fell over his right brow. I looked out through the partially misted-up windscreen at the lights that shone up from the buildings and homes below us.

"Quite a sight, even at this time of the day, don't you think?"

His congenial question to me was unexpected, and despite the diminishing light I continued to hold my gaze on the view beneath us, unsure what to say. Linney went on talking, unfazed that I had not replied to his question.

"I intend to build houses down there. Lots of them, and I'm building them for those who are currently living in run-down properties that barely survived the Blitz. You got six, seven members of a family all sleeping in a one-bedroom tenement, and who can't afford to pay the extortionate rents asked by greedy landlords, probably similar to your own, Mr Ellington."

Linney was on his soapbox and, like all politicians, he wasn't eager to get off.

"Did you know in between November 1940 and April of the next year the Nazi Luftwaffe dropped over 920,000 tons of bombs down there? They destroyed 82,000 homes and killed nearly 2,300 people. On the fourth of January 1941, Bristol suffered its longest raid: over twelve hours, they say. They even dropped an eight-foot bomb that never exploded. The disposal teams, who I'm told dug down over twenty-nine feet to retrieve it, nicknamed the monstrosity Satan. Amazing, don't you think, that a city can suffer such devastation, and return from the brink of destruction to such glory?"

"Oh yeah, I'm seeing all that glory, brother, glowing down there in them streets right now. What's your point?" I said sarcastically.

The old man went on, ignoring my question.

"On the thirteenth of February 1945, I was stationed at RAF Waddington in Lincolnshire, and part of the ground crew that loaded up some of the 4,000 tons of explosives that were dropped on Dresden in Germany over two nights of savage bombing. We tore the heart out of that city just as the enemy did to Bristol. I wonder if they managed to find an unexploded shell like they did down there and gave it a demonic title." Linney was quiet for a moment before looking at me and continuing. "My point being, Mr Ellington, that we all need to give evil a name, don't you think?"

He didn't give me the chance to answer him.

"Now let's hear this reliable information you have for me."

I told him how I'd been followed by the mystery fellow after our previous meeting and about my subsequent beating by him with the slapjack and how I suspected that he was a member of the Bristol constabulary. Then there were the details of the sighting of Stella at the shebeen and my chat with Jocelyn Charles at the Speed Bird club. I needed to keep on my toes with Linney and quickly fired off my next question to him, aware of how the old man liked to play a game of cat and mouse on his terms.

"You know a man named Otis Grey, most people call him Papa?"

"No, never heard of him. Should I?"

The alderman was quick to make it clear he wasn't acquainted with the Jamaican pimp. But it was too late: the look on his face had told me different.

"If you did, it would explain a lot. He's the kinda man who has a fairly limited social circle. You're not gonna meet him at the Rotary Club or Gospel Hall. Ting is, Stella was seen with him shortly before she went missing."

"And you think this Otis Grey or whatever he's called may have something to do with her disappearance?"

For the first time I saw Linney's cool demeanour waver. His nerve unsteadied at the mention of Papa's name, despite claiming he'd never heard of him.

"Could be, but I hope not fo' Stella's sake. From what I know of him, he's bad through and through. He's exists in the kinda world your Stella has no place being in. But it's why she was with him that's puzzling me. You t'row any light on that? Do you know if Stella had ever visited places like the shebeen?"

"Not to my knowledge, and as you only have the word of a two-a-penny call girl, it would be highly unlikely in my opinion. I'd treat Stella's supposed sighting there very suspiciously."

Linney was on the defensive and a little shaken by my questions, so I continued.

"Maybe so . . . but seeing as you said she barely left her house, its seems pretty damn strange to me that the only time she's been seen was with hookers and a man like Papa in a clip joint."

The councillor was shuffling uneasily in his seat and was tapping his index finger repeatedly on top of the dashboard. He'd lost some of his controlled composure, but I knew he was still holding out on me.

"You ever had problems with the police, given them cause to have you followed or me beaten up?"

"Don't be ridiculous. Why would the police need to follow me?"

Again, he was answering my questions by asking me one in return. I tried to remain calm, but his evasive manner was getting the better of me again.

"Is anybody into you fo' anyting?" I asked abruptly.

"Into me, whatever do you mean?" the councillor snapped back at me in an equally abrupt manner.

"Blackmail, someting in your past you want left alone, perhaps somebody you gone an' upset in a bidness deal, that kinda ting?"

"Of course not . . .What about the prostitute you questioned – can't you buy more substantial information from her other than the tittle-tattle she told you about seeing Stella in a house of ill-repute?"

"Well, I could if she was alive. She was found with her throat cut the day after I spoke to her. Jocelyn was one of Papa's girls, Mr Linney. I think it got back to him that I'd been talking to her, and she ended up being murdered fo' her troubles."

"Dear God . . ."

Linney slumped back into his seat, and for the first time since we'd met looked vulnerable. He put his hand to his mouth and gently rubbed at his chin while he thought. I remembered how before our meeting this evening I'd told myself that I needed to come away from my reluctant employer knowing more than he did and thought now was the time to chance my arm and see if I could get him to give me a little more.

"Does your wife know I'm working fo' you, that I'm trying to locate Stella?"

"She does not . . . nor does she need to. The last few weeks have been trying enough for my wife. I would not wish her to be upset any further with the news that I have had to employ a disgraced former colonial police officer because our own constabulary appears not to be taking the child's disappearance seriously."

If he'd wanted to put me in my place, he'd done so with all the malice of a man who saw those in his hire as nothing more than foot soldiers. I considered myself told and bit into my bottom lip. I didn't so much mind him calling me disgraced, it was the "colonial" remark that made my guts twitch. I wanted to smack him in his arrogant, self-satisfied mouth, but thought better of it and kept to my original plan to needle something extra out of the bastard. I had the weaker hand but it was time to play my best card.

"Stella was seen leaving the shebeen with a white guy, who may or not have been a copper. I'm waiting on a telephone call to help me find out who the man was and where he may have taken her. Now if I'm right, a lot of what may be going on revolves around whores and local law who are getting kickbacks from pimps like Papa Anansi. That means he can carry on selling sex and illegal booze without any worries. How Stella fits in to Papa's set-up, I don't know. But none of

116

it looks good. Now, befo' I start dragging my already bruised butt any further into your shit, do you have anyting useful you wanna tell me other than that you consider me a disgraced cop and only fit for shining your wife's shoes with a rubbing rag?"

Linney was silent. He stared hard into my eyes, his body tense, clearly unused to being spoken to by one of his paid hands in such a manner. I waited to see if he was a better gambler than me or if he was going to fold. I didn't have to wait for long. I watched as he reached into his inside pocket and pulled out the now familiar brown envelope. It wasn't what I was hoping for, and its contents were of little help in aiding my understanding of the bizarre inquiry that I had gotten myself mixed up in. It did make my empty wallet smile, though.

"I think you'll find this more than covers my commitment to support your endeavours to locate Miss Hopkins. Much as it may gall you, Mr Ellington, your naive questioning implying that my private life may be secretly in the gutter is way off the mark. I consider myself to be better judge of character than perhaps you've given me credit for. Now, continue with your investigation promptly, as I have instructed you. I'll expect to hear from you in due course. In the meantime, try not to ask the kinds of questions that see those answering them dead on a mortuary slab the next day. It may lead you into places you don't really want to be, don't you think?"

He suddenly looked forward, indicating our meeting was over. I leant across and grasped the door handle and pushed it open, letting in a cold breeze that felt as harsh as the alderman's tongue. He let me out, and I thought that I was financially better off, but none the wiser.

As I walked away, I heard him start the engine of his car and reverse before driving up alongside me, the window of the driver's side door partially wound down.

"And Mr Ellington . . ."

I stopped and turned towards him as he looked disdainfully at me through the gap he'd made by winding down his window.

"Should any of your snooping around happen for some godforsaken reason to lead back to me, I shall deny that you ever existed. Are we clear on that? Goodnight."

"Oh yeah . . . I got it, all right."

I let him drive away thinking that he thought he had once again outmanoeuvred me. But the nervous expression on his face after I mentioned Papa Anansi's name told me they had a shared history somehow and that Earl Linney's judgement of character was not as astute as he thought it was. And neither was the company he perhaps secretly kept.

16

I MADE THE SHORT journey back to St Pauls in the knowledge that Earl Linney and Papa Anansi were in some way connected. I just couldn't get a handle on how they were.

A day without food had left me feeling drained. I drove back into Bristol with the burning feeling of hunger in my belly and pulled over on Host Street, got out and ran across to Grace and Robert's fish saloon at the foot of Christmas Steps and ordered myself cod and chips. I ran my cold hands across the stainless steel and glass cabinets that were home to the crisp, golden-covered food, warming them on the hot metal top as I waited for it to cook.

Arriving back at my digs wasn't the welcoming pleasure that I wished it had been. The rooms were cold and there was always the musty smell of damp that I had never smelt until arriving in Britain. Like snow, damp's not something you get a lot of on Bim, even in winter. I went into my kitchen, grabbed a plate and ignited one of the hob rings on the oven, and placed the wrapped fish and chips and the plate inside to keep them warm while I filled the kettle with fresh water, let it boil and made myself a mug of coffee.

Turning the light on in my living room I was surprised at first to see my newly acquired sofa. I dropped my hat and coat onto the arm of my chair and walked across to the rusty electric fire and switched both bars on. I knelt down to my meagre record collection and pulled out Ray Charles's *The Genius Hits the Road*, blew the dust off of the vinyl, put it on to the Dansette's turntable, gently placed the stylus onto the second track and walked back into the kitchen to dish up my supper to the soulful strains of "Georgia on My Mind".

The lounge was starting to warm a little by the time I returned with my meal. I sat down on the surprisingly comfortable settee that till recently had belonged to good old Mrs Walker. I smiled to myself as I thought of Carnell Harris skipping, his big old gut flopping around as he jumped about in his futile attempt to lose weight. I then remembered the kind-hearted oaf's thoughtful gesture in loaning me his car. Without his wheels, today would have been far more hassle and I'd have been a lot colder than I already was.

I kicked off my shoes and moved my toes around inside my socks in front of the fire while I ate my fish and chips from the plate on my lap. As a child I'd caught fish from the sea and in the rivers surrounding my home. My first experience of eating this very English delicacy had been one of delight and revulsion in equal measure. Fish back on Bim was cooked fresh and simple. The use of batter to cover it before frying here in Britain was something I had not been used to and it took a while for my palate to adjust to the sometimes greasy texture of the flour-and-water coating on the fillet. Tonight, none of that mattered. I was so hungry I'd have eaten the damn thing with its head and scales still attached. I wolfed down my meal with all the cheerful abandon of a gluttonous gourmand.

I looked at my watch, which said it was just after seven thirty, and put my empty plate on the seat next to me, then closed my eyes. The room was starting to warm a little from the fierce, white-hot elements of the electric heater. I quickly drifted off to sleep as Ray Charles sang me a lullaby.

*

I was woken just after eleven by a repetitive, irritating knocking at my door.

I pulled myself off of the sofa and looked down the hall, wondering who the hell it could be. Through the stained-glass panels I could make out the slight figure of my elderly neighbour who lived downstairs. I opened up to find the old woman dressed in a long purple flannel dressing gown, a hairnet drawn over her thinning grey locks. Before I had chance to speak, she snapped at me like I owed her money.

"Mr Ellington ... I have been hammering away at your door trying to get you to hear me for the last five minutes or more. There's a coloured gentleman downstairs, says he wants to speak to you."

"Is that so, Mrs Pearce? I'm sorry, you caught me dozing. I'll be right down. Thanks very much. Did the gentleman asking fo' me say who he was?"

I tried to keep things polite, choosing to forget her earlier "coloured" remark.

"He didn't need to, Mr Ellington. It's your fat halfwit friend with the van. He's singing to himself out in the snow on my front porch. Do you know what time it is? Some of us would like a little undisturbed dozing of our own. Goodnight."

"Yeah, goodnight, sorry you were woken."

I followed her along the landing and down the stairs, listening to her mumble to herself, and went to let Carnell in as the nosy old crone watched me through the crack in her own door.

121

I could hear him whistling outside, and when I let him in he still continued to purse his lips and blow on, as if he been sent as some kind of late-night musical alarm call.

"What . . . ?"

My annoyance at being waken was now greater than my neighbour's earlier displeasure. Carnell stopped his racket, unsure why I had greeted him in such a bad mood. Rather than ponder on the matter for to long, he thankfully got to the point.

"Evening, JT. Vic asked me to come round say you need to git your ass round to him at his office at Cut Man's."

"Since when did Vic have an office at Cut Man's gym?"

I was as confused as I was tired.

"Ever since Vic and Cut decided to go into the import and export bidness,

I suppose. He says that important call you been waiting fo' came through and you need to git a buzz on."

The streets were quiet as I followed Carnell's van round to Cut Man's, parking the car at the rear of the gymnasium. I made my way up the fire escape and called out to Vic as I worked my way towards the front of the building. I found my cousin in the stock room that I'd last seen housing his knocked-off rum. He was sitting on the edge of an expensive teak desk, complete with a green baize ink pad and black Bakelite telephone. A high-backed leather office chair was tucked underneath the polished tabletop. Against the walls were a series of ex-army grey metal filing cabinets. A picture of Queen Elizabeth II adorned the back wall. I felt as if I'd just entered a very low-rent part of the Houses of Parliament.

"Hey, JT, so what you think?" Vic held out his hands, his huge open palms welcoming me to his new domain.

"Where the hell did you git all this stuff, Vic?"

I turned round full circle in front of him as I asked the question, taking in again the newly refitted storage area.

"Oh, I pick this shit up from all over, man. I got Cut Man in on a percentage of some of my bidness ventures. He obliged by renting me this office at a minimal cost."

"How much is minimal cost?" It had to be too good to be true.

"You think I pay that stinky fat old goat in her majesty's legal tender?" He nodded back at the royal portrait. "Fuck no! He gits a piece of whatever I'm shipping t'ru his door. He don't like it, he can go stick his big sweaty head up his fat old ass."

He laughed to himself as he walked round to the back of the desk, pulled out the plush executive chair and sat in it, reclining and rubbing his hands together before he spoke to me again.

"OK, we on at the shebeen, brother. I got the call from that skanky doorman 'bout forty minutes ago. He got two honkies that reek o' Bristol's finest in there at the minute. They waiting on Otis to arrive with a tasty piece o' skirt, then he says they move on real quick. We need to be outta here pretty lively to be on their tail. Find out where they taking the cock-rat to?"

"Thanks, Vic, but there's gonna be no 'we' tonight, brother. Look, I stood in this very same spot over a week ago and told you I had no right to be dragging you into trouble you had no place being in. You done enough fo' me, man, and I'm grateful, I really am."

"I ain't letting you—"

I interrupted him before he could finish. Earl Linney's bad habits were clearly rubbing off on me.

"I got myself into all o' this crap. I need to git myself out of it."

I smiled back at him before turning and walking away, seeing a look of disappointment and worry on his face. I closed his new office door behind me not giving him the chance to wear me down and change my mind, something I knew I could have easily done.

17

RICHMOND ROAD WAS covered in a heavy layer of frost that glistened on the tarmac and pavements. The tiny sub-zero filaments of ice were picked out by the glow of the amber streetlights as I sat waiting, my body dropped low in the driver's seat of the Cortina, which was parked far enough away up the street so as not to be obvious that I was staking the place out. I'd been watching for any sign of the crew-cut copper and his date to leave the shebeen for the better part of half an hour and the interior of the car now felt like a mobile fridge. It was after twelve thirty by the time the guy I was after finally showed his face at the front door, ushered out by Clarence Maynard, who I could see even at this distance was wearing a large Elastoplast strip across the bridge of his nose.

The honky copper leaving was the same guy who had beaten me with the slapjack after my meeting with Linney at Clifton. He waited at the foot of the steps as I watched Papa Anansi come to the entrance with a tall young black woman, perhaps in her late twenties. Papa lifted his right arm, the palm of his hand outstretched in a greeting, towards a parked car on the opposite side of the road. The girl cautiously made her way down the steps and placed her hand around the hooked arm of the awaiting plain-clothes cop. They walked quickly across the road towards the waiting vehicle, its headlights on, engine running, rear door already opened for the woman to get in. I waited for the copper to join them in the passenger seat before turning on my ignition and letting them get a little way ahead of me before beginning to tail them.

The roads were quiet, with little traffic at such a late hour; following them wasn't going to be easy. If I sat on their bumper I'd be spotted from the off, so I hung back and kept my foot off of the gas. Their car, a grey 1962 Mark Five Jaguar made its way out of St Pauls, through Bristol and out south along the coast road, where a little more traffic helped me out, stopping my quarry from picking me out as I was shadowing them. After around thirty miles the Jag began driving inland towards Taunton, taking me further into the wintry Somerset countryside, and a whole world away from my terraced digs and the bleak suburban housing.

I'd been driving for years back home, but had rarely been behind the wheel of a car since arriving in Britain and I felt a little rusty. The week's heavy snowfall and the icy roads were making it increasingly difficult for me to get a handle on manoeuvring the car in the kind of cold weather conditions that I'd previously only ever seen in picture books. After being on the road for over an hour my confidence improved, and I settled into the flow of handling the car on the iced-up roads.

I was now going east and the occasional road sign told me I was over twenty miles from Yeovil. It seemed I was driving further into the remotest edges of the county – probably closer to the back end of beyond than I realised.

I was still travelling a good stretch behind them, but they would've had to be blind to have not seen me tagging along by now. There had been few other cars on the roads for the last half an hour and the country lanes meant that my headlights could easily be seen. As I continued to stalk the Jag further along increasingly small country lanes, signposts were telling me I was heading towards an unusually named village called

Cricket Malherbie. The car in front was seemingly oblivious to me and I carefully hung behind it to see where I ended up.

The Jaguar made its way through the tiny village and out towards further open countryside with me in tow. I noticed large piles of snow had been ploughed off the road and into the hedgerow as I held back to let them get a little further ahead of me. I saw the red double brake lights of the Jag flash on and I pulled up, watching as it then swung right into a driveway. I turned both the lights and engine of the Cortina off and sat in the dark for a moment, watching the rear lights of the Jag disappear in front of me up the drive towards a large, well-lit country house. I restarted my car, keeping the headlights switched off, and turned back, driving the two hundred yards or so into the village and parking up at the side of the village church. I grabbed my torch from off of the back seat, then pulled on the leather gloves I'd borrowed from Vic, got out and made my way through the snow, back up the country lane towards the driveway.

The open wrought-iron gates that greeted me when I reached the gravel driveway that the Jaguar had turned into were flanked by two stone pillars and a large retaining wall that followed the perimeter of the property. Behind the wall, as far as I could tell from the light of my torch, was a lengthy, expansive lawn with the drive leading directly up to the property, which was elevated on top of a grassy bank. On the ground floor of the house, which resembled the old slave traders' mansions back home, were three large floor-to-ceiling French windows. Their drawn curtains prevented the light from escaping through them, but there was still a dull illumination that seeped through the fabric and it was just enough to let me to see where I was going.

I walked on the snow-sodden grass rather than the gravel to

mask my footsteps as I neared the property. I moved to my left and made my way along the side of the enormous building, which had the same style large windows, all with their drapes thankfully pulled to, allowing me fairly easy access to the rear of the building. I could hear the faint sound of classical music playing inside as I darted across to some out buildings; a single outside light shone, which gave me a clearer view of the back of the house. To the right of the building an open courtyard area was being used as a makeshift car park. Whatever was going on inside had dragged in quite a crowd for the night, judging by the number of flash motors that were hauled up at the rear of the building.

I turned off my torch and decided to make my way over towards what I believed was the kitchen and sneak a peek into the only windows in the whole building that hadn't been shrouded from the world outside by thick curtaining. I knew that there was no way I could get inside without being caught. The last time a black dude had been anywhere near the house he would probably have been dragged through the main gates on the end of a chain and collar. The place had me spooked, but I'd come this far and I needed something to show for my efforts. Whoever was holding the shindig inside certainly wanted to keep the get-together private.

The place was buttoned down like a prison. There wasn't a chance in hell that I was going to any further than the back door, but I would've liked to have taken a look at what was going on inside to find out why a woman had been brought from one party in St Pauls and driven nearly sixty miles to another in the middle of nowhere. I moved quietly between the parked vehicles and edged further towards the back of the house to get a look at what was going on in there. It was as I neared the rear entrance that I became aware of something behind me. I stopped dead in my tracks as I heard the low mumbling growl of a dog.

I turned slowly and watched as a large Alsatian came out of the darkness to face me head-on, its black and tan body lit up from the low-watt glow of the outdoor light. The dog's stance told me everything I needed to know and kept me firmly glued to the spot I was standing on. The flews around the top of his mouth were raised, showing a fearful array of sharp white teeth; its ears were raised forward; the big beast's dark, unblinking eyes penetrated deep into me, sensing my fear, awaiting my next move, its hardened gaze willing me to flee so that it could fullfil its natural instinct to protect and guard. I was now standing between the wing mirrors of two cars, with a further three vehicles parked parallel either side of me. If I ran to my right I had no idea where I was going to end up; my only realistic way out was the way I had come in. I knew there was no chance that I could outrun the dog back to my car, but at the same time I didn't want to be caught prying around in the dark at the back of the house by the staff if the damn mutt started to bark its head off.

With my head held low, keeping my eyes away from the Alsatian's angry stare and trying not to aggravate it further, I knew I had little choice other than to take off at a sprint and hope for the best. I took a deep breath and shot to my left, planting my foot onto the car tyre beneath the wheel arch, grabbing hold of the base of the rooftop aerial to pull myself up and onto the bonnet, and jumping across onto the second car as I heard the massive dog bolt forward while I leapt across the engine of the third and final vehicle in the row. I hit the icy gravel hard, running for all I was worth. Maybe it was fear that had messed up my hearing, either that or wishful thinking, but at first I thought the dog wasn't chasing after me.

I was about fifteen yards across the lawn heading full pelt for the wall, which was partially hidden by a row of trees, when I heard the heavy pounding of the dog's feet running at great speed behind me. I had no choice but to turn, face it and fight for all I was worth. I turned to face the dog, which was hurtling towards me and only a couple of feet away. I pulled my body in tight, clenching my fists in the leather gloves as it leapt towards my left arm. I instinctively swung away from its snapping jaw, its mouth snapping at my coat sleeve. I brought my left fist in hard into the side of its right ear as it luckily bit down into thin air. My blow made little impact on the animal but threw it off balance slightly and gave me enough time to kick into its guts savagely with my foot.

Raw adrenaline now racing through my veins had given me a second wind and I burst across the remainder of the open ground with the dog now barking as it came in behind me. I was only a few feet away from the line of trees and the wall when I felt it tear down at the hem of my overcoat, dragging me on to the slush-coated grass. I rolled over onto my back, my legs lashing out in every direction, my feet making contact with the Alsatian's muzzle a couple of times, provoking its aggression even further. It darted around to my side as I attempted to get to my knees, biting into my lower left arm. I yelled out in agony as it sunk its teeth into me. Taking a firm grip of my wrist, the dog began to shake its head viscously from side to side, my arm being thrown about like a rag doll in its mouth. I knew if I stayed on my knees I'd have no chance against its savage attack.

Going against all my instincts, I gripped hold of the Alsatian's ear, pulling its head towards me, pushing my arm further inside its mouth, so that it began to gag rather than continue to bite down on me. It gave me the briefest of chances to pull the dog towards the ground. I bore all the weight of my body down onto the bulky animal, and as I did, I beat at its ribcage with my fist repeatedly before bringing my right hand between its front legs, grabbing hold of the leather collar around its neck and twisting it tightly, choking the air from its throat. I felt it loosen its grip on me and I yanked my arm out of its mouth, then, with all the strength I possessed, I dragged myself and the dog up and in the same motion spun myself and the dog around, lifting it off of its feet and slamming it at waist height into the trunk of a tree. Rather than drop the beast and run, I let a blind rage enter my heart.

I continued with the bodily momentum I'd generated from the first spin and again tore the dog around for a second time, smashing it again into the side of the tree with a far crueller ferocity than the dog had previously inflicted upon me. I heard the crack of its spine snapping as it smacked against the dense bark. Releasing my grip on the animal, I watched it fall with a heavy thud limply at my feet, its legs giving short involuntary spasms as the last of its life left it.

I could hear the shouts of men behind me in the dark as I clambered breathlessly over the wall, dropping down into the ditch below. I scrambled up the other side of the waterlogged gully, running down the lane towards my car. I did not turn back to see if anyone was giving chase. I felt blood trickle down my arm, its sticky flow dripping around my cuff and over the back of my glove onto the snowy road as I ran, my heart pounding with such force I thought it was about to burst out of my chest.

18

I COULD FEEL THE warm wetness of blood around my left hand and fingers as it began to seep into the lining of my glove, my arm throbbing from the dog bite. I fumbled for the Cortina's keys in my jacket pocket and eventually pulled them out and rested my head on the roof of the car to get myself together and slow my breathing down a little. Whoever it was that had been running after me across the lawn appeared to have given up scaling the wall as I'd done, and the lane behind me looked pretty quiet.

I was soaked through to the skin and shaking from head to foot. A small light hung from outside the entrance to the village church gates opposite to where I had parked, and its orange shade glowed behind me but offered little assistance as I struggled to fit the key into the lock to open up the car and get myself the hell out of there. When I finally managed to get the key where it needed to be, I turned it quickly and yanked open the door, then sat in the driver's seat with my legs still hanging out in the street, my head dropping and chin resting on my chest, exhausted. I pulled off my sodden leather glove, dropped it onto the footwell of the car and watched as the blood continued to run down my hand and dripped onto the snowy ground at my feet.

"You all right there, sonny . . . ?"

Startled, I looked up to find an elderly man standing in front of me. His silver hair and bulky frame were covered by a thick black overcoat and his collar was turned up, which the man held around his throat to keep the night chill out. I could just make out his flushed, ruddy cheeks and bulbous nose from the glow of the gentle beam of the lamp behind him. He smiled at me, then looked down to where my blood was staining the white snow crystals.

"I've had better nights, if I'm honest." I looked back down at my feet.

"Well, it's not going to get any better with you bleeding all over the place like that, is it? From the look of you, you're in no fit state to drive anywhere at the minute."

The old man was right. The last thing I needed was a long drive back to Bristol wet, cold and leaking blood all over the inside of Carnell's car, but I'd no interest in hanging around any longer than I had to either.

I didn't fancy coming face to face with whoever had chased me from the grounds of the house and ending up in another fist fight. I decided to get moving, so I turned in my seat, pulled my legs into the car and fired up the engine. I was about to pull the door to when the old guy grabbed at the handle, his strength surprising me for a man of such advanced years.

"Please . . . don't be such a bloody fool, man. Look at you: you'll barely make it out of the village in that state. Turn off that damn engine and come with me, let's get you warm and cleaned up at least, shall we?"

Like a berated school child, I did as I was told and turned off the motor. I'd never been a man who trusted easily, especially white strangers, and that faithful instinct should have been no different tonight, but there was something about the old fellow, his smile, the placid look in his gentle eyes, that swayed me, and in truth I was in no position to

133

argue. As I sat staring weakly back up at him, I could feel my exhausted body closing down with the cold and pain. I switched off the ignition and pulled myself out of the driver's seat, holding onto the door frame to haul myself back up into a standing position.

"Come along with me, it's not far to walk, just up by the church there."

He pointed up towards a thin unlit path that ran between two high privet hedges. I had no idea where the dense gravel walkway would lead me and at that moment in time I didn't really care; I just wanted to get myself dry and take a look at what kind of mess my arm was in.

I followed the old boy up the path cradling my throbbing arm in my hand, and put my head down to prevent the wayward, untrimmed hedging from slapping me in the face as it bounced off the back of the stranger's shoulders in front of me. He stopped abruptly, and I lifted my head and was greeted by the subtle glimmering of lights that shone dimly behind small panes of glass from the two slim bay windows of the cottage that was set back at the top of the path. The stranger opened up a waist-high wooden gate, not bothering to look behind him to see if I was following, lifted a black metal latch on the front door and walked into the cottage, turning to face me and drawing me into the hallway with a single wave of his hand.

"Right, let's make you a little more comfortable shall we, Mr . . . ?"

The old man turned away from me as he spoke, unbuttoning his coat, pulling it from his shoulders and hanging it onto a single brass hook nailed into the hall wall, which was covered in yellowing, faded paisley wallpaper before turning back to me.

"The name's Ellington, Jose—"

I stopped mid sentence, staring in surprise as I watched the aging stranger as he pulled the clerical collar from his neck with nimble, long, bony fingers and undid the top button of his black shirt.

"That's better; I've had the thing on since six o'clock this morning. It normally begins to feel like a bloody noose around my throat by teatime."

He laughed to himself before raising his hand to greet me in a formal manner before realising I wasn't in any fit state to reciprocate.

"Oh, I am sorry . . . I can be an old fool sometimes. I'm Reverend Southerington, I'm the parish vicar here at St Mary Magdalene . . . but please, call me Philip; it's a little late in the day for the kind of strict formality that is calling each other by our surnames, don't you think? So did I hear you nearly say that you name was Joseph?"

"Yeah that's right . . . The dog collar t'rew me fo' a moment."

"Oh, you're not the first, my good man, happens all the time. People see the thing strapped to my neck and immediately become intimidated, I'm sure they think it gives me special powers over them or some other silly bloody mumbo jumbo . . . Now let's get you out of that wet coat and I'll take a look at what's going on with that arm of yours. Come on through into the kitchen and sit yourself down."

I followed the Reverend Southerington into his small kitchen, pulled off my drenched overcoat and jacket, dropped them on the floor, then sank down onto the wooden dining chair he'd pulled out in front of me and unbuttoned the cuff on my shirt. I rolled up the sleeve, revealing a nasty pair of puncture wounds from the dog's bite that were still oozing out a steady flow of blood from them.

"Been playing ball with a dog have you, Joseph ... and quite a big one from the looks of that bite?"

"Oh yeah ... It was sizable, that's fo' sure."

The reverend leaned to open a drawer by the side of him and pulled out a clean tea towel, then knelt down in front of me and placed it over my arm, applying pressure and making me wince in pain as he gently squeezed to stem the flow of blood.

"Only dog I know round about here that could inflict that kind if damage is back up on the Blanchard estate. It's kept up there for a reason and that's generally to keep people out ... especially in the wee small hours."

"I wouldn't know where it came from. Damn ting jumped out at me back up the lane as I was taking a pee in the hedgerow," I lied.

"Taking a pee, you say, then it's a bloody good job it was only your arm he bit, don't you think?"

The old vicar looked into my eyes, hoping for a reaction, then, seeing none, laughed again to himself at his witty remark to me.

"Here, put your hand over this cloth and hold it up while I go and get something to clean and bandage that arm with."

I did as I was told and watched him walk out of the kitchen and open a cupboard door by the entrance to the kitchen and listened to him mumbling to himself as he rummaged around inside. The kitchen was plain, clean and homely with a wood-burning fire that was kicking out a fair amount of heat. He returned carrying in his hands a tin box rusting at its edges with Camp Coffee printed on its sides and lid. He placed it on the kitchen table, then went over to a Welsh dresser that stood on the back wall and opened the small right-hand hatch door and reached inside, pulling out a large bottle of Bell's whisky.

136

"We'll have a nip of this in a minute."

He unscrewed the cap, placed it onto the kitchen table next to the tin box, then knelt down next to me again, lifted the cloth from my arm and poured the Scotch over it.

"Son of a bitch . . . !"

"Smarts a little, doesn't it?" The reverend winked at me as he put the bottle back onto the table and lifted the tin box onto the floor, opening it to reveal neatly wrapped white bandages and other medical supplies.

"Smarts . . . Shit, that's one word fo' it." I grimaced more from the fact that I had sworn in front of a man of the cloth than the stinging pain in my arm caused by the alcohol.

"Best thing to clear out infection, especially a dirty dog bite. Now let's have a closer look."

The old man took a swab of lint dressing, reached for the bottle and soaked it in Scotch, and dabbed in around the puncture holes.

"You're a lucky chappie, these bites have just punctured the flesh. Dog like the one the Blanchard estate owns would have done its best at taking your whole arm right off if it had wanted to; this is just a flesh wound . . . I've seen a lot worse."

"Oh yeah, so how come you're a dog-bite specialist as well as a man of God?" I remarked, still feeling the burn from the neat alcohol he'd doused me with.

"I've seen what damage a big dog can really do, though not in this country . . . somewhere else, a long time ago."

"Yeah . . . ? Where'd that be then?"

"Changi jail . . . I was held prisoner there after the fall of Singapore in 1942. The Japanese guards had a fondness for loosing the dogs off into the billets at night. Keep us on our toes, make us think twice in case we were thinking of escaping. Not that there was much chance of that. They starved the dogs nearly as much as they did us. I've seen them tear away the back of a man's calf from his leg as he tried to run from them before now."

The old man stopped cleaning at my arm for a moment and his stare remained locked momentarily upon my wound before returning to his story.

"The guards eventually stopped using their dogs to keep us in check. No need for them. Most of us were too weak to run anyway. The Japanese had a simple formula at Changi: if you worked you ate, if you didn't you starved. By 1945, when food became almost non-existent, to keep us working they fed us the dogs. By the time we were liberated we were just skin and bones."

"Jesus . . ." I muttered under my breath.

"Oh, I don't think Jesus would have fared any better than the rest of us did out there. He did, however, give me the faith to keep going when things became intolerable. But I don't think my faith's what actually kept me alive."

"Then what did, Reverend?"

"Luck, Joseph . . . it was pure bloody luck."

The old man took a lint dressing, a large crêpe bandage and small scissors from the tin. He placed the lint over the wound, which had all but stopped bleeding, and began to wrap the bandage around my arm, then took the scissors and cut down the centre of the end of the dressing, making two strips so as to tie it securely around my arm.

"There, that should do it. You'll need to keep it well cleaned and dressed over the next few days, but a young chap like you should heal up very quickly I should think. Now, let's not waste any more of my Scotch. How about that drink?"

The reverend stood, picked up the Scotch bottle and walked back into his living room, returning with a pair of cut crystal tumbler-style whisky glasses, which he sat on the kitchen table. He poured two large measures of spirit into them before handing one over to me and raising his own glass in a toast.

"Down the hatch, Joseph."

"Cheers, Reverend."

I knocked back the amber malt in a single swig and let it tickle and burn the back of my throat; its warmth travelled through my insides and hit my belly like a slug of lead out of a fired gun. The reverend picked up the bottle and I lifted my glass towards it as the old man poured me another two fingers of Scotch. This time I took a single slow sip and savoured the flavours a little before cupping the glass in both hands, my body shuddering in the damp clothes I was still wearing, before returning the glass to my lips and sinking the rest of the malt so it could continue to warm my insides.

"Now, let me see if I can find you something to change into . . . You don't want to be catching your death from cold now."

The reverend returned a short while later with a pair of tan trousers, a plaid black and grey shirt, a brown Fair Isle jumper and a pair of brown wool socks, which he laid out on the back of one of two high-backed upholstered chairs that stood in front of the fire.

"I'll go and find a bag for your wet clothes while you get into those. They're not the height of modern fashion, and judging by your height the trousers are going to be a little short in the leg, but they'll do you for tonight and get you home dry." He smiled at me again, then left me alone to change.

When he returned around ten minutes later he had in his hand a Navy-style dark-blue duffle coat and army-style webbing rucksack. He threw the coat over to me, then bent down, picked up my wet clothing from the floor and stuffed it into the rucksack before placing the bag onto the kitchen table. He walked across to me, sitting in one of the armchairs in front of the fire.

"Joseph, grab that bottle and our glasses, will you, then come and sit yourself down and have another snifter with me and, if you will, tell me a little about yourself."

Again, I did as I was told: collected the cut crystal and the Scotch, and joined the old fellow by the fire. I poured another two large measures into each of the glasses, handed one over to him and sat the bottle in the hearth of the fireplace before taking a hefty gulp of my drink.

"There's not a lot to tell, Reverend."

"Is that so . . . Well, I already know that you like a drink . . . Tell me, where are you from, Joseph?"

"Barbados . . . Been over here 'bout a year."

"The Caribbean, very different from this green and pleasant land, I'd say. You must be finding it hard with this awful bloody weather, more used to the sun and blue skies I should think, hey?"

"Hard is an understatement, that's fo' sure . . . Never seen snow until less than a month ago. I seen pictures as a kid; never thought I'd feel it soaking through the soles of my feet, though."

"Quite, quite . . . So what brought you to Great Britain, Joseph?"

"I was told the streets were paved with gold . . . Thought I'd take my chances, see if I could find me a stash of it."

"And have you?"

"Oh yeah . . . I got me a back bedroom full o' the stuff."

"And you were panning for a little more of the glittering gilt out in the snow earlier tonight, were you?"

The pastor took a sip of his liquor and sat back in his chair, waiting for me to answer him. I remained tight-lipped, unsure if the conversation might take me into areas I didn't want to go. But the old man wanted to continue with his questioning . . . only this time he was a little more to the point.

"So where are you living now and what are brings you out to Cricket Malherbie on a cold winter's night?"

"St Pauls . . . I travelled down from Bristol earlier this evening . . . I was told I may find someting I was looking for in your village."

"And did you find what you sought?"

"No . . . only a big dog with a bad temper."

"Out at the Blanchard estate?"

"It coulda been . . . but I think that dog was most probably a stray. Maybe I was just in the wrong place at the wrong time."

"Does that happen to you a lot, Joseph?"

"Does what happen to me a lot, Reverend?"

"That you find yourself in the wrong place at the wrong time?"

"That seems to have been the case this last week or so."

The padre changed tack, throwing a fast ball and knocking me off kilter with his new line of questioning.

"What did you do for a living back home . . . on Barbados?"

"I was a policeman."

The reverend was still for a moment, thinking carefully about what I had just told him. He took another short sip of whisky before carrying on.

"A police officer . . . And did you retire from the force?"

"Not really . . . more pushed out."

The whisky was starting to loosen my tongue.

"And you miss the force?"

"No . . . I miss the sun on my back and hearing the song of the Aruban birds early in the morning, but not being a copper."

141

I suddenly fired a question back at the old man to get the spotlight off of me.

"Tell me, who lives up at this Blanchard estate you keep taking about?"

"Terrence Blanchard . . . He's a silk, I believe."

"Silk . . . What the hell's a silk?"

"Queen's Counsel, my dear fellow. Blanchard is a barrister. A very successful and expensive one, so I'm reliably informed."

"That so . . . It would explain the big house and the even bigger dog," I laughed to myself.

"And your difficulty in being able to enter it without an invite, I would imagine."

I looked at the old man, I was puzzled by and anxious about the way our conversation was going. I watched as he put his glass down at his feet before he turned back to question me yet again, and this time his enquiry hit hard at the core of my heart.

"Are you married, Joseph?"

"No . . . I came to Britain alone."

"And have you always been alone?"

"No . . . not always."

"Family, loved ones?" the reverend persisted.

"Wife . . . I had a wife . . . She's been dead nearly eighteen months."

"I'm sorry to hear that, Joseph, never easy to lose a loved one. You must miss her greatly. I know a little of loss and how grief can eat at the insides of a man. I've seen how it can burrow into the soul and take the unkindest grip at a person's very being. You know, I believe God doesn't want us to feel that grief forever. He wants us to believe in the truth of the everlasting spirit and that our salvation is found in the all-encompassing truth of his word. He wants us to redeem

142

ourselves in seeking out his love. What are we without faith, without redemption? It's not part of his great plan for us to be alone, to be unredeemed, you see."

"I don't think God has any further plans fo' me, Reverend, and if he has I suggest he keeps 'em to himself. I think it's time I was on my way. I wanna thank you fo' your kindness, Philip. I'm gonna bid you a good night."

I stood up and took a final draught of the Scotch, then placed it onto the white cloth-covered table in front of me, picked up the duffle coat and pulled it on, then grabbed the rucksack filled with my wet clothes, slung it over my shoulder and made my way quietly out of the kitchen towards the front door.

"Whatever darkness you left back on that island is still eating at your heart, Joseph. I saw it in your eyes earlier, just like I saw it in the eyes of those poor souls dying of cholera and dysentery in Changi. Don't allow anger and hate to destroy the decent man inside. You need to forg . . ."

I shut the front door and let his final words fall away silently, unheard to me as I dropped the latch into its holder and walked back along the path towards my car. But in truth, his last warning to my barren, faithless spirit had already begun to etch itself deep within my being and the old vicar's closing sermon to me echoed inside my head like the final toll of a death knell.

19

THE DRIVE BACK TO Bristol in the dead of night took forever. The roads were treacherous with fresh snow and black ice, my arm throbbed, and I had been left unsettled by the well-meaning reverend. He had touched upon locked-away feelings I didn't even want to acknowledge, let alone discuss, and tonight I'd done as I always had since I was a young boy: I'd simply clammed up and walked away. My dead wife, Ellie, only ever came to me in my dreams and nightmares. I denied her memory entry to my waking world and refused my inner need to openly grieve her death. To function on a daily basis I shut her out, wiped the past out of my mind and never spoke openly of her past existence or the wonderful life we had once shared together.

But tonight in the reverend's home, comforted by the smouldering warmth of his fire, with whisky masking some of the pain and driving its calming influence through my bloodstream, I had permitted myself a brief moment of remembrance and thought again of what I had lost and how much I missed her. By the time I pulled up outside of my digs on Gwyn Street it was after 5 a.m. and I was beat. I walked into the brittle chill of my rooms inside the terraced house, dropped the rucksack with my wet clothing by the door to my bedroom and walked in without turning the light on. I kicked off my sodden brogues and undressed out of the mismatched clothes I been given, leaving them in a heap on the floor, and crawled into a cold bed, lying on my side and pulling the sheet and blankets across my bare shoulders. I closed my eyes and felt the angry sting of fatigue burn into them beneath my heavy lids, then reached out my arm underneath the bedclothes in the futile hope that for once I would find Ellie there again waiting to draw me close into the safe warmth of her body. My palm skimmed the icy material that covered the hard mattress and found nothing. I whispered her name, withdrew my hand and placed it against my chest, and let the release of sleep finally guide me into the darkness towards the shadowy places I only inhabited during my nocturnal respite.

*

It was after 2 p.m. on Sunday afternoon by the time I woke and I cursed myself for wasting the better part of a day by sleeping in for as long as I had. I hauled myself out of bed and pulled back the curtains. Outside, the gentle afternoon sun shone and a slow thaw had set to turning the pavement and gutters in the street into a thick, grey slush.

After making myself a black coffee, I let the immersion heater warm up and drew myself a hot bath, had a shave and dressed. My arm was not as bad as I had first thought, Reverend Southerington had been right. The swelling around the puncture holes of the bite had reduced a little, and a heavy blue-yellow bruise was starting to take shape and was about to join the other shades of the many contusions that covered the various parts of my now-battered body.

I sat on one of the rickety dining chairs in my kitchen, thinking and going over in my mind what I'd achieved in the last twenty-four hours. I still knew so little about the disappearance of Stella Hopkins and why she had gone missing in the first place. It seemed I was only any good at scrambling around in the dark and getting nowhere. Somebody out there had the answers; I just needed to find that somebody. And from where I was sitting at the minute, that was turning out to be no mean feat. The St Pauls community was as tight as a drum: either they knew nothing or didn't want to talk to me. If Stella had been involved with the pimp Papa Anansi and was turning tricks for him then how come none of the local call girls recognised her as being on the game?

The murdered prostitute Jocelyn Charles had seen her at a party, so Stella had been with Papa that night at the shebeen then walked out with a white guy . . . But where had she gone next: to his house or had she gone all the way out to the Blanchard Estate? If so, what was a young black girl, deaf and mute, doing with a bunch of country toffs in the small hours of the morning in the middle of the Somerset countryside? What connected her to the girl I had followed last night? The one new thing that I'd come away with was the name Terrence Blanchard, an apparent mover and shaker in the world of British law, well known and respected in his field. And from the look of his home and the motors parked at the rear of his house, he and his associates were well heeled too.

I'd known men like Blanchard all my life, whether they were running local businesses back home on Barbados or the political affairs of state from the High Commission building in Bridgetown, or my superiors when I was a sergeant on the force. They had one thing in common: power and a deep desire to keep it close to them.

As far as I was concerned they were all cut from the same cloth: they were egotistical and cash motivated with a generally pretty low regard for the black workers who toiled for them. I didn't trust any of 'em and saw no reason to think Blanchard would be any different, and I'd as yet never even set eyes on him, let alone met the man.

Despite finding out where the girl who got into the car outside of the shebeen last night had been taken, I still had no idea who she was or why she'd been driven all those miles out to that big house. I could have hung around and hoped to have tailed her and the white guys back to Bristol, but I knew I'd have been spotted by the occupiers of the car I'd been following, especially if they were cops. I had been lucky tailing the car to Blanchard's; now I needed to locate the girl in the car, and quickly. She could tell me what the hell was going on down there, which could possibly lead me to Stella. There was only one person I knew who could point me towards her . . . the bulky paedophilic doorman at the shebeen on Richmond Road: Clarence Maynard.

I also needed Vic. He was sure to know of Maynard's address and, if not, a man who did or could easily put his feelers out to his contacts on the streets to find it quickly. I certainly didn't fancy going toe to toe with the bouncer on the street, my business with him needed to be out of the public eye, but none of that mattered for now.

My hardest task at the moment was finding my itinerant cousin on a Sunday. At best he was likely to be still shacked up in the bed of any one of a number of the countless floozies he hung around with or at worst he may be sleeping off a night of hard drinking and weed smoking at one of his many business associates' joints in either St Pauls, Montpelier or further across town. I decided to take a ride over to Carnell Harris's house and see if he could point me in the right direction before I started going door to door around the area in search of Vic. If anybody could pinpoint Vic for me quickly, it was sure to be Carnell.

As I pulled up outside of Carnell and Loretta's basement flat on Brunswick Street I could hear the dull thumping of music outside through the closed windows of the Cortina. By the time I'd gotten outta my car and was walking towards the front door of their home, I had no doubt where the sound of James Brown's "Papa's Got a Brand New Bag" was coming from. I stood and hammered repeatedly at Carnell's door with my fist in the hope that somebody would hear me inside and come and open up. Finally, after around two or three minutes of continual heavy knocking, Carnell's wife, Loretta, opened up.

"Hey ... if it isn't Joseph Tremaine Ellington hanging on my gate door ... What you doin' here, baby?" she shouted at me over James's frantic wailing.

"Is Carnell in, Loretta?" I shouted back.

"Sure is, honey ... Step on inside."

I stamped the wet snow off of my feet on the hessian mat and walked in, kissing Loretta on the cheek as she closed the door behind me. She moved in closer towards me, raising her voice over the heavy volume of the music

"Is that little peck on the cheek the best you got fo' your old friend, lover boy?"

As she spoke, she ran her fingers teasingly along the inside of my left thigh and groin. I drew my arm around her curvy ass and snatched her closer towards me, taking her by surprise, seeing a look of sudden shock on her face as I did so and smelling the scent of marijuana in her hair and clothes, which would explained the reason for her teasingly cavalier behaviour towards me.

I took her chin in my hand and drew the side of her head towards my lips, gently kissed her ear and spoke into it.

"Now you're too much woman fo' me, baby ... I'll leave keeping you sweet to that man o' yours."

I let go, then winked at her playfully.

"So where is the old fool?" I bellowed over the music.

Loretta straightened her dress, then smiled back and called for me to follow her with the silent curling motion of her index finger down the hall towards where the music was coming from in her living room. She threw open the door and strode in, and I followed. Loretta stood staring across the room at Carnell, who was fast asleep, lying outstretched on the sofa in front of the electric fire, which was knocking out all three bars of heavy heat. The room reeked of the heady whiff of dope and Carnell's sweaty feet. He lay dead to the world, hands rested on top of his enormous belly, head flopped to one side perched on a red cord cushion, his chin covered in a thin layer of dribble that was leaking from his partially opened mouth, from which his slightly bucked, yellowing teeth protruded.

Loretta walked over to the record player and turned the volume right down until James Brown was only a murmur in the room and the sound of her husband's heavy snoring was the major noise to be heard. She stood over her sleeping man, hands on her hips, head shaking disapprovingly from side to side before deciding to announce my arrival to him.

"Carnell, git your fat ass up offa that sofa, you lazy muthafucka . . . You gots somebody here wants to see you."

Carnell shot bolt upright on the sofa, rubbing his sweaty face and scalp frantically with his big hands, confused and sleepy.

"Loretta, honeybunch, what the hell you doin' scaring me like that? I nearly gone and messed myself, you shouting so loud down at me."

"Mess yo'self . . . You could lie in your own shit fo' a month and not wake up unless you needed to stuff that big ole face o' yours!"

Carnell, still rubbing his eyes, peered across the room towards where I was standing, his face breaking out into a big smile once he recognised me.

"JT ... Hey, it's real good to see you. How's everyting going, brother?"

"Everyting's cool, Carnell ... Yo'self?"

Carnell didn't get the chance to reply to me, with Loretta quickly answering for him.

"That idle bastard's always good. He gits t'ree square meals a day and my pussy to pound ... He ain't got no reason to complain, that's straight."

"Honeybunch, you know how grateful I a—"

Loretta cut her sluggish husband off in mid sentence.

"Don't you honeybunch me, and never mind how grateful you think you are, mister. You need to haul all that blubber you got stored round your gut off that foam-covered bench once in a while and help me out. Shit ... that settee got an imprint o' your fat ass so big on it that I couldn't knock the damn ting out with the back end of a grave digger's spade!"

Loretta turned away from Carnell and faced me, all sweetness and light on her face, and smiled. I laughed under my breath at her bad-tempered berating, then sniffed enthusiastically.

"Loretta ... What's cooking, girl? Whatever you got going on back there smells so fine."

"We having ourselves some brown down chicken and rice ...You wanna stop and eat with us, honey? You most welcome to."

"Yeah, JT, do you wanna stop and ..."

Again, Loretta viciously interrupted Carnell before he could finish what he was saying to me.

"Shut your shit, Carnell ... I'm doin' the cooking and I'll be doin' the inviting. You keep your big fuckin' nose out of it."

"Loretta girl, I ain't refusing your cooking, baby ... but I'll only stop if you got enough to go round. I don't wanna deprive Carnell of his evening meal. That boy, he needs to be keeping his strength up to be taking you on."

"Keep his strength up ... that fat fucker been chewing down on my food all weekend. It'll do him good to share it around a little."

She laughed at her slothful spouse, then leant forward and kissed him gently on his balding head while rubbing the edge of his perspiring temple with the back of her hand and whispering to him.

"I'll go set the table fo' our friend, honey ... Dinner be ready in ten minutes."

The smile on Carnell's face was a picture of contented happiness as his wife walked out of the room, leaving us alone together, and in that brief moment I envied the love that they shared. And somewhere in my own carefully locked-away memories, the similar feelings I had once known with Ellie returned to my recall and would haunt the remainder of my waking day.

20

WE SAT AND ATE AT the kitchen table, and my belly ached after consuming three bowlfuls of Loretta's wonderful brown down chicken, a rich, spicy stew that reminded me of my late mama's fine cooking. During the meal Carnell and I each drank Guinness stout from bottles, and by the time I'd finished eating my stomach was bloated up like a farmyard hog's. Carnell raised his big bulk off of his chair, the end crust of the loaf of bread in his hand, and peered into the duchy cooking pot that stood in the centre of the table. Loretta sat and watched her man with a beady eye, her arms folded across her shapely breasts, as her ever-hungry man checked for any leftovers before snapping her disapproval at him, making him jump back into his seat.

"What the hell you staring down into that bowl fo', Carnell, damn it. Ain't your guts ever filled?"

"I was just gonna mop out the gravy with this piece o' bread, Loretta honey."

"Mop it out . . . If you try and wipe anyting else outta that pan I'm gonna pick it off the table and crack the fuckin' ting across your big, fat, greedy head. And if you think I'm doing those damn dishes sat in front o' you then you stupider than you look!"

"Ain't no need to be speaking to me like that, Loretta, with JT here; you know I'll sort the dishes and tidy round."

Carnell tried to placate his wife with his best patter, stroking the back of her hand with his stubby fingers. She quickly snatched it away from him, leaving Carnell to tap the table playfully. He was fooling nobody, least of all Loretta.

"Carnell, I know you too well where you and washing dishes is concerned. You told me the other night you'd scrub that old copper pot I use to braise plantain in. Fuckin' ting still sat in the sink fo' four days and I had to chip all that shit outta it with a chisel, took me near on a half-hour to git it clean. Now I'm gonna take my VP sherry wine, put my feet up fo' a change and paint my nails while you see to that lot." Loretta pointed at the dirty plates with an outstretched finger. "JT, just you make sure he starts on those pots befo' my ass hits that armchair out there, you hear me?"

"Oh, you got it, Loretta ... Carnell here's gonna be scrubbing them plates and pans and have this kitchen clean as a new pin in the hour. I give you my word."

I kept a straight face as I answered and winked at her as she sauntered in her best Sunday heels out of the kitchen and away into the living room.

It was after six thirty that evening before talk finally got round to Vic and where he might be hanging out. I'd picked up a tea towel and stood next to Carnell, who was leaning over the sink, wearing a pair of yellow rubber washing-up gloves stretched tight across his massive hands. The bowl was overfilled with dirty pots and too much Fairy Liquid; he clumsily splashed himself and the floor with water as he rubbed away at the crockery with a long, wooden-handled dish mop before rinsing off each of the plates and handing them over to me to dry.

"You got any idea where I can find Vic tonight, Carnell?"

"Sure, he'll be hanging out in the Western Star Domino club in town later. I was gonna try and catch up with him myself, play a coupla hands of poker, see if I can fleece him of some of his cash."

He laughed to himself as he thought about the possibilities of scoring a couple of flushes out of his friend and cleaning up a tidy sum of money for himself. It was unfair to describe Carnell as a degenerate gambler; rather he was a clever odds man whose skill and success at the card tables across Bristol and further afield had become legendary. When Carnell wasn't filling his face with Loretta's home-cooked food you could normally find him at the various dog tracks, bookies' shops, race meetings or card schools, where he would be plying his trade and generally coming out a winner.

He was also an accomplished sleight-of-hand man and a renowned pickpocket who targeted wealthy "marks" on the street to supplement his gambling income.

"I'll tag along with you later, but don't you think I'm about to sit with you at no card table, I got little enough money in my hip pocket as it is and I ain't about to lose any of it to you."

"OK ... Let's finish off in here and I'll put me on a clean shirt and splash a little Bay Rum around to freshen myself up, then we'll hightail it outta here."

He smiled back at me.

"If you thinking o' going out, Carnell, you sure gonna need more than Bay Rum to jazz up that stinky hide o' yours. Git in that tub and let your ass see some soap befo' you think of walking outta this house with JT ...You hear me?"

Carnell winced at being overheard as Loretta screamed her orders at him from the comfort of her armchair.

★

It was just after 9.30 p.m. by the time Carnell and I pulled up outside of the Western Star club. Carnell had done as he was told by Loretta and had taken a bath, and he looked and smelt a hell of a lot better by the time we were greeted by Benton Barrow, the doorman who allowed punters access to the gambling house. Benton was from the island of St Kitts and was a stocky, passive dude with a whispering, effeminate voice whose general calm exterior and gracious manner to those he met at the club's entrance and inside immediately made you feel welcome. You felt at ease as soon as he put out his big hand to greet you. But there was another side to Benton Barrow, the nasty side, which made him an effective and feared bouncer with a reputation for stopping trouble with a pair of four-inch brass knuckledusters that downed his opponents in a single, swift blow. Tonight Benton was· on cheerful and ingratiating form, wearing a blue velvet dinner suit, bow tie and black shades, which even at such a late time in the evening made him look strangely cool. He outstretched his arm to welcome us as we walked into the foyer.

"Hey there, Carnell, JT . . . How you boys doin' tonight?"

"We're both good, Benton . . . thanks," I chipped in real quick, knowing that if Carnell had replied he woulda started up a fifteen-minute conversation with the man that would have most likely ended up going nowhere other than keeping us hanging about and freezing our asses off at the main door. I kept things speedy and the conversation light. "Hell, it's cold out there, Benton . . . My cousin Vic in this evening?" I rubbed my hands against each other as I awaited his reply.

"Yeah, JT . . . Last time I seen him he was at the bar with a honky chick with titties on her the size o' watermelons. I don't know how he manages to hook up with some o' the skirt he brings in here. Must have a dick on him as big as a mule."

He laughed to himself as he opened the inner door to the club, nodding a good evening gesture to the both of us as we walked on through.

Inside, a thick blanket of cigarette smoke hit me square in the face and I resisted the urge to cough as my eyes adjusted to the low lighting of the large room. Derrick Harriott and the Vagabonds' "I Care" played on the old jukebox, and I stood for a moment trying to locate Vic. Carnell moved out in front of me, having already spotted Leroy Ward, a fellow card sharp and gambling buddy. He turned on his heels, walking backwards as he spoke to me.

"JT . . . I'll catch you later. Join us at the tables when you find Vic, yeah?"

He winked at me before turning back to join Leroy, who greeted him like a long-lost brother rather than the man he was going to lose all his money to later that night.

I eventually found Vic sitting at a small circular table on the left-hand side of the room. He was glued to the busty barmaid that he'd had his eyes on the other evening when we were in the Prince of Wales pub in St Pauls. She was draped over him the worse for wear after too much Cherry B, the empty bottles littered across the table. She was nibbling on the fleshy lobe of his left ear, one red leather-booted leg was hooked over his knee, and her skirt had ridden up, which gave the rest of the men in the club watching her playful antics a cheeky glimpse of her stocking tops and white panties. She was a class below Vic's usual kind of woman, but her ample chest was obviously the magnet for my wayward cousin. Vic caught sight of me walking towards him and pushed his amorous companion off of him and stood up. He was wearing a dark purple shirt and white neckerchief, held loosely around his muscular neck with a gold loop, and black corduroys. His long leather coat opened to reveal a large silver horseshoe-shaped belt buckle with a pearl centre that had a tiny scorpion in its setting. The woman with the big breasts spat out a disgruntled comment at him as she fell away from his shoulder, which had been propping her up. All six foot four of his frame hovered over her as she grumbled some obscenity at him. A stern look of disapproval on his face had already put the busty woman in her place, but Vic still insisted on further berating her.

"Git the hell out my face and go put some lipstick on in the ladies' room. I got me some bidness to attend to here."

He turned from her and she got up, kicking her chair back as she did so, a look of nasty dissatisfaction on her face as she stumbled off towards the toilets muttering drunkenly to herself.

"JT . . . and it's 'bout time too, brother. I started to think you'd got yourself a piece o' skirt and was bunked up somewhere after tailing that cock-rat across country. Where you been, man?"

He slapped me hard with his hand on the side of my arm where the dog had bitten me, making me flinch from pain.

"What the hell you been getting yourself into now?"

"Tings got a little rough . . ."

Vic lifted his palm in front of me, stopping my answer to him in its tracks. He raised his eyebrows and a massive smile erupted across his face, before he put his arm around my shoulders and drew me in towards his bulk.

"So tell me, you end up at some mattress house, git yourself laid?"

"I got myself bit."

"Man . . . If that kinda shit gets you off, it don't matter a ting to me."

157

"Not by a woman, a dog . . . and a goddamn big one too!"

"Dog . . . what the hell kinda dog got the better of you? Just hold it right there fo' a minute. I'm gonna git us a drink . . . I just gotta hear this bullshit . . . C'mon, you go an' git that free table by the right-hand side of the stage over there. What you wanting to drink?"

"I'll have a pint o' Dragon Stout . . . Make sure it's cold."

"Ain't nobody stupid enough to serve me warm beer in this place. You should know that."

Vic returned from the bar carrying my pint of Dragon and a saucer glass of Babycham, with the yellow deer printed on its side, which he sipped from as he sat down beside me. He swirled the bubbling, golden liquid a couple of times before knocking it back in a single gulp, then took another nip bottle of the sparkling perry from his jacket pocket and put the bottle cap in his mouth, pulling it off with his teeth.

"Do you have to do that, Vic? Damn, it turns my guts."

He smirked to himself as he poured the fizzy drink into his glass, before sliding the little green bottle into the centre of the table and taking a drink.

"So how'd you git mauled by some skanky dog then?"

I told Vic about the young girl who had got into the silver car on Richmond Road with the white dude and how I'd followed her out to the village of Cricket Malherbie and the Blanchard estate, how I was attacked by the guard dog while snooping around and having to kill it, then the brief meeting with the kindly old vicar. My cousin sat looking none too impressed with my poor night's work.

"Shit . . . I went to all that fuckin' trouble putting the frighteners on that big bastard doorman at the shebeen fo' you to git yourself dragged about on the lawn of a stately

158

home by some mangy old mongrel? Man, you didn't even git a look at the girl properly or find out her name? Damn, some Dick Tracy you are!"

I pinched my eyes hard, rubbing at my mouth with the palm of my hand before looking up at my irritated kin and risking further scorn with the question I had for him.

"I need to find out where Clarence Maynard lives."

"What you want with that filthy kiddie fucker now?"

"He knows more than he's letting on, Vic . . . like the name of the girl in the back of that car I followed, probably her whereabouts too."

"Yeah . . . and how you gonna git him to spill his guts?"

Vic's face had gone from disdain to concern. He knew only too well what Maynard was physically capable of.

"You let me worry 'bout that. Can you find out where the big bastard lives fo' me?"

"Brother, I don't need to ask anybody a damn ting. That sick son of a bitch lives in some shack in Montpelier, up by the railway tracks on Mina Road. He's got himself a dope-selling ting on the side. It all goes down from that hovel he nests in, everybody but the police knows that . . . shit."

Vic picked up his drink and knocked it back with gusto, then took a beer mat and split it down the centre with his thumbnail.

"You got anyting on you I can write with, Mister private detective?"

I pulled a lightweight chrome propelling pencil that had belonged to my late wife Ellie from the inside of my jacket pocket, then passed it to Vic, who took it from me sheepishly, recognising it immediately. He stared at it briefly, saying nothing, then wrote on the card beer mat in block capitals Clarence Maynard's address in the Montpelier district. He pushed the mat across the table towards me, giving me a hard look as he did so.

"You want me to come with you . . . watch your back?" Vic asked me.

"No . . . we've been over this befo'. Thanks fo' the offer, cous'."

I gave him a sharp nod in further grateful appreciation.

"You watch that nasty prick, JT . . . If you put that fucker in a corner he's gonna come at you like a trapped rat in a pipe. Make that dog you went head to head with the other night look like a puppy chasing its tail."

"Don't worry . . . I ain't gonna screw this up, Vic. Now git back to your lady friend befo' she thinks better of it and stands your mean ass up."

I rose from my seat and clasped his broad shoulder with my hand, then smiled at the man who was both a brother and true friend before turning and walking away through the tables of domino and card players.

"Hey, JT!" Vic bellowed out to me, making the room go silent and the heads of the men around me rise from their hands of cards and spotted ivory blocks. I turned to face him with everyone in the room seemingly staring at me, dreading what was about to come out of his foul mouth next.

"What the fuck are you wearing on your back, man? You look like you some damn down-an'-out. Git yo'self sharpened up next time you wanting to hook up with me."

He slapped hard down on the table and laughed out loud as I stared at him, shaking my head. He reached down into his jacket pocket and pulled out another small bottle of Babycham and again cracked off the top with his teeth and raising it in a toast to me.

"Cheers, brother."

The room filled with laughter as I turned away from Vic. I yanked at the hooded collar of the tatty duffle coat that the Reverend Southerington had given me, drawing it around my face, putting my head low down with embarrassment as I strode quickly out of the club, making a mental note to go buy myself some new clothes the first chance I got.

21

CLARENCE MAYNARD LIVED in a run-down Victorian tenement that resembled the kind of slum hovels I'd once patrolled around back home. It was the last property in a row of eight and stood out as a rathole even in the dark.

I was sitting in the Cortina parked across the road from the house, which stood in darkness, apart from the gentle orange glow of a street light that illuminated part of the gable end of the building and also exposed a slim alleyway that I assumed led to the rear of the house.

My fingers gently drummed on the steering wheel as I thought to myself how to play things with Maynard. Vic's brute force and blackmail had worked for him a few nights ago in getting the big man to cooperate with us and his threat to disclose to the outside world Clarence's carnal interests in children was a motivator for the doorman to toe the line and spill his guts. If I was to achieve anything tonight and obtain the information needed to find the woman who I'd followed out to the Blanchard estate, I would need to be a little more subtle and take a different tack with the big guy.

I got out and walked round to the boot of the car, opened it up and rummaged around until I felt the cold touch of a metal tyre iron, pulling it out and hooking it inside my belt, hidden from view by my newly acquired duffle coat. If my subtlety idea didn't work then I'd have to resort to something a little more basic to get what I wanted.

One way or another, Maynard was going to talk to me: it was as simple as that. I'd become tired of being given the runaround and was in no mood for any bullshit, so it was important to make sure Clarence knew I meant business. Closing down the lid of the boot, I made my way across the road towards the shabby house and its unwelcoming façade of grey stucco.

Stepping over an empty milk bottle on one of the three granite steps that led up to the paint-peeled front door, I peered through a small circular glass panel in its centre to check if anyone was home, but struggled to see anything. The dark curtains across the large front window obscured any further chance of observing if someone was inside the house.

I decided to take a look around the back of the place and climbed over a small red-brick wall that separated the building from the street, and stood peering in the blackness down the covered entry towards the other end, which was made visible by a low shaft of light that gave a dull glow at the bottom of the alleyway. I carefully made my way down the passage and came out into a small yard. The dull glow that lit the outside was coming from the kitchen window; I took a peek through the filthy net curtain inside. Hung from a ceiling rose, a single light bulb was burning away with no shade covering it, and again no one appeared to be about.

Directly opposite the window stood the back door, which I could see was slightly ajar. I opened it up wide and walked on in. Inside, the house stank of the funky stench that only comes with the daily smoking of weed. It permeated every fibre of the place and reminded me a little of Carnell's place, but unlike the Harris's home, which was spotlessly clean, this joint was a shit box. Leftover uneaten food stood on a chipped blue ringed plate on the draining board, and the sink was piled high with used pans and dishes that sat in dirty water, its surface covered in a floating layer of light-yellow fat that clung to the sides of a grimy old red washing-up bowl. Three separate ashtrays, each almost over flowing to their brims with the butts and roaches of marijuana joints, were left on the dining table and on the shelf of an old Welsh dresser. On the back wall, next to what looked like a small walk-in pantry, stood an old electric cooker, its hob covered in the grime of spilt food.

Approaching the pantry slowly I was greeted by the familiar but unwelcome rank fragrance of death, which had been until now masked by the powerful and lingering aroma of ganja. The experienced voice of ten years' policing spoke out to me from inside my head warning me to forget it, to back away and to get out of the damn place, but I'd never been too good at listening to my own advice back then and wasn't about to start now. I took hold of the handle of the door, then looked down at my feet and saw the pool of dark blood that was seeping slowing underneath. I steeled myself before opening it up.

Inside the pantry, his hands and arms bound by thick rope to one of his own kitchen chairs, were the naked remains of Clarence Maynard, his head viciously dragged back, revealing the gapping cavity of his slit throat and exposing the severed trachea. His fast-flowing blood had quickly drained out of his body and after running down his bare chest, legs and tightly tied ankles had filled up the floor space around him and then settled at his unshod feet before slowly leaking out further across the linoleum of the kitchen floor towards me.

I stared at what remained of the big bouncer's face, which was barely recognisable as belonging to the man I'd come up against with Vic forty-eight hours or so earlier. Both his ears had been cut off, and his forehead, cheeks and chest were covered in numerous deep lacerations cut by the same sharp blade that had almost severed his head from his body. I fought off the urgent desire to throw up and concentrated on the gory sight in front of me, looking on the blood-soaked floor for his amputated ears, which were nowhere to be seen. I dropped to my haunches, slowly scanning the back of the large cupboard, double-checking and taking care not to stand in the dark-red body fluid creeping towards my shoes.

"Well, he sure as hell ain't looking too hot."

The shock of Vic's voice from behind gave me a scare, and I cursed out loud as I spun around to face him.

"Jesus Christ, Vic! What the hell are you doing here?"

"I don't remember and at the minute I don't care. You really think I was gonna let you come out to this crap shack on your own, just what kinda brother you take me fo', JT? Shit . . . looks like somebody gone and cut Clarence there a new ass'ole."

Vic moved closer towards me and the corpse and stood directly over where I was crouched, a large smile on his face.

"Damn, and from now on he's sure gonna struggle to listen to Jimmy Ruffin, that's a fact!"

"Give a rest, Vic. What a fuckin' mess this is."

"Yeah, mess is one word fo' it. Personally I think it couldn't o' happened to a nicer guy. He wants to count his blessing: least whoever chopped him up didn't scalp him too. He goes to his grave knowing nobody messed with his oiled-up quiff."

Vic started to laugh, expecting me to join him. When I didn't, he looked at me like a confused teenager who'd just been scolded by his parent before returning his gaze to Maynard's body.

"You think this bastard didn't have this coming to him, all that nasty stuff he'd been getting up to over the years? Come on, it was only a matter o' time, man." Vic was still staring at Clarence as he spoke to me.

"I don't think this has anyting to do with Maynard's involvement with underage boys, Vic, this is someting more than vengeance, this is—"

Vic interrupted me in mid sentence.

"What the fuck is that sticking outta his mout'?"

We both moved in closer, standing on tiptoe to avoid the blood, leaning our bodies over towards the heavily butchered face of the dead bouncer. Protruding ever so slightly out of the right-hand corner of Clarence Maynard's barely opened mouth was what looked like a piece of black ribbon. Vic leant across my shoulder, balancing on the balls of his feet, and reached over to pull it out. Maynard's jaw had locked and Vic struggled to draw the foreign object free. He looked over at me, a smile on his face, before speaking quietly.

"You take hold of his chin and pull down those big lips so I can drag out what he's got stuck between his teet'."

I blew out a long breath of air, then, doing as Vic had told me, I put my thumb flat onto Maynard's chin and gently pushed down onto his jaw, opening his mouth as I did.

Vic carefully withdrew the dark ribbon; attached at the end of it, coated in saliva and blood, was a chicken's foot. We both stepped back, watching our feet as we did, taking care not to stand in the leaking red juice all around us. Vic watched my nervous reaction to the superstitious significance of the rooster's appendage, its meaning to those who either practised or believed in the dark religion we had both grown up around, and swung the bird's foot close to my face, knowing it would further unsettle me.

"What ... Tell me you ain't scared o' this shit, JT? Just

a bunch o' old bitch's horseshit, it don't mean a damn ting unless you want it to."

"I'm not so sure, Vic. I think somebody out there wants everyone to know that he had one big blabbermouth."

"If that's the case, whoever cut this boy up was aiming fo' Clarence to be found by one of us. You tell me how many honky coppers gonna know 'bout voodoo and how to connect this tatty piece o' hen's hoof and that dead fool's loose tongue?"

Vic was right. Bristol and the south of England was hardly a hotbed of knowledge for the practising of an ancient West African religion. Whoever had rammed the fowl's foot inside the dead man's mouth clearly knew about the practice of voodoo and the violent threat associated with it. Perhaps they would have hoped that the police would finally issue a statement to the press informing the public of their findings, or that word would have been leaked out onto the street by a none-too-discreet bobby and that the news would then filter through the Caribbean community across the districts of St Pauls and Montpelier. But perhaps it was hoped that Clarence Maynard's butchered remains would be found by a person who knew exactly what the true meaning of the hen's foot warning really meant – somebody like myself.

"Vic, put that damn ting back inside his mouth," I snapped at him.

"The hell I am ... Fuck knows what's been in that creepy brother's mout' befo' now. You want it back in there, you do it, fool!"

Vic tossed the chicken's foot across the kitchen towards Maynard's body. I watched it bounce off of the dead man's chest and fall into his bloodstained lap. Vic sucked air through the gap in his front teeth while glaring at me before speaking again.

"Come on, let's git the fuck out here ... This place is starting to give me the creeps!"

"Just hold on ... I wanna take a quick look around the place."

"Jesus, JT ... Why'd you wanna look around this craphole fo'? Place stinks like a slaughterhouse. We don't need to be found in here by anybody, especially the police. If you gotta nose around, just make it quick, will ya?"

I opened the hall door, flicked on the light switch and made my way down into the front room, which was in pretty much the same filthy and dilapidated state as the kitchen and stank just as bad. The bare wooden floor was strewn with old coffee mugs and empty bottles of beer and rum. A half-dozen large church candles, the wax almost burnt down to the tiles, sat in the hearth of the rusting black fireplace, its grate piled high with ash. A pair of moth-bitten, deep-purple velvet drapes were drawn tightly across the front window, keeping the world shut out. Not that the world would have given a damn about this place and that's probably just how Clarence Maynard had liked it. I walked across to the living room door, opened it and went out into a tiny hallway and the steep uncarpeted stairs to the rooms above. I again flicked on another light and made my way quietly up them. At the top, the bathroom door stood wide open. A cracked single-pane mirror caught my reflection as I walked in. Ignoring the image that bounced back at me, I took a look in the bath tub, which had a tidemark round it that looked like it had been drawn on by a six-inch charcoal stick. Unflushed dark-yellow piss stagnated inside the toilet bowl, and I retched at the rancid fumes it gave off as I walked out.

The landing led towards a further single room, its door closed. I opened it up and was immediately taken aback by the heavy aroma of incense, stale sweat and a cruel, never forgotten aroma that brought me right back to Barbados's Glendairy Prison on Station Hill and the men who were penned up inside it.

I felt for another light switch in the semi-darkness, finally locating it on the side wall beside the door frame. I clicked it down: nothing. I turned and walked back to the top of the stairs, calling Vic. He wandered into the tiny hallway, looking impatiently up at me.

"Ain't you done yet? I'm getting sick of staring at that ugly stiff back there in the kitchen."

I ignored his whining.

"Vic, grab me one o' those candles in the hearth back there; light it and bring it on up to me."

"You want me to mash you up a coffee while I'm at it?"

"Just do it, fo' Christ's sakes."

I walked back to the bedroom and waited.

Vic brought the lit candle up to me, held high in front of him, its wick flickering in front of his face, his tongue stuck out at me, eyes bulging, a gurgling noise coming from his throat. He once again resembled the child I'd grown up with, trying to spook me, just as he had always done each Halloween.

"Stop fuckin' around and give me that," I snapped.

"OK . . . Take it easy, brother; you don't wanna go upsetting ole Clarence downstairs; you be looking round his boudoir like this in the dark, it's gonna upset that unsettled spirit o' his."

He raised his eyebrows repeatedly, a massive grin on his face as he did.

"Just shut up fo' a minute, let me take a look in this pit."

I walked into the bedroom, the light from the landing bulb and the candle flame offering me the chance to see a little better now. A stained double mattress was pushed up against

169

the skirting board of the far wall, its bedding and pillows littered around the floor. A Red Stripe Jamaican beer poster was sellotaped above it; clothes and shoes were thrown all over the place.

"Hey . . . Joe Friday, check out this shit behind you," Vic called over to me.

At first I thought it was going to be another one of his lame pranks until I turned and saw what was facing me. Tucked in neatly against the wall where an old fireplace had once stood was a small handmade wooden altar for the practising of voodoo. It was really nothing more than an old chest of drawers that stood at around four feet in height and was draped in a white linen cloth.

A series of small unlit black and white candles were positioned on the top along with a number of small porcelain saucers, which held oils and herbs, rotting vegetables, dead flowers, old bones, coins, silk handkerchiefs, feathers and beads. Twelve brightly painted bottles containing God knows what also adorned the shrine. A large child's rag doll, undressed and with its hair pulled out, was at the centre of the altar next to a sepia-toned photograph of an elderly woman, which had been turned upside down and had a cord tied around its middle, hiding the mouth of the subject. Small red stones and shards of broken glass were scattered all around the base.

"Looks like Maynard had a ting going with the loa, JT."

"Sure looks like it," I replied quietly, my eyes drawn towards the doll at the middle of all the paraphernalia.

I knew that loa are spirits, which can be good or bad, and that those practising voodoo believe these entities to be sacred: some are revered, others feared. A worshipper's altar represents the crossroads between reality and the spirit world and draws the loa towards it. I also knew that it's considered

170

highly disrespectful to touch, add to or take anything from an altar, and that the penalty for committing such an act against these unwritten spiritual laws was to risk the awakening of the all-consuming wrath of the loa. I was about to tempt fate by breaking two of the three laws.

"Here, hold this fo' me a minute, Vic." I passed the candle to him, walked over to the altar and reached for the doll, picking it up carefully so as not to disturb anything else. It was nothing to look at, but for some reason my gaze had been guided to it and I found my gut instinct had paid off as I gently squeezed at the torso of the toy and felt something hard inside. I turned it over, lifted the flap of cloth in its back and pushed three of my fingers inside the stuffing and pulled out a small pocketbook no more than three inches in length.

I pushed the stuffing back into the doll and placed it exactly where I'd found it, back into the centre of the altar.

Vic and I walked out onto the landing. He blew the candle out and shut the bedroom door behind him while I opened up the pocketbook and began to read its contents.

At the top of each page was written a date, starting in the June of 1963. Below were a series of names: women's names, surname first, followed by Christian; then on the far right-hand side of each page behind a faint margin an amount of money allocated to each woman. None of the names were recognisable to me, but for Vic it was a different matter. He snatched the book out of my hands and ran his big index finger down each row of names, flipping over the pages and shaking his head, tutting to himself as he did so.

"JT, you got the names o' more whores in this book than there were on the streets o' Sodom. From the looks of it ole Clarence was taking himself a piece of each o' these girls' action and then passing it on to his boss, Papa."

171

"How you know these ain't Papa's girls in the first place?"

Vic smiled at me and winked before answering.

"See this initial by each of the payments: HSD . . . That, my man, has to be Hoo Shoo Dupree."

I took the pocketbook from Vic and stared at him gravely before putting it into the inside pocket of my duffle coat. I then went back down the hall and wiped the door handle of the bedroom to remove any of our prints from the surface and did the same for anything else we may have touched, turning out the lights of the rooms as we did, before leaving Clarence Mayfield's mutilated carcass to begin the slow process of rotting in the dark.

I left the back kitchen door ajar, as I had found it and followed Vic down the damp, murky entry and out into the street. As we drove away, I felt the unwelcome presence of the loa seep into my superstitious psyche and I began to wish I'd left well alone back there in the dead man's house.

22

CLEMENTINE "HOO SHOO" DUPREE was what my Mama called a "traiteur", the French-Arcadian name for someone born with the ability to heal the sick or mentally infirm by laying their hands upon them. As their special gift was considered God-given, traiteurs would traditionally refuse the offer of payment and so Clementine would never take remuneration from any poor soul who sought her help. But then she didn't need to. Hoo Shoo made her living in a far more unpleasant, dark way.

In her late sixties and originally born in Martinique, Hoo Shoo lived a solitary existence in a rented three-storey Edwardian town house on Melita Road in the St Andrews district of Bristol, about a mile and a half from St Pauls. From inside her sandstone-bricked residence she ran a discreet and highly profitable prostitution business with a large client group and countless girls on the streets, and which rivalled Papa Anansi's in both size and monetary success. But unlike Papa, Hoo Shoo Dupree's relationship with her staff did not require her to use the brutality of physical violence for which her competitor was infamous; women that worked for her on the streets had a different reason to dread the wrath of their employer. Clementine simply used her knowledge and reputation as a powerful voodoo mambo, which brought forth veneration and terror in equal measure.

It was after midnight by the time Vic and I pulled up outside of Hoo Shoo's home and place of work. Sleet and hail fell out of the night sky and pinged off of the windscreen and roof of the Cortina as we sat in silence and I thought about the best way to question someone who, despite her advanced years, had a reputation for vicious malevolence through powerful magic.

"Are we gonna sit in this fuckin' car all night or knock on that old bitch's gate door and git some answers outta her?" Vic asked me aggressively.

"Oh no, there is no 'we', not in there anyway. I want you to stay in the car and wait here fo' me. I'm gonna be twenty minutes, max . . . you hearing what I'm saying?"

My eyes bore down on my cousin as he lounged back in his seat, biting at one of his fingernails.

"Yeah, yeah . . . I hear ya. Just don't be trying to smooth-talk that crazy old woman. She's more on the ball than most people give her credit fo'. She'll tie you up in knots with all her magic shit talk, so don't you be falling fo' it now. You have any trouble getting inside, give me the nod and I'll come over and bust in fo' you."

"I'm hoping that won't be necessary."

"You can hope all you like . . . if Hoo Shoo don't wanna talk, she won't . . . You just remember that when you playing the nice guy on her stoop up there." He nodded towards the entrance to the venerable sorceress's home.

I got out and left Vic to sulk, and walked up the red-brick steps that cut through a well-kept front garden to the large front door that had two pretty red-stained glass panels at its centre. A table lamp behind them gave off a comforting smoulder of light, which felt quite welcoming. I grabbed hold of a brass knocker in the shape of a lion's head and gave it a couple of heavy belts, then stood back and looked through the hardwood sash-style windows into the candlelit living room. I returned my gaze to the door and watched through the stained glass, and could see the tiny frame of an elderly woman making her way down the hall towards me to open up. She stood for a moment, looking at me through the illuminated lead lights, before drawing a bolt across from the inside and opening up a mere six-inch gap, just enough to allow her to get a better look at who was calling on her at such a late hour.

"Miss Dupree?" I asked politely.

"Yeah ... it is. You better have a damn good reason fo' wanting me at this time of night."

She opened up the door a little more and steadied herself up on a slim African hardwood cane with a crystal handle shaped like a hummingbird.

"I'm hoping you can help me; I have a couple of questions I'd like to ask you."

"You wanna ask me questions, son, then you come back when the sun's way up higher in the sky and the cock's crowed its last holler."

She went to slam the door on me and I stuffed my foot inside the hall and grabbed hold of the frame.

"It's funny you should mention a cock crowing, cos I had me a nasty experience with part of one earlier this evening. I think you best hear me out, Hoo Shoo."

She stared up at me for a moment before releasing her grip on the door and swinging it open.

"Hear you out, should I? Well, you better come in and spill your guts, mister ... ?"

"Ellington ... my name's Joseph Ellington."

I walked on in and she shut the door behind me and leant herself against it, looking me up and down and twisting her cane in her frail fingers on the polished tiled floor.

175

"Well, to start with, Mr Ellington, you can start by addressing me as Miss Dupree; you don't know me well enough to be using the name you just called me by."

I put my hand inside of my coat and pulled out the tiny pocketbook and gently shook it in front of her. She stared at it with a jaded look on her face.

"This little old book came into my possession earlier tonight. I think you're gonna be interested to know what's written inside it."

"Don't you be too sure that I'm gonna be interested in anyting that's scrawled on those pages. If somebody needs to be scribing 'bout me they gonna need a bigger book to tell it in. Now what you here fo', Bajan?"

I was taken aback by the old woman's correctly telling me my previously undisclosed nationality. I tried to stay focused, so opened up the pocketbook and slowly began to read out loud from the tiny pages.

"Freya Robertson, two pounds; Isabella Cray, t'ree pounds; Rose Williams, two pounds . . ."

The old girl stood quietly as I continued reading the women's names to her. Finally she raised the palm of her hand to silence me. The stern gesture worked and I shut up, but a look of curiosity on the elderly madam's face told me that I'd now got her full attention.

"Let me see that, Mr Ellington."

She reached out her skinny arm towards me to relieve me of the pocketbook. I snapped it shut and held it like bait between my thumb and forefinger in front of her.

"I'll hold on to it fo' a little longer, if you don't mind . . . Miss Dupree?"

The traiteur frowned and stood quietly for a moment, weighing me up in her suspicious mind, then, smiling, decided on a different tack.

"As you wish . . . Come on through to the sitting room, Mr Ellington . . . You'll take a drink with me?"

It was clear that Clementine Dupree wasn't somebody you said no to, well at least not too often.

"Why not? I could do with someting to take the ice outta my bones."

I followed her through into an immaculately furnished and tastefully decorated lounge. Two plush red high-backed velvet armchairs sat opposite each other, and on the floor an ornate Tabriz fringed rug was laid out in front of a well-stocked coal fire that burnt fiercely. Its amber and blue-tinged flames licked around each other and a heavy plume of smoke was being dragged up the chimney. A black iron poker sat in an etched copper pot that stood next to the chiselled fireplace. The old woman stood in front of a large mahogany drinks cabinet, her back to me, pouring spirits into a couple of glasses.

"So I'm assuming that little book of yours contains more names?" Her voice was playful and I didn't feel like I was being asked a question. Perhaps this was what Vic had meant about her tying people up in knots with her wily way of going about things.

"Yeah, and more payments by those other names too . . . and the initials HSD."

"And you put them tings together and came up with me, yes?"

She turned to face me, a coy smile on her face and a knowing in her eyes that made me feel a little uncomfortable. She'd filled two delicate cut-glass tumblers with Jamaican white rum and raised one of the glasses for me. I walked across the room and carefully removed the glass from her frail-looking hand, feeling her cold fingers brush against mine as I did.

"Thank you, Miss Dupree."

"Please take a seat."

She ushered me and my glass of rum over towards one the comfy armchairs by the fire and joined me in the one opposite. I undid the old duffle coat, sat down and for the briefest of moments thought of the Reverend Southerington and our similar meeting a couple of nights previously.

"I have to say that it didn't take much detective work on my part to work out that the names of the girls listed in this book and your initials were connected, Miss Dupree."

I thought of Vic and his quickfire deduction as to who the initials HSD belonged to and how they linked up to the local call girls in the pocketbook. I also thought of him freezing his moody butt out in the car outside and smiled to myself as I knocked back the warming rum.

"And that's what you are, Mr Ellington, is it . . . a detective?"

Raising her slender arm to the back of her head as she spoke, she pulled out a long wooden pin that had been holding up her grey cornrow-plaited hair. I watched as her thin mane fell around her shoulders before answering her question to me.

"Let's just say I'm a man who's being paid to snoop around a little."

"So that book filled with names you think I know has brought you to my door. You said you had questions fo' me . . . so why don't you fire away and git along with more of that snooping."

"The girls I mentioned from the list inside of this book: they work fo' you?"

"They may do . . . I have a small cleaning bidness . . . Most of my staff are ladies," she lied, then began to roll the crystal glass in the palms of her hands as she waited for my reaction to her answer. She took a sip of her rum and

178

I noticed two crudely drawn figures that looked like stick men had been tattooed in red and black ink on the inside of her tiny wrist.

"Let's cut the dust-and-polish routine, shall we? You know as much 'bout running a cleaning bidness as I have o' being the next heavyweight great white hope of British boxing."

Miss Dupree smiled, then put her expensive glass to her mouth, took another sip and let me continue.

"So these are your whores in here." I placed the notebook on the arm of the chair and tapped the maroon fabric cover with my finger as I spoke. She gave a single nod in agreement to my question. "Have you any idea why there should be different amounts of money by each of their names?"

"No . . . makes no sense to me. Those are some of my best girls you mentioned in that book you have there. They never tried to be underhand with me, they knew better than to do that. They always paid up what they owed and if any of them were skimming off the top of what they were making outta the johns I'd have soon picked up on it."

"Well, I've got a feelin' the money listed is a record of a series of pay-offs."

The old woman snapped at me suddenly. "Now who'd be giving my girls money I didn't know 'bout and what the hell fo'?"

Dupree's lip twitched.

"I don't think anybody was giving them a ting . . . but I'm pretty sure somebody was taking cash off of 'em."

"Would take a fool to be messing with my girls, making demands on them fo' cash . . . Where'd you git that damn book from anyway?"

She was clearly irritated by my questions, so I asked her another, just to watch her lip twitch again.

"You know a man called Clarence Mayfield?" I asked bluntly.

"The thug that's got a ting fo' child flesh, he works fo' Papa . . . What about him?"

"I found this notebook into the back of a rag doll that was the centrepiece on an altar he was keeping fo' the loa up in his bedroom. I think he was putting the strong arm on your girls, collecting on a protection scam he decided to git going fo' himself; he put the frighteners on them and collected a monthly fee just because he could. They didn't tell you because they were more scared of him than of you."

I watched as Clementine Dupree stared into the fire, her focus fixed deep into the white heat of the burning coals, and saw that her hands shook with rage. When she finally looked back up at me her eyes had changed, and unwillingly I felt a cold shiver run through me. The image of the flames had been fixed into the centre of her pupils and her slight frame had stiffened and appeared stronger. She seemed to have absorbed a vengeful inferno from the inglenook and then replicated it within her to become a fearful force to reckon with. I broke away from my desire to stare at her and shuffled in my chair. When she finally spoke again, her voice had become deeper and more stern.

"You need to hand that tiny book over to me. I'll pay you handsomely fo' it; you won't be leaving here outta pocket, Mr Ellington, I can promise you that. As fo' the pervert Mayfield, I'll be dealing with him privately."

"You gonna be wasting your time going down that road. Somebody beat you to it."

"What'd you mean?"

"I found him earlier tonight in his kitchen pantry tied to a chair with his throat cut from ear to ear . . . well, that's if he'd had any ears to cut to. Whoever slaughtered him sliced those off and most probably kept them as a souvenir."

"Nobody weeps fo' the severed head of a serpent, Mr Ellington . . . I still want that book."

She pointed at it and shifted in her seat, then moved towards me and balanced the middle of her hand on the crystal handle of her cane.

"You can want all you like. I didn't come here to sell you a book . . . You ever heard of a girl called Stella Hopkins?"

I followed her lead and brought myself forward out of my chair, replicating her posture, standing my ground.

"Only what I hear the gossips talk 'bout. She's the missing mute child outta St Pauls . . . What's she gotta do with Mayfield?"

"I think he was probably one of the last people, along with Papa Anansi, to see Hopkins befo' she disappeared."

I continued to watch the time-worn juju woman as she considered my words. Finally she spoke without looking at me.

"You give me that notebook, I'll tell you someting that could help you along a little."

She put out her wizened hand to collect what she'd demanded.

"OK, Miss Dupree . . . You tell me what you know and I'll hand it over to you. You can ease up with the dramatics, I don't make a habit o' welshing on my deals."

I sat back and waited for her to get on with it.

"Papa's got a ting going with the Babylon: the police leave him alone fo' a reason, and over the years he's cast his net out far and wide and caught himself some powerful and influential allies. Now he's got his claws into a lot of tings . . . let's just say that one of 'em is supplying good-looking,

181

clean girls to well-heeled white men who want someting a little different."

"How you mean, 'different'?"

"These men I'm taking 'bout, they ain't looking fo' no cush-cush. They're wanting a special kinda woman, one who's innocent, pure and, most importantly of all, they gotta be black."

"Say what?"

"You heard me, Mr Policeman. You think you can come into my home an' fool me with your talk. I could smell the self-righteousness of a white man's law coming off your hide soon as you step' over my gate door. I can see inside o' you like you opened up your insides to spill 'em in front o' me."

She flicked her tongue over her top lip a couple of times as she gauged the reaction off of my face. I still played it cool and kept pushing her.

"So none of your girls ended up with these white fuckers?"

"Course not, you fool . . . but I may know of one who did."

"Give me a name . . . and where can I find her?"

"Not until you give me that book," she growled.

"Why you holding out on me? You ain't afraid of Papa or anybody else from the look o' you. You got the gift . . . Play ball with me and you git what you want. We both come away from this happy. So, her name . . . please." I threw in some good manners to sweeten the deal.

The old woman stared out across the room towards the window for a while, then said, "Child's name's Virginia Landry, lives out on Wellington Hill; she's in a little council place opposite Horfield Church. One o' my girls, Carla Havers, she beds down at the house; Landry sublets a back room out to her and makes a little extra cash on the side. One morning, couple of months back, Virginia Landry rolls into her place at the crack o' dawn, scared outta her mind. She tells Carla 'bout some place out in the wilds where she's been taken night befo', said she'd been blindfolded then driven there, said she could only tell she was not in the city by the smell o' the fields and the chattering o' the birds in the early morning. Carla said the girl was just too plain scared to tell her anyting else . . . and that's all I know. You want more, you go to the horse's mouth and git it . . . Now gimme that book."

I rose from the chair and stood over Dupree while she went back to looking at the fire and put the notebook back into the inside pocket of my coat.

"You'll git this book after I've spoken to Virginia Landry and she confirms what you just told me is the truth!"

I began to walk across the sitting room to leave, but the silver-haired old hag wasn't going to let me get away that easily and soon stopped me in my tracks.

"You from the little Island, ain't you? You a Bajan?

"Yeah . . . That's right, what about it?"

"So you know 'bout the Heartman?"

"Yeah . . . I know it's some mumbo-jumbo boogey man that my mama used to scare me 'bout when I was a kid. She said that the Heartman would come into our home in the night and steal me and my sister's souls if we misbehaved. I may have believed it existed when I was eight years old, but I sure as hell don't now."

"Oh, you need to believe in him, brother, you surely do. The Heartman's grasp is closer to you than you think, and he's been close to your kin too . . . Close to that dead woman o' yours. She no more at peace as a fly is round a bowl o' mouldy fruit. She clings to your rotting soul just waiting fo' you to join her in the white heat."

I turned on my heels to face her, and as I did the old woman threw what was left of the rum in her glass onto the blistering cinders in the grate of the fireplace, erupting the ashes into a ball of cobalt blue and red flames bringing me to a dead halt on the edge of her fine rug. Dupree pointed at me and then back into the fire.

"She with the Heartman and she burns in there with him, her skin blistering off her back, hair crackling in a furnace o' torment, and she screams out your name now, just like she screamed fo' you back then, when you did nuttin' to try to save her or that poor child cooking in her scorching belly, she gon—"

My right hand was around Dupree's throat and I was squeezing the breath outta her before she could say another word; my other hand took up the slack of her shiny locks and I drew the old woman close towards my face, my teeth so tightly clenched with rage that I could barely talk. I saw the fear awaken in Hoo Shoo's eyes as she stared back up at me, and at that very moment her bladder gave way and the strong stink of piss crawled up my nostrils as it fell down the inside of the old woman's legs and splashed off the toe of my brogue. I released my grip on her neck, flung her into the armchair and stood back away from her as I tried to contain my wrath. I looked down at the urine-drenched rug and saw Dupree's cane, then bent down and picked it up. I held it at its tip and slowly shook the end of it in front of the shocked madam's face before pushing the crystal handle of the stick hard into her breast.

"You ever speak o' my wife again and I'm gonna t'row you on that fire myself, then watch you kick and thrash about on those searing coals. See how you like the white heat."

I flung the cane across the room and left Dupree sitting in the wetness of her leaked, reeking body fluid, the beast inside of me restrained, but only just.

23

It was after two in the morning by the time I dropped Vic off outside Gabe and Pearl's house on Banner Road, and other than to tell him that I'd got the information that I needed from the old woman, we barely spoke again as I drove back into St Pauls. I knew that my cousin sensed that something bad had gone down back at Hoo Shoo's place, but he had the good sense not to ask me about it. After Vic had got out of the car, he turned and stood with his elbow resting on the roof, peering back in at me, a look of unease etched upon his face. I put my hand inside my coat and pulled out the pocketbook.

"You know where to stash this fo' me till I need it, yeah?"

"Sure. No problem. You got any plans fo' tomorrow night, JT?"

"No . . . Why'd you ask?"

"I gotta spot o' bidness with Hurps down at the Speed Bird, selling him some hooch. Meet me there after ten, we can kick back, have ourselves a few rums and take it easy . . . OK?"

"Sounds like a plan."

My cousin went to walk away and I called after him before he had chance to leave.

"Hey, Vic . . . Thanks, man."

I nodded my head at him in gratitude for being around for me earlier that evening.

"Don't sweat it, brother . . . Just do me one ting befo' we meet up at Hurps' place tomorrow, will ya?"

"Yeah, what's that?" I asked him cautiously.

"Git rid o' that nasty fuckin' ting you been wearing on your back and sharpen yourself up, brother. You'll be giving me a bad name if I have to be hanging around with you looking like you just got off of some crab trawler."

He tapped the roof of the car with the flat of his hand a couple of times before slamming the passenger side door shut and walking away, his head shaking slowly from side to side, those massive shoulders rising up and down as he laughed to himself in the street.

★

I woke early on Monday morning, after a poor and short night's sleep that was disturbed by the visitation of my usual nightmares. I drank a mug of hot coffee, had a wash and a shave and was outta my digs before 9.30 a.m.; then I drove into the centre of Bristol, parked in a side street behind St James's church and walked up through the Haymarket to Lewis's department store. I took the lift up to the men's outfitters on the second floor to spend some of Earl Linney's cash and kit myself out with some new threads.

I'm no eager shopper and wanted outta the place real quick. I picked up a couple of pairs of military-cut navy trousers; two cotton sports shirts, one in light blue and another in white; and black leather oxford brogues to replace the pair that were leaking slush and iced water through to my socks at the minute. But it was the charcoal-grey wool herringbone overcoat that really caught my eye and that I just had to try on. I pulled it over my shoulders, doing up one of the buttons, and stood in front of a large mirror admiring myself for a moment, immediately feeling at home in it. I dismissed the hefty twelve-pounds price tag, concentrating on how good it felt on me, then took it along with my other duds up to an effete shop assistant who looked at me as if I was about to rob him blind. I paid the man without hardly a word said between either of us, then got back into the lift and pressed the button to take me the two floors up to the Pageant Café.

It came as no surprise to me to find that mine was the only black face in the place. Unlike some of the local pubs, there was no sign up to say I wasn't welcome, but it was pretty clear from the reaction of the white clientele that I was not. The lunchroom that I had just walked into, which had been busy with the gossiping chatter of diners, was now silent. I stood in the small queue, waiting to be served, and glanced around at the staring faces. A young woman holding the hand of a pretty little girl came to join the line of patrons, saw me and walked out again.

When it came to my turn to be served a middle-aged woman, a bitten-down pencil and jotter in her hands, asked what I wanted without even looking at me. I ordered a pot of tea and a bacon sandwich and took a seat at the back of the place and stared at a large portrait of the Clifton Suspension Bridge that hung on the wall opposite me. An elderly couple were watching me as I put my bags down at my feet and I heard the old man mutter the words "dirty fuckin' monkey" under his breath to the woman next to him. I ignored his offensive comment, thinking it better to disregard his ignorant and malicious remark, and kept looking at the picture of the famous Bristol landmark.

The food and drink I'd ordered was brought over to me by a middle-aged brunette with bad teeth and the kinda attitude that required no words to tell me how unwelcome I was dining in her establishment. She handed me a cheque for one and six. I reached into my wallet, put the coins onto the paper bill and thanked her. She gave me a pinched smile before quickly sliding my money across the Formica into her cupped hand at the edge of the table and dropping it into the pocket of her apron. She wiped her hands on a pristine-looking white cloth that was looped through the belt of her pinafore, then strode away from me, taking the cash and leaving her prejudice behind to keep me company.

I deliberately took my time over my late breakfast, pulling the crusts from my bread before eating the sandwich, aware that I was being watched as I ate. I was thinking about Clementine Dupree and the things she'd told me last night. The fact that she knew so much about my past simply reinforced my own superstitious belief in the power of voodoo and I was having trouble shaking the old girl's words outta my head. I finished the last of the tea in the pot and picked up my bags, and as I got up from the table I gave a polite wave of thanks to the waitress at the serving counter who had brought my refreshments over to me earlier. She ignored my gesture of gratitude, but watched me suspiciously as I walked out of the restaurant. The bitter stare of her bigotry burnt into my back as I got into the lift to leave.

*

It was just after midday by the time I drove out to Horfield. The roads were quiet and the last of snow had been blown off the roads and was thawing in the gutters. I pulled up on the opposite side of the road outside of the old church only a few yards away from the home of Virginia Landry. There been little more snowfall over the last few days and a slow thaw had started to turn the ground to slush. The harsh brightness of winter sunshine crept out from behind grey clouds above me. I'd stopped off at a stationer's on the way over and bought myself a small black flip-over police-style notepad, which I picked up off of the passenger seat and slipped it into the inside pocket of my second-hand duffle coat. Despite Vic's hatred of the thing, I was increasingly growing fonder of it and saw no reason to discard it for the moment, despite just forking out twelve notes for a classier new one.

I got out of the car and wandered over towards the sandstone two-storey house with a lime-green door that stood behind a wild spread of weeds on an uncut lawn and a multitude of overgrown rose bushes in the small, unkempt garden. I approached the tired-looking door, the paint peeling off it in big thick strips, gave a sharp knock, then waited.

24

I WASN'T STANDING THERE for long before the door was wrenched open by a nervous-looking small, skinny white girl in bare feet, who I assumed to be Carla Havers, the prostitute in Hoo Shoo Dupree's employ. She was no more than sixteen or seventeen years old and dressed in a tired-looking grey dressing gown, with an off-white towel wrapped around her head soaking up the wet residue of her recently washed hair. She looked me up and down for a moment, her fingers tapping on the unpainted woodchip in the hall, getting the measure of me, and soon gained confidence once she realised that I wasn't the kind of guy who was calling to arrest her. She threw me her best "I couldn't give a shit who you are" face and leaned against the wall, not taking her eyes off of me.

"What d'you want?" she spat at me as she drew her dressing gown closer across her chest.

"I'm looking fo' a Miss Virginia Landry."

I spoke lightly and smiled as I did.

"Yeah, and who the hell are you?"

"My name's Ellington . . . I was hoping to have a moment of her time to ask a few questions."

She kept her face hard and I felt compelled to try to reassure her a little.

"I ain't the police and I'm not looking to git her into any trouble."

"Well, that's big of you. What kind of questions you wanna ask?"

"That's between me and Miss Landry . . . Is she in?"

"No, she ain't, but I'll tell her that you called when I see her."

The young girl went to slam the door on me, but I caught it just in time and held it open, going with my gut instinct and taking a chance, calling out down the hallway to anybody else who may be listening in the house.

"Well, when you do, let her know your boss Clementine Dupree told me where I could find her and that I'm looking to find out what she might know 'bout a trip to the country she took a short while back."

I let go of the door and felt the force of its closure on my mug. I began to walk back to my car, thinking whether or not to sit and wait outside of the house for the rest of the afternoon for Landry to perhaps return when a woman's voice called across the road after me. My gut instinct had paid off.

"Hey, you . . ." she called to me from across the street.

I turned around to face a young mulatto woman who was standing in white stilettos on the kerbside outside of the house whose door had just been pushed into my face. She was around twenty-five years old, petite, and wore a pretty white dress with green and yellow flowers on it. She looked cold as she held the lapels of a lemon-coloured cardigan tightly across her breasts. Her attractive elfin looks were set off by stunningly high cheekbones and a tight afro that was cut close across her scalp.

"I'm Virginia Landry . . . Seeing as you're letting the world know my bidness, I suppose you best come on inside." It surprised me when she smiled and outstretched an arm, the palm of her delicate hand guiding me back towards the house. I returned the smile and followed her as the heels of her shoes tapped hypnotically on the concrete path. She held the door open as I entered, and I put out my hand to properly introduce myself.

"Hello . . . My name's Ellington."

She gingerly took my hand and shook it briefly before closing the door.

"So you said a moment ago when you were quizzing Carla. I don't know what you want from me or what you think I can tell you, but I'd prefer it if you didn't feel the need to raise your voice again trying to find out."

She looked at me severely and her pretty hazel-coloured eyes attempted to mask the fear my unwelcome visit had brought about in her.

"I'm sorry, Miss Landry. I was just hedging my bets a little back there. Hoping you may have been earwigging in on the conversation. You proved me right and I'm grateful fo' your time."

She nervously rubbed at the back of her hand as I spoke, clearly unsure of my intentions. Carla Havers stood at the bottom of the stairs, one hand on the large domed sphere of the wood-turned banister; she was guarding the entrance to the property with the same kinda determination as the damn dog that had bitten me had done a couple of nights before. My hand unconsciously took hold of the top of my arm and I briefly rubbed at the healing wound over the fabric of my coat.

"You better come on through, but I can't give you very long. I have to be at work fo' one o clock. Carla, it's OK. Mr Ellington's only stopping fo' a short while, you go on back up and dry your hair befo' you catch your death, child."

She pulled back the sleeve of her cardigan to look at her

watch, which read twelve twenty-five, then turned the handle on a door that opened up into a small sitting room as the young Havers girl made her way sullenly back upstairs. I followed Miss Landry in and she pulled out a rickety metal chair with red foam back and cushion from underneath a brown glass-topped dining table for me to sit on.

"Where is it you work?" I asked inquisitively as I tried to make myself comfortable on the chair, which I seriously doubted would take my weight for long. She joined me, sitting with her arms rested on the table in front of her, answering me as she stared at her reflection in the glass.

"The Bee Hive Inn; you passed it on the way up here. I'm a barmaid there; I don't normally do the lunchtime shift. Today's a favour fo' one of the girls who normally works during the day: she has some appointment and I'm covering fo' her. I normally work from 6 p.m. till closing time."

She lifted her head and stopped gazing into the glass, and swallowed hard as she looked at me.

"I don't know what you've been told about me by Miss Dupree, Mr Ellington. I've never met her, and other than the fact I'm aware of her unpleasant bidness dealings through a friend of mine, I fail to see why she should feel that I could possibly help you."

"By friend . . . you mean Carla upstairs?"

Virginia Landry didn't answer and returned to staring at the tabletop.

"Look, it's like I said earlier at your door: I ain't here to make trouble fo' you. But I think you may be able to help me out."

"How . . . ?"

She kept her head down, her hands still unmoved from the table.

"Carla Havers, Your house guest, flatmate or whatever you wanna call her, works the streets fo' Hoo Shoo Dupree, right?"

"I think so . . . yes."

She was cagey in answering me, confused and still uncertain as to why I was asking the kinda questions I was.

"Well, I heard that while you were at a party in St Pauls some time back you met a white guy who drove you out into the middle of nowhere, perhaps to another shindig but with a more, how can I say, a more upmarket clientele. I also heard that you got yourself blindfolded in the back of that car. I'm trying to find out who took you there and what goes on inside that house."

"And why would you wanna know that, Mr Ellington?"

"Cos I believe you weren't the first to be taken out there. I'm looking fo' a missing woman who may not have been as lucky as you were in getting home."

Virginia Landry lifted her head and stared back at me, tears welling in her eyes, her lip quivering. I reached across and placed my hand on the back of hers, but she snatched it away, folding her arms protectively across herself and sitting bolt upright as a single tear fell and ran down her cheek and stopped briefly on her chin before falling to the floor.

"How'd you find yourself in the back o' that car, Miss Landry?"

I waited, letting the girl fully absorb my words, hoping that she'd come clean. My patience was finally rewarded when she took a deep breath, wiped her eyes with the back of her hand and began to speak.

"'Bout four weeks ago, Carla took me to an all-nighter in Montpelier . . ."

"Was this all-nighter held at a shebeen on Richmond Road?" I interrupted.

194

Landry nodded and I watched as she recounted the facts in her head before beginning to talk again.

"Believe it or not, but I'd never been to a shebeen befo', until I met Carla that is. She came into the Bee Hive one night 'bout six months ago with some guy who ended up knocking her about in the car park after she tried to pick his pockets. She was in a bit of a state and came home with me so I could clean her up. She stopped that night and she's been coming back here on and off ever since."

She shook her head to herself as she spoke.

"Carla invited me to a private party at Richmond Road. It was a Saturday evening and I had the night off, I thought, 'A free night out, what the hell, why not?'"

"Yeah, why not . . . I agree. I spent my youth hanging round the shebeens back home; it's a right o' passage where I come from." I smiled to myself as I thought of those happy times, now long gone.

"Where's home, Mr Ellington?"

"I'm from St Philip parish, Barbados . . . and you?"

"Tortola on the British Virgin Islands; my mama worked as a cleaner in a couple of bars in Road Town. I never knew my father. He was in the Royal Navy. Believe it or not, when my mama passed away five years ago I decided to come to Britain to start afresh and try to find him."

"And did you?"

"No . . ."

She cursed to herself under her breath at her past naivety before continuing.

"He was long gone and never wanted to be found, I'm pretty sure of that."

"So tell me 'bout what happened that night at the shebeen."

I reached into the inside pocket of my coat and pulled out

the black notepad and Ellie's propelling pencil, opened the cover and prepared to write. Miss Landry stared at the pad suspiciously.

"Don't worry; it's just so I can remember what you tell me. You don't git mentioned in this . . . I promise. If I write some of what you tell me down in this book, it helps me out later, that's all. My memory's starting to slide . . . it's an age ting."

I smiled at her and Virginia Landry's blank face looked again at the notepad on the table like it was some kind of instrument of torture.

"You were going to tell me what happen while you were at the party . . . at the shebeen?"

"That's just it . . . Nuttin' happened at first. I smoked a little weed, drank some Bacardi, danced. It was a nice night. Then, just befo' I was getting ready to leave, Carla brought this big guy over who'd been stood outside at the front of the house letting people inside when we arrived. This guy gave me the creeps, he said he'd got somebody special that wanted to meet me, said I'd no need to be afraid. That he was a bidnessman and that he ran the all-nighters at the shebeen. Carla said I'd be fine, that she'd come with me, and by this time I'd perhaps overdone it a little with the drink and dope. I wasn't thinking straight. We went with the creepy guy upstairs, and he took me along the landing to a room at the rear of the house; that's when he told Carla to go on back down to the party, that he'd look after me. I was taken through into this badly lit little bedroom and that's where I met him."

"Met who, Miss Landry?"

"The man they call Papa . . . Papa Anansi."

She swallowed hard. Her face had turned pale and sickly, her brow perspired a little. I needed to keep her on track, so I pushed her to go on.

"What did Papa want with you?"

"At first he just sat on the end of what looked like a child's bed, staring at me. He never said a word . . . just looked at me. I got scared and tried to git outta there, but that big guy had locked the door from the other side. I just stood facing it. I was too damn scared to call out, to scream fo' help. I was praying to myself fo' a hole to open up below me, to let me fall through it and take me outta that place. I closed my eyes and that's when I heard him git up off of the bed and speak fo' the first time."

"What did he say to you?"

I wrote as she continued to recount what had happened.

"He said how he'd seen me working behind the bar in the Bee Hive. That I was beautiful and made fo' better tings and that if I wanted, he could offer me better. He said he had a bidness proposition fo' me, that I could earn myself some real big money and that I'd be a fool to refuse him."

"What was this bidness proposition?"

"He told me that he had some special 'associates', as he called them, men who enjoyed the company of attractive black girls and that they paid a lot of cash out fo' the pleasure of having refined female company. He said I'd be perfect, said all I had to do was spend the evening out in the country with these 'associates' of his, drink fine wine, eat some nice food . . . talk, that's what he said. Told me it would be like being on a date and that I'd enjoy myself and that I'd come away richer in my pocket fo' giving up my time fo' a few hours. I said I wasn't interested and wanted to leave and that's when . . . that's whe . . ."

Miss Landry began to cry again, tears streaming down her cheeks; she put her head in her hands and sobbed.

I heard Carla Havers running down the stairs and by the time she barged through the living-room door she was itching for a fight. I'd got up outta my chair and quickly moved away from her as she faced me full of bile and spite, an empty bottle of Johnnie Walker Scotch clenched at the neck in her right hand and the stink of the joint she'd just smoked hitting my nostrils square on. She glared across the room with doped-up eyes and flashed a vicious, accusatory look at me.

"What the fuck do you think you're doing, making her cry like that? Take that pad and pen and piss off outta here, you black cunt!"

She raised the whisky bottle and came closer towards me, and I could smell the booze roll off of her breath. I lifted my hand in front of me; my index finger stretched upwards towards the ceiling and I held a hard gaze on the stoned hooker.

"You take another step towards me waving that length o' glass around in your hand and I swear to you that I'm gonna break every bone in your face befo' you can drag it above your head. You hear me?"

I curled my finger back and balled a fist with my elevated hand. Carla hesitated just long enough for her friend to intervene.

"Stop it, both of you! You hand that damn bottle over to me right now . . . Do as I ask or you can say goodbye to our friendship and the roof you have over your head, I swear, Carla."

Virginia Landry stood calmly by the agitated young hooker's side. She carefully wrapped her hand around the bottle and slowly pulled it away from Carla Havers' fingers and dropped it on to the table.

"Mr Ellington didn't start anyting here. He was just asking me a few questions, I became upset, but I'm all right now . . . see?"

She placed her fingers underneath Havers' chin and made eye contact with her.

"Look at me, no harm done. Now you go back upstairs to your room and git some sleep, Carla. I'll see you later."

The young call girl was reluctant to leave at first and stared back at me, the dissipating fury in her eyes barely sated.

"Do as I say now, please . . . Everyting's just fine."

I watched in admiration as Virginia Landry closed the living room door as the young girl passively returned back to her room. In an unruffled manner she had managed to halt a potentially dangerous situation and turn things round for the better, and that had surprised me. It was a stark contrast to the woman who had sat weeping in front of me a moment ago.

"Thank you."

"Would you have really done to Carla what you threatened to, Mr Ellington?"

"I'd hoped I wouldn't have had to, but if she'd have forced my hand, she'd have left me with little choice. I didn't fancy having my face split open like a busted-up plum."

Miss Landry raised her eyebrows sharply as she looked at me, then sat back down, surprising me again with her willingness to recommence our previous conversation and go over the incident that had aroused so much fear and sadness within her.

"While I was standing in that dirty little back bedroom with my eyes shut and my back turned away from that animal Anansi, he walked over to me, took me by the scruff of the neck and slammed my face up against the door. He's not a man who likes to be refused, Mr Ellington. He told me that I had no choice and that tomorrow he'd make it known to my pastor and the congregation at my local church that I hung out in shebeens with whores and dope addicts and that I was no better myself. He said that he'd see to it that I lost my job at the Bee Hive and said he'd make sure that somebody lied to the landlord of this place, saying that I'd been bringing men back here and having them pay fo' sex. He said he'd see me out on the streets."

"So you did as he asked . . . Yes?"

"Of course I did . . . What the hell was I supposed to do? Carla said he's got people everywhere. That he's a dangerous and powerful man. That if I had refused him, the tings he'd threatened to do to me would seem like nuttin' by comparison once he'd finished with me."

"What happened after you agreed, Miss Landry?

"Oh please, enough with the Miss Landry. Call me Virginia. You're starting to sound a like a nosy copper."

"Funny you should say that . . . I was once upon a time."

"You were a copper?"

"No . . . I was just nosy."

I grinned at her, and the graveness on her face was lifted for a moment by the briefest of smiles at my juvenile joke before she continued.

"If I tell you what happened . . . when I've finished, I want you to do someting fo' me."

"OK, if I can."

I sat back on my chair and closed the notepad, resting it on my knee.

"Befo' Anansi let me leave that damn room, he said that somebody would be in touch with me at the Bee Hive and that he'd have me picked up from my home and I'd be introduced to his 'associates' in the near future. Sure enough, less than a week later the big bastard who stands guard outside of the shebeen called on me while I was at work, said I'd be collected on the Saturday at 9 p.m., that I was to wear someting elegant and no make-up. On the night I'm picked up at nine on the dot and taken over to Richmond Road, where Papa's waiting in that stinky old room again. He tells me how beautiful I look, that I've pleased him and that his associates will be pleased too. He takes a small envelope outta his pocket and tells me, 'This is fo' you, baby, spend it wisely,' then we went back down stairs and joined the party fo' a while."

"How much money was there in the envelope, Virginia?"

"Forty pounds. It's still sitting in my chest of drawers, been there since I got back from wherever I was taken. I don't wanna ever have to touch it again."

"I'm sorry that I have to ask you this, but it's important . . . I need to know what happened after you left the shebeen."

"At around eleven thirty I'm sitting with Papa. He hasn't spoken a word to me since handing over the money, and through the crowd some white guy heads over towards with us. The white dude's just standing there, the pair of 'em don't speak to each other, but Papa looks at me and tells me that it's time fo' me to leave and to have a good evening. I'm taken outta the shebeen across the road to a car, I'm put into the back, and the white guy gets in beside me and pulls out a piece of cloth and tells me that I have to wear it across my eyes, that I'm safe and no harm is gonna come to me. I let him put the blindfold on me, he clips the seatbelt across my lap – and that's when he did it."

"Did what?"

"He injected me with some kinda drug, powerful enough to stop me from making a fuss. It was starting to wear off a little by the time we arrived at the house."

"And then?"

"And then what happened next I just wanna forget about, OK?"

"Somebody hurt you?"

"Like you wouldn't know, Mr Ellington ... Like you wouldn't know."

"What the hell happened to you, Virginia?"

The young woman started to shake.

"What, are you sick in the head or someting? Do you need it spelling out to you, giving you a kick to hear this stuff, is it? Jesus, you're as bad as those dirty perverts, stood pawing over me like I'm some piece of meat on a butcher's slab, hiding behind those masks."

"Did you say masks?"

"Yes ... crazy carnival masks. The white guy in the back of the car, he took me down some steps into a room; there was very little lighting and it was cold. He stripped me outta my clothes and I was pushed onto some kinda bench. My wrists were tied and then he took the blindfold off of me and stuffed it into my mouth, then he left me there alone. That's when the men in the masks came in."

"How many men do you think there were?"

"Oh fo' Christ's sakes, I don't know. Ten, fifteen ... more ... and there was the woman."

"There was a woman?"

"Yeah ... She was a young black woman. I can remember her being dragged in front of me and pulled onto her knees, and they made her watch, they held her face next to mine and they made her watch as they ... Well, you can guess the rest, surely. I could hear the mumbled voices of the men. I don't recall a word any of them said, but the one ting I do remember is that young woman never made a sound, she didn't call fo' help, scream out ... nuttin'."

I began to feel sick at what she had told me. My head was struggling to comprehend the inhuman cruelty she had endured.

"How'd you git back to home?"

"I can't remember; I think I was drugged up again, probably driven back same as befo'. I woke and found myself outside, propped up against my front door."

"And other than what you've just told me and Carla, nobody else knows what those bastards did to you?"

"Of course not . . . Do you think I'm mad, who the hell is going to believe a story like that?"

"You need to tell the police about this, Virginia. You can't keep this a secret, and you hide it inside of you like it never happened, it's going to haunt you fo' the rest of your days."

"But he'll kill me if I go to the cops!"

"Think, girl . . . The police can protect you. What if Papa is about to seize another woman and then puts her through the same horror as you suffered? You don't wanna have that on your conscience. You've been through enough, surely?"

Virginia Landry sat looking up at me. It was if every fibre of her humanity had been stripped from her as she had narrated the vile abuse that had been inflicted upon her.

"You needn't worry 'bout my conscience or if another woman is going to suffer at Papa Anansi's hands, Mr Ellington. He already has his next woman fo' those twisted bastards . . . You're looking at her."

25

I STOOD LOOKING THROUGH the frayed net curtains out into the quietness of the street as Virginia Landry sat, motionless, behind me. Neither of us had spoken for the last couple of minutes and her fear pervaded the little sitting room like an unwelcome relation had just joined us, giving me a real sense of unease as I tried to take in all that she had just told me. As I continued to stare out at the greyness outside, lost for a moment in my thoughts, a lone magpie flew down onto the church wall opposite. It steadied itself on the arch of the stonework, then began to clean its beak on the edge of the blue masonry before raising its head to study its surroundings; it peered across the road towards the house and bent its head ever so slightly, as if it were trying to get a better look inside at me through the translucent fabric.

"Hello, mister magpie, how's your wife and kids?"

I was brought back to reality from my preoccupied thinking with a start as Virginia Landry suddenly spoke. I had not heard her get up, but she was standing directly behind me, watching the large black and white bird over my shoulder.

"You should salute it now."

"What?"

"That's what people say over here when they see a magpie alone. It's an old English superstition, Mr Ellington."

She smiled at me before returning to her chair and sitting down.

"It's only a bird . . . Why'd they say that to a bird?"

"Maybe it is only a bird . . . but I'm told they're supposed to mate fo' life. When you see one on its own that means the bird is mourning the loss of its partner. You salute it to show sympathy fo' the magpie's loss."

I turned and looked back out into the street to catch another glimpse of it, but the feathered creature that provoked such unusual sentiments was gone. I felt a sharp shudder run through me as I walked back across the room and stood in front of the frightened young woman, gently resting my hand on her shoulder.

"You said earlier there was someting I could do fo' you once you'd finished telling me what happened . . . What was it?"

"If you find the missing girl you're looking fo' and she turns out to be the same poor child they had in that room, the one those bastards were holding and forcing to watch as they did what they did to me . . . You tell her I was sorry."

She stared down at the floor and I watched as she softly tapped the toes of her white patent-leather shoes together.

"Sorry . . . What you gotta be sorry fo'? There was nuttin' you could have possibly done to have helped that girl."

I knelt down in front of her and rested my arm across my knee as I looked back up at her tired, anxious face. When she finally answered me, her voice was tense and subdued, as if the words had been attached to barbed wire and her edgy utterances were being cruelly dragged out of her throat one by one as she spoke.

"No . . . You don't understand . . . You see . . . While she was being held by those men . . . she smiled at me. It was the kinda smile that I'm sure was trying to tell me that everyting would be all right . . . that it would soon all be over . . . I was just too scared to smile back . . . to give her the same feelin' in return. All I had to do was smile, Mr Ellington . . . but I just couldn't."

She returned her gaze to the floor and I laboured to think of what I could say without appearing to be insensitive. At that moment I felt anything I said to try and offer solace or sympathy would perhaps feel hollow and senseless to her. When I finally spoke, it was from my heart rather than my head.

"When bad tings happen to us, we never know how we're going to react to them. You're being real tough on yourself, girl. You did what you had to do to git outta that place in one piece and I'm gonna see to it that you ain't going back there."

I took out my notepad back and wrote my name, address and Vic's telephone number back at Cut Man's gymnasium for her to leave a message for me should she need to. I tore the page from the small lined book, folded it in half and gave it to her.

"I'm gonna be sorting all o' this . . . You need me, that's where you can find me, OK? In the meantime I suggest you lay low fo' a few days. You have anywhere else safe you could stop fo' a time? Some place away from Bristol perhaps?"

"I have a friend used to be at my church. She lives in Birmingham now. Or maybe Carla could find . . ."

"No . . . not Carla. The kinda circles she moves in, you can be sure she's soon gonna be getting stoned again and be talking to people who you don't want knowing your bidness . . . Do you have any way of getting in touch with your friend in Birmingham?"

"Yes . . . I have her phone number, but I—"

I put my finger to her dry lips, interrupting what she was saying and silencing her words. I fished my wallet out of my back pocket and took out a five-pound note, placing it on the table in front of her. She looked at the cash, then pushed it back across the polished veneer towards me.

"I'm not taking your money . . ."

"Oh yes you are. I'm the one telling you to leave. Take it and git away from here . . . Do you understand me?"

I got up from kneeling in front of her and saw the graveness on her face lessen slightly.

"OK . . . I'll call her when I git into work . . . which reminds me, I gotta go or I'll be getting the sack."

She stood up and smiled hesitantly at me.

"Do you really need to go into work this afternoon? I suggest you make a move outta here sooner than later."

"If you say this is going to be sorted, then when I return I'm going to need a job to come back to, Mr Ellington. At least I can square tings there befo' I leave. I git back around four; I'll pack a bag and try to make the earliest train to Birmingham that I can . . . If I'm having to run, at least I'll do it at my pace, if that's all right with you?"

The way she asked the question made me realise that there was a stronger person hidden away than inside of her and that made me feel a little less anxious for her well-being.

"I don't think I have any choice, from the sounds of tings . . . but just make sure you do as you said and be on the next train you can and git yourself long gone fo' a while. Next time we speak, with any luck your life should be returning back to the way it was."

I shot her a look that exuded the kind of confidence I knew she need to see, even if my insides couldn't back up the outer sureness of my conviction. I took the handle of the sitting-room door in my hand and opened it slightly before turning back to Virginia Landry and smiling at her.

"Watch your back. You take care now . . . yes?"

"I'll be careful . . . I promise. Thank you, Mr Ellington."

"It's Joseph . . . Call me Joseph."

I nodded my head in farewell and walked out into the hall and made my way towards the front door to leave.

"Joseph . . ." Virginia Landry called after me weakly. "There's someting I forgot to tell you, it's about the young girl that was there with me, the one that never spoke down in that godawful place I was taken to."

"Yeah . . . what's that?"

"While those men held her in front of me, she was clutching hold of some sort of child's cloth toy. Had it clasped to her chest like she would never let it go . . . no matter what."

I stared down at the floor thinking for a moment, remembering the photograph I'd found back at Stella Hopkins' place of a young child sitting on a man's lap with the toy rabbit in her tiny hand. I shook my head gently from side to side as I thought of the man and the little girl in the picture, then swung open the front door and, without looking back or saying another word, I walked out into the street, closing myself off from the damaged soul inside and wishing there was more I could have done for her.

I walked back to the car, my guts churning and my head filled with the horrific images that had just been revealed to me. From its telling I felt dirty and selfishly craved the memory-purging burn of a stiff drink to flush away my thoughts of the women's misery. I got into the Cortina and sat numb for a moment before sticking the key in the ignition and driving away, unaware of the two men who'd been on my tail since I'd left my digs earlier that morning who sat part hidden, parked in the driveway of a house across the road.

★

Before heading back to my place I stopped off at Cutman's gym and left a message with its sweaty proprietor for Vic to meet me at the Speed Bird club later that night. I knew Vic would turn up, but I knew that arranging a get-together with my unpredictable cousin had to be based on the understanding that he'd turn up when he was good and ready. Vic didn't believe in rushing for anybody unless you happened to be female, attractive and inviting him into your bed.

By the time I pulled up outside of my place on Gwyn Street it was after two thirty and I was nursing a headache and in a sombre mood. After grabbing the bags from the boot of the car containing the new clothes I'd bought myself, I trudged up the eight wet stone steps of the large Victorian two-storey property that I was still failing to call home. I opened up and came face to face with my elderly neighbour, Mrs Pearce. She had the kind of darkly welcoming expression on her face that you only see when calling on the services of an undertaker and it made me wish I'd chosen the pub to go back to rather than my pokey, cold rooms.

"Mr Ellington . . . I've had to take in a parcel for you."

She looked towards me like I wasn't there, refusing to make eye contact and shuffling nervously where she stood, keeping her distance in case she'd maybe catch something off of me.

"You have?"

I was as surprised to hear the news as she was put out in having to tell me it. I rarely received letter post, let alone a parcel.

"Just wait there."

I did as I was told and watched as the mean-spirited old woman went back into her flat to retrieve my mail and returned a few moments later holding it cautiously at arm's length in front of me. The expression on her face had gone from mildly disgruntled to deeply annoyed as she held a small package with the tips of her fingers.

"Is somebody sending you food parcels from wherever you came from?"

"Food parcels? No why?"

She was starting to get my back up. My head pounded and I just wanted to eat two aspirin, knock back the remaining half-bottle of Vic's rum and sleep for the rest of the afternoon.

"Well, whatever is wrapped up in that box has gone off. I couldn't have it stinking my hallway out, so it's been sitting in the yard since it was delivered by a coloured gentleman this morning."

"Coloured gentleman . . . so not the postman then?"

"Do you see any stamps stuck on that box, Mr Ellington? It was hand-delivered. I was out scrubbing down the front when he arrived. He asked if I'd seen you; I said that I hadn't; he asked would I take it in and see that I gave it to you as soon as you returned. That's what I'm doing now."

She stuck out her arms towards me again with a violent shove, commanding that I unburden her of her responsibility. I took the box from her and my nostrils got a hit of the offending smell that she was wittering on about.

"Well, I'm grateful Mrs Pearce . . . Thank you."

She snapped around on her heels and returned back to her now odour-free dwelling. I began to climb the stairs to my room when she shouted up to me.

"Just you see to your own deliveries in the future, Mr Ellington, I'm not your paid servant you know."

I ignored her comment while thinking to myself that in the eyes of my neighbour, the only form of domestic servitude she'd truly approve of would be me being the toiling minion doing her bidding.

I dropped the bags containing my new clothes onto the floor in the hall and took the parcel into the kitchen, leaving it on the draining board. I took off my coat and hung it on the back of one of the dining chairs, then went into the bathroom and grabbed a couple of aspirin from the medicine cabinet. I filled up a glass of water from the kitchen tap and knocked back the two tablets, then took out the sharpest knife I owned from my poorly stocked cutlery drawer and carried the lightweight package over to the kitchen table and sat down. The parcel was no more than ten inches long and neatly wrapped in brown paper, held together with carrier's string around its centre and with my name and address clearly printed across the top in blue ink. I cut the string and wrapped it around my hand, then threw it into the grey bin by the sink. I tore the paper from around the box and took the blade and cut along the Scotch tape that sealed the two adjoining lids of the packet and opened it up. A strong, overpowering smell of decay hit me, instantly making my eyes smart and my head jolt back. I peered back into the opened box: inside was a black velvet cloth, bunched up at its edges and tied with a short length of dark-red ribbon. I lifted the cloth out of the box with my finger and thumb and placed it on the table, then pulled at the ribbon drawstring to release the corners, letting it unfurl in front of me. There, splayed out across the sable fabric and carefully positioned either side of a chicken's foot, were two pieces of human flesh. I had little doubt they were the bloodless, severed ears of Clarence Mayfield.

26

"MR ELLINGTON!"

It was my name being called from outside on the landing that broke me from an almost trance-like state as I stared at the sheared-off remains of the dead doorman. Mrs Pearce was screeching for me with all the vocal ferocity of a distressed jay whose fledgling had just fallen out of its nest. I quickly grabbed the cloth from off of my kitchen table and gingerly picked up the dismembered ears and chicken's foot and dropped them back into the box, and stashed it out of plain sight in the cupboard under the kitchen sink. Then I went out onto the landing and stretched over the banister of the staircase and looked down to where my elderly neighbour stood just as the old woman hollered out for me again.

"Mr Ellington, are you there?"

"Yeah, I'm here . . . What's the problem?"

"The problem is that I'm doing your donkey work for you again. You have a gentleman caller at the door."

If it had been either Vic or Carnell down there, old Mrs Pearce would have reluctantly let them in and they'd have come straight on up to me. The fact it wasn't immediately made me edgy.

"OK, thanks, Mrs Pearce, I'm on my way down, I'll take it from here."

I ran back into my kitchen and picked up the knife from table, then slid it through my belt, covering it with my shirt tail. As I walked nervously down the stairs towards the front door, I could hear the old girl mumbling to herself as she went back into her room. I reached the bottom step to find that she'd closed the front door on whoever it was calling on me; my fist clenched as I uneasily walked across the austere lobby and opened up.

"Your housekeeper seems a little tetchy this afternoon, Mr Ellington."

Earl Linney stood in front of me, his impatience at being kept waiting outside etched on his irked face. He didn't wait for me to ask him to come in and strode through into the hallway, then turned on me like a rabid dog.

"You better have some damn news for me," the old Jamaican snapped.

"And it's good to see you too, Mr Linney . . ."

I flashed a false grin towards my cantankerous employer. My headache continued to throb, and I was in no mood for the sarcasm and short temper of the alderman.

"I'm not here to make pleasantries and small talk with you, Ellington, just tell me what you've found out. I haven't heard from you in days. What the hell's been going on?"

He'd stopped addressing me as mister, so I assumed it was all downhill from there.

"You best come on up; we can talk with a little more privacy then."

I cocked a sneer at Mrs Pearce, who I could clearly see was eavesdropping from a gap in her door. I made my way back up to my digs and could hear Linney following, his laboured gasps and heavy-footed gait buffeting the wooden panels of the stairs as we climbed the flight of steps. I waited at the top, then gestured with an outstretched arm for my crabby guest to enter my cold flat. I showed the alderman into my austere sitting room.

"Excuse me a moment. Why don't you take a seat?" I went out to my kitchen, pulled the knife from my belt, returned it to the open cutlery drawer, slammed it shut and then called out to Linney.

"You want a drink?"

I tried to offer my hospitality in a civil tone, but it probably failed to convince.

"No. I have a meeting in Bristol at four thirty. Let's get straight to the point: what have you got for me?"

When I returned to my unwelcome caller, I found he had decided to remain standing and was rubbing his hands together with his back towards my electric fire, which was switched off. I smiled to myself as I sat down in my armchair, thinking where to begin.

"A lot has happened since we last spoke and I've gone and opened up a big can of worms looking fo' Stella. What I've found out ain't pretty, but since you paying fo' this you better brace yourself."

"I'm not a weak man; don't underestimate me, Ellington."

"OK ... I followed the information I got from Jocelyn Charles, the murdered prostitute, back to the shebeen on Richmond Road. I grilled the doorman of the place, a guy named Clarence Mayfield. He finally coughed up that he knew of some 'special' girls who didn't normally work the streets and were perhaps being taken from the shebeen and delivered to some place out in the Somerset countryside. Mayfield contacted me the next time one of these girls was taken out there; that was last Saturday night. I hung around outside the joint and waited. Sure enough, a woman left with a big white dude: he turned out to be the copper who beat me with a slapjack after our private meeting up on Clifton downs. They got into a car all cosy and I followed it fo' over

214

sixty-odd miles to a crazy-named place near Taunton, called Cricket Malherbie . . . You ever heard of it?"

"No . . ." He barked out his reply and nodded at me to go on.

"I trailed them a short way outta the village to an old country house that's owned by some legal big shot called Terrence Blanchard . . ."

"Terrence Blanchard, are you sure?"

I'd suddenly got Linney's full attention. The alderman look startled and took a seat on my tatty sofa, looking up and waving his hand towards me to continue.

"Yeah . . . I'm sure. I had it confirmed to me by the local village padre. He gave me the rundown on who this Blanchard was and what he did. You know him?"

"Yes . . . We've met on a number of occasions at the council chambers. He's the chair on the planning committee. I believe his family were prominent landowners and he still has substantial ownership of a number of land banks in and around the city. We had a disagreement some time back when I tried to buy land he owned in Bishopston for a housing project. I believe he scuppered the negotiations when he realised I'd be creating council housing for black folk like you, Ellington."

I assumed by his "like you" jibe he meant anybody who didn't bow down to his high and mighty posturing.

"What do you think the connection is between Blanchard and these 'special' girls that are taken there?"

"Well, I'm pretty sure he ain't having 'em over fo' tea and cakes."

"Don't be so bloody flippant . . . just tell me all you know . . . the facts!"

Linney rested himself back into my settee and exhaled deeply in irritation, waiting for me to go on.

215

"Well, I took a look around the outside of his place, I couldn't see inside or who was in there. I heard loud music and at the rear of the building there was a lot of cash tied up in the flash vehicles his visitors had parked up behind the plush mansion he owns. I tried to get a closer look, but I met up with Blanchard's security."

"Security, by that you mean you were seen?"

Linney leant forward, agitation in his voice.

"No . . . I was attacked by a dog."

I waited for Linney's impatient annoyance to erupt a little more. I was starting to enjoy myself a little.

"A dog . . . ?"

"Oh yeah, and it was a hefty one too. Blanchard clearly likes his privacy and obviously used a guard hound to maintain it. I had to kill it."

"You killed Blanchard's dog!"

"You heard me . . . Man, that big mutt had me dragged down on my ass in the snow and it damn near tore my arm outta its socket. I wasn't about to let it rip me to pieces."

I watched as the alderman rubbed his brow in exasperation and decided to keep going with the just-the-facts patter, knowing that the rest of what I had to tell him was going to antagonise him even more.

"I got outta there with my tail between my legs, my clothes in tatters and a mauled arm. I came back to Bristol and after digging round a little deeper I managed to locate the young woman I followed out to the Blanchard estate on the Saturday night. Her name is Virginia Landry; you ever heard of her?"

I was prepared for his answer even before I got it.

"No."

As usual, he left me little room to pry.

"Well . . . Miss Landry was approached by a local lowlife, Papa Anansi. He put the strong arm on her during an all-nighter party at Richmond Road. During their chat he offered what he called a bidness proposition. He told her how she could earn some 'easy' cash by attending an invitation-only shindig held by some of his affluent 'associates', as he called them, out at some country spread."

"And this would be at the Blanchard estate?"

"You got it . . . When Miss Landry told Papa to stick his bidness proposition, he turned nasty. He'd got his blackmail spiel worked out upfront and put the squeeze on her. I'm pretty sure he'd marked her out as being a prime candidate way befo' she ever turned up at his knocking shop. He threatened to expose the poor child to her local Baptist minister and let the congregation know she like to party her evenings down at low-rent shebeens. Now the fact was she'd only ever set foot in one that night, but that didn't matter to Papa. He told her that he'd let the world know she spent her spare time with addicts and whores."

I noticed Linney wince at the mention of the word "whore" and carried on appraising him.

"Miss Landry told me that Papa's so-called associates sought out 'special girls': attractive, pure black women not tainted by the streets like his hookers are. Once he'd got his dirty claws into her, she had little choice but to attend and was picked up the next weekend. She was taken blindfolded out to the Blanchard place and hauled down into a basement and raped."

"She was raped! Oh sweet Jesus."

Linney rubbed repeatedly at both temples with the tips of his fingers as he took in the severity of my account.

"Yeah, well, Jesus, he wasn't around to help out that night. In my experience he never is when the shit's about to hit the fan, Mr Linney."

"Keep your blasphemy to yourself."

He pulled himself up out of his seat, stood upright and starting brushing out the creases in his gabardine overcoat with the back of his hand.

"This young woman, Landry . . . Did she . . . er, go to the police, report what had happened to her?"

"No . . . she did not. Seems that she was popular on the night with the white gentry and they sure wanted a quick return from her in the future. She was so scared of Papa's threats that she agreed to his demands to go back there some time soon."

"She must be insane . . ."

"No, Mr Linney, she ain't insane, but she was scared outta her mind at the thought of what Papa was gonna do to her if she refused to go back. I gave her some of your money to git outta Bristol and lay low fo' a while till this is sorted; with any luck she'll be on a train going north some time later today. Anyhow, there's more, Mr Linney . . . Virginia Landry said there was another young woman who was being violated in that basement. She'd been stripped naked and then held in front of Landry and made to watch the assault. Now this other young woman, she didn't scream, cry out or attempt to break free. She stood there silent, and not as much as a peep came outta her."

"My God . . . You think . . . she could be my Stella?"

The agitation the alderman had felt previously had now been replaced by distress, which was clearly engraved upon his face.

"Well, she's deaf and dumb, ain't she . . . Why else would any woman who's being subjected to that kinda misery not cry out . . . unless she can't?"

I watched as Linney got up and began to pace the short

length of the room, his hands clenched together behind his back, his head sunk low, eyes focussing on the threadbare carpet. His mind seemed to be locked away in a room of disquiet and pain. I broke his anxious concentration with another query.

"You sure you've never had any dealings with this Papa Anansi guy?"

"Absolutely . . . I've told you befo', until you turned him up, I'd never heard of the man."

"So tell me . . . How the hell did Stella hook up with him, Mr Linney? If what you've told me is on the up and up, then it don't make a bit of sense that a young woman you say was shy, reserved, scared of the big wide world and who barely left the house other than to work under your wing at the council offices should ever end up in the company of a lowlife criminal like Papa."

"Just exactly what are you saying here, Ellington – that I've been lying to you?"

"I ain't saying nuttin', I'm just trying to fathom out how a guy like Papa manages to meet a girl like Stella. Those two should never have crossed paths. Somebody had to have introduced him to her . . . Ting is, who?"

"Can't you put a little more pressure on this Mayfield fellow, see if he knows more?"

"That would be difficult."

"Look, if it's a question of money . . ."

Linney reached inside into his coat. I raised the palm of my hand, stopping him in his tracks.

"No amount of money in this world gonna make Clarence Mayfield talk to me, Mr Linney, he's long gone. I found him all butchered up and stuffed in his kitchen larder with his throat slit night befo' last."

I ignored the old councillor's shocked reaction to hearing of the doorman's death and continued laying it on the line for him.

"Now, somebody already knew Mayfield had been talking to me. I'm guessing it was Papa . . . Look, man, since the day I took this job on, I've been chasing my tail, either being given the runaround, threatened or having the crap beaten outta me. I finally find out there are black woman being used as top-grade call girls fo' some wealthy white guys, one of them you know, and that Stella may have been one of those girls. It all stinks, and at this point I couldn't tell you whether she's dead or alive. The one ting I do know is that there are two murdered people linked to all of this and I could easily be put in the frame fo' killing them. If you got anyting else to tell me 'bout what's going down here, then you better cough it up now, cos brother, I'm ready to walk."

At that moment I wanted to stick the photograph of the young child sitting on a man's lap that I'd found hidden in Stella Hopkins bedroom in front of his face, but something told me to hold off and to trust my old policing instincts for just a while longer.

"Everyting I've told you is the truth. I'm shocked to hear how Stella could have become mixed up with this man Papa and his seedy little businesses or why she would have chosen to associate with the kinds of people you find in a shebeen. My reasons for originally employing your services were based on my desire to uphold a promise that I made a long time ago: I swore to take care of the child's well-being . . . to protect her. I don't intend to go back on that promise . . . I know she's out there somewhere and I'm asking you to find her for me. Do you understand what it means to make the kind of vow I have, to safeguard those you care about, Mr Ellington?"

220

Linney looked at me with the kind of eyes that were holding back a river of tears. There was something in the way he'd just spoken about Stella and looking out for her that had reached inside of me, and I realised that he was telling the truth.

"Yeah . . . I understand."

I dropped into my armchair and watched as the old man took a fountain pen and a small crocodile-print leather diary from the pocket of his jacket. He wrote inside one of the back pages and tore it out, reaching down and giving to me.

"This is my home address . . . Whatever other information to have, you bring it to me there."

"OK."

I folded the piece of paper and placed it on the arm of the chair as Linney returned his pen and diary to his pocket, then withdrew his wallet and took out a wad of banknotes and placed on top of the lid of my Dansette record player.

"I'm a rich man, Mr Ellington. This means a lot to me . . . Here's a further one hundred and fifty to keep you motivated. Locate Stella, bring her back to me and I'll give you another thousand pounds."

He pulled his trilby down over his eyes, then drew the lapels of his coat across his chest and left, letting himself out as I sat in silence, staring at the pile of cash next to me, wondering whether in accepting it I'd just bought myself a one-way ticket to the hangman's noose.

27

As soon as Earl Linney was out of my front door, my thoughts returned to the mutilated body parts of the late Clarence Mayfield that were sitting stinking underneath my sink and how the hell I was going to get rid of them. I looked at my watch: it was just after 4.30 p.m. and the onset of dusk. Whatever I was going to do with them, I knew that the nearing nightfall would be a welcome ally. I hesitantly returned to the kitchen, lifted the box with its sickening contents and put it onto the table. I stared at it for a moment and the hairs on my forearms and neck stood on end. I must have stood staring at that box for damn near ten minutes when a name from the past edged into my brain and showed me a way out. A guy called Brian Dulland had worked with me in the stores at Wills' cigarette factory and had a habit for rattling on about useless trivia and an unhealthy obsession with coarse fishing that drove me and anyone unlucky enough to be in his presence to despair when he'd catch you during your lunch or coffin-nail break. But for once I was grateful for his aimless meanderings. He'd told me about a place called Bathurst Basin and his unsuccessful attempts to fish in it.

"There's s'posed to be bream and roach in that dirty old sump pit, but I've never caught a bloody thing in it. Only fit for dropping a corpse in is Bathurst Basin, only a corpse!"

At the time I had taken little notice of Brian's rambling,

222

but now his macabre recommendation had a weighty persuasiveness about it. The basin joined the main harbour in the city. Brian had told me that it had been built on an area where an old millpond once stood and had lost its water supply when the New Cut river was created, which, unlike the River Avon, was not tidal. With no current in its flow, what went in the water stayed in the water.

I went into my bedroom, opened the bottom drawer of the battered Schreiber dressing table and pulled out one of Aunt Pearl's pillowcases that she had given to me when I first moved in, then walked out of my digs and downstairs into the street and walked across the road towards the dilapidated wall that surrounded the run-down corner tenement building. I checked behind me to see if anybody was about or if my downstairs neighbour Mrs Pearce was snooping from her front window. When I was sure no one was watching, I felt along the crumbling masonry of the top layer of red bricks and found one loose; it pulled away from the old, loosening cement easily and I walked away back towards my bedsit with the block held partially out of sight behind my leg. I returned upstairs and back into my kitchen, put both the box and brick into the pillowcase, and drew the fabric of the cotton pillowcase together in one hand. Then I picked up the string that had previously been looped around the box and tied it all together tightly in a series of heavy knots. I grabbed my coat, car keys and my Bristol street map from the sitting room, then picked up the box and walked out of my bedsit feeling like a low-grade Sweeney Todd.

It wasn't difficult to find the basin. I drove the two miles from St Pauls across the Prince Street Bridge and parked my car up close by on Lower Guinea Street. I got out and suspiciously looked up and down the road, which was thankfully free of human life. I'd been fortunate not to be caught during my earlier vandalistic activities obtaining the brick. I was hoping that my luck wouldn't run out now. The last thing I needed was to be stopped by a copper and found in the possession of a number of severed body parts and a rotting chicken's limb all bundled up in a box. I leant back into the car and lifted the grisly contents that were housed in the cardboard and Irish cotton sarcophagus from off of the passenger seat and quietly closed the car door, then briskly walked across the road and followed the river's-edge path opposite the run-down warehouses that had once been a hive of Victorian commercial activity. I made my way over the old iron bridge on Commercial Road and continued travelling on the opposite side of the embankment towards the far end of the jetty. My urgent desire to rid myself of the contents I carried was less about ridding myself of incriminating evidence and more about my lifelong dread of the power of the hex and the voodoo magic associated with the warning I had been given. I was about to send them to a secluded and nameless grave.

After about fifty yards I turned to check that I was still alone, then walked over to the edge of quay and without any hesitation slung the bagged-up box of chopped-off auricles and the intimidating chicken's foot as far as I could and watched it rapidly sink into the gloomy waters of the basin.

I returned to my car with my flesh crawling, the stink of human decay lingering on what I was wearing. My nostrils retained the unwelcome odour of death and I had a bitter taste in my mouth that I associated with both my previous visits to a morgue while I was a cop back home and the putrefying appendages I had just dispatched to the bottom of the cavernous marina. I spat out saliva onto the cold pavement and felt the urgent need to scrub both my clothes and skin. But the primal, superstitious fear that that I had known since childhood and which now clung to my insides as I drove back to St Pauls would not be so easy to wash away.

28

THE FIFTEEN TEN-POUND notes were still sitting in a neat bundle on top of my old record player when I returned from disposing the body parts that had belonged to the dead doorman. The money was a stark reminder as to how far down a very murky road I had gone in my search to put hard cash in to my wallet. I felt grubby and strangely corrupted by my earlier actions and needed to wash away the sullied deed that I had just undertaken.

I returned to my sitting room after having a shave and a hot bath. I felt cleaner but still strangely tainted by what I had just done. I'd lain in the tub for the better part of an hour trying to forget about the malevolent reminder of Clarence Mayfield's murder and the voodoo chicken's foot warning I'd been sent, as well as the matter of Stella Hopkins' disappearance and the further sizable retainer that my wealthy employer had left for me earlier. But I still couldn't get my mind to settle and I again began to question what the hell I'd gotten myself into and why the taciturn alderman was prepared to cough up his hard-earned riches for me to do his bidding and why he needed to keep the local law on the back burner. In the short time that I had been searching for the missing girl, two people had been murdered and I been beaten up and attacked by a dog. Moreover, it was likely that there was a group of local bigwigs that were up to their necks in seedy acts of depravity, and their shady activities were probably being covered up by bent law who were most probably on my tail and attempting to warn me off with hacked-up flesh and black magic. If I'd had any sense left at all I would have heeded their threats and left things well alone, but I'd never liked being threatened and I never could let sleeping dogs lie.

I genuinely believed that Earl Linney's need to find Stella was heartfelt and sincere. During our last two brief encounters he'd fleetingly shown to me an inner vulnerability that from my policing experience I knew was only visible when an individual had their back against a wall, was desperate and with nowhere else to run. I kept asking myself what Linney's story was in all this. The photograph I'd found at Hopkins' place made me question whether he was more than just Stella's guardian. If he was her real father, if in fact they were kin, then what kind of parent allows a stranger to try to locate his lost daughter while he hides in the shadows? None of it weighed up. If that had been my kid out there lost, not seen for days, I'd have been tearing up both the streets and anybody that had got in the way of finding her. I knew one thing for sure: I'd certainly unsettled Linney when I'd informed him of my belief that the wealthy lawyer Terrence Blanchard could possibly be involved in Stella's disappearance.

I knew deep down in my guts that the wily Jamaican councillor was still holding out on me about his true relationship with the slick honky barrister and I was damn sure it went deeper than the two of them sitting cosy around a table at a town-planning meeting at the council chambers. I knew I needed to start digging a little deeper and try to find something else that linked the two of them together in all of this mess.

To bring that kind of information out of the woodwork would require me to start nosing around again, and that in turn would invariably lead me to me getting beaten out of joint for my trouble. I rubbed at my brow with the tips of my fingers, wondering what to do, then looked back down at the tidy bundle of dough on the lid of my Dansette player and decided that for the kinda cash I was being offered, my nose could take another beating to find out what I needed to know.

I walked into my bedroom with the money in my hand and dropped it onto my bedside table, then pulled on my new strides and took the blue sea island cotton shirt from off of its hanger, which was hooked on the handle of the door, and put it on, noticing as I did that the swelling on the lower part of my left arm from the dog bite had gone down nicely. In years past when I was still on the force I'd taken my fair share of beatings and had always healed up real quick. The bite on my arm was proving to be no different. It was another war wound to add to a collection of many scars, which seemed to increase as each of my years passed. I looked into the mirror on the front of the wardrobe and carefully knotted my knitted navy tie so that it sat flush in the centre of my collar. I rubbed Bay Rum through my hair and then massaged a palm full of Old Spice aftershave into my stubbleless jowls before pulling on the shiny brogues I had bought earlier and tying them in tight double knots. I stretched out on my tiptoes to start to break in the new leather a little.

The stiffness of the hide pinched at my ankles as I took the first few steps across the room to collect my hat and grey herringbone jacket from the bed, and I reminded myself that I'd need to buy some sticking plasters later to prevent the inevitable painful blisters from erupting on the sides of my feet. I slipped my jacket on, collected the cash from the bedside table, folded it in two and put it into my inside pocket. I dropped the black felt trilby onto my head, pulling its brim down low across my eyes, and walked out into hall, turning off each of the room lights as I made my way towards my front door. I felt in the dark for my newly acquired hand-me-down tatty old duffle coat that was hanging on the hat stand and threw it over my shoulder as I closed up and made my way downstairs. Outside in the street, I stood for a moment taking in the peaceful calm of the winter's night; then from the corner of my eye I saw my elderly neighbour Mrs Pearce watching me suspiciously from her living-room window. I waved up to her as she eyed me in the street and I felt the top of my lip break out into a riled sneer as she quickly darted back behind the curtain, embarrassed at being caught spying on me. I slipped my arms into the threadbare sleeves of the coat, pulling it across my back and buttoning it up. A rebellious smirk crept across my face as I thought of Vic's appalled reaction later to what I had to tell him, and to the fact that I was still wearing the garment that he detested so much.

I'd decided to walk the short distance from my place to the Speed Bird club on Grosvenor Street. The night air was cold and a sharp frost had begun to set in; the pavements were starting to freeze over again, making walking on them difficult, other than at a snail's pace. As I cautiously stepped out onto the harsh hoar surface I thought to myself that no matter how long I'd be living in this godforsaken country I would never get used to the bone-chilling winters or get the hang of keeping upright on an iced-up sidewalk.

By the time I reached the Speed Bird it was after nine and I wasn't surprised to see that the place was quiet. The club did its major business at weekends, when the regular punters happily spent their meagre wages Friday through to Sunday evening. Good times were to be had by those wanting to imbibe in the heavy alcohol of over-proofed rums. This was when the place would be packed to the rafters and throbbed with the sound of soul music while the basement club would be filled with the heady, herbal fragrance of ganja. Over the years the penetrative hemp aroma had seeped into every nook and cranny of the cellar room and its intoxicating effects would've comforted many from the painful homesickness they would feel after leaving the sunny Caribbean islands on the promise of an even better life to go to in the land of a falsely welcoming empire. No more than a handful of drinkers, all black dudes, were in tonight; most were sitting quietly hunched over their half-filled glasses as Don Covay and the Goodtimers' "Mercy, Mercy" played at low volume.

All but one of the booths were empty: a heavyset Jamaican I didn't recognise sat in one of the far-end cubicles on the back wall with a slight, mousy-looking white girl who looked scared to death at the thought of being in the joint and I guessed was only there in the first place because she knew there was nowhere else they could to outside of St Pauls without causing trouble for themselves. Openly dating a black guy meant a woman risked being subjected to the kind of vicious scorn my people had put up with for centuries. I was of the opinion that if any woman was prepared to take that kind of crap on a day-to-day basis then she was to be respected; it was a damn shame that the girl looked so ill at ease in a place that welcomed both the courage of her convictions and the money in her purse. I casually smiled at her as I walked to the bar and as I did I got the disgruntled attention of her big suitor. I offered him a friendly "How you doin'?" to placate his irritated demeanour and he returned my greeting with a fiercely dark look of pent-up aggression that I ignored.

I stood patiently at the bar and waited for the barmaid to look up, as she was lost in a world of her own, filing her crimson-painted nails with steady, rhythmical strokes. She was well into her sixties, white peroxide-haired and wearing a cheap purple satin low-cut dress. I stared at her and finally had to tap the bar real hard with my knuckles to get her attention. Not at all pleased at being interrupted from beautifying her talons, she looked up from her chair with a powdered face like thunder, but when I flashed a grateful smile her sour appearance quickly altered. When she spoke it came as a surprise to find her tone less aggressive than I'd expected it to be. The warmth of her Bristolian accent instantly put me at ease as I took a seat across from her, folding my arms on the bar, maintaining a cheerful beam on my face when I flashed her a grateful smile that I traditionally broke out for mean-tempered women who were about to reluctantly serve me a drink.

"Sorry, lovely . . . Now, what'll you be havin'?"

She put down the nail file next to a half-finished mug of tea and returned my smile, showing off a double row of badly kept teeth. A single gold tooth caught the beam of one of the club's dimly flickering lights; it glinted back at me from the left-hand side of her lower gum and she reminded me of an aging, bleached pirate. I kept a fixed grin and tried not to let my dislike for the gilded crown show on my face.

"Pint o' stout and a couple of fingers of Mount Gay rum in one of those pretty crystal glasses Hurps keeps hidden way under this old bar of his. Where's your boss tonight?"

"He's outta my way, thankfully, and a bleedin' good job too. The times he is down here he's making a nuisance of himself. If he ain't got his hand up my skirt he's in the till raking the takings out to put on the next bloody horse race that takes his fancy. He'd be a rich man if he spent the same amount of time grafting behind this bar rather than trying to get his mucky paws inside my knickers or betting on the next losing nag out of the stalls . . . Know what I mean?"

She winked at me, and I shuddered at the thought of the kind of antics that she'd just described between the over-amorous club owner and the scary-looking sexagenarian pint-puller. I paid for the rum and stout chaser and retreated over to one of the booths, took off the heavy duffle coat and sat down with my back against the wall so that I could keep an eye out for Vic.

An hour and another pint and double measure of rum later, my cousin finally sauntered through the door and greeted me from across the room with an embarrassingly mighty holler, which nearly knocked the blonde-tinted pirate from behind the bar off her perch and made the few remaining customers jump with fright. Vic was dressed all in black: a polo-neck sweater, kid leather flared pants and his matching knee-length leather coat. He made his way to the bar, engaging the lady with the gilded gums with his flirtatious banter while he waited for his drinks. I watched as he paid up, then caressed his fingers with his lips and blew a kiss, which he guided towards the old barmaid with his massive hand. He casually strolled over towards me chuckling to himself as he held the two pints steadily between his huge stubby fingers. Hauling his big frame into the seat opposite me, he placed the two jug-handled glasses of darkened ale on the table, then reached into the side pocket of his leather jacket and pulled out his silver hip flask. Unscrewing the tiny cap in a couple of twists, he then poured a large measure of rum into my empty crystal tumbler before taking a hefty swig of his favourite tipple. I watched as he carefully screwed the top back and then returned it to the deep pocket of his coat. When he finally spoke, his voice was filled with the sense

232

of mischievous fun and joy that I remembered with such fondness from our childhood.

"Shit, JT, did you see that? Where the hell did Hurps git that ugly old fucker behind the bar from? She's got a face on her like a pig pissing, damn near turned that beer sour as she pulled it up the pipes."

He made a squirming face of disgust before taking a long draught of his pint, then laughed again to himself no sooner than he'd gulped it down.

"Hey . . . Now I gotta say, you is looking real sharp tonight, real sharp. I was starting to think you was considering a life as a hobo from the shit you been wearing on your back lately."

He put both hands flat out onto the table and pushed himself up, peering down in the low light of the club to get a better look at me, nodding to himself in approval at my new clothes. His cheery outlook was brutally halted when he caught sight of the tired old military-style overcoat nestled beside me on the seat.

"What the fuck you doin', man, bringing that tatty rag windcheater out with you? Didn't I tell you to lose that piece a shit? Makes you look like an outta-work Paul Robeson . . . There ain't no way I'm being seen anywhere with you if you thinking of putting that shagged-out pelt on your back again, no way!"

"It keeps the cold out and I don't see no point in t'rowing away a good jacket like that when it's still got some life in it."

I watched as my vexed cousin struggled to comprehend what I was saying, trying not to laugh as he seethed silently to himself at my apparent lack of fashion sense.

"Oh, it's got some life in it all right . . . enough to let the damn ting crawl off o' that seat on its own with all the nasty shit that's probably nesting in it."

Vic grimaced at the thought of what he'd just said and sat back in disgust, staring at me. I cheekily winked across to him as I took a sip of my pint and watched as his eyes widened with the realisation that I'd been pulling his leg. He looked down at the table, slowly shaking his head from side to side, laughing quietly to himself, relieved that I'd been having him on. When he finally looked up and spoke, his face had hardened and his voice had a matter-of-fact, determined edge to it.

"C'mon ... I wanna know, let's hear what's been going down since I last seen you."

I took a mouthful of beer and began to recount to Vic how I had been sent the sliced-off ears belonging to Clarence Mayfield and the chicken's foot, and how I'd disposed of them earlier.

"It looks like you're making some real nasty friends in real low places, brother. Whoever it is that cut Clarence up wants you off their case and they've sent you a pretty straightforward message to back off. I suppose I'd be wasting my breath if I told you that you should back down on this shit."

"Would you?" I asked, hoping to get the further benefit of my relation's streetwise wisdom. I then regretted asking such a dumb question to somebody like Vic, who didn't know the meaning of the term "back down".

"Hell no! I'd find whatever gutter-crawling bastard had sent those ears to me an' I'd be stuffing them down their t'roats and the chicken's foot up their ass."

I chose to ignore Vic's advice and concentrated on telling him what I'd found out over the last few days: how I'd followed up the leads Hoo Shoo Dupree had given to me, my meeting with Virginia Landry, the visit I'd received earlier that afternoon from Earl Linney, and my unsubstantiated belief

234

that he and the barrister Terrence Blanchard were linked in some way. Vic listened patiently, not making eye contact with me while I spoke, weighing up in his head what I was saying and considering the implications of my words.

When I'd finished, he waited for a short while, mulling over the facts of my report to him before asking me a question.

"So tell me, this Landry chick . . . she a stunner?"

He pumped his eyebrows up and down a couple of times in quick succession while drumming the edge of the table with the flats of his hands.

"C'mon, cough it up, I needs to know if she's hot, brother!"

"Jesus, Vic! Can't you think of anyting else? All that stuff I just laid on you and all you can think of is whether the damn woman's hot or not. She was a decent lady, fine-looking, that's all I gotta say."

I picked up my glass and sank the rest of my stout, and dropped the empty pot back onto the table, unable to hide my frustration at my cousin's glibness.

"Fine-looking lady, is that so?"

I felt Vic staring across at me while an invisible flush of warmth hit my cheeks as I reluctantly recollected Virginia Landry's waiflike beauty, and he mischievously ribbed me some more.

"Man, I git the feelin' this fine-looking lady floats your boat; tell me I ain't wrong? And befo' you git on your high horse, brother, that's cool, cos it's 'bout time you got your hands on a piece o' tasty skirt, put some life back into . . ."

Vic stopped himself mid sentence and I looked out across the empty dance floor and shuffled uncomfortably in my seat as the heated embarrassment leaked out of me. He realised he'd touched a raw nerve as soon as he'd made his flippant remarks and leant over towards me, placing his hand on my arm gently as I continued to gaze out into the uneasy emptiness of the night club. When he spoke and broke into my silent state it was with a surprising tenderness that I did not expect or honestly believe him to be capable of.

"JT, I wish I could take the hurt away, brother, I surely do. You know I gotta real big mouth sometimes and I don't know when to keep it zipped. I never meant to mess with your grief."

His head dropped and we both sat silently for a moment. I turned back to Vic and watched as he slowly rose from his seat and carefully collected the empty glasses from the table. There was an unmasked sadness in his eyes as he nodded an unspoken apology towards me. He walked over to the bar, shaking his head from side to side, and I knew that he was privately punishing himself for his ill-chosen quips. He strode across the floor unable to hide his anger at himself, his huge shoulders hung down low like a dejected prizefighter who was reluctantly leaving the ring after losing on points in the twelfth. When he returned a few minutes later with our glasses refilled, his mood had lightened and it was as if the brief, awkward conversation that had just taken place between us had never happened and that the ghosts from my past that he had accidently awoken within me had been exorcised from his memory so as not to cause me further injury. He put the pint of stout in front of me with one hand, then jovially slapped my shoulder hard, his huge hand knocking me forward in my seat. If there had been any bad blood between us, then the simple gesture of offering me another drink and a swift manly clout across my upper body was how he expected what had passed between us to be forgotten. It was a simple and effective act of contrition that I could not deny him.

When Vic finally spoke again, he chose to return to the subject of Earl Linney.

236

"Why'd you think that two-faced Jamaican Linney got you involved in this mess in the first place? He came outta nowhere and he's been slinging greenbacks at you like he's got a fuckin' printing press in his back yard ever since. Just think on about the kinda weird shit he's been laying on you these past few weeks; it reeks o' trouble, man. I'm telling you, I wouldn't trust the bastard as far as I could t'row him. Hell, every word that spills outta that old nigger's mouth sounds like one big pack o' lies. If you ask me, he's gonna let you take the fall fo' someting he's most probably up to his thick neck in."

Vic didn't give me a chance to reply or interject an opinion. He was on a roll and intended to stay on it.

"Another ting, there's this honky lawyer you found living out in that big joint in the country. Linney tells you he barely knows him, yet you say he nearly messed his britches when you mentioned his name. You tell him there's been a sighting of the damn mute he's paying you to find and that this Blanchard dude is having scrubbed-up cock-rats run down to his place by what has to be bent law, just so that he and his loaded brethren can stick their dicks into a little piece of forbidden ebony cooch. The fact he still wants you to go it alone and not come clean with what you know to the local police is another crock o' shit . . . Brother, that bird, he don't fly straight, I'm telling you fo' sure."

"Maybe you're right, Vic, maybe Linney is involved in Stella's disappearance, maybe he is setting me up as a patsy or perhaps what he's been telling me all along has been the trute. All I know is that I have to do what I think is right and try to find out what the hell has happened to her."

Vic was about to interrupt me, but I lifted my hand to prevent him from butting in and continued speaking.

"If I find that the alderman is dirty in all o' this then I'm gonna make damn sure that he spends some time behind bars. I can't explain it any better, but I've come this far and I need see it through to the end – you gotta see that?"

"JT, I told you befo', you ain't a copper no more. Git real on this. You've been up against bent law and men with money and power once befo': that ended real bad fo' you. Don't you be repeating the same shit twice, man, it ain't worth it, only person that's gonna git hurt in all this is you."

Vic blew out a heavy breath of air, knowing that his words were falling upon deaf ears. He rested back against the red vinyl-covered seat and stared back at me, his frustration evident upon his chiselled features. I finished the rest of my beer, stuck my hand into the inside pocket of my jacket, pulled out the money that Earl Linney had given me earlier and slid it across the table towards Vic, who whistled quietly to himself at the bundle of notes that sat in front of him.

"Stash that with my other stuff."

"No problem . . ."

He picked up the cash, folded it in half again and got up outta his seat, putting the wad of notes into his coat pocket as he took himself out of the booth.

"Now, you sure you don't wanna keep a bit of this back, git some style in the rain mac department? You can sling that other old rag out fo' the bin man."

He grinned at me as he turned up the collar of his own flash coat and walked out of the club without looking back, seemingly without a care in the world. But in truth I had unsettled him with my bravado talk of taking on another man's problems and possibly going toe to toe with a faceless enemy that I knew so little about and who was clearly capable of doing me great harm.

29

AFTER VIC HAD LEFT I bought myself another pint and sat thinking about his advice and mulling over his words of caution and whether he was in fact right about how I should throw in the towel and get the hell out of Earl Linney's spiral of chaos as quick as I could. What Vic had said made a lot of sense, but I'd rarely taken the counsel of others, well meaning or not, and my cousin's advice to quit while I could had failed to make the impact he'd hoped it would. Something inside of me told me that I needed to see the job through to the end and find out the truth regarding Stella Hopkins' disappearance.

Sitting slumped in the booth, I felt my eyes struggle to stay open as the need for sleep overwhelmed my thoughts. I jerked my body into an upright position along with my sluggish consciousness and swirled the last dregs of my beer around the bottom of the glass before tipping it towards my lips and downing the remainder in a final draught, then sat the empty glass in front of me as a veil of fatigue washed over my weary body. My watch said that it was just after midnight. I grabbed my coat and pulled it on, then made my way upstairs out into the dark, bitter chill of the early hours.

I stood and briefly looked up and down the still quietness of Grosvenor Road, taking note of the solitary but familiar car parked further up on the opposite side of the street. The blue neon sign of the Speed Bird club buzzed and flickered above me as I slowly did up the buttons of the dog-eared duffle and drew my trilby across my face before starting off back towards my digs, fully aware that from the silver Ford the unmistakable faces of Elrod "Hurps" Haddon and the crew-cut cop who had attacked me with the slapjack were watching me disappear into the night.

I was too full of beer and rum to think straight any more. My body ached and was so dead-beat tired that by the time I got back to my bedsit all I was fit for was taking a quick pee, kicking my clothes across the floor of my room and falling into bed. Any thoughts of Elrod Haddon and the crew-cut cop sitting back in that car on Grosvenor Road were quickly eradicated from my consciousness as my body submitted to its natural desire to sleep.

★

Ellie's nocturnal homecoming to me is always the same. She appears out of the penetrating firestorm and into my waiting arms as I rest, taking advantage of the privacy that heavy slumber allows, empowering within her the ability to reach into the unseen protected sentiments of our cherished past and permitting us to return to the shared love we swathed ourselves in when she freely walked upon the earth and we believed our happiness had no end to it. Now, in the darkness of my dreams, that joy is scattered into fleeting moments of idyllic reverie. My once flawless memories of her are now frequently tarnished by the cruelty of my waking into a world where she no longer exists and I remain, tormented and alone. But for tonight we return to each other and briefly exist at our most contented, reliving a seamlessly perfect memory of a perfect day.

The splendour of this time is always shattered by the returning bouquet of smouldering ash and charred human flesh, but on this occasion my nightly delusion is somehow different and I feel the presence of another soul who remains anonymous and silently stalks our intimacy in the previously impenetrable and private Eden that my mind has created.

We walk barefooted, as we always do, along the pink sands of Needham's Point towards the makeshift beach house, with its roof covered in heavy layers of palm fronds and with its slatted wood floor, which I would cover with a couple of red and green checked woollen blankets so that we could stretch out together. Now protected from the rays of the strong midday sun, my back propped up against the back of the shack with Ellie lying between my legs and her head resting against my chest, I gently caress her arm with my fingertips and the sweet aroma of coconut oil and ozone drifts from the jet-black curls of her long hair as we look out of the open doorway towards the gently breaking waves of an azure sea.

I close my eyes and feel the warmth of a gentle breeze that blows in from off of the sombre shoreline and I allow myself to drift deeper towards a sense of a shared tranquillity that is conveyed by the ebb and flow of a placid tide. As I lose myself in the stillness of the hushed moment, then for the first time in my secluded dream state I sense a tiny hand gently take my own and feel the lips of a child touch my ear and whisper, "Sing to me, Daddy, sing me the song that sends me to sleep."

*

It was the sound of splintering wood and the bouncing rattle of the Yale lock spinning across the polished floorboards of my hall way that sent her soothing voice back towards the timeless hideaway I was being drawn from. I shot up naked off of the mattress as the multiple thuds of heavily studded boots made their way at speed towards my closed bedroom door. I leapt towards it in the hope of rolling the bolt across to lock myself in, to give me a little more time to work out an exit plan, when with two hefty strikes to the edge of the doorjamb it was nearly kicked off its hinges by the intruders on the other side. I instinctively backed up as two uniformed police officers burst through the two-foot-wide gap of the now unsealed doorway and ran at me, slamming me down hard on to the mattress of my bed. I shouted out and fought to try to free myself from their grasp, and one of the cops drove his clenched fist into my guts, winding me.

They spun me over onto my stomach, grabbing hold of my wrists, burning my skin with their leather-gloved hands and yanking both my arms out behind my back to restrain me. A further two coppers sped through the door and grabbed at my flaying legs, pinning them down to the bed by my ankles. I was held tightly at the neck in a pincer grip by one of the officers and my right cheek was pushed into the mattress, and I watched as the distinct outline of a fifth man calmly walked around the periphery of my vision, then stood over me watching as the four others held me down. I tried to relax my body against the powerful grasp of my captors and found sufficient breath within me to speak again just as the unknown figure took a clump of my hair in his hand and with brutal force wrenched my head back so that I was staring into the emotionless, hard eyes of what had to be a plain-clothed officer.

"What the fuck's going on?"

I spat out my demand towards the scarred face of the man who had my locks tightly in his grasp.

"Are you Joseph Ellington?" The plain-clothed copper asked me the question with the kind of assured timbre in his voice that told me that he'd been doing the job for a long time. I replied with an attitude and tone that showed little deference to his time served or rank.

"Yeah, that's me . . . What the hell you doin' busting into my pad at this time o' morning?"

"I'm arresting you on the suspicion of the murder of Virginia Landry. You do not have to say anything if you do not wish to do so, but anything you do say may be used against you in a court of law. Now get a pair of drawers on this coon's arse and run him back in the Maria pronto down to the nick . . . And nobody speaks to this black bastard until I get back to the station, is that understood?"

A Black Maria was the nickname for secure police vans with separate locked cubicles, used for the transportation of prisoners. The name was said to have come from a large and powerful black lodging-house keeper named Maria Lee, who helped constables of Boston, Massachusetts, in the USA in the 1830s when they needed to escort drunks to the cells. And so it was with a touch of twisted irony that I was flung unceremoniously into the back of the infamous police vehicle whose origins had gained a notorious reputation via the deeds of one Maria Lee, an American black woman feared by both crooks and police in the 1820s for her use of violent force to catch local miscreants.

My elderly neighbour Mrs Pearce stood on the pavement along with a sizable array of curious onlookers who gawped at me from outside of their homes. The gathering was tutting and nodding at my apprehension as I was led handcuffed towards the opened rear doors of the polished navy-blue vehicle. Oblivious to the crime I was accused of committing, each of the spectators seemed to share a certainty in their expressions as to my obvious guilt.

I wondered if the colour of my skin influenced their opinion in the matter of my alleged culpability and felt that perhaps little had changed in the hundred and sixty-five years since the abolition of slavery. I was certain of one thing no matter how much time had passed: whether we were secured in handcuffs or chains, if the accused were black, you were damn sure to be in one hell of a lot of trouble.

I was driven at speed the short distance out of St Pauls to Bridewell police station on Nelson Street, barefooted, a blanket wrapped around my partially clothed body, with the four coppers who had busted into my flat sitting at either side of me. The harsh echo of the klaxon rattled alongside the aura of confusion in my head as it rapidly travelled through the early morning fog-bound streets of the city. It wasn't long before the Black Maria broke sharply and the driver shifted the gears and quickly reversed the paddy wagon.

The ear-piercing whine of the engine reverberated throughout the interior of the Austin van as it accelerated backwards towards my final destination. It came to a juddering halt, and the doors were thrown open and I was led from the police carrier into the rear of the station house by one of the officers along a series of spotlessly scrubbed-down corridors, each decorated with the kind of uniform olive-green paint work that could be found adorning the walls of nicks and jails spanning the four corners of the known colonial empire.

The copper leading me through the maze of passageways finally came to a standstill at a large iron door, which we waited briefly at until it was opened by another fresh-faced bobby who took me by my left elbow and walked me towards a chest-high counter. I watched nervously as a burly-looking desk sergeant with a balding pate appeared behind it, shirt sleeves rolled up, his arms revealing two blue-inked tattoos:

a pair of crudely drawn crossed Gurkha kukri blades on one, and the emblem of a sphinx surrounded by a knitted ring of oak leaves and with the words "Egypt" and "Gloucestershire" inscribed underneath on the other. He gave me the once-over, not speaking, before returning his attention to the young constables who had brought me in and were standing behind me. When he finally chose to speak, he directed his question to his youthful colleague at my rear, his eyes showing that he was ignoring the fact I was even in the room but I knew from the way he held himself from behind his coveted place of power that he'd already got my card marked.

"Who've we got 'ere then?"

He made his enquiry as he began to write something in a large red-bound ledger in front of him.

"Joseph Ellington. The old man says he wants him banged up and not interfered with till he gets back."

There was an apprehensiveness in his reply that gave away his lack of experience on the job and the intimidation he felt when addressing the no-nonsense desk officer.

"Not interfered with, is that so? Well, that's fine by me; I've no interest in making small talk to a bloody wog at this time of the morning. Did the governor say whether he wanted his fingerprints rolling?"

"No . . . He didn't mention anything 'bout prints, just to get him in a cell."

"If it's a cell he wants him in, it's a cell he gets."

I watched as the canny copper lifted a thick pottery tea mug to his mouth, swigging back the last of his breakfast cuppa before lifting a large set of brass keys from off of a hook at the side of his desk. He open up the bar hatch and strode out in military fashion to where I was standing. I could smell the stale odour of cigarettes and the cold tea he'd just consumed

245

on his breath as he squared up to me, the edges of his spit-polished shoes no more than an inch from my bare toes.

"Right … Let's find this gentleman a nice comfortable room, shall we?" He winked cruelly before turning on his heels. "This way."

He marched me towards another sealed entry, which he unlocked with one of the fat keys, and I was escorted along a dim, short hallway towards the lock-ups. The duty officer's martial stride was curtailed as we reached the end of the jail block. He opened the door to the final cell, held out his hand for me to enter, and flashed a wide grin at me as I was pushed inside by the copper behind. I sat on the edge of a concrete bench and stared down at my cold, exposed feet, my broken spirit left in no doubt as to the certainty of my detention and the swiftness of my confinement.

30

A LENGTHY PERIOD OF time spent in a cell alone allows a man to do one thing well, and that's to think. The solitude that comes hand in hand with any incarceration sanctions the mind to consider, reflect and deliberate the whys and wherefores of a life gone bad. It is not unnatural for an individual who finds himself imprisoned to question what has brought him to such a desperate end and what he could have done to alter the course of his felonious actions. Few at the time of undertaking such lawless acts would have accepted that their servitude to crime would be their undoing until they found themselves caged. My time as a police officer had allowed me to witness in many souls all number of reactions to their confinement, from the old-time lag who craves the security of his repeated custody to the first-time offender who begs to be released from the barren, foreboding confines of his captivity. Our freedom, normally always taken for granted, is never really appreciated until we are denied it. At least I knew that my false internment was not due to any crime I had committed and that I was innocent of the charges that I had been accused of. But knowing one's own guiltlessness stands for very little when you find yourself detained at Her Majesty's pleasure and the incriminating facts are lined up against you, and I was still very much in the dark as to what evidence there was linking me to the murder of a woman I'd met only once.

As I sat alone in the six-by-eight-foot cell, my own gloomy thoughts were mulling over the death of the beautiful Virginia Landry and how I had perhaps unwittingly played a part in her murder. Whoever had taken the poor girl's life obviously wanted to silence her from divulging any further information about the brutal experience she had endured at the hands of a bunch of degenerates out at the Blanchard estate. Whether it was Papa Anansi, crooked coppers or Terrence Blanchard's henchmen who had tailed me, I had stupidly led them straight to Virginia's door and she had suffered at their brutal hands and paid the price for my questioning. Try as I might to deny it, I had her blood on my hands.

I stood up from the stone bench and pulled the blanket tight around me in a poor attempt to stave off the shivering that quaked through my unclothed body. The cell stank from the fusty-smelling piss that had been sitting in a galvanised bucket for days and I was beginning to gag from the intense, ammonia-like smell that was saturating what little fresh air there was to breathe in such a confined space. I paced the short length of the chamber to try to keep warm, counting out in my head the seven steps it took to pace from door to wall. I kept that up for a good ten minutes, finally stopping when I heard the sound of a key being turned in the lock.

In silence, with my wrists still handcuffed, I was escorted by a constable from the depths of the lock-up area to a drearily decorated interview room on the second floor of Bridewell station. As we entered, I noticed the straightened backs of two police detectives who sat in silence at a large polished timber desk; neither got up nor spoke as I was shown to a seat on the opposite side of them. The initial muted eeriness of the situation abruptly changed as one of the officers, who I recognised as the guy who had grabbed me by the hair earlier, casually excused the copper who had brought me up from my cell by jabbing his thick thumb towards the exit. In front of them were a couple of Manila folders and two fountain pens, their caps still firmly pushed on, next to an unopened packet of ten Park Drive cigarettes. The clock on the wall above the two men's heads said it was just after two in the afternoon. We continued to sit in hushed quiet apart from the second hand ticking away. I placed one hand on the desk and covered the back of it with the palm of my other; the brass links of my handcuffs clinked together as I did. I stared down at my lap and waited for them to begin their interrogation. I didn't have to wait long.

"Mr Ellington . . . You don't mind if we call you Joseph?"

The scar-faced detective asked me the matter-of-fact question in the kind of way that told me he wasn't used to being refused too often.

"You can call me whatever you want, man, just as long as it ain't coon."

I guessed from the look on the detective's face that my reply to him wasn't what he'd expected to hear. I watched as he blew out a hefty draught of air, his middle two fingers tapping the edge of the frame of his chair as he inwardly tried to reign in his still-hidden quick temper. He leant towards me, stroking the five o'clock shadow on his squared-off chin with his thumb and forefinger before sitting back in his seat and staring at me. Rather than stare back and antagonise him further, I returned my gaze to my lap. I had, however, in the short time I'd been in their presence got a pretty fair idea what I was up against. The first dude, the one asking the initial questions, was clearly the superior in rank of the duo. He was a big-set guy whose broad shoulders struggled to fit into a tight tweed jacket. I'd noted that his trousers had seams pressed into them that could have sliced a loaf of bread real thin and that his black Oxford brogues were polished so that the fluorescent strip light's glare bounced back off of the pristinely buffed-up toes. His greying hair, complete with lengthy, immaculately trimmed sideburns, was cut neat into his neck, and his greased locks were combed back tidily, the faint hint of Brylcreem and Wright's coal tar soap his only concession to male grooming. He must have been in his late fifties and carried the soldierly air of a Second World War veteran, which would most probably explain where he had acquired the deep three-inch scar that ran from his right temple to the centre of his cheek.

The other fellow was even easier to read: he was a skinny detective constable, in his mid twenties, new to the job, with a shaving rash stretching down his neck, and he was in awe of his gaffer. I'd come against his kind a hundred times before. He was the sort of copper who was dangerous to a man in my position because he was most likely to be ambitious, and devious to boot. His need to carve himself a name that would be respected with his boss and fellow officers would be high on his agenda. Integrity was rare in a beast like him, and I chose to mind what I said if I had to engage in conversation with him. His scar-faced superior decided to break the silence with an introduction.

"Joseph, my name's Detective Inspector William Fletcher, and the gentleman sitting to the right of me is Detective Constable Nathanial Beaumont. We need to ask you a few questions, if you wouldn't mind?"

"Oh, I mind . . . but that ain't gonna cut it with you guys, is it?"

I waited for Fletcher to answer me; instead, he reached over for one of the Manila files and opened it so that all I could see were the sides of the blank brown covers. He began to read, taking his time over the content. He snapped the folder shut and dropped it back on the desk before speaking to me again.

"Where'd you know the deceased from, Joseph?"

"You talking 'bout Virginia Landry?"

I kept my cool and bounced off my reply in as relaxed a manner as I could summon up.

"You know any other dead women, Joseph?"

The DI uttered my Christian name with friendly warmth in his voice that belied his true intentions in questioning me.

"Course I don't . . . Hell, the first I knew that the lady was dead was when you guys came crashing into my place like you was out to get public enemy number one this morning."

Fletcher reached over to the cigarette packet and pushed the base up, revealing the ten fags. He pulled one out and placed it between his lips, then produced a brass Ronson lighter from his jacket pocket and lit it, drawing hard then pushing out a heavy plume of smoke into the room. He rolled the lighter round in his hand for a moment, looking at me, before returning it to his pocket.

"What's your relationship to the deceased?"

Fletcher's phrasing of the word "deceased" had a heartless finality in its intonation. I thought of Virginia, her body lying cold on some mortuary slab, the elegant life force she'd possessed ripped out by a senseless, violent act. I swallowed hard and answered.

"I met her in the place she worked; she was a barmaid at the Bee Hive pub in Horfield. I was drinking in there one afternoon, the place was quiet, we got talking, and I asked her to come out with me. Gave her my name and a number she could git a hold of me on . . . She said she might call; she never did, guess I wasn't her type . . . That's it."

"How long ago was this?"

Fletcher kept the manner of his questioning light. He'd started to play the game and at this point he didn't realise I knew that or that I understood the rules.

"'Bout a week an a half ago, I'd say," I coolly lied. The detective constable reached into the other Manila file and pulled out slip of paper, which I recognised as mine. Sure enough, he turned it over to reveal the torn-out sheet from my notepad that contained the contact details I'd given to Virginia Landry.

"Is this your handwriting, Mr Ellington?" the snotty DC demanded. He spat out my surname when addressing me and clearly wanted to keep our interview on a professional level. I leant over and drew the slip of paper closer to me, scrutinising what was written on it for a moment before answering the jumped-up bobby.

"Yeah, that's my scrawl."

"Well, the piece of paper that you have just admitted has your handwriting on it was found with a number of other personal effects next to the body of the deceased. Tell me ... where were you last night?" DI Fletcher asked me the question straight off the bat and caught me off my guard. Not wanting to involve Vic, who was only too well known to the police, I stumbled for a second to reply to his query with the fast-paced certainty I'd previously had.

"Er ... I was with my uncle Gabe and aunt Pearl, over at their place in St Pauls. Yeah, me an' old Gabe we played cards and I drank way too much of his rum. It ended up me sleeping off the booze fo' a while on their sofa. I woke up around 3 a.m. and made my way back to the digs."

"And I suppose these relations of yours can corroborate your whereabouts, can they?" the snide DC interjected. His brashness was starting to piss me off, but I tried not to show it.

"I'd sure as hell hope so; if not, I'm in a stack o' trouble."

"You ever heard of a local hooker called Jocelyn Charles?" Fletcher asked.

"No . . . Am I supposed to?"

My third lie: it was starting to become a habit. I just hoped that the pair of them were buying into it.

"She was found dead just over a week ago in Montpelier, dumped in undergrowth by the railway sidings with her throat slashed. You ever visit Montpelier, Joseph?"

It was the detective inspector's first stupid question, but I went along with his idea of good sport to keep him happy.

"Not to butcher women I don't."

"Of course you don't . . . Our man here's not that kind of fella, far too bright to be hanging around filthy murder sites and women of ill repute. Is there anything you should be telling me, hey . . . Joseph?"

Fletcher was casting his line out, hoping to get a nibble on his hook. I wasn't biting and I sure as hell didn't like the bait. I preferred the idea of keeping my mouth shut, composed and unobtrusive. That was the key to their game: let them get hot under their collars and keep 'em thinking they'd got me on the ropes.

"What do you do for a living, Joseph?"

I'd seen this one coming.

"I used to pack boxes of smokes in the warehouse at Wills' until I had a falling-out with a foreman on the shop floor. I'm looking fo' someting that better suits my previous kinda of work."

I decided to try a little fishing of my own, see what I could haul in: I'd nothing to lose.

"And what kind of work would that have been, Joseph?"

DI Fletcher had took a chunk outta my lure. It was time to reel him in.

"Your kind . . ."

I watched as the two copper looked at each other, confused and unable to quite accept what I'd just implied.

"What . . . you're telling me that you were a po—"

I interrupted him before he choked out the word that he could not associate with the man he was questioning.

"Policeman . . . Yeah, that's right, man. Sergeant Joseph Tremaine Ellington, Barbadian Police Force, working outta Central station, Bridgetown. And as a sergeant, that made me t'ree stripes higher than your boy there." I nodded over to the sullen-guts detective constable who looked like the world had just dropped outta his bowels. "Now I don't know what else you think you got pinned on me, but I'm telling you straight, I don't knock around with whores and I met that poor girl Virginia Landry as she was pulling a pint o' stout fo' me. I asked her fo' a date, she said she'd think about it, I wrote my name and number on that there scrap o' paper you got. That was the last I seen of the woman and I sure as hell never murdered her."

Those last three statements were fact and it felt good to know that I'd managed to utter a little truth finally.

DI William Fletcher sat scowling at me from behind his station, trying to weigh up the truth of what I'd just told him. He swallowed hard and drummed the desk at varying speeds with the flat of his hand before knocking his chair backwards as he rose to his feet.

"Get this cocky bastard back to his cell while I check out his story; give him his bloody clothes and something to eat."

The detective inspector stormed out of the interview room, slamming the door behind him, leaving his ill-humoured subordinate to do his dirty work. I grinned at the boyish underling and thought to myself that getting the shit end of the stick was the same the world over.

254

31

THE LONG NIGHT SPENT in the cell had deprived me of sleep as well as my liberty. A constant metallic drip-dripping outside the door, which did not let up during the hours of darkness, became the least of my worries as various new inmates were brought into the lock-up, each adding to the increasingly high levels of intolerable rows as the evening progressed into bedlam. Swearing, screaming, the punching and kicking of cell walls and doors: all contributed to the relentless din, and by the time the change of shift had come on duty and had lifted down the hatch in the pokey to check on me, my head was pounding and every inch of my body ached.

Earlier, while that entire racket went on around me, I tried to switch off from it and returned my thoughts to the murdered girl Virginia Landry and how the paper with my name had conveniently been found next to her body. It had to be a plant, and I was now certain that Papa Anansi and the crew-cut cop had to be involved in my false arrest. My interfering had thrown a proverbial cat among the pigeons for them. Their paymaster had no doubt demanded that any loose ends should be tied up quickly and they had been very quick in dealing with the thorn in their side that I had become, perhaps less than eight or nine hours since I'd spoken to the terrified girl at her home. I began to realise how stupid I'd been in thinking that my search for Stella Hopkins was just about finding a lone missing deaf, mute girl. Was she just the tip of the iceberg?

I was obviously uncovering somebody's dirty linen and they would do anything to prevent it being laundered in public. If Terrence Blanchard was as well connected and powerful as I believed him to be, then perhaps the rough detective grilling me last night was in his pocket too? I don't know what I'd hoped to achieve by disclosing that I had been on the force back home to DI Fletcher: it was a wild card. With my back against the wall and facing a murder charge, I needed some personal leverage with which to approach the seasoned plain-clothes officer regarding my guiltlessness. Why I chose to tell him about a part of my life that I had until then been trying so hard to forget was perhaps less to do with my belief in the universal brotherhood of policing and the professional camaraderie we might share and more about how desperate I was to show my own integrity and virtue, which derived from my past employment as a copper. Let's face it: just because I was once a law-enforcement officer didn't preclude me from committing murder, but I was hoping that the shrewd scar-faced investigator may think twice before judging me and go with his instincts after I'd protested my innocence.

Apart from knowing that it was Wednesday, I'd lost track of the hours and had no idea what time of day it was when Detective Inspector Fletcher opened the door of my cell and crabbily walked in, bringing his short temper with him. I remained seated on the end of the cold bunk, ignoring his presence, looking at the floor as he lit one of his unfiltered cigarettes and then leaned against the cell wall, staring at me. When he spoke, his deep, booming voice echoed around the stonework of the cramped jail room.

"I've just got off of the phone with a stiffened shirt who runs the nick you used to work in back on that godforsaken place you used to called home: a Superintendent Mackinnon."

"Never heard of the man," I snapped back.

"No? Well, he sure as hell has heard of you and he wasn't too happy to hear your name being bandied about by another copper from the better part of four thousand miles away. It looks like you left that island under a bloody big cloud, my son; in fact, from the sounds of things you kicked up more crap back there in the tropics than a cesspit shoveller on overtime. Now this Mackinnon fellow says that he's just been shipped to his new office from the London Met and that he's just taken over from your old governor, some bloke called Alexander. That was the name of your gaffer, yes?"

I nodded at Fletcher in agreement and he quickly carried on with his sermon, not missing a beat.

"Anyhow your old chief has apparently taken early retirement, lucky bastard. The new superintendent went on to tell me that he knew very little about you and what he did know was from the tales some of your ex-colleagues had been telling him since his arse first hit his chair. Most of them seemed to think that the name Ellington was bad news."

When I heard him say that, I immediately went on the defensive, pointing my finger at the preaching detective, about to give him a piece of my mind and my version of events when he raised the flattened palm of his hand, stopping me in my tracks.

"Now hold on there, mouthpiece, let me finish before you get on your high horse and start spraying the walls with spittle. Mackinnon also went on to say that he'd heard from other officers that you were an honest copper, that you never took a penny on the job, had an even temper with the rouges you pinched and were meticulous in your investigative skills.

"I asked Mackinnon for something a little more concrete about your background and time on the force. He said that he'd do a little discreet digging around at the station and he'd call me back. Guess what? Just over an hour later he's back on the blower, full of himself with your big, thick file in front of him. He said that you made very interesting reading. You had an unblemished record with just over fifteen years' service tallied up, reaching the rank of sergeant and with several commendations for bravery to boot: impressive stuff, Joseph. Then things go belly up when you apparently, for whatever crazy reason, decide to take on a local drug kingpin who may have had some of your high-ranking workmates in his pocket and that you started a one-man war against him and his operation. You made a lot of waves, and because you did, this crook got nasty and tried to take you out at the neck. Only rather than putting you in a box, he ended up killing people close to you. Mackinnon said that you lost your wife and young daughter in a fire at your home, and that before you could seek revenge this mobster had you connected to some trumped-up illegal activities at your station and eventually, from what he can gather, you were given two pretty desperate choices. It was either a lengthy spell in a sweaty Caribbean nick or the chance to get off the island on the next ship out to Blighty. You obviously saw little chance to clear your name or seek retribution for the tragic loss of your kin and took the boat trip out of there. Pretty miserable stuff, son, pretty miserable."

Fletcher looked down at me; the hardness in his glare had disappeared. He returned his hand to his jacket pocket and pulled out his cigarette packet, shook one partially out and offered it to me.

"I don't smoke . . . but thanks anyway."

Fletcher smiled to himself and tapped the cigarette back into its box, returning it to his pocket.

"The superintendent went on to say that he'd had a word with an old chum of yours from the time when you and this bloke both patrolled the streets of the poxy shanty town you used to call home. This geezer got the wind up him when your name was mentioned and wanted to remain anonymous, even with you long gone and on the other side of the planet. This is on account of possibly getting himself in the muck with some his mates on the job, or perhaps this thug you went up against may still have his digits on some dirty cops where you used to work. This nameless wonder told Superintendent Mackinnon that you had a reputation for sniffing out trouble and that you were often like some mangy dog not wanting to give up a bone when you went up against villains and that you didn't back down when things got hairy. He also said that for as long as he knew you, you'd never needed to pull out your service revolver in defence of yourself and would do anything to prevent a situation from going bad. He also added that most of the local felons would stay clear of you if they could. He was also of the opinion that he doubted that you were a whore-killer and that you'd more than likely been playing the defender of some damsel in distress or two-bit loser and had perhaps returned to your old ways and gotten involved in things you had no business being mixed up in.

"So Joseph . . . You tell me, is that what you've been up to? You been sticking your big black conk where it don't belong again? Cos if you have, whoever's bidness you've been prying into has gotten mighty pissed off with your over-curious behaviour and dropped you into a big, steaming heap of monkey shit for your trouble."

"Like I said to you in that interview room yesterday . . . I took a chance on asking a beautiful lady fo' a date. I left my particulars with her. She never rang, wrote or stood on my front doorstep to take me up on the offer. I never saw her again after I walked outta that public house and I never took her life."

I stared up into inspector's eyes, my glare hard, filming over with tears.

"What my police file says and everyting else you just said 'bout my past is the truth, except fo' one ting."

"Yeah ... and what's that, Joseph?" Fletcher asked. The uncertainty in his voice crackled as he waited for my reply.

"I once pulled my service revolver and used it in my defence. I shot and killed a young kid who was attempting to rob the takings out of a cash register in a liquor store. He was no more than seventeen years old and was high on dope and booze; he had a knife to the shopkeeper's throat and I knew he was going to cut him up. I blew a hole in that kid's face the size of a cricket ball. I regretted having to fire my pistol then and I still do to this day."

I looked back down at the floor and bit at a hangnail on my thumb. The same feeling of emptiness now gnawed at my gut in exactly the same way that it had on the night I'd taken another human being's life. I heard the cell door open as the laces from my shoes and the belt from my trousers fell at my feet.

"I'm going to be keeping a real keen eye on you, Joseph Ellington ... Now get the hell out of here."

When I looked up, the scar-faced detective was gone. I sat staring out of the opened door as I listened to the studs on Fletcher's soles clip down the corridor and was about to call out "thanks, man", but my lips would not open nor my tongue form the words to speak. Did I really want to offer up my gratitude to a man who had just taken the darkest moments from my past and spilled them out in front of me so that their cruel memory could inhabit my sentient and leaden soul? I picked up the meagre belongings that my earnest inquisitor had just thrown down in front of me, got up off of the solid bench and followed after his footsteps, leaving my unwanted and haunting reminiscences in the bleak cell behind me.

★

It was after two in the afternoon by the time I was finally released and I walked out of the main doors of Bridewell police station. A heavy fog had dropped outside, making it difficult to see more than six feet in front of me. I walked down the granite-flagged steps into the smog, which smelt of gasoline fumes and chimney smoke, and inhaled the first kind of fresh air I had breathed in over twenty-four hours. I didn't care about the filthy pollution I was drawing into my lungs, I was just grateful to be out of the clutches of the police.

I rubbed at my face with the flat of my hands in a desperate attempt to shake off the fatigue as the harsh chill of the winter's day blew right through my cotton shirt and trousers to the goose-pimpled skin of my upper body and legs. The burning-cold gusts nipped at my sockless feet and I began to shiver from head to toe.

"Vic said you'd be needing this; that boy was sure right."

The familiar, lyrical voice of my uncle Gabe emanated from the murkiness before his physical presence became visible to me. He slowly walked towards me through the pea-souper; his left arm was outstretched and in his hand he held the old navy-blue duffle coat that the kindly reverend had given to me.

"He said someting 'bout you saying to him that it was lucky. Shit, brother, from the look o' this old cagoule it don't look like it can offer you much good fortune. Maybe you shoulda been wearing it in bed yesterday morning, then the police might not a' been beating in on that gate door o' yours wanting to sling your ass in the slammer."

He laughed as he hooked the battered old coat over my shoulders, drawing me towards him in a protective hug.

"Come on, let's git you back to your aunt Pearl, git some of her chicken and rice and peas inside your belly. I got Carnell Harris round the corner in that flash jalopy he's gone and lent you, he'll git us home real quick. That man, he ain't the sharpest knife in the drawer, but he cares 'bout you and he's been worrying his guts since he found out you'd been lifted yesterday. Friends like that are hard to come by, Joseph, real hard to come by."

We walked together in the heavy, impure mist. The profound gratitude I felt inside at that moment for those who so clearly cared for me was truly indescribable.

32

EXHAUSTED AND COLD, I sat on the back seat of the Cortina trying to stay awake. The only thing that kept me from nodding off on the short journey back to my aunt Pearl and uncle Gabe's place was Carnell's bad driving. In less than two miles he'd managed to find every pothole in the road so that each time I closed my eyes and surrendered to my desperate need to sleep, my weary head would either crack against the window or be thrown back and forth as we hit another rut in the tarmac.

"Damn it, Carnell, you ain't motoring down no dirt-track road. Who the hell taught you to drive a car, boy, your blind grandmama?" Gabe snapped at our hapless but well-meaning chauffeur, who was by now gripping at the steering wheel of the Ford for dear life. His body was rooted to the edge of his seat as he nervously peered forward through the windscreen out into the dense murkiness of the smog. Carnell glanced across at Gabe in the passenger seat, my uncle's face raw with irritability.

"Sorry, Gabe . . . You know how I hate having to drive in this shitty weather. Gits me all worked up, and this fog's sure making it hard to git a handle of where I'm headin'."

"Just keep your stupid, squinty eyes on the damn road befo' you run this heap into the side of a wall and git the t'ree of us killed, you fool!"

Gabe frantically rubbed at his balding scalp and shook his head slowly, mouthing further insulting obscenities to Carnell before swinging around to brusquely speak to me.

"You been kicking up a shit storm from the look o' tings. Vic says to tell you that he's got Leroy Granger, the joiner on Gatton Road, to go see to those busted doors back at your place; he's putting you a couple o' new locks on and all. Your aunt Pearl, she's already been round to your place with Loretta and cleaned up what the police t'rew about while they was pulling your digs to bits. You really gone and upset somebody with your busybodying, boy. Time you thought 'bout a different kinda work, Joseph."

It was the second time in less than twenty-four hours I'd been told that my prying was making me enemies. It was sounding like old news to me and I switched off from any further exchange with my elderly relation by not making further eye contact with him, instead looking out of the side window into the mist-filled street as we drove back into St Pauls.

Gabe turned back to face Carnell and disapprovingly shook his head at him again before removing his ill-tempered gaze from my good friend and staring down at his feet in the foot well of the car, the awkward silence a cruel companion until we pulled up outside my relatives' house on Banner Road.

The first thing that hit me when I walked through the front door and into the hall of my aging kin's home was the delicious smell of the pepperpot beef stew that was cooking on the range in the kitchen. I took off the old duffle coat and hooked the hood over the wooden ball of the banister post at the foot of the stairs and followed the warming aromas through to the scullery. Aunt Pearl was standing in the centre of the room, topping up an ancient tin bathtub, carefully pouring scalding-hot water from a brass kettle that she had already half-filled. A pile of fresh, clean towels sat on top of a kitchen dining chair next to it with an amber bar of Wright's coal tar soap sitting squarely in the centre of the fluffy bath sheets. She looked up at me and smiled before decanting the remainder of the boiling liquid into the bath, then turned to the sink to refill the kettle and sat it back onto the waiting blazing gas flame on the hob of the stove.

"I thought you'd be needing to git yo'self scrubbed up after spending a night in that pokey the police been holding you in. Joseph, take those filthy rags of yo' back and I'll see they git washed. I brought you back some of your tings to wear. I ironed 'em up and they hanging on the back o' that door fo' you."

She pointed past me to where my freshly pressed clothes were hung with her long, time-worn finger before setting her knowing eyes on her husband and Carnell, who stood close by at the entrance to the cramped kitchen door.

"That pepperpot cook-up sure does smell fine, Mrs Pearl!" Carnell piped up hungrily from behind me.

"Oh, I know it does. You ain't never gonna change, are you, boy? Food and cards only tings that stupid head o' yours has ever been interested in. I don't know why Loretta puts up with your gluttonous and gambling ways; she must be witless! Yo' know, I could hear those guts o' yours rumbling after that chow I got bubbling away on that oven no soon as yo' came strolling t'ru my front gate door."

She laughed to herself as she lifted the kettle off the hob again and tipped it into the bathtub, then came over to me and gently kissed me on the forehead before leaving the room and turning her attention again to the audience at her kitchen door.

"Now you two let this man git himself cleaned up; then we can all sit and eat."

"Lord have mercy!" I heard Carnell call out with ravenous joy, and he clapped his hands together as he and my uncle

265

Gabe followed Pearl back down the hallway towards the sitting room. "Hey, Gabe, you wouldn't happen to have a bottle o' stout hanging round that we could open up, celebrate old JT's return to the fold?"

The three of them broke out laughing as I closed the door behind me and began to undress, the warmth of their continuing laughter from the other room a welcome respite from the twenty-four hours of misery that I'd just endured.

I didn't mess around getting myself clean. After I'd scrubbed off the stink of the police cell from my skin, I quickly dressed and called Carnell to come and give me a hand to lift the heavy tin bath filled with my grimy water and suds. He joined me in the kitchen, took a hold of one of the looped handles at the edge of the bath, and we carried it outside, then threw the mucky bathwater into the yard. I took the old metal tub back into the outhouse, where it was normally kept, and hung it on a large nail that was hammered into the red-brick wall. When I came out, Carnell was still standing at the kitchen door looking at me with a witless smile on his fat face, which usually meant that he was about to say something stupid. I was freezing standing out in Gabe's tiny garden and couldn't be bothered to wait for one of my friend's senseless observations, so I cut to the chase.

"What the hell are you smiling fo', Carnell . . . You won yourself some cash at the dog track today or someting?"

Carnell laughed out loud at me before answering, his voice soft and reflective.

"You gotta be kidding, no such luck, brother . . . I just got to thinking how pleased I am that you're OK. Say, you free to meet me later in the Star and Garter, say around nine o'clock? I got someting I need to talk to you about, it's . . ." He paused for a moment, thinking to himself before finishing what he was about to say to me. "It's kinda important, JT."

The inane smile then returned back to his face as he waited for my reply. I again began to feel my body and mind aching for sleep and I rubbed the weariness out of my brow before answering him.

"I'll see you in the Star at nine, and you're buying the damn beer!"

It was the first time Carnell had ever asked to speak to me about something that he regarded as important, and despite his mindless and childish ways sometimes, I knew he would not have made the request unless it was something significant that he had on his mind, and despite how much I longed to lay my dog-tired carcass down on that bed of mine, I just didn't have the heart to refuse him.

"Thanks, man." He slapped the wall with the flat of his hand and turned and ambled back through the kitchen, calling back to me as he did, "C'mon, let's go and git some o' that pepperpot stew in our bellies, I'm starving!"

The four of us sat and ate at the kitchen table. I was listening to my aunt Pearl and Carnell yakking on enthusiastically about the kinds of food we used to eat back home, plantain, yams, mango, and how much they missed them and why it was a shame that they couldn't get them here in England. I remained mostly quiet during their colourful conversation, chipping in occasionally and enjoying the cheerful banter between the pair of them.

But Gabe's mood had changed and he sat in silence, picking at the food in front of him, his discontent seeping across the table towards me. After we had finished, Gabe got up and without speaking picked up his paper from the arm of the chair that sat besides the range and returned to the sitting room. Carnell rose from his seat shortly afterwards, sensing the awkwardness in the air, and leant down and put his muscular arm around aunt Pearl's slight frame and hugged her. She brushed him off, dismissing his affectionate embrace of gratitude with the back of her hand.

"Git on wid you, boy, I don't want you soft-soaping me!" She smiled at him as his bulky frame stood over her.

"That was some fine pepperpot stew you served up there, Mrs Pearl . . . surely fine."

Carnell rested his hand on my shoulder and looked down at me. "JT, I'll see you at nine then?"

"You sure will, Carnell . . . See you later, brother," I replied keenly as I got up and collected each of our plates from the table and took them over to the sink, which was already filled with hot, foamy water. I heard Carnell bid farewell to Pearl and Gabe, but their genial guest did not receive a reply from my uncle.

I stared down into the dishwater, aware that Gabe's taciturnity was of my doing and my mind pondered on how I could approach my disgruntled relative. Pearl spoke, breaking into my troubled thoughts and bringing me promptly back to the then and now of the matter.

"Your uncle Gabe, he means well and he's been worried sick 'bout you, Joseph. Whatever trouble you got yourself messed up in has got him all riled up and you know he tinks the world o' you. You're more than just flesh and blood to him, JT, he treats you like you was his own son. And he knows you ain't like your cousin Vic. He was so proud when you made the police. You always been on the right side o' the law; he's always respected that, took pride in it. Now you go in there and speak to him, you hear me, boy?"

I took a blue and white checked tea towel from off of the draining board and dried my hands with it, folded it, then sat it back next to the sink. My aunt Pearl stared down at the table, and as I walked past her she gently touched my arm as if to say something, then turned away and faced the wall as I left the kitchen to face her troubled spouse.

Gabe was sitting reading the sports page of *Bristol Evening Post* in one of a pair of green cord armchairs that directly faced the freshly made-up coal fire that was now throwing a welcome amount of heat into the small sitting room. A single standard lamp behind him shone an amber glow of light around his head and onto the back page of the newspaper.

The woody aroma from my uncle's cigar combined with the sooty scent that was slowly wafting up from the hearth lent the room a strangely welcoming ambience. I took a seat opposite and looked over towards him as he took a heavy draw on the thick cigar that was hooked into the left-hand corner of his mouth. Gabe stared back at me, then exhaled a thick spiral of smoke up into the air, and the dense beam of light from the lamp caught the grey vapours that were beginning to float around the room. When he finally spoke to me, his timbre was brittle and short.

"I suppose this is what the police was questioning you about last night, was it?"

He closed the paper, then threw it over to me, and I lifted it up in the half-light. The bold print of the newspaper's headlines stared back at me cruelly from the front page: "Woman Found Dead in Grounds of Ashton Court". I swallowed hard and reluctantly began to read the grisly account.

> The body of a young woman has been found in the densely wooded area known as Clarken Coombe in the grounds of the Ashton Court estate on the western edge of the city late on Monday evening. The shocking discovery was made by two wardens who were patrolling the parkland as part of the council's attempt to prevent the poaching

of the country park's deer. The Evening Post
can confirm that the identity of the deceased has
been ascertained by Bristol City Constabulary. DI
Fletcher, who is heading the inquiry, told the post
earlier today, "At this stage in our investigations we
are not prepared to release further details regarding
the discovery of the body found last night due to
the brutality of the crime and the significance
of evidence found at the scene. I can assure the
general public that everything is being done to
apprehend the perpetrator of this atrocious crime.
We are at the moment exploring many avenues of
inquiry and will be issuing a further statement to
the press shortly."

I folded the newspaper and dropped it at my feet, sickened
at what I had just read and at myself, knowing that my brief
involvement with the dead girl had most certainly contributed
to her untimely and horrific murder.

"The girl they found out in that wood . . ." I pointed down
at Gabe's paper, which sat at my feet. "Her name was Virginia
Landry; I met her earlier this week. She told me she believed
she'd seen that missing girl I'm looking fo'."

"Seen her where?" Gabe took the stubby stogie out of his
mouth and rested it between two of his fingers.

"You really don't wanna know, Uncle Gabe"

"Don't wanna know or you ain't gonna tell me?"

Gabe sat back in his chair and took another drag on his
cigar, waiting for me to answer him.

"The less I tell you, the less mess you can git yourself into."

I knew I sounded glib, but my sentiment was sincere.

"Don't play games with me, boy. I got myself into your
mess as soon as that snotty lookin' copper came knockin' at
my door askin' if I knew where you were on Monday night.
He was wantin' to know all kinds of tings 'bout you, so I just

played along with that bobby. He looked at me thinking I was nuttin' but a miserable, scared ole nigger who was gonna tell him how I hadn't seen hide nor hair of you in days, then put you in the frame for whatever he wanted to finger you fo'. You shoulda seen his face when I told him you was here all night playing cards with me. Anyhow, I stood on that step out there in the street and lied my ass off, so you try tellin' me I ain't in enough o' your mess as it is. Besides . . . you really think I'm gonna let my brother's boy sit rottin' away in some police cell?"

"Years ago, when I was a child, my mama told me that you would always use the 'we were playing cards all night' number when the law came lookin' fo' my papa when he'd been up to no good. When I asked you last year 'bout it, you said you couldn't remember ever doing it, said my mama had been pulling my leg. I sure am happy as hell you did the same fo' me."

My uncle smiled at me and leant forward in his chair, weighing up whether I was just placating him with a little of my usual charm.

"Boy, I know you ain't murdered no young woman, but I'm in the dark 'bout the rest o' what's been going on . . . So why don't you tell me what all this madness is about, Joseph?"

He again rested back in his seat and rubbed at his top lip, waiting for me to begin my account of what had happened to me during the last ten days or so. A stern look of determination was etched upon his heavily lined face, which I recognised only too well. I took a deep breath and spilled my guts, leaving nothing out. Afterwards he continued to mouth and suck on what was left of his cigar, puffing out more clouds of thick smoke around us, mulling over what I had said. When he finally spoke, he surprised me with what he had to say.

271

"Joseph . . . You took a big chance when you came over here to start a new life fo' yourself. Now, your aunt Pearl and I knew you never had any choice but to leave Barbados. We knew you were honest, knew you weren't nuttin' like that rascal brother o' mine. Your papa was as crooked as the hind leg of a mule and as mean-tempered too. But you were never like him – Vic maybe, but never you. We knew you wouldn't be on the take like some of ya colleagues back in Bridgetown and I knew you could never turn a blind eye to all the illegal stuff that was going on around you. We were proud when we heard you made a stand, son, real proud. Ellie, she wrote to us time and time again.

"That girl told us everyting that was going on. How stubborn you had become and how determined you were to bring down those crooks on the force you was working with. Ellie knew you wouldn't give in. She was scared fo' you and fo' herself and fo' ya children, Joseph, but she respected you fo' not turning the other cheek and fo' standing up against that bastard thug who had his hand in all those other policemen's pockets back at your station house . . . What was his name?"

Gabe's question caught me unexpectedly and I instinctively pushed my tongue under my top lip, not wanting to utter the name of the man who had caused me such pain.

"Monroe . . . His name was Conrad Monroe."

I fell silent again.

"Yeah, that's it, Monroe. Well, you don't need me to tell you how that bastard destroyed everyting you held dear. He took your old life, your wife, the child growing in her belly and your six-year-old daughter. You think I'm getting any pleasure saying this stuff to you? Look, I know you've been trying to do what's right, you trying to find this lost mute woman an' all, but if you think playing at being a policeman again is going to give you the chance to right old wrongs from the past, then you fooling yourself, Joseph. There are bad guys the world over and you can't think you can take every one of them on because you still hurting fo' the bad tings that have happened to you, boy.

"Monroe and this man, Terrence Blanchard are the same, bad through to the bone, and there you sit thinking you've got nuttin' to lose, and all because of that damn stubborn streak you got . . . But men like Blanchard will find someting to cause you some more pain . . . and you know why he will?"

"No, Gabe . . . Why?"

"Because like that bastard Monroe, he can, Joseph . . . because he can. It's as simple as that, boy."

Gabe rested both of his arms on his legs and drew himself forward, then patted my arm while he stared into the dying embers of the fire. It was the second time such a tactile and caring gesture had been shown by a member of my family in such a short space of time. I knew that both Pearl and Gabe cared about me dearly, but tonight, for the first time, I realised that they shared the burden of my own grief in a way I had not until now fully recognised. Earlier when Aunt Pearl had touched my arm I had braced myself to prevent any show of my real feelings, but now the truth of Gabe's words had reawakened all of the pent-up guilt and grief from my recently tragic past I had hidden and shattered the defences that kept those who knew me isolated from my true inner heartache. I began to sob such uncontrollable tears that I thought they would never stop.

33

THE WARMTH OF THE sun caught the side of my face as it shone through the open window of our room. The temperate balminess of a Barbadian summer's morning cosseted my body as I lay alone in the large rattan bed, a thin white sheet pulled down low across my hips, and I could hear the whisper of the cicada's song hypnotically mixing with the gentle sound of waves lapping against the shore of the golden-sanded beach that rolled up towards the edge of our tiny garden. Outside my bedroom I overheard the comforting chatter of familiar voices coming from the kitchen and the tempting smell of breakfast cooking. A calming sense of contentment enveloped me as I relaxed with my arms splayed out across the bed, my hand stroking the warm mattress where my wife had been lying next to me. I looked up at the ceiling and watched as a swallowtail butterfly floated gracefully above me; I followed its unmapped journey across the room until it drifted down to the edge of our dressing table to rest.

My wife Ellie and six-year-old daughter, Amelia, entered the room. My little girl carried a glass of mango juice, which she carefully brought to my bedside. I pulled myself up the mattress by my elbows and propped my back against the headboard as the two of them joined me, their heads resting on my chest, nestling closer into my body as I wrapped both arms around them and drew them towards me. I closed my eyes as Amelia began to sing to me, while my wife ran her fingers tenderly across the back of my hand, but her touch began to fade as the nursery rhyme my child sang grew more distant. I felt the two of them draw away from me, and the once gentle warmth of the morning sunshine suddenly burst into the unbearable heat of a firestorm as my wife and child screamed out. In panic, shouting their names, I tried to pull myself up from the bed, but my powerless body was held down by a weighty invisible pressure and I was forced to watch in horror as my two beautiful girls were dragged into the flames that were about to engulf our bedroom.

"Joseph . . . Joseph, are you all right there, son? You were shouting in your sleep."

Pearl was kneeling at my side as I sat slumped in the armchair. Disorientated after being woken, I wrenched myself up in the old chair and rubbed my face with the flats of both hands and felt the coarse stubble on my clammy cheeks and chin with my palms. My eyes gradually refocused on their surroundings in the weakly lit room and I once again felt the unsympathetic heat from the coal fire discharging towards me.

"Yeah, I'm OK . . . What time is it, Pearl?"

I sat forward in the chair and felt the damp wetness of my shirt pull away from the sweaty skin on my back.

"It's just after six . . . You been sound asleep this past hour or so. I heard you calling out for Ellie and Amelia, bless them. Gabe and me could hear you rambling away to yourself from where we were sitting back there in the kitchen. I really didn't wanna wake you, but you were starting to scare me, hollering out like you were."

Pearl lifted herself back up from where she had been kneeling next to me, put her hand into her front pocket, pulled out a brass Yale lock key and held it in her hand in front of me.

"Here, take this: your cousin Victor came round earlier to give you this, said you'll need it to git inside your digs tonight. You got yourself a new door and Loretta and me cleaned up after the police had made all that mess in there. Vic wanted to wake you, but I told him to leave you be while you was sleeping, says he'll catch up with you tomorrow. Now let me git you a cup o' coffee; it'll bring you back round to the land o' the living."

Pearl's face flushed and she tried to hide her shame at using the word "living" by quickly getting up to avoid my eyes. As she was about to leave, I took hold of her delicate hand and gently squeezed it in my own.

"Yeah . . . That'd be great, Aunt Pearl, and thanks fo' what you done fo' me."

She brushed my hand away, making a series of huffing noises as she ambled out of the sitting room to make me the hot drink that she hoped would revive my spirits.

At that moment in time, the land of the living was the last place I wanted to be. I'd grown used to the nightmares and how they relentlessly permeated my sleep and they were now the companions of the daylight torment of my conscious being. I believed that there was nothing that could have drawn me away from the contrition and anguish that would continue to dominate my waking hours, and I once again felt the urgent desire to inflict my wrath upon those who had taken my wife and children from me. But I knew that it was too late for such aimless thoughts of vengeance. In truth, I'd had little time to plot my method of revenge against those who had killed my wife and children and had razed my house to the ground. It had only taken a few hours for my shady superiors to make me falsely complicit in my own family's tragic demise and they had quickly hung me out to dry on trumped-up charges of murder. I was handcuffed and taken out to a remote station house in Bathsheba, on the eastern side of the island, and after days of being grilled by white detectives about my supposed involvement in the killing. During my questioning, I had continuously denied any wrongdoing. I was interrogated for hours and then returned to my cell, where I was not allowed to rest and was instead hosed down with heavy jets of cold water. In my despair, I imagined that I would eventually be killed and my body dumped down a drain that would finally wash my corpse out to sea. But I had continuously denied any wrongdoing and their determined grilling was just part of a plan conjured up by the man I had been trying to uncover as running a drug ring along with a number of officers in the police department. Conrad Monroe was determined to see me broken and humiliated, and after days of being beaten and deprived of sleep, in the end it came down to a simple ultimatum.

I was told that the charges against me would be dropped if I agreed that the fire at my home was the result of human error and that the deaths of both Ellie and Melia had been a tragic accident. My lengthy investigation into the drug kingpin and his organisation was to be closed. I was ordered to make a statement saying that I deeply regretted pursuing a long-time personal witch-hunt against a local businessman, namely Conrad Monroe. On top of that I had to hand in my resignation, losing the job I'd proudly held for over fifteen years, and get off the island on the next available boat.

The crooked bastards had got it all worked out and I'd had little choice other than to run with my tail between my legs. The alternative would have been to spend the next twenty years in a Bajan prison shacked up with many of the violent criminals who I had probably pinched.

On the long journey at sea, alone in one of the cramped shared cabins of a battered, rusting old freight ship that would eventually bring me to Great Britain, I thought of nothing other than vengeance and much how better I would have felt if I had been rotting away in a cell with Monroe's blood on my hands. But at night, unable to sleep, the doubts crowded in thick and fast. An ex-copper locked up with mainline crooks: how long could I have lasted inside even if I'd kept my head down and my wits about me? Alone with my miserable thoughts, I continually asked myself whether the twenty-year sentence that I would have received for taking out the men who had murdered my loved ones would have been worth it. The answer was always the same: yes, I'd have happily done that lengthy stretch and been willing to have lived or died in jail if there had been the slightest chance to avenge my kin. Monroe and his minions would have been dead and that would have been the end of it, the score settled. But that was not to be; I had not been able to exact the kind of swift revenge my wife and daughter's violent deaths had demanded, and the cowards who had murdered them would continue to hide behind the corrupt fellow police officers I had once worked with and be protected by the powerful drug lord who would continue to control them. I had tried and failed to do my duty as an honest police officer and in my failure I had paid the highest price.

Staring blankly into the fire in front of me, I thought about Stella Hopkins: could I save her? Had she already succumbed to the same vicious fate at the hands of ruthless men in the same way that Virginia Landry had? I sensed a tight knot develop in the pit of my stomach, and felt my throat tighten and the my fists instinctively clench as an overwhelming fury ascended from some place deep within me, and at that moment I swore that I would not be as restrained in seeking out those who had snuffed out Virginia Landry's life so cruelly and that my retribution against them would be merciless.

★

Heavy sleet bounced off the windscreen as I sat in the Cortina across the road from the Speed Bird club and waited. Something I'd learnt many years ago was that patience was a police officer's best friend and that the ability to attain a sense of forbearance when dealing with the criminal classes was a valuable partner. I didn't know how far up the club's owner, Elrod "Hurps" Haddon, was on the lawless ladder of crime or what his involvement with Papa Anansi, Stella and the deaths of two innocent woman was, but patience or not, I was damn sure I was going to find out.

The one fact I did know was that I'd seen old Hurps with the crooked copper who had given me a beating a couple of nights ago sheepishly sitting in a motor in almost the very same spot that I was now parked up in. I glanced at my wristwatch when I saw Elrod hauling his big butt down Grosvenor Road; it was just after seven thirty. My eyes skipped between the sweeping movement of the wiper blades that were knocking the slushy rain onto the pavement as Hurps Haddon fumbled in his coat pockets and finally drew out a big bunch of keys. I quickly got out of my car, pulled the old duffle-coat hood over my head and ran across the street while Hurps was unlocking the front door to the club, and stood close behind him as he opened up.

"How's tings going, Hurps?" I called out to the burly landlord as the sleet pelted down in the street. He almost jumped out of his skin with surprise.

279

"Jesus . . . What the . . . Is that you, JT? What the hell you doin' creeping up on my ass like that? You scared the shit outta me!"

"You look like you just seen the bogie man, Elrod . . . I was just passin' by an' seen you 'bout to open up your doors fo' the night. Though I'd git myself a rum, try to warm up my bones."

I moved closer towards him, rubbing my hands together and feigning a chill that tonight I didn't feel.

"We ain't serving till Dolores gits here, an' I got my books to account fo'. Why don't you come back later, I'll git you a Mount Gay in; you tell that old bitch behind the bar it's on me."

He flashed a smile at me, turned and began to walk inside, his hand already on the edge of the frame, ready to slam the door in my face when he was safely behind it. I grabbed hold of the door just above where Hurps' hand was and thrust the toe of my shoe hard into the back of his knee, bringing him down on to the floor and making him howl out in pain. I pushed my way in, slammed my fist into his neck and the side of his face a couple of times, then kicked his now hunched-up body further into the corner entrance so that I could close the door. Once it was shut, I fumbled around on the wall in front of me until I found the light switch. I flicked it on, then leant down and dragged Haddon off the floor, pulling him down the stairs by the collar of his heavy coat towards his empty bar.

"C'mon, brother, don't git all mean on me. Now you can git me that drink; all that tussling round outside your gate door has given me one helluva thirst."

Hurps gasped. "You bastard . . . Where the hell you git off tinking you can knock me 'bout outside my own place? If you got ideas 'bout robbing me, then you don't know whose money you gonna be messin' with, you stupid prick!"

"Take it easy, Hurps, only ting I'm interested in taking from you without paying fo' is that shot o' rum you just promised me now."

I hauled his weighty carcass across the small dance floor, then slung him into one of his booths and watched his hefty arms and legs flail about as he desperately tried to right himself in the tired crimson leatherette seat.

"You sit yo' ass still, while I git the drinks in."

I strode back towards the bar, opened up the hatch and walked the length of the antique counter to pick up a bottle of Barbadian rum from off of the middle shelf. I noticed the cricket bat that Hurps always kept underneath the cash register in the event he ever had any trouble from a drunken punter. I grabbed for the bat and put it under my right arm, then lifted the bottle to my mouth and pulled off the stopper with my teeth, spitting it out on to the floor, taking a hefty swig as I made my way back towards where Hurps was sitting, rubbing at his aching knee. He looked up at me and at the bat under my arm and decided to get wise with me. It was a big mistake.

"What the fuck you think you gonna do wid that paddle?" he snarled at me. "You think I'm scared o' you cus you used to run with the police back on that poxy island you got kicked offa? You start gittin' rough wid me and you gonna wish you never set a foot t'ru my door!"

The sizeable ex-boxer squared up at me in his seat, then thought better of it: tough as he had once been, he was in no fit state to go head to head with me, and he knew it. He'd already seen the look of the devil in my eyes and gambled that his best bet was to make sure his oversized backside remained glued to his chair.

281

He thought he'd wagered well by not rough-housing with me, but his decision wasn't going to do him any favours – no way was I going easier on him just because he'd backed down. I took another slug of the rum and sat the bottle down on the bench in front of Hurps, then pushed the curved end of the bat underneath the heavyweight's massive double chin.

"I want you to tell me what you know 'bout a missing young woman called Stella Hopkins and why you been seen hanging round with the kinda jazzed-up lawmen that like to mix it up with whores and pimps?"

I released the pressure on his flabby gizzard to let him speak.

"I don't know what the hell you talkin' 'bout; you a damn' fool. Why don't you sling yo' skanky pig hide outta my place befo' I—"

He found a little courage and tried to defiantly raise himself up from where he was sitting, but I forced the end of the bat harder into the fat man's throat, pushing him back down into his chair.

"Befo' you do what? Start hollering out fo' that pox-faced ponce who's got you in his pocket? You hoping he's gonna come and heave you outta the big pile o' shit you got yourself into? How long you been in cahoots with ole Papa, Hurps?"

"Cahoots . . . What kinda shit is that? I ain't got nuttin' else to say to you, Ellington . . . Crazy talk 'bout me and whores, you stark raving mad . . . Take a hike!"

Hurps stared up at me insolently and lifted his head away from where I held the tip of the bat at his neck, then proceeded to drag a wad of snot from the back of his throat and spat it out in a huge globule of green phlegm at my feet.

"Now that ain't polite."

I lifted the bat and smashed it across Hurps' right kneecap, making the chubby innkeeper scream out in agony. I raised the club above my head and let it hang menacingly above his skull.

"I ain't fuckin' about with you, Hurps," I warned. "What you got going down with Papa Anansi and that bent copper? C'mon . . . I seen you and that crew-cutted blond fucker that calls himself a police officer sitting in the silver wheels he drives about in. You were having it up real good outside o' the Speed Bird the other night. What was going down?"

"Noth—"

I snatched the bat back sharply, ready to bring the flat side of it around the back of the pudgy liar's thick head.

"Papa brings his girls in here all the time . . . You know that, JT!"

"Cut with the 'JT' shit . . . I ain't interested in making nice with you no more, Hurps, start giving me someting I don't already know. Did he ever bring Stella Hopkins down here?"

"I don't know . . ."

He began to lie to me again, but I was getting real sick of hearing his bullshit. I swiftly carved the bat through the air and slammed it down onto Hurps' left shoulder blade, snapping his clavicle in two. The old boxer bellowed out an ear-splitting scream that echoed around the basement room and then disappeared into the dark obscurity of the night.

"I'm gonna ask you one last time, Elrod. Did Papa ever bring Stella Hopkins to your club? Now think hard befo' you speak, because if you keep lying to me you're gonna end up a cripple. You dig me?"

"You talkin' 'bout that creepy deaf bitch?"

A smacked-up knee and a broken collarbone and he was still brainless enough to get mouthy with me.

"Oh, you really testing my patience, Hurps."

I grabbed hold of one of his thick earlobes and yanked him up from where he sat, then heaved him back across the dance floor and shunted him into his precious bar.

"Did he bring her in here?"

I shouted so loudly at him that he covered his head with his arms and curled himself into a ball on the floor. I leant forward and wrenched him back to his feet, taking his jaw in my hand and squeezing it until the veins on either side of his temples looked like they were about to explode. The canny old prizefighter was starting to get the message.

"Yeah, yeah . . . He brought her in here just the one time, some time last month, I think. He was showing her off like some circus freak."

"And where'd they go to after they left here?"

I squeezed a little harder into Hurps' jaw and could feel his molars pressing onto the tips of my fingers from inside of his mouth.

"To his shebeen on Richmond Road, I suppose, same place he always takes those girls."

"Those girls . . . what you mean by 'those girls'?"

"Fuck it . . . No way, you had all you gonna git outta me, Ellington. You think I'm gonna dig my own grave spilling my guts out to you so that Papa can fill it in when you done with me? Shit man . . . you got another think coming, you think I'm that crazy?"

I took a hard look at the scared face of Elrod Haddon and knew that he was right. In my experience, there comes a point when a man who lives constantly in the company of true malevolence and now facing a new threat will seriously consider what he fears more: the demon he knows or the monster staring back at him. Tonight, for Hurps it was a simple case of the lesser of two evils, and I'd just crapped out.

But I had one ace left up my sleeve. If you can't hurt the skin and bones, hurt 'em in the pocket.

I wandered back round the bar and stood admiring the rows of expensive cut glass and lead crystal that were Hurps' pride and joy and worth a pretty penny. They were neatly lined up on three shelves between the optics of martini, vodka, whisky and gin.

"This is some snazzy glassware you got here, Hurps."

I lifted my arm, bat in hand, and brought it down on the first row of finely etched goblets, shattering them across the dance floor and across the back of Hurps' head and neck.

"Oh you prick!"

I lifted the bat to start on the rest of Hurps' chalices, to given him a chance to recant his last comment and tell me what I wanted to know. But something inside of my head snapped and I unleashed all my pent-up anger on the rest of the club owner's precious collection, then started on the bottles of drinks and his beloved aged teak bar. Glass shards, alcohol, optic heads, bent-up metal and splinters of cracked wood were strewn all over the place. I finally flung the bat into the large glass mirror that hung as the centrepiece of the bar, then turned and grabbed Hurps by his lapels and heaved him close to me. The aged boxer finally submitted to the inevitable.

"Papa brings his special girls in here, the ones he picks to visit some white cats out in the sticks. He gets Warren to take 'em out there once they're boozed up or as high as a kite."

"Who the hell's Warren?"

I shook the old prizefighter, bringing him closer towards me, slapping him hard across his face to keep him focussed and scared.

"Mickey Warren . . . The honky copper you saw me out front with. He's the middle man between Papa and the countryside

285

club all those honkies meet up at to mess round with black chicks. One night he came down here, got himself filled up with ale and Scotch, sat in one o' them booths over there and started telling me 'bout this place he takes these special girls of Papa's. He said they call it the Erotica Negro!"

"You better not be shitting me: they call it what?"

I drove my fist into the side of Haddon's head and watched as his eyes rolled uncontrollably round in their sockets.

"No . . . stop, I swear that's the name the place goes by. The Erotica Negro club. All I know is it's a strictly invite-only kinda place. Papa picks up hot-looking coloured woman, clean and no previous dealings with johns on the streets. These honeys are definitely not his usual cock-rats, they're all top grade, and he arranges fo' 'em to do the dirty with a bunch o' well-heeled dudes who pay him a hefty sum fo' the privilege."

"What's your end in the deal?"

Hurps wilted at the bar.

"I keep an eye out fo' any fresh skirt that comes into here. I give 'em some shit 'bout looking fine and how they could earn themselves some easy money. I introduce 'em to Papa if they take the bait: that's it, I swear."

"How does Stella Hopkins fit into all this, Hurps?"

"I don't know . . . your guess is as good as mine. I only seen her the one time. Like I said, Papa brings her in, it was a Saturday night. He was as high as a kite on grass and he has her sat at his side at that table he always sits on by the door. I knew someting wasn't right with her, though."

"How come . . . Tell me, what was different 'bout her?"

"Well, she was dressed up to the nines, face full o' make-up that even an old bastard like me could tell she never wore. Ting is, she still looked like a child. You could tell she was outta her depth . . . real scared. She just sat there next to Papa

286

stiff as a board, drinking a Britvic orange and clutching hold of a teddy bear or someting."

I let go of Hurps and he slid to the floor with a heavy thud. I bent down and picked up the phone from underneath the bar and dropped it on the counter before walking back round to Haddon, treading broken glass under my feet as I did, and stood over him.

"You're gonna call Papa. You tell him that I'm onto him, that I know that he's involved in the disappearance of Stella Hopkins and the murders of Virginia Landry and Jocelyn Charles. Let him know that if he's got an ounce o' sense in that drugged-up head of his he'll meet me in the back bar of the Star and Garter pub at ten o'clock tonight."

I lifted the phone off the bar and dropped it into Hurps' lap, then walked back up the stairs and out into the sleet-drenched street, leaving Haddon to make the call.

As I drove away, I was unaware that my demand to meet Papa would set in motion a series of tragic events that would haunt me for the rest of my days.

34

It was just after eight fifteen by the time I got to the Star and Garter. Outside it was still hammering down with heavy sleet and yet another blanket of thick freezing fog had dropped over the streets. I was grateful to get inside and out of the constant downpour of watery snow.

I walked over to the bar and was confronted by the pub's grumpy landlord, Eric, who was ready to take my order, a pint pot glass already held in his big mitt.

"What d'you want?"

It was the kind of warm welcome that kept me coming back to the place. I was still fired up after just tearing the Speed Bird to pieces and nearly putting Elrod Haddon into hospital, but I had no quarrel with Eric and chose to ignore the gruff publican's manner. I leant at his bar and flashed him a smile to try and lighten his mood; it had little effect.

"Evening, Eric, I'll take a pint o'Dragon . . . Thanks."

I watched as the miserable licensee clasped at a ceramic and copper-tipped beer pump and drew up the dark, treacle-coloured stout from his cellar. He let the liquid settle for a moment and then topped up the remainder of the pint before setting it down; the tanned head spilt over the side of the glass and the residue was soaked up by a cloth bar towel that had the word Guinness printed on it.

"That'll be one shilling and three pence."

Eric held out his huge calloused hand palm up, for prompt payment; his other was tightly gripped in a distrusting manner around the pint of ale until I'd paid up. I fished about in my wallet for the right money and slapped the coins down into his eagerly waiting paw, then took my beer into the snug in the back room to wait for Carnell while Eric went about polishing the part of his bar I'd been leaning on with an old rag.

My friend didn't keep me hanging around for long and it was just before nine when Carnell showed up through the pub door. He stood for a moment at the entrance to wipe the wet sleet that had drenched his face. He wore a dark-brown velvet jacket and matching pants, with an open-necked purple flower-print shirt. He was soaked through from head to foot. It came as no surprise to find that despite leaving his house in a winter storm, he'd not thought before walking out that he may need something on his back that would protect him from the dire weather, such was his eagerness to get to a poker table, never mind to meet me. I thought of my aunt Pearl and her comment about him earlier that day and smiled to myself: "Food an' cards only tings that stupid head o' yours has ever been interested in." She was probably right, but that's what made Carnell such a good guy: what you saw was what you got, and it was why his wife, Loretta, loved him so much.

I watched him from the snug as he casually brushed off the wet snow that had accumulated on his jacket and trousers with big strokes of his hand, and laughed to myself as it flew across the pub, splashing the other customers who'd been sitting quietly supping their drinks until Carnell had showed up. Eric mean-spiritedly leant across the bar and pointed a stubby finger at his most recent but unwelcome customer.

"Oi, jungle bunny!"

Carnell looked up and then around himself, unsure if it was he that the none-too-pleased landlord was so rudely addressing. He gestured to himself with his own hand, confused.

"Yes you, Nat King Cole, if this lot in 'ere had wanted a bleedin' bath they'd 'ave bloody well stopped at home . . . Pack it in, slinging all that crap round my lounge, you arse'ole!"

"Oh, I'm sorry Mr Eric . . . I didn't mean to cause no offence."

Carnell circled the room on the spot, waving apologetically at the other customers, who grumbled and groaned under their breaths, before walking up to the bar to get his order in. He peered through the serving hatch in the wall behind the bar into the room where I was sitting and grinned at me. Drips of water continued to run from his face, head and clothes and splashed down onto Eric's polished bar. Carnell good-naturedly attempted to wipe the mess up with the sodden sleeve of his jacket but was making more trouble for himself. Eric seethed, and I watched in amusement, desperately trying not to burst out laughing again.

"Come on . . . Stop buggering about, do you want a drink or what?" Eric snapped impatiently at my beleaguered buddy.

"T . . . two pints o' Dragon, please, Mr Eric," Carnell stammered. He dropped his head in embarrassment and stared at his feet while Eric pulled the two glasses of beer and again shot out his greedy hand for payment.

By the time Carnell finally came and pulled up a stool and sat across the table from me in the snug, he had successfully managed to upset every punter in the pub and had given the place a good washdown. Eric stared suspiciously through the serving hatch at the two of us, and I grinned back at him, then raised my glass to sarcastically toast our cantankerous host. Eric blew out a contemptuous jet of air from his inflated cheeks and went back to polishing his bar.

"Cheers, Carnell."

I put my arm out towards him and he did the same, beers in hand as we clinked our glasses together to salute our camaraderie before necking back the ale.

"That Mr Eric, he sure is one sour old muthafucka, ain't he, JT?"

"Oh, he's sour all right, Carnell; take no notice of the fool, he just full of his own spite and bile, that's all. So c'mon, tell me, what's so important that you need to bring me into this nasty rathole on a miserable night like tonight?"

I watched as Carnell nervously squirmed about on his seat before setting down his drink in front of him and placing his hands flat onto the table either side of it, considering carefully what he wanted to tell me.

"Come on, out with it; I ain't got all night, brother."

"It's Lor . . . Loretta . . ." he stammered again. Unusually for Carnell, he'd said his wife's full name rather than Lolly or honeybunch or any other of the stupid names he would normally address her by. The expression on his face was solemn and reflective, very unlike the look he normally carried.

"What 'bout Loretta, she caught you sticking your hand in her purse again? Cos if you have, I'm surprised you've manage to walk in here with a set o' balls still attached to that fat ole dick o' yours."

Carnell laughed at me before replying and winced as he thought about his ill-tempered wife.

"No . . . I ain't been pinching her housekeeping; you really think I'm that stupid, JT?"

I kept my mouth shut as he smiled to himself briefly before his face became serious again.

291

"So what you so vexed about? You look like you damn near fit to shit."

"Lor . . . Loretta's gone and got herself pregnant."

He flung the words out of his mouth like they didn't belong in there.

"Yeah?" I gasped out in surprise. "Who the hell by?"

"Me, you damn fool, who'd you think?"

He huffed about like a sullen teenager before the penny dropped and he realised that I was having him on.

"Git the fuck outta my face, who by . . . You a real bastard sometimes, JT, you know that, don't ya?"

We roared with laughter, our thunderous merriment causing Eric to stick his head through the serving hatch to complain.

"You pair, keep the bleedin' noise down. This happens to be a public house, not Saturday night at the London Palladium."

"Hey Eric, be cool, man, can't you see we celebrating here? Carnell just found out he's gonna become a daddy!"

Eric gawped at the two of us in dismay, an abhorrent look on his face. He shook his head slowly from side to side before adding his heartfelt congratulations to Carnell: "Not another o' you black bleeders to contend with." He turned to his regulars on the other side of the bar and cursed again before bellowing out across his pub to his unsuspecting punters, "I warned you lot this is what we'd have to put up with years ago." He pointed to a mystified old fella who was sipping his pint of mild in a seat by the door. "What'd I say would happen if we let all these coons shack up here? That there'd be thousands of the buggers crawling about the place in no time; well, I was right, St Pauls has gone to the shithouse!"

Still happy at Carnell's' news, I got up and took his big chubby cheeks in my hands, squeezed them then planted a big kiss on top of his head. Eric was furious, staring back at us through the hole in the wall, and when I winked at him he promptly threw his cloth onto the floor in disgust.

One pint later, I nervously looked at my watch. It was just after nine twenty-five. I reckoned I'd got around twenty minutes before I expected Papa Anansi or one of his dogsbodies to hang about early, then stride through Eric's gate door at ten and turn the place sour. I didn't want Carnell to be around when somebody too shady showed up, but at the same time I felt bad about asking him to leave after he had told me about Loretta and the forthcoming birth of his child. I decided to get another round in to further celebrate Carnell's good news and I returned to where we were sitting with more stout.

"Here's to Loretta and the little one, Carnell. You one lucky fella, you know that, don't ya?"

He grinned at me, and nodded in agreement, then put the glass to his lips and swiftly sank the pint in a single draught. I decided now was the best time to tell him that he needed to be on his way.

"Carnell, seriously, brother, I'm really pleased fo' you both, it's real great news. Look, I got a spot o' bidness I gotta deal with. There's a guy meeting me here in around five minutes or so. I think it'd be better if you got yourself off to that game o' cards you were telling me about earlier befo' he shows up here, hey?"

My friend stared stonily back across at me.

"JT, if you in trouble I don't mind hanging about to watch your back, you know that, don't ya?"

"Course I do. Hey man, it's no sweat, I got this covered, thanks fo' thinking of me, but you know I'm gonna be fine."

Carnell nodded at me, then rose out of his seat and stuck his hand out to say farewell to me. I raised my arm and we shook our goodbyes without speaking. I could hear the sleet pounding outside against the pub's windows as Carnell turned to leave. I stood up, took off my old duffle coat and threw it over to him.

"Here, you chump; you can't show up at no card game looking like some drowned rat. I got your car parked down the street; at least I can git back to my place dry in it!"

I laughed as he fumbled to catch it, then struggled to put the ill-fitting coat on. He buttoned it up and it looked like it was about to burst at the seams before he drew the hood over his head. I sat back down and lifted my glass up to him in a final tribute of congratulations and took a sip of the darkened ale before he left.

"Thanks, man . . . that's real kind o' you."

He raised his hand and waved at me almost like a child would when saying farewell to a parent at the school gates. Then my friend cheerfully walked out into the frozen rain and dense smog. His simple words of gratitude to me would be the last I'd ever hear him utter.

35

THE WORD "ANANSI" means trickster. I'd been a fool to think that Papa Anansi would agree to my demand to meet in plain sight and I should have realised that men like Papa never take commands from people they have little or no regard for. Elrod Haddon would have made the call warning Papa that I had paid him a visit, smashed up his bar and beat him around his club with a cricket bat, but it had been foolish to think that Papa would have been spooked enough to meet me. I'd waited for an hour and a half hoping he would show so that I could put the squeeze on him. I'd let my quick temper and hunger for retribution cloud my judgement. The Caribbean folklore title that Papa had adopted had a great deal of veracity behind it, even though I didn't know it as I left the Star and Garter and walked back to my car.

The sleet had stopped hammering its way out of the night sky, but the thick smog still floated about the streets in thick, impenetrable swathes. It was just before eleven o'clock when I pulled up outside my digs and made my way up to the front door to let myself in. I stuck my hand into my back pocket to pull out my keys but realised that they were still in my room and that all I had with me was the brass Yale key that Aunt Pearl had given me for my new bedsit door. Mrs Pearce, my cranky old neighbour downstairs, was most certainly in bed, but unless I wanted to spend a night sleeping in the car I had little choice other than to rap her front window and get her to let me in. I leant over the wall and gave her sitting-room window three hard knocks, then stood back. A few moments later the curtain was pulled back and her grumpy, wizened old face appeared behind the glass and she peered out suspiciously at me.

"Go away . . . before I call the police."

Then once she'd recognised who I was, she flung her arms in the air. "Oh it's you . . . Locked out, are we? Do you know what bloody time of night it is?"

She tapped at her skinny old wrist to a watch that wasn't there, then slung the curtain back at the glass, leaving me to stand like a fool on my own doorstep. I leant against the front door and waited while the minutes passed until I heard her lift the latch on the door; I stood away from the entrance and waited to face her displeasure at me for getting her up at such an ungodly hour. As soon as the door was unlocked, she started on me.

"Eleven o' bleedin' clock it is . . . What d'you think you're playing at getting an old woman out of her bed at this time of night? You ought to be ashamed of yourself, do you hear, ashamed!"

She stood to one side to let me in and I sheepishly walked through into the hallway as she slammed the front door behind me. I turned to face her, about to apologise, but was stopped in my tracks as she continued to berate me.

"I could smell the ale coming off you no sooner than I'd opened that door. Just out the bloody clink and straight down the pub. What would your mother think, police knocking bloody doors off their hinges in the early hours, half the street gawping at you as you were marched out into a Black Maria in handcuffs; no job that I know of, too; odd men calling at all times of the day and night. You need to take a bloody good look at yourself, young fellow, get your act together. Just look at the state of you. It's freezing out there, you've no coat on your back, man. I'd have thought where you came from you'd feel the cold!"

At less than five feet tall, she stood scarily glaring up at me in her worn cord slippers and duck-egg-blue dressing gown, her silver locks dragged back and covered in a green hairnet. I was in no fit state to argue with her. She studied me as I stood in front of her like a scolded child before speaking again.

"Well there's no point in going on about it, I suppose. Make sure it doesn't happen again, do you hear me?"

Despite her vicious tongue, there was something about the look in her eyes that told me she wasn't all bad. I remained silent, with my head down and took her reprimand on the chin, then began to make my way upstairs to my room.

"Mr Ellington?"

I turned and stared down to where she was standing at the foot of the stairs looking back up at me. The tone of her voice had softened.

"Are you sure you're all right, Mr Ellington?"

"Nuttin' that a good night's sleep can't cure . . . Thanks fo' asking, and fo' letting me back in, Mrs Pearce. Good night."

"Goodnight, Mr Ellington, sleep well."

I watched as she returned to her flat and quietly shut the door behind her. I continued to climb the stairs back to my own room, thinking that I may have just made myself a new friend.

★

"JT . . . JT!"

It was Vic's voice bellowing out my name and his desperate, heavy-handed pounding on my door which woke me with

297

a start from a sound sleep that, for the first time in many months, had not been plagued with nightmares or visited by the restless, tormented spirits of either my wife or daughter. I reached for my watch and saw that it was just after seven thirty.

I got up, grabbed my dressing gown off of the floor and made my way down the hall with each of my footsteps appearing to be syncopated with the frantic thuds from my cousin's fists on the door. When I opened up, Vic reached out to me and took a hold of both my shoulders firmly. He stared blankly at me, his eyes red, tears streaming down his face, his body shaking with anger. Mrs Pearce stood a few paces behind him on the landing, a look of concern and confusion on her face.

"What the hell's going on, Vic?"

My cousin drew me towards him, cradling his huge, muscular arms around my back so that our chests touched and I could feel his heart beating against my skin. He forced my face deep into his neck and put his mouth close to my ear, his breath laboured. When he finally spoke I had already anticipated the pain of his words as he whispered them to me.

"Carnell's dead, JT . . . He's dead, some bastard's gone and cut him up from behind."

I felt my cousin's grip on me loosen as he slowly started to slump to the floor. I held on to each side of the door frame as his powerful bulk dropped, his hands desperately clawing at my body as he fell. Now hunched at my ankles, I watched powerlessly as he wept uncontrollably at my feet.

★

Vic and I sat at the kitchen table. Neither of us had spoken since I'd helped him to his feet and brought him inside. I heard the *tap, tap, tap* of Mrs Pearce's shoes on the floorboards in the hall as she made her way down to us holding two delicate china cups filled with tea.

"Here now, drink this: best thing for shock is tea."

She placed the cups in front of us and I thanked her. Vic maintained his hard stare, and I got up and walked my elderly neighbour back down the hall to see her out.

"If I can do anything for the pair of you, you just let me know."

She smiled at me and patted the side of my arm before leaving.

When I returned to my cousin, he had got out of his seat and was standing resting his arms over the sink, running the cold-water tap. The empty teacup was sitting upside down on the draining board.

"You know I could never stand to drink tea."

I walked back into my bedroom and brought back what was left of one of the bottles of rum that Vic had given me. I unscrewed the cap and handed it over to him.

"Here, git a drop of this down you."

Vic took the bottle from me, lifted it to his lips and gulped backed the remainder of the contents in four solid gulps. He walked back over to me and dropped the empty bottle on the kitchen table before telling me what had happened to Carnell.

"Police knocked on Loretta's gate door at around four this morning and told her that he was dead. Just like that. Some old guy had found him laying face down in the gutter on Dean Street. Some son of a bitch drove a blade so far into his back that it came t'ru the front of his guts.

"The police recognised it was Carnell: shit, everybody knew Carnell. They took the pastor from the City Road Baptist church with them when they broke the news to Loretta. Her neighbour Carmen heard her screaming; she saw the panda car parked outside her house and went straight round to see what all the commotion was about. It was Carmen who came running round to my place to let me know what had happened. I went straight over to see Loretta: she was a mess, wailing and screeching out Carnell's name, pulling out her hair in great big clumps. There was no way any of us could console her. In the end, the police called for a doctor to come out and sedate her. That's when I left. I don't understand it, JT. Why, why'd somebody do that to Carnell? That dummy, he'd never hurt a fly."

I watched has Vic's shoulders slumped and he began to weep again.

I knew that Carnell was dead because of me. He cheerfully walked out of the Star and Garter wearing my coat and in a cruel twist of fate was killed in my place. It seemed Papa Anansi had taken me seriously after all; he'd waited in the shadows and fog to snuff out my life, armed with the large, cold steel machete that he was notorious for using. He was going to make sure that what I knew about him and his involvement with Terrence Blanchard, the murders of two people and Stella Hopkins's disappearance was going to be information that I'd take to my grave. In his eagerness to get rid of me, he'd silently crept out the darkness and brutally extinguished a life that he believed to be mine.

Papa could not have known he'd slain the wrong man. He had struck in the most cowardly way, from behind, and had left Carnell, his head most likely still covered by the hood of the duffle coat, to bleed to death in the street. He'd walked away thinking I was dead, and in the next few hours I would make sure his arrogant false sense of certainty would be his final downfall.

Carnell's murder hit Vic hard. Since we were young kids I'd never seen him this hurt. We'd been through a lot together, and in all those years of hardship we'd stayed loyal, stuck up for each other when things got tough and never kept a secret from each other. I wasn't prepared to jeopardise that strong bond. I needed to tell him how I had again unknowingly played a part in the death not only of an innocent but also of somebody whom we both loved dearly.

Although he had been living in Britain at the time both Ellie and Melia had been murdered, I knew that Vic had mourned their loss greatly. He had once told me that I was blessed and that I possessed what he had always wanted: a beautiful wife and a daughter that doted upon me. I sat back at the kitchen table and called over to him to come and join me. He drifted over and dropped into the chair opposite, wiping away the tears and the snot that ran from his nose with his sleeve. He looked up at me and saw the tortured anguish in my eyes, then, surprisingly took my hand in his and spoke quietly to me.

"What d'you need to tell me, Joseph?"

I told him the events of last night: what had happened at the Speed Bird club and the futile threats I'd made to Papa Anansi, and my meeting with Carnell at the Star and Garter and the wonderful news that he'd shared with me. Then I told him as he'd left I'd offered him my old coat, which he'd taken and which I believed had ultimately led to Carnell's murder. I recounted my terrible story like a sinning man in the confessional. I watched as Vic kicked his chair back from under him, grabbed the empty rum bottle from the table and flung it at my kitchen wall, sending pieces of broken glass across the kitchen.

"That muthafucka Papa . . . I'm gonna waste that nigger's worthless ass!"

301

He paced the short, cramped length of the galley, crunching broken glass under his feet as he spat out threats and obscenities at the world. I stayed in my seat, knowing better than to get in my volatile cousin's face when he was raging. He came to a sudden halt in front of the kitchen cupboards and began to kick at the panels furiously, and continued putting the boot into them until he'd busted one off of its hinges and knocked an eight-inch hole in the other. Finally he calmed a little and rested his forehead on the kitchen door before speaking.

"All this bullshit is because o' you, man. Carnell should never have been involved in any of this, you know that! You nearly four thousand miles from home and still got it in your head that you can push people about like you still got heat. Well, you ain't no cop no more, JT. You caused a shit storm back home on Bim, then come running from the last jive-assed bastard you pissed off and you still tinking you can be the only honest marshal in town. Damn fool, same old Ellington, same as you were when we was yout's, thinking you can fight the good fight, sticking your finger in the bad guy's eye then wondering why you leave a trail o' blood and misery in ya damn wake. Well, I'll tell you straight: I'm gonna finish this, you gonna see some blood run when I git a hold of that pox-faced Jamaican ponce. You should o' let me take him out at the neck after we found that pervert Mayfield carved up and he tried to put the frighteners on you by sending you his damn ears in a box!"

I'd heard just about enough of his ranting and got to my feet, my temper about to boil over.

"Damn you, Vic, tell me what good would it have done if you had wasted Papa?"

"Carnell would still be alive if I'd have put a bullet t'ru Anansi's ear. You know that one less wufless shitbag on the street and it would o' sent a message to the prick you trying to lean on to find that damn mute woman. Damn you, fo' all you know she could o' been dead fo' weeks an' be dug down deep in some field!"

"She's not dead!" I snapped back at my relation.

We started to square up to each other like prizefighters about to knock gloves.

"If she's dead then why is everybody who had any contact with Stella Hopkins lying behind sheets up at the morgue? Clarence Mayfield, Jocelyn Charles, Virginia Landry all dead cos they knew someting they shouldn't have. When I first started poking about all I got was the runaround. I took a beating from a dirty cop, then got lifted on suspicion of murder when I was getting too close to the trute. Somebody out there doesn't want Hopkins found, dead or alive! I don't know yet what it is that's so special about a girl who Earl Linney claims is nuttin' more than a simpleton, but I'm sure as hell gonna find out."

"Linney . . . that Jamaican fucker that don't fly straight and you know it. He's had you dangling off a short lead from day one. How'd you know he ain't killed her?"

"You got it wrong, Vic . . . Ask yourself this: what would be the point of Linney employing an ex-copper to look fo' a missing woman if he'd already had a hand in her disappearance? Why would he set himself up to take a fall? It don't make a damn bit o' sense. Surely he ain't that stupid?"

"How the hell do I know, JT? Stupid or not, I told you befo' everyting that comes outta that cat's mout' is a pack o' lies. He's been playing you since he first offered you a wad o' cash to find that damn retard."

"Look, Linney ain't the source of all this mayhem, I know it. Papa's just a foot soldier, a gofer doing the dirty work fo'

303

a man who thinks he can play with people's lives. He's a little fish in a big sea. It's the shark I need to go after."

Vic pushed his face into mine.

"I don't give two shits 'bout no shark ... I want that murdering nigger Papa's head on a pike. He's mine, you hear me?"

"And you can have him, but please, Vic, don't blow this fo' me, not now. I know I'm close; I just need a little more time to solve this and work out what the hell is going on."

Vic stared back at me for what seemed like forever.

Slowly he began to calm and sat back down on his chair, put his head in his hands, then frantically started rubbing at his scalp in frustration, then all of a sudden froze, his fingers still hooked into his hair. When he spoke to me, his head was still pointing down at the floor.

"OK, Mr Detective, when you was tearing Hurps' a new ass'ole back at the Speed Bird and he thought you were gonna rob his cash register, what was it you told me he shouted at you?"

"That I didn't know whose money I was gonna be messing with. Why?"

Vic looked up at me.

"By 'messin' with', who'd you think he was talking 'bout?"

"Well ... Papa, I suppose."

Vic laughed to himself, shaking his head to and fro.

"Papa's got his dirty hands in lots o' people's bidness: not in the Speed Bird, though. Hurps don't like people knowing, but he's got himself a silent partner in that underground shithole of his, he always has had."

"Yeah ... Who's that?"

"Cut Man Perry."

Vic got up without saying another word; he grabbed his

coat from where he had hung it on the edge of the kitchen door, then turned to me as he was putting it on and nodded toward the hallway as an indication that we needed to haul our butts. Confused, I was about to ask him what the hell was going on when he barked out at me impatiently.

"C'mon, drive me round to Cut Man's place. I got someting you need to take a look at."

36

Cut Man Perry didn't believe in opening up for business until after midday. The slothful proprietor of the only gymnasium in St Pauls was renowned for his love of two things: sleep and food. How he'd become rich remained a mystery to many, as he rarely rose from his pit before eleven and had never appeared to work a full day in his life. But behind this façade his business ventures were both varied and almost always illegal in one way or another. Those who knew the stinky fat man well enough never tried to contact him until after he had eaten his lunch or attempted to do business with him thinking they would get the best end of a deal.

Cut Man was astute in all things fiscal, a miser who was rumoured to keep his ever-increasing amounts of capital in various dubious businesses, which he may or may not have owned. He refused to trust a bank and loved the thrill of being able to barter for what he wanted. He would have happily been at home doing business in a Moroccan souk or in any of the hundreds of money-lending houses across the globe. Never shy at courting friendships with those who wielded power or influence, Cut Man trod a fine line that sat somewhat uncomfortably between gregarious entrepreneur and just plain shifty.

I parked the Cortina in a side street across the road from Cut Man's gym. Vic was on a mission: he slammed the door behind him, ran over the road, unlocked the gym's door and

306

was impatiently waiting for me by the time I'd caught up with him. He walked in and flicked a switch on the wall; a series of unshaded hundred-watt bulbs sprung to life and brightly lit up the stairwell in front of us. I watched my cousin sprint up the flight of stairs, taking the steps two at a time to the top of the hallway.

"C'mon, fool . . . We ain't got all day."

I hesitated, then followed his lead. We passed the office that he was supposedly "renting out" from the fat man and made our way down the corridor to Cut Man's workplace. Vic reached Perry's door but put his back against the wall and with one swift, violent kick smashed it open. He looked at me and winked.

"What was I supposed to do? I ain't got no key fo' this rat'ole."

Vic strode across the room in the dark to Cut Man's desk, leant across it and turned on a small lamp with a flexible stand. He picked it up, then set it on the edge of the table and directed the strong beam of the spotlight onto the far wall, where the gym owner's collection of fight posters and memorabilia was pinned up. Vic walked over to the floodlit wall and jabbed his finger at a large black and white photograph that was partially hidden between a cut-out newspaper picture of Sonny Liston and a local Masonic Lodge dinner-dance invite.

"Here . . . You come take a look at this."

I joined Vic as he pulled the photograph off the wall and held it closer to the strong shaft of light.

It was a recently taken photograph of Cut Man standing with both Elrod Haddon and the white cop Mickey Warren, as well as a group of men and a woman I didn't recognise. Cut Man, Haddon and Warren were standing either side of a white guy who was probably in his fifties and a well-dressed black woman. Vic stuck his big finger on the face of Mickey Warren and tapped at it repeatedly as he asked me a question.

"Tell me who you think that ugly-looking honky is with the crew-cut trim job?"

I looked back at him and smiled.

"That's the dirty cop that tried to put my ass out to grass with a slapjack."

Vic pushed the photograph hard into my chest and let it go. It stuck to my raincoat for a moment before it started to fall to the floor. I caught it as floated to my feet and looked again at the faces in the picture. Vic picked up the phone on Cut Man's desk and began to dial a number.

"I think we need to have a serious word with the fat man," he said, the bloodlust in his voice barely hidden. "Hey, Cut Man . . . How you doin', brother, it's Vic." I could hear the oily businessman complaining from across the room.

He was banging on 'bout how pissed he was at being woken at such a ridiculous time of the day. My cousin interrupted his whining on the other end of the line by giving him a tall tale that he knew would silence the flabby old goat.

"Man . . . Will you shut yo' big, saggy-assed mout' fo' one goddamn minute. I just got to the gym to pick up a couple o' boxes of hooch. Ting is, when I gets here I finds the back door 'as been jemmied open and all my Mount Gay rum has took a walk. The ting is, from where I'm speaking to you now and from the size o' the hole in your office wall, so has your damn safe too!"

Vic pulled the receiver away from his ear just in time as Cut Man bawled a series of crude expletives at him. The line went dead and we sat and waited in the semi-darkness of his stinky office for him to arrive.

37

THE SOUND OF A breathless Cut Man running up the stairs announced in no uncertain terms that he had arrived. He marched down the hallway towards us, continuing to swear and curse in between bouts of hacking and wheezing.

"What muthafucka tinks he can come in my place and steal from me!"

He stormed into his office and came to a grinding halt, looking straight ahead at his back wall expecting to see his precious safe gone only to find it untouched and Vic sitting at in his best leather recliner with his feet resting up on his desk. I stood out of sight behind the opened door, my back against the wall, and waited.

"Hey, Cut Man, it's good a you to show up so promptly, brother."

Vic smiled at him for a moment before his face became blank and stern.

"What the fuck you playing at, dragging me outta my bed fo' some damn stupid prank, how the hell you git in my office?"

Cut Man gingerly walked towards Vic, angry but not stupid enough to challenge him outright.

"One o' the rats that you shack up here with let us in."

I closed the creaking door behind him as he moved forward, and a surprised Cut Man turned indignantly to face me. Livid, he snapped at me like a chained-up bulldog.

"What the . . . ? Not you too. What is this, some kinda Ellington family git-together?" He pointed at Vic. "Next ting you'll be telling me you got that miserable ole bastard of a daddy and uncle o' yours in my shitter back there!" He crudely stubbed his thick thumb over his shoulder towards the WC to make his point.

Vic bolted out of his seat, flew round the desk towards Cut Man and stood right up close in his face.

"Now you mind your big mout' what you saying 'bout my daddy . . . You hear me?"

Cut Man backed away from Vic and found himself caught between the two of us. The original whiff of unpleasant body odour that had originally hit me when Cut Man first walked in had now erupted into the pungent stench of nervous sweat. At first the perspiration that was running down his forehead, nose and cheeks had been caused by the excursion he had made to get to his beloved coffer, which he thought had been fleeced; now it drained out of him from pure fear.

"What the hell are you two pair o' bastards playing at?"

I leant over Cut Man's shoulder and hung the photograph of him and Hurps Haddon with the bent copper in front of his clammy face.

"Tell me 'bout the people standing with you in that photograph, Cut Man."

"What'd you wanna know that shit fo', JT?"

"Cos I'm t'rowing a party . . . Who are they?"

"They ain't nobody, just some moneyed-up honkies and an ole nigger bitch I met at the Masonic hall last year . . . What the fuck is it you on with? You bustin' into my place, asking me questions 'bout tings that are none o' your goddamn bidness!"

Cut Man fell silent. He'd been directing his anger at me and he'd briefly forgotten Vic standing behind him . . . It was a big mistake. Vic swung him round by his lapels, then hammered two swift direct blows to his gut. Cut Man doubled over and threw up over his carpet as Vic pulled him over to his desk, pinned his head to the green baize ink-blotting pad with one hand, then pulled his right arm out straight, turned it so his palm faced upwards and angled the foul-smelling fat man's elbow on the edge of the table. Vic held Cut Man's wrist tightly and applied pressure, bending his arm towards the floor, making him cry out in pain.

"Now you listen to me, you stinky fat bastard. You better start answering my boy's questions with a little bit more accuracy and good manners, cause if you don't then I'm gonna pop your elbow outta its socket like a fuckin' chicken wing. You hear me?"

Vic applied more pressure to Cut Man's arm, making him squeal out like a pig.

"Yeah . . . yeah, I hear you."

Vic loosened off the pressure, but only a little. I bent down so that Cut Man could see my face, then held up the photograph in front of him again.

"Now . . . I'm gonna point at every one o' these people in this picture that I'm interested in an' I want a name fo' them. You under understand me?"

I watched as Vic pushed Cut Man's arm towards the floor a little, making him wince.

"OK, OK, I . . . I understand."

I pointed at the first face.

Cut Man snapped at me. "Oh fo' Christ's sakes, you know who that—"

Vic leant down on Perry's arm again.

"It's Hurps . . . Elrod, Elrod Haddon."

Sweat continued to fall from Cut Man's face onto the desk.

"Like I said . . . every face I point to gets a name." I directed my finger to another face, this time to one whose name I already knew.

"That's Mickey Warren, he's a fight fan."

I looked up at Vic and nodded to him to do his thing. I heard the rim of the desk creak as Vic bent Cut Man's arm hard down towards the ground.

"It's Warren . . . Mickey Warren, he's a vice copper, works outta Bridewell station, we drink together sometimes."

"Is that so . . . is that so? You doin' good, Cut Man. Keep this shit up, we going be out your hair in no time." Vic grinned down at the squirming lowlife, then turned and cruelly winked at me.

"That's just nice, ain't it, Vic? What you doin' drinking with vice cops, Cut Man? You started adding police officers to your wide circle o' friends now?"

"In my game I have to drink with everybody . . . I'm a bidness man; you know that, JT, I mix with all kinds o' folks."

I nodded, then pointed back at the print to a silver-haired white man dressed in a dinner jacket and bow tie.

"Who's this serious-looking dude?"

"That's . . . Terrence Blanchard."

"How'd you know Blanchard?"

"Warren introduced me to him a while back at a prissy knees-up at the Masonic hall on Park Street . . ."

Vic interrupted. "You a Mason, Cut Man?"

"Hell no . . . ! Those bastards won't let no black man be a Freemason, you know that."

"So how'd you git to be at a Mason's Lodge fo' some good-time knees-up then?"

"I gits invited all over; Mason's Lodge ain't no different to the Speed Bird, if you got money to spend and a little juice!"

"You do any bidness with this Blanchard fella?"

"No . . . never."

Vic could smell Cut Man's lies like he could smell the stink of his sweat. Out of nowhere my cousin forced himself down onto Cut Man's arm; I heard an almighty crack as the portly gym owner screamed out in agony and fell off the desk and began to roll around in his own puke, cradling his broken limb in his crook of his other elbow.

Vic dragged everything that was on the desk and threw it across the office in a single stroke of his massive hand, then grabbed Cut Man and hauled him off the floor. Slamming his back onto the desk, Vic delivered a vicious series of blows to his stomach, chest and face before grabbing the wrist of his other arm to repeat the process.

"OK, you lying, miserable prick. You gonna be having to pay somebody to git yo' next handjob, cos I'm going break this other fuckin' arm off if you don't start being straight with us!"

Vic pressed down on the other outstretched arm.

"Stop . . . stop! What you want from me . . . what you want?" Cut Man shouted out. He began to bawl, panic set in his eyes like he was a rabbit trapped in front of the beam of a motor car headlights, his legs began lashing out all over the place. Vic applied more pressure, and as he did Cut Man's bladder gave out and a stream of yellow piss fell down from between his legs and flowed along the inside of his trousers, spilled out onto the carpet and began to mix in with the puke.

"Blanchard . . . Tell me everyting that you know about him and his connection to Mickey Warren and the whoremonger Papa Anansi."

Cut Man blew spittle and blood from his mouth; he coughed then spat out a mixture of the two across the desk and wall. He was close to passing out. Vic gave him a slap to bring him round. His eyes sparked up in their sockets and he reconnected with the conscious world and, looking, at me began to talk.

"He's a big-time player . . . a real piece of work, loaded. He owns thousands of acres of prime undeveloped land here in Bristol and further out into Somerset."

"Oh c'mon . . . ! Tell me someting 'bout him I don't know, Cut Man."

Vic slapped him across the face again, only harder this time; the sound of skin connecting with skin recoiled around the small office, which was starting to stink like a latrine.

"He knows Papa cos he's into whores, but not just any kind: rumour has it he like 'em young and clean."

Vic applied a little more force to Cut Man's other outstretched arm to keep the information flowing.

"And it's not just girl's he's into. I heard talk that he's game fo' anyting that moves, a real sicko!"

"That's rich coming from you, Cut Man," Vic interjected.

I shook my head at him and he went back to pushing on the fresh arm.

"Tell me 'bout Warren."

"Warren is on the payroll from Papa, has been fo' years. Warren gets a cut from the dope and girls that Papa peddles and he's got a couple of guys on the force who moonlight fo' him when he needs some grunt work doing, but as far as I know they're pretty low grade . . . they ain't players, not like Mickey is."

"What's your end, Cut Man . . . ? You gotta have an angle to know all this."

"Me and Hurps, we let Papa use the Speed Bird fo' private functions: you know, gala nights, soirées, somewhere with a bit

314

more class than the shebeen Papa hangs out in on Richmond Road."

Vic laughed. "Yeah, I could see all that class last time I was hanging down at the Speed Bird, Cut Man."

I shot Vic a pair of hard eyes and shook my head at him again.

"You ever hear of a place called the Erotica Negro Club?"

"Yeah ... some gentleman's club ... Blanchard's behind it; he holds these hot parties at his country pad, gave it some jazzed-up name, but it's just a place fo' him and his rich honky cronies to fuck black bitches."

"And Papa Anansi?"

"Papa makes his money outta Blanchard; he scours the streets, clubs and pubs lookin' fo' fresh meat fo' him fo' his damn club!"

"What you know 'bout a girl called Stella Hopkins, Cut Man?"

"The deaf mute that went missing from round these parts? Nothing ... why?"

Vic went to break Cut Man's other arm.

"No!"

I shouted at Vic and pushed my hand against his tensed shoulder, holding him off from doing any more damage. I leant down towards Cut Man's face and hung the photograph in front of him one more time.

"Who's the woman standing in between Blanchard and you?"

He squinted at the photograph and blew out warm air, his appalling halitosis almost knocking me on my back.

"That's the alderman's wife ... That's Alice Linney."

38

I SAT A PETRIFIED Cut Man in his plush chair, grabbed the telephone from off of the floor and put it in his lap. He stared down at it as if I had just presented him with some kind of strange, poisonous fruit that I was expecting him to eat. I perched myself on the edge of his desk and he looked up at me with eyes that told me that he was beat. Vic stood behind me, leaning against the door of the office. I noticed him staring at Cut Man, his eyes hard and dangerous. I looked back at Cut Man, rocking in his seat, holding his broken arm against his chest. Beads of heavy sweat dripped from his brow. He gave a little scared smile when I eventually spoke to him again.

"Last night I went to see Hurps down at the Speed Bird and, like you, he wasn't too hot 'bout me paying him a visit. Got himself all worked up and nasty just because I wanted to ask him a few damn silly questions that he didn't wanna answer. I had to do some serious persuading with the man to get him to answer what I wanted to know. Now, I told ole Hurps to git a message to Papa Anansi 'bout how I wanted to meet up with him at the Star and Garter later last night, only he didn't come in and face me; the nasty piece o' shit waited outside in some back street hoping to take a knife to me in the dark when I left the pub. Ting is, in his eagerness to take me out he gits the wrong guy. He guts Carnell Harris and leaves him to bleed out in the gutter like a stuck pig."

I paused for a moment, giving Cut Man time to take in what I had said.

"Now as you can imagine I'm pretty eager to reconvene that engagement I shoulda had with Papa and I need you to help me reschedule it. You getting my drift, fat man?"

Cut Man winced and began rubbing at the top of his shoulder with his hand, hoping that it may offer some relief from the pain he was in.

"Yeah . . . yeah, I git it. But Papa don't take too kindly to people putting the screw on him, making him do stuff he don't wanna."

"Yeah, I kinda got that feelin' as I sat in the pub last night. That's why I want you to ring that bent cop Mickey Warren. "

"What, Warren? Why the hell should I call him up?"

"Cool it, Cut Man, I don't wanna have to let Vic git heavy on your knees cos you starting to git all shirty with me again. You're gonna call Warren and I want you to tell him 'bout how I've been here this morning, what I've said to you 'bout Stella Hopkins and how I know 'bout him being on the take and his dirty work fo' Terrence Blanchard. Tell him I know he's up to his neck in it and if he wants to settle this with me then he needs to drag his worthless ass and Papa's out to meet me out at Blanchard's place at six tonight . . . You got that?"

"Yeah . . . I got it."

Cut Man wriggled uncomfortably in his seat and slouched forward, grimacing in pain as he did.

"Good . . . Then do it now, brother."

I nodded towards the phone, which was resting on his knees.

"Look, JT, I'm in pain, I ain't thinking straight, I can't talk to no police . . ."

Vic shut Perry up as he walked towards the desk, took out his knife from the back pocket of his jeans and released the blade, then slipped the razor-sharp edge up underneath Cut Man's throat. He nervously lifted the receiver and made the call to Mickey Warren.

It was a short phone conversation, but it was done. Mickey Warren sure got the message real quick. The fear in Cut Man's voice and his repeated insistence that this was serious got across to the crooked copper, and the line went silent. I leant towards the phone in Perry's hand in time to hear Warren suddenly shout, "You see that black bastard befo' I do . . . you tell him he's dead meat, you hear me?" before slamming the phone down on him.

The portly gym owner looked up at me, his face etched with pain and dread, the receiver still gripped in his trembling hand. Vic withdrew the knife from Cut Man's throat and turned to me; he rested his huge hand on my shoulder and whispered into my ear.

"I'll be back in a minute; I just need to git me a few tings outta my office. Befo' we leave I need to have a private word with my friend Mr Perry there."

Vic smiled at Cut Man and walked out as I took the receiver from him and picked the phone out of his lap.

"OK . . . Now give me Terrence Blanchard's number."

Cut Man gave a heavy, pained sigh before bringing himself forward and nodding over the desk towards the carpet.

"It's in that grey Rolodex that ape of a cousin o' yours just t'rew across my office floor."

I rescued it from underneath a heap of paperwork, set it down on the desk and leafed through it until I found two numbers for Blanchard: one his home number with a Somerset dialling code and the other his business contact details in Queen Square in Bristol. I tapped down on the phone's cradle to get a new line. The receiver made a familiar burring sound as I spun the numbers on the rotary dial and waited for a reply.

"Blanchard Stewart partners, can I help you?" A young woman's voice chirped at me from down the other end of the line.

"Good morning. I'd like to speak to Mr Terrence Blanchard please."

"I'm sorry, Mr Blanchard is with a client at the moment, can I take a message, and get him to return your call later?"

The young woman was precise, efficient and obviously good at cutting to the chase. I was staring to dislike her already.

"No, but I need to speak to the man now. So you go tell your boss that you have a Mr Joseph Ellington on the telephone and that he would like to urgently discuss the important matter about his club with him. Now, you be sure to tell him my name and that it's urgent, got that?"

The other end of the phone went silent for a moment as the switchboard operator mentally went over her options before replying to me.

"Mr Blanchard isn't able——"

I interrupted the receptionist before she had a chance to give me any more of her pre-scripted spiel.

"Look, I ain't interested in what he isn't able to do, sweetheart. I just wanna hear his ten-guineas-an-hour voice on the end o' this phone in the next two minutes or tings are going to start getting real awkward fo' the man. Now, write this down so you don't forget: you give Blanchard my name – it's Ellington – and tell him that I wanna talk to him about the Erotica Negro. He'll know what I mean."

I heard the telephonist cover the mouthpiece of her receiver and waited for a few moments before coming back to me.

"I'm just putting you through to Mr Blanchard now."

319

I was about to thank her, but she nervously cut me off before I could express my gratitude.

"Good morning, Mr Ellington, this is Terrence Blanchard speaking. How can I possibly help you?"

His voice was calm, cool with a hint of patronising, arrogant superiority inflected in the way he addressed me. He reminded me of nearly every white officer who had casually flipped me an order back when I was on the force. I didn't reply and instead waited for a moment before speaking, trying to get a measure of the man by how patient he was.

Patience clearly wasn't one of Terrence Blanchard's best qualities. I didn't have to wait long before he snapped dismissively at me down the phone.

"Now look here, I don't know what this is all about. My girl said you wanted to speak to me about something she could barely pronounce. What is it that you want exactly, Ellington?"

Blanchard spoke my name as if it were a reminder not to step into something unpleasant in front of him. But despite all his self-assured public-school bullishness, I could tell he was bluffing. And for a man who spent his working days pulling the wool over the eyes of his fellow legal opponents in the Crown Court, he was pretty easy to shake up.

"Erotica Negro . . ." I said the two words slowly, sounding them out in a way that gave Blanchard no uncertainty that I knew what their true meaning was.

"I have absolutely no idea what you're talking about, and if you think that you—"

I interrupted the slippery barrister, quickly looking at my watch. I realised that time was against me and that once my call to Blanchard was over the clock would be ticking and every second was going to count if I was to nail him.

"I think you best shut your mout' and listen up, Mr Blanchard. Now git this straight: you stop playing games and I'll tell you how it is. You may not want to admit it right now, but you know me and you know why I'm on the other end o' this damn phone, don't you?"

Terrence Blanchard was silent, just a trace of his breath on the other end of the line. I continued.

"Ting is, you hoped that I'd never git the chance to make this call. You thought that with the help of a little bent law and a few well-placed scumbags to scare me off or frame me fo' a crime I didn't commit that you could draw me off your scent. Well, surprise, surprise, Mr Blanchard, guess what? Your scent stinks a whole lot more that you thought it did."

"Now look here . . ."

He was about to come back at me, but I didn't give him the chance.

"Shut up and listen. I know 'bout your place in the country and those invite-only parties you've been having. You do know the ones I mean, don't you, Mr Blanchard, the Erotica Negro parties? I met one of your lady guests from one of those knees-ups, a Miss Virginia Landry. You remember her? She was a sweet ting, beautiful. Ting is, she was murdered and dumped in some godforsaken coppice in the middle o' nowhere a few days back. Befo' she died I had a real good chat with Miss Landry: she remembered you, remembered you well."

I lied 'bout Virginia seeing the barrister, but I didn't care; I just wanted to get Blanchard all wound up, and I was. I kept on at him.

"Now I just got off the phone talking to another friend of yours, a sack o' shit that pretends to be a police officer, by

321

the name o' Mickey Warren. Anyhow, we got to talking 'bout another guy who finds you all those pretty tings: girls like Virginia Landry and the others that you take a shine to. This fella drops them off at your gate door, fo' a price, of course . . . goes by the name of Otis Grey."

Blanchard remained silent. I kept winding him in.

"Oh, course . . . you may not know him by that name: truth is he don't normally answer to what his mother first called him the day he crawled out from between her pussy and the best part of him slid down the inside of her leg with the afterbirth and dropped onto the floor."

"I don't have to listen to this filth." Blanchard went to slam the phone down on me, but I soon stopped him in his tracks.

"Stella Hopkins . . . Let's talk about Stella," I bellowed at him.

The barrister remained on the other end of the phone; I could now hear his breathing quickening as he waited for me to continue.

"She's the reason I got messed up in all your crap, Mr Blanchard. She went missing a few weeks back, I was paid to find her, and the more I look, the more shit I find myself in. Now, I know you know someting 'bout her disappearance, so I've decided that I best come down to see you in that pretty old place o' yours, sort this mess out. I gonna be waiting around fo' you when you git back this evening, see if we can find her. I assume you'll want to bring your hired help along, so I've invited Papa Anansi and Mickey Warren to hold your hand."

Blanchard was silent.

"That's fine by me, we'll have ourselves a coupla drinks, hey? Let Papa and Mr Warren in on the party, they'll keep us both company."

322

I heard the barrister take a sharp breath before speaking to me; when he did, his tone was concise and brittle.

"Mr Ellington . . . I warn you, if you choose to go down the path of trying to illegally enter my home then you will be making a very big mistake. I'm not a foolish man and I'll be taking precautions to see to it that you won't be a nuisance to me, is that understood? Be aware, my property is very well protected. You'd be a fool to attempt a break-in or to think you can put the frighteners on me. I'm not easily threatened, Mr Ellington."

Like a great chess grandmaster he'd made his move and was now patiently waiting for my response. I didn't want to disappoint him.

"But I ain't threatening you, Mr Blanchard. You need to understand, I've gone way past the point of issuing threats. I know that Papa Anansi and Mickey Warren have been doing a lot of grunt work fo' you: supplying your so-called 'Erotica Negro' evenings with top-grade, good-looking black girls, drugs, maybe some illegal hooch and then taking to butchering anybody who displeased you or stuck their noses too far into your seedy, secret little world.

"But last night one of those goons of yours went and killed a friend o' mine. Those bastards took the life of a good man that never hurt a soul and who sure as hell didn't deserve to end his days being run through by one o' your hired blades. Well, I got news fo' you: I'm 'bout to pull the plug on what you and those killers you pay off have been up to. You git into your head real quick how serious I am 'bout all o' this. I ain't just coming to pay you a visit 'bout Stella Hopkins; I'm coming to settle what you and your people did to my friend Carnell Harris and to those poor young women. So don't be thinking I'm just spouting hot air here; you in some deep shit mister and I'm 'bout to bury you in a whole lot more of it. So why don't you git your ass into the back o' your limousine and git your driver to get you home real quickly.

"You wanna call the police to fight your battles, that's fine by me, bring 'em along, but I'm thinking you probably wanting to keep this mess between us."

I could hear the barrister breathing hard through his nose. When his reply came it was far calmer than I'd expected to be: cool, in fact.

"Very well, Mr Ellington, we'll see you later. I'll look forward to it."

He was about to cut me off.

"Oh, and Mr Blanchard?" I called down the phone after him.

"Yes, Mr Ellington?" He remained as cool as ice as he spoke.

"If you considering letting another dog out with those two thugs that are in your employ, then take my advice and git yourself a bigger one. Cos that last fucker I came up against at your place, he wasn't up to the job!"

I slammed down the phone and then looked across to Cut Man Perry, who was staring back at me with a look of horror and disbelief on his pallid, pained face.

Vic walked back into the office with a large khaki ex-army-surplus bag; he held it out in front of him and nodded at me to take it.

"No peeking inside now. I'll meet you back at the car; I just need that quick word with Cut Man here. And don't worry . . . I ain't gonna be long."

I did as he asked and left Vic alone with Cut Man. I walked out of the stinking office, back down the hallway and made my way out to the street towards the car, knowing that behind me back in the gym my cousin could be committing any number of cruel acts of violence against the immoral aged businessman, and as I dropped the heavy bag into the boot and slammed down the lid, I realised that today I didn't give a damn.

39

I SAT IN THE DRIVER'S seat of the Cortina waiting for Vic. True
to his word, he didn't take long having his "quick" chat with
Cut Man and I watched in the rear-view mirror as he sprinted
across the road with a rolled-up document in his left hand and
a big smile on his face. My stomach stopped knotting itself up
and I relaxed a little, in the hope that that my unpredictable
cousin hadn't caused the carnage back at the gym that I was
dreading he would. Vic came round to me and opened up the
door, still smiling.

"Hey, where'd you stash that bag, man?"

"It's in the boot, why?" I asked suspiciously.

"Why you always asking damn fool questions? Just git your
sorry ass outta that car and follow me, will ya!"

He winked at me, then walked around to the back of the car
and popped open the boot. I could hear him opening up the
bag as I made my way round to him. Vic glanced behind him
shiftily as I joined him at the rear of the motor. I looked at me
and grinned, then pointed into at the opened holdall.

"I got us a little main-line protection on board, brother."

Inside the bag, mixed up in between a couple of large
torches, several lengths of heavy-duty naval rope, a tyre iron
and a pair of ancient-looking binoculars, were a trio of what
had to be unlicensed firearms. Two Colt 45 army-issue pistols
sat next to a cut-down Spencer pump-action shotgun, with a
half-dozen boxes of mixed ammunition thrown in for good

measure. Vic closed the bag and dropped the hood of the boot back down, tapping the top of it as he walked whistling to himself back round to the passenger seat of the car and got in. I joined him and looked over at my cousin, who was drumming his fingers on the dashboard excitedly.

"Look, Vic, I ain't gonna ask you where you got all that firepower from, but you can at least tell me why you're holding that ream o' paper like it's made of sheet gold?"

"I just made me a new deal with Cut Man. I told him that I could keep his name outta all this mess he's got himself in if he considered his options carefully."

"Yeah . . . and what were they?"

"He could either sign the deeds of his gym over to me or I could make sure the law found out his name was linked to drugs and dead whores. He came to a real quick decision and you're looking at the new owner of Perry's gym." Vic shook the deeds in front of me cheerfully. "Now let's git movin'; you can fill me in on what goes down next while you drive."

Before going into detail with Vic about what was about to go down, I drove round to my digs, left the engine running in the street, and ran up to my bedsit to pick up my wallet, little notebook and the slip of paper Earl Linney had given me a few days back with his address and contact numbers on.

When I got back into the car, Vic looked at me, then nodded his head towards my digs and laughed.

"Shit . . . I thought you'd gone inside to bring that mean ole bitch of a neighbour o' yours as some extra back-up!"

I looked out towards my front door and saw Mrs Pearce standing in her bay window. She held the curtain back and stared down at me, then raised the palm of her hand and rested it on the glass pane of the window and mouthed the words, "You take care, Mr Ellington," before she slipped back

327

behind the curtain. I turned to look at Vic, who shook his head in bemusement.

"You sure like hangin' round with some funny old muthafuckas, you do know that, don't ya, JT?"

We burst out laughing at each other as I drove away down the road, both embracing a brief moment of lightheartedness and realising that the next few hours would hold little laughter for either of us.

★

It was after twelve thirty in the afternoon when I stopped just outside of Bristol at a petrol station and filled the car up with fuel. I then got on to the main A38 road out of the city and started at speed on the fifty-mile-plus journey down to Cricket Malherbie and Terrence Blanchard's home. Vic sat peacefully next to me with his eyes closed; his hands on his stomach, fingers knitted together, his chest rising up and down slowly.

"Hey, you asleep?"

Vic opened one eye and peered over to me, a none-too-happy look on his face.

"Shit no! Asleep? I damn well ought to be, the way you chugging along in this ole hearse . . . Can't you git a bit more poke outta it?"

"Poke, I've been pushing the damn ting to its limits fo' the last ten miles; this ain't no Ferrari GTO, you know!" I snapped edgily at my cousin, and I gave the accelerator another push towards the floor.

"It ain't no car either, brother, it's a piece o' crap. You need to git yo'self a set o' decent wheels when all this bullshit is over, you hear me?"

Taking no notice, I drove on through the bleak wintry

countryside, telling him how I wanted things to play out when we got to Blanchard's place. Vic was looking out of the passenger side window when I'd finished what I was saying. He didn't turn to look at me when he decided to speak.

"What makes you think that this Stella Hopkins is still alive, JT? If Blanchard's as nasty a piece o' work you say he is, then he's gonna have had her wasted by one of his punks as soon as he got wind that you were on to him."

"I don't know fo' sure, Vic, but I gotta a real strong gut feelin' 'bout all this. I have to find her, and Virginia Landry said she saw a scared young woman who never spoke and who was made to watch while she was molested. Stella's mute, so who's she gonna tell 'bout the evil tings she's seen? She can't speak and she sure as hell can't hear anybody ask her questions 'bout what's could o' happened to her. No, Stella's useful to a warped bastard like Blanchard. It's about power and control and the fact they thought they could git away with it."

Vic stayed staring at the passing countryside.

"I gotta ask you this, brother . . . What's she to you?"

"I don't know. Maybe just cos she needs my help but can't ask. I do know there's a heap o' people interested in her fo' different kinds o' reasons, and a wealthy guy wants to pay out a heap of cash fo' me to try to find her and to keep the police outta the picture. I got so many damn questions I can't answer, Vic. I wish I could, but I can't. All I can say to you is, I'll find the truth . . . You gotta trust me, cousin . . . You just gotta trust me."

I looked across to him and he stared back at me, shaking his head slowly, tutting to himself.

"Shit . . . You don't need to talk 'bout trust, JT, we is family."

Vic smiled, reminding me of the little boy who I had grown

up with, before he frowned and his placid features changed suddenly and he became severe, savage almost.

"You just remember what I said 'bout Papa earlier: he's mine. He made the play on Carnell and he's gonna pay fo' what he done to him, you understand me?"

I said nothing, but nodded sharply at Vic and returned my eyes back to the road, and I kept looking straight ahead of me with neither of us speaking again for the rest of the journey.

Outside, snow still lingered in the fields and hedgerows. I gripped at the steering wheel as an unnerving, eerie presence clutched at my chest as I drove. The bleak feelings of tragedy and death were now an unwelcome companion on our journey, my kin and I approaching ever closer both to an adversary who would seek to destroy us at any cost and to a cruel truth I would find hard to understand, let alone accept.

It was just after three o'clock when we drove through the Somerset village of Knowle St Giles and into Cricket Malherbie and out along the single-track road towards Terrence Blanchard's imposing estate. I pulled up outside of the property next to the impressive wrought-iron gates surrounded by the high sandstone wall that secluded the wealthy barrister from the rest of the world, and the thought hit me that in the cold light of day the place was a lot bigger than I had remembered. Vic pursed his lips and whistled as he gazed up the gravel drive towards the mansion.

"This dude Blanchard really knows how to live; how'd you think he'd react if Mum and Dad and me decided to move in next door?"

He slapped the dashboard with the flat of his hand and beamed a toothy grin at me. I moved off and drove further along the badly maintained road, until around three hundred yards after the retaining wall had ended I came across a small dilapidated barn that was sitting in a grassy field behind a large old wooden gate. I pulled in beside the gate, got out and climbed over it into the field, and walked towards the barn. It was red-brick built with a short pitched grey slate roof, around twelve feet long by nine feet wide, with no windows to see inside and double doors that were practically dropping off their hinges. There was no lock and it had been poorly secured by baling twine that was loosely knotted in a futile attempt to keep both panels closed.

I untied the knot and opened up one of the doors. I took a look inside the almost empty outbuilding. A few spades, scythes and oversized iron sieves where hung on rusting nails from the heavily cobwebbed walls. At the back of the barn was a selection of what looked like ancient ploughing machinery, but there was little else. The most important thing was that there was more than enough space to hide a Cortina inside. I dragged the large door panels carefully back, walked to the gate and pulled it open. Vic looked bemused as I reversed the car the short distance into the waiting deserted storehouse. He then wound down the window, stuck his head out and shouted, "You thinkin' o' making an offer on the place, JT? It sure is a step up from the tatty rathole you're dossin' down in at the minute." He chuckled to himself and got out, slamming the door behind him.

"Sshh! Keep it down will you."

I shook my head to myself as I went to draw the barn doors to.

"Who they hell am I supposed to be disturbing out here, fo' Christ's sakes, the rabbits? We're in the middle o' nowhere!"

"I don't care, we need to keep a low profile . . . You know that."

Vic ignored me and walked round to the rear of the Cortina, popped open the boot and leant inside. He returned with the two Colt automatics and the shotgun, and dropped them ceremoniously on the bonnet of the car, then pulled out a couple of boxes of ammunition from each of his coat pockets. He threw a box over to me, then picked up one of the handguns and held it by the barrel in front of me.

"Here, you still know how to use one o' these?"

"Yeah . . . You don't forget." I took the blued-steel Colt from him and cradled the walnut grip in the palm of my hand, getting used to the weight, then pushed the small button at the back of the trigger guard to release the magazine. I took eight bullets from one of the boxes, slid them into the clip and snapped it into the stock, pulling back the slide, and put a round into the chamber. I slipped the gun into my waistband at the back of my trousers and watched as Vic loaded a handful of twelve-gauge shells into the shotgun's magazine; then he rapidly worked the forestock back and forth, sending a cartridge into the elevator ready to fire. He rubbed his hand appreciatively along the length of the barrel, then placed the gun back onto the bonnet of the car and began loading the other Colt automatic's magazine with bullets.

"You ready to roll, JT?"

I nodded that I was.

"Good, I'll go git the bag from the boot, then we can git the fuck outta this oversized pigsty and go find ourselves some bad guys."

We closed up the barn doors, hiding the Cortina from view, then Vic and I walked across the field and through a small wooded area and back towards the boundary wall of the Blanchard estate. Vic walked on in front of me along the perimeter, hoping to find a suitable entrance to get us inside.

Disappointed that he couldn't find one, he turned to me and pointed to the top of the wall.

"Looks like we gonna have to haul our butts over this old pile o' brickwork."

"It ain't the first time I had to do it, brother. C'mon, let's git on with it."

We clambered over the wall into the grounds of the estate and followed its edge until we could see the great house in the distance. Vic and I made our way across open land and into a small coppice that sat around sixty yards or so from the stable block and outbuildings at the rear of the property. It gave us a good view of the main gates, driveway and the house. I looked at my watch: it was four twenty. Dusk was slowly falling and the temperature was beginning to drop. In another couple of hours it would be well below freezing. I hoped that we wouldn't have to be sitting out in the cold for too long. We found a spot close to the edge of the thickly wooded thicket that was sufficiently sheltered from prying eyes and would keep the icy wind off our backs. Vic looked across towards the house, a confused look on his face.

"Just tell me what the fuck we're doing standing out here like a couple o' stiff pricks? Let's git our freezing batties inside that spread and jump the bastards from inside when they turn up. At least we can fight 'em in the warm!"

"No . . . That's what Blanchard will be expecting; he'll have it in his head that I'll be waiting fo' him inside one of the dozens of rooms he's got in that place. I want him spooked, so we stay put here and wait it out, then we can see who's going to roll up that drive and what we'll be up against."

We had to wait for just over another hour before a familiar grey Jaguar pulled into the driveway; it was followed by an expensive-looking Bentley S Two Flying Spur with blue and grey two-tone paintwork. I snatched Vic's binoculars from the bag and focused on the slow-moving vehicles. Even in the failing light I could see the buzz-cut hairstyle of Mickey Warren at the wheel of the Jaguar and behind him the prickly, hawk-like features of Terrence Blanchard as they made their way up towards the house. The two cars came to a halt outside of the main doors. Both men got out of their motors and I watched as Mickey Warren stayed back, suspiciously scanning the boundary of the property before he joined his master on the large stone steps of his grand home. Blanchard was shouting and aggressively throwing his arms about, pointing to different parts of his property and the surrounding land.

I couldn't hear what he was saying to Mickey Warren, but from the look on the bent copper's face he was being put through the wringer. I watched as Blanchard walked up the remaining steps and disappeared inside. Warren returned to his car, opened the rear door and pulled out a canvas rifle case. He leant against the wing of his Jag, unzipped the case and removed what looked like a Lee-Enfield bolt-action rifle, then threw the case onto the ground. Warren drew back the bolt, eased a round into the chamber and wrapped the sling round his right forearm, then started to make his way along the side of the house towards the rear of the property.

I dropped the binoculars back into the holdall, then whispered in to Vic's ear.

"Looks like Blanchard was getting hot under his collar out there. We ready to move?"

"Yeah, I'm ready ... but if you say Blanchard's looking vexed then watch out – man like him's dangerous, you need to remember that!"

Vic was agitatedly looking out towards the two cars that had parked up.

"JT, I only saw two honkies git out their cars; where the hell's that bastard Papa?"

"Who knows? Maybe he got scared, cut his losses and done a runner cos he knew I was on to him 'bout Carnell?"

"Nah . . . Not that, brother; he don't run from anyting. You watch your back when we git ourselves in the thick of it up there: Papa, he's like herpes, man, once you got him, you can't git rid o' him!"

All the time Vic was talking to me, he had been following Mickey Warren's movements.

"That the copper that beat you 'bout with the slapjack, JT?"

"Yeah, that's him."

"Don't you think it's time fo' a little payback?"

Vic looked across to me and back over to Warren, who was making his way towards the large stable block.

"Let's git it on!" Vic whispered and nodded over at me to follow his lead.

I watched as he released the safety catch on the shotgun and, crouching down low, we started to walk along the edge of the thicket towards where it broke out into open ground. I noticed Vic continuing to stalk the copper's movement. When Warren disappeared into the block of horse stables, we sprinted across the lawn and made our way around the rear of the stabling yard towards the other entrance and waited. We stood flat against the side wall of the stables; across from us was the gravelled courtyard that had doubled as a car park on my previous visit. I remembered beyond that were the kitchens: the perfect place to enter the house. I reached into my coat, pulled out the Colt from my waistband and raised it against the side of my face, and waited.

Warren's footsteps grew louder as he clomped on the concrete inside the stable block. I heard him stop for a

335

moment and turn on his heels as if he was going to return the same way he had come. I looked at Vic, who just put his finger to his lips and gently nodded at me to be cool. Then Mickey Warren's pacing started up again; the man's heavy footfall left the hard concrete surface and his tread touched the gravel in the open paddock. Instinctively I shot out from behind the wall and slammed both my clenched fist and the butt of the Colt into Warren's face, knocking him senseless to the floor. Vic came from behind me like lighting, and I heard the familiar swishing sound of his flick knife releasing itself from its hilt; he dropped to his knee, stuffed his hand over the incapacitated cop's mouth and went to sink the six-inch blade into Warren's guts. I grabbed at Vic's arm, preventing him from finishing him off.

"No Vic . . . Not him, we bag his ass up. Whatever happens from now on, we still got ourselves a crooked lawman to t'row into the ring. Listen, he's gonna keep me and you outta jail, if tings git shitty later . . . Trust me, brother."

I put the Colt back through my belt and then hooked my hands under Warren's arms and dragged him into the stable block. Vic watched me for a moment, rubbing the stubble on his chin, then followed me in, dropping the holdall at his feet. He then reached down into it, pulled out the two lengths of rope and threw them over to me.

I began tying Mickey Warren by his hands and feet in a series of tight fishing knots that a grizzly bear would have struggled to break free of, then squeezed his cheeks open and stuffed my handkerchief into his mouth. I called over quietly to Vic.

"Here, gimme a hand to sling his butt into this horse stall."

I knelt besides the unconscious body of the copper and I watched as Vic went and retrieved Warren's Lee-Enfield rifle from off of the ground in the paddock. He unclipped the magazine and pulled the bolt back to receive the unspent cartridge, then slipped both sets of the gun's ammunition into his pocket and slung the rifle over his shoulder.

"OK, Dick Tracy, what next?"

"I want you to go round to the front of the house and make sure neither one o' those flash motors is fit to drive outta here. I don't want Blanchard to be able to make a run fo' it. When you've finished putting the jalopies out o' action, you scout round and keep a sharp eye out in case Papa decides to show after all, got that?"

Vic nodded, but was clearly unhappy that I'd made the decision for us to separate.

"Now gimme that iron so I can jemmy open the kitchen door."

Vic reached into the holdall and handed over the short metal bar with the flattened, hammered end, and a torch.

"You may wanna take one o' these too. Just watch your back in there with that slippery muthafucka Blanchard. If you in any doubt 'bout how its gonna play out when you finally git to him, and if he gives you any shit at all, you put a bullet in his head or holler out and I'll come do it, you hear me?"

I looked at my cousin gravely, shaking my head.

"I hear you . . . Look, I'm sorry I got you into this mess, brother, even after I'd stood in front of you and said I wouldn't."

Vic looked at me and shrugged to himself, then winked.

"Shut your fool mouth . . . Now let's finish this shit!"

Vic raised the shotgun on to his hip, smiled at me, then walked out into the darkness.

I leant against the wall at the back of the house and fitted the jemmy as far as it would go into the frame of the door, next to

337

the handle and lock, and wrenched it open with a single firm yank. I stepped inside the unlit kitchen and switched on the torch, scanning the beam around the massive scullery.

At the left-hand side of the room was a short corridor that led towards a door. I walked along the corridor, took the brass door handle in my hand and opened it up.

On the other side was another, larger corridor that was lit by small wall lights. I followed the length of the passageway, which finally brought me to a second, more ornate doorway. I quietly opened it up and stepped out into the main reception hall of the house. At my feet, an impressive white tiled marble floor stretched out in front of me; it was intercut with black diamond shapes across its width and breadth. I turned off the torch and put it into my jacket pocket, then stood for a moment and admired the cut crystal hanging from the chandeliers and the expensive oil paintings and portraits that hung on the flock-wallpapered walls around me. The room was filled with the fresh scent of lilies, lending it the atmosphere of a high-end funeral parlour. In the centre of the baroque-style vestibule stood a large, crimson-carpeted staircase. I walked to the bottom of it and looked up towards the second floor; a gallery ran around the entire length of the upper floor, looking down on to the atrium below. I began to make my way up the plush matted steps and wondered if Blanchard employed staff to run such a large place, and if he did, then why were none of his aides about? Perhaps he'd decided to give them the night off on account of my unexpected social call. The stillness of the building was giving me the creeps, so when I reached the top of the stairs, I took the Colt automatic from my waistband and pulled the slide back.

Holding the grip firmly in my right hand and keeping the pistol at chest height, I began to walk along the left-hand

338

side of the gallery towards a passageway that had a series of rooms.

"You'll only find the guest bedrooms in that section of the building, Mr Ellington!"

I spun around and aimed the Colt 45 directly towards Terrence Blanchard, who stood on the other side of the staircase. He showed no sign of alarm at a gun being pointed at him, and he smiled at me. Blanchard sure wasn't pretty. He had the caustic appearance of an aging bird of prey: all hook nose and sunken eyes. His silver hair was combed back across his scalp and his pastel-soft skin stretched across his bony face, which gave the impression of a lost soul that had received early mummification. He was suavely dressed in a violet cravat, quilted dark-purple smoking jacket with gold-braid piping around the collar and cuffs, and a pair of bespoke grey pinstripe trousers. Between the tips of two fingers of his left hand he pinched an ivory holder; attached inside it was a freshly lit unfiltered cigarette. He put the pale holder to his lips and inhaled, then blew out a haze of thick smoke towards me.

"My study is just to the right, please . . . Mr Ellington, this way."

Blanchard held out his right hand to guide me towards his private quarters. I kept the Colt trained onto his upper torso and apprehensively walked towards him as he carefully backed up and stopped outside the large open doorway to his study, the pale-skinned palm of his hand again gesturing to me to enter.

"After you . . . Mr Blanchard."

"Thank you . . ."

Blanchard walked into his study.

"You're quite a cautious chap, aren't you, Mr Ellington?"

"Pays to be cautious with strangers, even well-dressed ones: my mama taught me that."

"Quite right, quite right, my dear chap. 'How prone to doubt, how cautious are the wise!' as they say."

I followed the barrister in and took a good look around the room, which was badly lit by various candles. Two of the walls, one on the right and the other behind me, were draped in thick, dark-red velvet curtaining; there were no windows visible. To my left stood an enormous black wood ceiling-to-floor bookcase filled with leather-bound tomes; on the wall directly in front of me a coal fire roared inside a massive granite fireplace. Blanchard walked over to a small Victorian oval drinks cabinet, opened up the door and took out a bottle and two small brandy balloons.

"I was about to enjoy an early Armagnac; would you care to join me?"

"I'll pass, thanks . . . but you go right on ahead."

"Yes . . . Yes, I think I will, if you don't mind? Mr Ellington, it would appear that you and I have gotten off on the wrong foot after this morning, as it were. I was hoping I could rectify our little misunderstanding."

Blanchard poured himself a generous amount of his high-priced French brandy, put the stopper back into the bottle and returned it to the cabinet, then walked a few more paces towards me, stopping by the edge of his desk, and raised his glass.

"Chin-chin."

He took a delicate sip of the spirit before returning his bird-like gaze towards me.

"By 'misunderstanding' I presume you're talkin' 'bout my interest in your little members' club, Mr Blanchard?"

"That, and my other personal affairs: affairs that I'd prefer remained out of the public domain. So rather than protract the situation, perhaps making it difficult for both us in the future, I thought that as gentlemen we could come to an agreement?"

"What kind of agreement you suggesting we come to?"

I kept the gun loose in my outstretched hand, the barrel pointed directly at the devious lawyer's chest.

"Well, perhaps 'agreement' is too vague a term; maybe 'settlement' would be more appropriate: a financial settlement?"

"An' I suppose you had a figure in mind that would reflect upon my future silence in regard to your personal affairs?"

I watched as Blanchard walked slowly towards me. He took another pull on his cigarette, then came to a sudden halt. I glanced quickly around the room, then took a few steps back and shifted my weight from one leg to the other, keeping the handgun directed towards him.

"I was thinking in the region of, say, five . . . No? As I'm fond of informing some of my less educated but wealthy clients, 'silence is often the answer'. Let's say ten thousand pounds or guineas: could that buy a silentious disposition, sir?"

"I don't even know what those words mean let alone whether ten grand could buy it, Mr Blanchard."

"We could consider a larger amount if you thought you were being unfairly coerced into making a rushed decision?"

He smiled at me again, which sent a chill through me. I felt an acidic taste at the back of my gullet, which I hacked at to clear.

"Perhaps you'll take that drink with me now, knock that frog out of your throat?"

He turned to walk back to his mahogany drinks cabinet. I cocked the hammer of the 45 all the way back, stopping Blanchard in his tracks.

"I won't be taking that drink from you, or your lousy money. Just hand over Stella Hopkins to me."

Blanchard raised his arm and threw both his finished cigarette and its holder into the fire, then slowly turned to face me again, his angry eyes smouldering in their sockets as he glared into my own, his hands bunched into tight fists at his side.

"I'm afraid that outcome simply isn't possible, Mr Ellington. You and I are not that different, I'm sure. Name your price, but Stella stays here with me. You see, I consider her to be a very precious asset."

I gripped the gun tighter in my hand and took a step towards Blanchard, not taking my eyes off him for a second.

"Well, that's where we differ. Stella's not a piece of property, she's not some slave, and she's coming with me whether you damn well like it or not!"

I watched as Terrence Blanchard nodded to himself slowly, taking in my determined words. Then he spoke through gritted teeth.

"Mr Ellington, let me explain something: it took me quite a search before I was fortunate enough to come into possession of Miss Hopkins, a unique beauty. I first saw Stella last summer with her guardian, Mr Linney, a man I know you are well acquainted with. From the moment I was introduced to her, I knew that I wanted her . . . and to get to know her more intimately. However, I knew Mr Linney was a pious man and that it would take the most delicate tact and diplomacy to get near to his ward.

"I also knew he was eager to purchase a sizable amount of land in my ownership in the Filton area of Bristol. You see, Linney's honourable but rather naive intention was to create a small housing development that would allow those from

342

the . . ." – Blanchard considered his words for a moment – "from the colonies, people like you, Mr Ellington, so that they may procure their own homes in the future. So one evening while we were both attending a rather ghastly charity dinner, I took Earl to one side and quietly suggested that if he was happy to allow me contact with Miss Hopkins that I would be prepared to offer my land for a less costly figure. It was an exciting proposition, hard for him to turn down."

"You're telling me that Earl Linney went ahead and sold Stella to you so he could build houses for coloured people?"

I could barely believe what I was hearing.

"Well, that's what happened in the end, only in a roundabout way. Things are never what they seem, Mr Ellington! As it happened, Mr Linney refused me outright. Now, as with all men who are cursed with having the need to stand on the moral high ground and repent their sins in deed or thought, Earl felt compelled to seek atonement for even being party to what he considered to be improper. His conscience demanded it of him, and that's when he made his fateful mistake."

"Yeah and what mistake would that have been?" I was growing tired of Blanchard's monotonous lecturing and wanted him to cut to the chase.

"Earl Linney told his wife, Alice, Mr Ellington and she was far more understanding than her spouse. I was rather taken aback at first when she first contacted me in such a surreptitious manner to request that we meet. A convergence after dark in a secluded part of the county: it was all very covert, I have to say. Alice drove a hard bargain: she clearly had no affection for Stella and offered to bring her to me on request. All I had to do in return was to reoffer the land sale to the alderman and create a convincing scenario in which our subterfuge would be accepted by her husband. Of course, I concocted some cock-and-bull story, sold him the land cheap and he swallowed my story hook, line and sinker. There was, however, a small caveat: I informed Alice that Stella must remain with me, until . . . well, until I'd finished with her. It seemed only fair after I'd had to lose a great deal of money . . . but I have to say I have had my money's worth.

"You've been flailing around in the dark all this time, having scraps of misleading information dropped into your lap, and those deceptive inaccuracies have led you to a very dark place where you really don't belong. You've come for the wrong person, Mr Ellington; you should be talking with Alice Linney at this moment, not me. She's a rather devious lady, you know; I was rather impressed with her, deadlier than the male, all that sort of thing.

"It's a pity that because of her there have been so many unnecessary deaths, so many deceits. She is clearly the one with the real business acumen in the marriage, you know. And she has a much darker talent for treachery than I would never have credited a woman with possessing. Alice Linney is quite a cruel beast. I wonder if her poor husband knows that."

40

I WAS HAVING REAL trouble taking in everything that Blanchard had been telling me.

"I don't believe anyting you've just said, Blanchard, and if I did it don't explain why you'd need to keep Stella like she was some caged animal. You didn't need to keep her under lock and key. Let's face it, you hadn't any worries about her blabbing to anybody, she can barely read or write. Who could she have betrayed you to fo' Christ's sakes?"

My mouth was dry and my body trembled with anger.

"Let's just say that I prefer to keep my personal life away from the prying eyes of others. I wasn't concerned about betrayal, but I was concerned about putting myself at any risk. Mistakes are made, accidents happen, people talk, Mr Ellington."

"That's not what I've heard 'bout the private parties you been holding here of late. They seem to have a lot of prying eyes taking part in them. Tell me, did you pass her around to your buddies or just keep her to yourself?"

"That's an interesting question coming from the man who's supposedly here to rescue her. Stella's an asset to my little fellowship. All precious items draw the attention of interested parties. The discerning guests who attend the Erotica Negro are no different. They appreciate items of quality and distinction. It would have been churlish to have denied them the pleasures of Stella's individual peculiarities."

"You sick son of a bitch, how'd the hell you sleep at night with all that crap rattling round in your head? You may be dressed like a gentlemen but you got the scruples of an alley cat, mister, you know that? I've had enough of this . . . It'll be a pleasure to drag your ass into Bridewell police station later. I know a Detective Inspector Fletcher there who will be real interested to meet you and that shitbag Mickey Warren. By the way, if you're thinking he's gonna come running to your rescue in a minute you got another think coming. He's sleeping off a smack in the mouth I gave him in your stables out back. Now take me to where Stella is!"

Blanchard walked back to his desk and leant against the front of it, then looked at me head on his furtive eyes that I knew were looking for a chink in my armour, a weakness that he could take advantage of. Like all predators, he was out to make a kill.

"As I said to you a moment ago, Mr Ellington, handing over Stella to you was never going to be an option. Surely you didn't think I would confess the truth to you without considering the implications of such a precarious decision. I have what you would call a back-up plan. But I'll let Mr Grey tell you all about that . . ."

For a split second from the corner of my right eye I saw the razor-sharp blade of a machete coming towards my outstretched arm as the colossal frame of Papa Anansi appeared from behind the velvet drape and charged towards me. I instinctively threw my body backwards as Papa Anansi lashed out and fell past me, but his machete made contact with the barrel of my gun, knocking it out of my hand and spinning it across the room. Seeing this, Blanchard sprinted towards the bookcase, stumbled, then disappeared down steps behind a concealed door in one of the panels. I recovered just

346

as Papa came at me swinging the knife viciously at my chest and head, and I backed closer up towards the fire. He lashed the bush-cutter close in front of me a couple more times, and as his arm drew back to come at me again and I dropped down low and struck out hard at his shin bone. Papa wailed out in pain. I saw a brass poker sitting in its stand in the hearth only a few inches away from me, and grabbed it and managed to block the Jamaican killer's next ferocious blow towards my head with it. I struck out with the metal spur but missed him, then as I went to strike at his shoulder Papa sidestepped me and smashed his boot into my stomach, sending me across the room and knocking the wind out of me.

I knew I was in trouble and, gasping for breath, I tried to crawl across the carpet on my elbows to create some distance between me and the giant, but he came back at me with tremendous speed. I kicked out at him weakly, and as I went to hit out again Papa growled at me, "Stay on yo' ass, you piss ant!" He savagely put the boot into my chest, doubling me up in pain. I lay on the floor helpless as he stood over me. I could see his cold, black, shark-like eyes staring down at me unemotionally from behind large strands of matted dreadlocked hair that hung over his pox-scarred face. He shot me a look of merciless scorn, then dragged a throatful of mucus into his mouth and spat it at my chest before raising the machete above his head, ready to unleash his rage down on me.

"You are one dead Bajan pig!"

I shut my eyes, dug my fingers into the carpet and waited for the razor's edge to slice into my flesh.

The unexpected noise of the shotgun firing was deafening. I felt warm, sticky liquid splatter across my face and neck, and the harsh stink of burnt meat and cordite filled my nostrils.

347

I opened my eyes to find Papa Anansi still standing above me; his muscular arms were now hanging loosely at his sides, the machete still limply held in his hand. I stared at the jagged twelve-inch gaping hole where his guts had once been before the pimp fell to his knees in front of me. Both eyeballs protruded as dark blood oozed from his mouth, and he let out a final desperate gasp for life. It was the last thing Papa did as he hit the floor dead at my feet. I heard the familiar to-and-fro action of another cartridge being loaded into the pump-action's breech and saw Vic standing in the doorway, gazing down at the man he had just killed. His face was hard and resolute.

He casually strolled across the room and picked up the Colt 45 pistol, then returned and stood over me, holding the gun by its barrel for me to catch hold of. I reached up for it and took the walnut grip in my trembling hand. Vic let go of the barrel and gestured with his outstretched palm to help me up. I felt a sharp pain in my ribs as my cousin got me to my feet, and we stood looking at each other for a moment before Vic spoke.

"I thought I told you to holler out if you got into trouble, fool!"

I pointed to the door in the opened panel of the bookcase. "Pass me a torch, Vic, Blanchard's disappeared down here."

We made our way down the stairs with the faint light of the torch. I gripped the 45 in the other hand as we warily made our way towards a glow coming through an arched doorway at the bottom. Vic was a couple of steps behind me and held the Spencer shotgun shoulder height in front of him. As we neared the foot of the stairs, he put his hand on my shoulder as a warning: that's when I got the first unmistakeable whiff of gasoline. I gestured to Vic with the flattened palm of my hand to get him to stay where he was, then made my way down towards the open door and walked into yet another large, poorly lit room.

"Be careful where you're standing, Mr Ellington, and I'd advise you not to take another step – not unless you want to go up in flames, that is."

Terrence Blanchard stood drenched to the skin in fuel in the centre of an alabaster-walled cellar. From its low ceiling hung a series of candelabrum fittings each lit with a series of candles. In the walls around, five feet up, were a series of small recesses that all held large wax lights, their tapers glowing, helping in a small way to illuminate the miserable-looking crypt. I looked down at my feet to find that I was standing in a pool of gasoline, then stared back up to Blanchard, who was now holding a silver cigarette lighter at arm's length: his thumb was sitting on the plunger button and a discarded jerrycan had been emptied then flung across the floor.

"I'd be correct in assuming you've come looking for your prize?"

Blanchard slowly took a couple of steps to his right to reveal a large white stone platform, around three feet high, with a mattress at its base. Curled up in a ball on top of it was Stella Hopkins. A long length of iron chain had been bolted to the wall; it ran along the base of the plinth and was attached securely to her slim ankle.

"She's quite all right, Mr Ellington, sedated, but quite all right. She means more to me than you will ever understand. When Stella is resting, as she is now, I always like to think of her as being a princess in a fairy tale: a real Sleeping Beauty, don't you think?"

"I think she looks like a young black woman who's been chained to a wall!"

349

I took a step forward; my hand squeezed at the grip of the 45.

"Don't take another step, you bloody fool, not unless you want the whole place go up like a scene from Dante's *Inferno* . . ."

Blanchard raised his left arm, the palm of his hand outstretched.

"'I come to lead you to the other shore, into eternal darkness, ice and fire.'"

"What the hell are you talkin' 'bout, man? Now put that lighter down on the ground real slow and back away over to that side wall."

I nudged the barrel of the 45 towards where I wanted the barrister to move, but he ignored me.

"Interesting that you should mention Hell . . . Well, I couldn't have put it better. Dante once said that the hottest places in hell are reserved for those who in a period of moral crisis maintain their neutrality. Neutrality! That's what I've been trying to achieve while you've been sniffing around, Mr Ellington, to maintain a sense of the impartial, to be . . . detached. I've let others concern themselves with the complications that have arisen from Stella being here, with me.

"I have mixed in circles you cannot imagine, Mr Ellington, from princes to the kings of the underworld, and I know a lot about the criminal mind: too much, you might say. Suddenly you realise there is no difference between them; all have their failings, their weaknesses, so it was easy to find people to supply my private little gatherings and the discreet errands I needed carried out using men like Mr Grey, or Papa, as you know him. I take it from the strident gunshot that I heard resonating around the building a short while ago that Mr Grey has joined his . . . fellow lowlifes, in Hades. That's a pity, but no great loss in the grand scale of things. However, the gun you're holding

350

in that hand of yours didn't create such a deafening noise, that came from a more powerful weapon, no doubt fired by the other black bastard that tags along with you."

Vic swung around from behind the wall and slowly came and stood at my side, the pump-action pointed directly at Blanchard's head.

"You want me to blow this crazy ole fucker's face off, JT?"

Blanchard didn't give me the chance to reply and took a step forward with the lighter poised in front of him.

"Stop right there! At your feet and liberally dispersed around this room, and doused over myself and young Stella there, is enough petrol to eradicate any trace that any of us have ever been here. I have no intention of letting either of you walk out of here alive, and I do not relish the thought of having to face any of my fellow barristers in court, so, as I said before, one has to have a back-up plan."

Blanchard swiftly put his hand in to his pocket, drew out a small slip of paper and held it out at arm's length, and then pushed down the plunger of the lighter. A small blue and yellow flame flared up into the air. Vic edged forward and Blanchard drew the paper towards the short jet of rising fire, holding them inches apart. I held out my arm to keep Vic from moving any further.

"So, gentlemen, enough is enough, this is where it all ends . . . I don't know about either of you, but I'm not afraid to die. And the truth is I like secrets and I think I've told enough of them tonight . . . Goodbye!"

Then before either of us could say anything to him or move, Blanchard touched the paper into the lighter's flame, then dropped both at his feet, igniting his whole body in a ferocious ball of fire. The floor awakened and erupted into a carpet of flames.

Blanchard's piercing screams were lost in the commencement of the firestorm; now, with his arms reaching out, his engulfed form began to run towards me. Vic stepped in front, knocking me out of the way, and pulled the trigger of the pump-action, hurling Terrence Blanchard's fire-consumed body across the cellar and slamming it into the wall.

I snatched the shotgun out of my cousin's hands and screamed, "Git the fuck outta here, Vic!" Then I burst through the intense blaze towards where Stella was shackled. I forced another round into the pump-action's breech as I ran and fired towards where the chain was secured, blowing the manacle out of the wall and releasing the heavy metal restraint. I threw the gun down at my feet and stood over Stella's fragile, unconscious body. I grabbed up the blanket at edge of the mattress and covered her with it, then hooked my arms underneath her back and drew her slight frame close to me.

When I turned to face the bonfire that was raging all around me, I could just about see Vic through the choking smoke and brimstone. He was yelling out to me from the doorway, but I couldn't hear what he was saying over the conflagration that was exploding in front of where I was standing. In my head I heard the cries of my wife and child, calling out to me to come for them. I closed my eyes, pulled my coat over the back of my head the best that I could, then ran out into the fiery holocaust. As I launched myself across the burning room through the scorching heat of the cellar, I could feel the intense heat burning at the tail of my coat and the skin starting to blister on my calves. Then Vic's huge hands reached out to me from the doorway and we fell into his waiting arms. He yanked Stella from me, then turned and carried her up the stairs towards Blanchard's study.

I tore off my burning coat and turned to follow Vic up the stairway. It was then that I saw, standing in the furthest recess of the cellar, my wife, Ellie. She was holding the hand of our little girl Amelia. I screamed out their names and went to run back into burning catacomb, but Ellie calmly raised her hand to stop me, shaking her head, telling me to come no closer. She smiled and drew our beloved child close to her side. Amelia held on tightly to the crisp white linen of her mother's long, flowing skirt with her tiny fingers. Then I watched as they both disappeared into the flames.

41

OUR DRIVE BACK TO St Pauls was made in silence. The only noise that disturbed our otherwise peaceful nocturnal journey came from the intermittent banging that occasionally emanated from our fellow passenger, the crooked cop Mickey Warren, who Vic had dumped, bound and gagged, into the boot of the Cortina. We had left the Blanchard estate at speed and drove out into the night with the house ablaze, the fire destroying any trace that we had ever been there, just as Terrence Blanchard had foretold.

I was sitting on the back seat being shunted to and fro as Vic sped through the darkened country lanes. I was holding Stella in my arms, and she was still out for the count from the soporific drug that Blanchard had given her. Looking at her sleeping face, I could not imagine the cruelty that she must have endured, and I drew her close to me like a parent with a sick child.

It was just after ten thirty by the time Vic pulled up outside my digs. He got out and opened up the rear door, and I slid out, still holding onto Stella tightly. As we began to walk towards my front door, I felt something drop from out of the blanket and fall to the ground. Vic bent down and picked up a small cloth rabbit. He looked at it, then handed it back to me, shrugging his big shoulders, puzzled. Something told me I'd seen the toy before somewhere as I tucked it back in between the blanket and let it nestle close to her. I stood in the street, thinking for a second or two.

When I looked down at the toy again I realised it was the same as the one in the photograph I'd found underneath the wardrobe in her house a short while ago. Stella was the young child sitting on the knee of the guy who resembled Earl Linney. I lifted my head and looked across at Vic, who said nothing but nodded towards my bedsit. Standing there, with her frail hand opening the door for us, was Mrs Pearce.

I lay Stella on my bed. Safe now and gently breathing, she looked to be in a dreamless sleep. I chose to let her rest for as long as was necessary before calling for a doctor. I closed the bedroom door behind me and walked into the kitchen, where Vic and Mrs Pearce sat across from each other at the small dining table.

"Mrs Pearce . . . Can you do me a small favour?"

I stood over her tiny frame and smiled down at her.

"Is it to do with that poor girl? Your cousin 'ere says she's had a bit of a time of things. What is it you want me to do?"

"Yes, Mrs Pearce, Stella's a little shook up, but she's fast asleep now. Could you stay here? Then look in on her in the next quarter of an hour to check she's OK, but I'm sure she'll be fine. I need to go with Vic to the family, but I won't be long . . . I promise."

"She'll be fine with me, Mr Ellington . . . You run along now, I'll see you shortly."

She nodded at me gently, and I looked over at Vic to let him know I was ready to leave. As we were walking out of the kitchen, I stopped and turned to my neighbour.

"Oh, there's another kindness you could do fo' me, Mrs Pearce."

The old woman looked up at me. "And what's that, Mr Ellington?"

"Call me JT . . . All my friends do."

Vic and I sat in the car outside of my place on Gwyn Street. He looked across at me from the driver's seat.

"OK . . . JT, what do we do now?"

I took in a deep breath, working my game plan out in my head.

"Listen, Vic, I want you take that bastard we got stashed in the back o' the boot and drive him over to Bridewell police station. You leave the motor outside in the street, find the nearest phone box, then call the operator and ask to be patched through to the station. When you git through, say you wanna speak to Detective Inspector William Fletcher. Tell 'em that it's real urgent. If he ain't there, you say to whoever's on the front desk to go git him, no matter where he is! Understand?"

Vic nodded at me.

"Then tell 'em that Fletcher needs to git his ass outside the nick and that in the boot o' this Cortina is Mickey Warren, awaiting arrest for his involvement in the murders of Carnell Harris, Clarence Mayfield, Jocelyn Charles and Virginia Landry and the attempted murder of Joseph Ellington. Fletcher's gonna shit when he sees a serving police officer tied up in the boot of a car on his doorstep and he's bound to come looking fo' me soon afterwards. I'll worry 'bout all that later. Once you done that fo' me, you don't say another damn ting and you walk away, you hear me?"

"Yeah . . . I hear you. But I ain't too pleased having to be so close to no police station, let alone speaking to 'em. I'm only doing it cos you my kin. I woulda slit that pig Warren's throat and not thought another ting 'bout it. You know that, don't ya?"

"I know . . ."

I put my hand into my jacket pocket, pulled out my notebook and flipped over the pages until I found the slip of paper with the address I needed on it. I tore it out and passed it over to Vic.

"Now take me to this place in Montpelier, brother."

I sat back in my seat and shut my eyes. The thought of what I had to do next was eating at my guts as Vic pulled away and drove me over to Earl Linney's home.

★

It was just after eleven as I watched Vic pull away, leaving me outside of the Linneys' house. A hard frost had crept in and the ground below me sparkled with ice crystals as I made my way across the road to the old Georgian town house that stood behind a tiny garden, which was surrounded by a four-foot-high red-brick wall. I opened the gate and walked down the short path to the front door, then took the brass lion's head knocker in my hand and let it fall against the door a couple of times. A few moments later a light came on and shone out through the stained-glass panel above me, and a small, thin, well-dressed black woman opened the door. She peered out at me suspiciously over her half-rim reading glasses. I stared back at the slight and unassuming lady who faced me and wondered if this could really be the inhuman monster that Terrence Blanchard had described to me earlier. I stood back from the doorstep and tried to force a smile, but failed.

"Mrs Linney . . . ?"

"Yes, can I help you?"

Her tone was polished and formal, and she spoke without the Caribbean accent I'd previously heard when she'd answered the telephone to me a few days previously. She nervously stood back into her hallway, unsure of my reason for calling at such a late hour.

"Good evening, Ma'am, I'm hoping to speak to your husband on an urgent matter. Is he in?"

"I'm sorry, no, he's not. He'll be on his way home shortly; he's attending a social event at the council chambers. Can I tell him who called?"

"My name's Ellington, Joseph Ellington ... I've been working fo' Mr Linney these past few weeks. You and I spoke recently on the phone, I don't know if you remember me?"

"No ... No, I'm afraid I don't remember, Mr Ellington ... Would you like me to pass on a message to him when he returns?"

Her tone had hardened, like she was suddenly ready to be rid of me.

I decided to play my ace and walked up onto the step directly in front of her.

"Yes, if you don't mind. You can tell your husband that I've found Stella."

Alice Linney took another step back from the door, visibly shaken. I watched as she swallowed hard, then, without being asked, I walked by her into the hallway and set the door ajar to allow us a little privacy.

"I don't know what your game is, but you can get the hell out of my house!"

I ignored her and continued to walk boldly on through into the cosy sitting room; then I felt her fingers jab into my arm. I turned to face her as she waved an accusatory finger in my face.

"Who the hell do you think you are pushing your way into my home at this time of night? I'm going to call the police."

She spun on her heels, marching back towards the telephone in the hall. I called after her, stopping the old woman in her tracks.

358

"Make sure you ask fo' a Detective Inspector William Fletcher out at Bridewell station. Now, I know he's gonna be busy tonight, but he'll sure be mighty interested to hear your story, Mrs Linney, I can promise you that . . . After you git round to telling him that you got an unwanted guest in your house, don't forget to mention to him 'bout how you took young Stella and hocked her on to a depraved animal like Terrence Blanchard!"

Alice Linney turned to face me, then slowly walked back into her living room and stood a few feet from me, her face contorted with anger.

"What d'you want from me . . . money?"

Her clipped colonial true-blue accent used for guests and callers had been lost and replaced by a more familiar Jamaican twang.

"No . . . I want what I've been looking fo' this past few weeks: just simple bit o' truth."

"The trute . . . oh you want the trute, do you, Mr Ellington? Well, the trute can be twisted in all kinda ways. You wanna hear my side o' tings or the man who's been payin' you your wages?" She sneered at me, her eyes burning with anger and contempt.

"I wanna know how you could sell a pretty young woman's freedom to an insane pervert like Terrence Blanchard and think you could git away with it, fo' a start."

"You call Stella pretty? She a lot tings, brother, but she ain't pretty . . . She a stupid dirty girl! Ever since she was a little pitney, she was trouble. Always messin' her drawers, needing attention and to be bathed every couple o' hours, constantly crying and causing trouble. Couldn't do a damn ting fo' herself; she put me t'ru hell!"

She jabbed her skinny finger at me like she was about to sentence me to the gallows.

"What you talkin' 'bout? Why would she put you through hell? Yeah, the little ting was deaf and dumb . . . but that wouldn't make her a monster. Stella hardly came into the world blessed, did she?"

"Stella shouldn't o' come into this world at all, damn retard! Victoria, her mama, she couldn't cope with her when she was a child, had some silly kinda breakdown. Doctors t'rew her into the nuthouse at Stoke Park; she was locked up with the rest of the mental defectives inside o' there fo' nearly ten years. My husband said he wanted to help, and like a fool he told the authorities that we would bring her up here with us, in my home. In the end it came down to me to wipe her filthy arse, comb the lice outta her hair, make sure she wasn't stinkin' while her worthless mama rocked away in that loony bin and I took care of her brat . . . Woman only took the child back when all the hard work was done!"

I was confused; none of what was being said to me made any sense.

"Why'd your husband agree with Stella's mother to look after her? She wasn't your kin . . . I don't understand, Mrs Linney."

"Why would you?"

She walked over to the far side of the room, took a photo frame from the back of a teak sideboard and returned with it outstretched in her hand and shoved it at my chest.

"Here . . . here's ya damn trute!"

I took the recognisable photograph from her. It was the same as the one I'd found in Stella's bedroom. I looked up at Alice Linney, who stared back at me bitterly.

"So Stella . . . is Earl's daughter?"

"Don't be a bloody fool, man . . . That's not my husband in that damn picture . . . It's his brother, Patrick!"

I stood motionless, staring down at the snapshot, while Alice continued to rant on at me.

"Patrick was in the Royal Air Force same as my man, Earl. The two of 'em was the only family either of 'em had, an' they was inseparable. After the war they both went back home to Jamaica. Earl an' I married, an' his brother met a lovely woman from Spanish Town, they got hitched and Patrick became a Baptist minister. We all came to Britain in 1948. Within months, Patrick had met Stella's mama, Victoria, starting seeing her on the quiet. Stupid fool, he got her pregnant and she refused to git rid of it. Patrick panicked, packed up everyting he owned and took him and that poor ignorant wife o' his and sailed back to Jamaica. Earl, being so close to his brother, made him a promise: he told him that he'd keep an eye out fo' the child. We ended up doing more than that ... Earl treated that ting like it was his own, and my feelings were never considered, not fo' a moment. He stupidly thought that I'd be agreeable to his madness and took it fo' granted that I'd go along with it all, just like he does with so many other tings.

"Patrick came back to Britain in 1955 to see her, the year that photograph was taken. Only time he ever saw Stella. He gave her that damn silly cloth rabbit she carries round with her. It's never left her side since the day he gave it to her. We told everybody Stella was our ward, that we were fostering her. It was easier to lie than admit the trute 'bout how we'd ended up stuck with the child. It also allowed my husband an excuse to not have to face the trute 'bout me. You see, I'm what you call a barren woman, Mr Ellington. Earl and I could never have a child of our own. So he took to caring fo' another woman's bastard offspring!"

I could feel her stare burning into me. I kept looking at the picture in my hands and I stumbled for the words when I spoke.

361

"I found a copy of this photograph at the back of an empty scrapbook in Stella's bedroom a short while back. I thought that the man in the photo looked like your husband, but I was wrong."

I kept staring at it and spoke to Mrs Linney without raising my head.

"Stella's home, it was filled with bleach and other kinds a cleaning stuff, it was all over the place . . . Why'd that be?"

"Her useless mama died in that house . . . in that very same room riddled with cancer, she was. The stupid girl used to try and scrub the stench o' death outta that place day and night. Even took to washing down her skin with it, but like I told you, she was always a dirty little ting, so a bit a bleach wasn't gonna harm that thick witless hide o' hers!"

I began to shake my head at her bitter words.

"So because you thought that Stella had been a thorn in your side fo' so many years and a constant reminder of the child you couldn't have, you decided to palm her off to some crazed old bastard to defile and abuse . . . What the hell were you thinkin', woman, how did you really think you'd git away with such madness?"

"I didn't have to think, man! You haven't had to suffer the humiliations I have. I was tired of seeing the foolish child's face about and my man still doting on her like he was her daddy all these years later. I encouraged Terrence Blanchard to renegotiate the land deal with my husband after he'd previously turned his offer down. Earl has had great plans to offer many people in the community a better chance of owning their own homes. I didn't wanna see his dreams tumble just because some old racist didn't wanna part with a few thousand feet o' dirt to a black man. Stella was the key to realising those dreams fo' my man. So I parlayed another deal with Blanchard using that worthless deaf simpleton as surety to git what I needed. He promised me that she'd be well looked after and I believed him when he said she'd be cared fo'."

Alice Linney tried to justify her actions with an arrogant belligerence that I'd never seen in a woman before.

"Cared fo' . . . You sick, evil old bitch, Blanchard couldn't have cared fo' any living soul, no more than a gator could keep his mout' away from dead meat! You knew when you made that trumped-up land deal with him that you were selling that poor child into a living hell!"

I felt the fury tighten in every muscle in my body and my fists clenched. Something snapped inside my head and I shot towards Alice Linney. My arm outstretched, I grabbed hold of her clothing and pulled her towards me. She screamed out as I lifted up my bunched knuckles ready to rain down my rage upon her slight body – then I froze as I saw Earl Linney standing in the doorway of his sitting room, neither of us aware of how long he had been there. I held onto his wife tightly, my breathing heavy and laboured.

"Where's Stella, Mr Ellington?" He spoke softly, the water welling up in his eyes.

"She's sleeping over at my place. I gotta friend of mine watching over her."

"Take me to her . . . please."

Earl Linney looked at his wife; with a face past pity and hate . . . Loathing was what came to my mind. She threw out her chest at him defiantly. His head sank to his chest as the tears began to flow from his eyes, and I watched as he slowly walked back out of his home and into the street. The sound of his desolate sobbing would stay with me till the end of my days.

I offered to drive Earl Linney's Austin Cambridge back to my place. He threw the keys over to me as we neared his motor and got in, and he stared straight out of the windscreen, his body trembling. During our ride I asked him how much of my conversation with his wife he had heard.

"I heard enough," was all the man whispered to me.

The car journey seemed endless. A fresh dusting of snow began to fall out of the sky as the car wipers worked hard to knock it away. I knew what it felt like to have your life taken from you: one day we think we have it all, then when it is gone we wonder if it was all just a dream, a mirage.

It was just after midnight by the time we reached my bedsit. Earl was out of the car and standing impatiently by my front door before I had even got the key out of the ignition. I walked up the steps behind him, leant over his shoulder, put the key in the lock and let the two of us in. I climbed the stairs with a foreshadowing sense that something was not right, an ominous feeling that I put down to fatigue. The small blisters on my calves from the fire earlier stung with each step I took, and as I reached the top of the stairs I saw Mrs Pearce waiting for me.

"Is everything OK?"

My aging neighbour walked towards me, a look of concern on her face.

"Oh, thank goodness you're here, Mr Ellington. It's the strangest thing. I did exactly as you said . . . I went and checked on the child fifteen minutes after you and your relation had left. She appeared to be fine . . . Sound asleep, just you like you said. Then I went to check on her about five minutes ago and I couldn't get into the bedroom. The door appears to be locked."

Earl Linney pushed past the two of us and ran down the

hallway, and I followed close behind him. Linney became agitated.

"Where the hell is she, Ellington?"

I managed to catch hold of him by the elbow just as he reached my bedroom door.

"She's in here."

I took hold of the door handle to my bedroom, turned it and pushed. It was locked, just as Mrs Pearce had told me.

Linney, panicking, grabbed me by the shoulder and yelled, "Kick the damn thing in, man!"

I put my back against the wall opposite, then booted at the lock and handle. What confronted us as the door flew open was more disturbing than anything we could ever have expected. Hanging from the iron curtain rail by the cord belt of my dressing gown was the lifeless body of Stella Hopkins, her eyes open, looking directly at us.

I stood staring for a moment, horrified at what I saw, before Earl Linney edged past me and slowly walked across the room. He dropped to his knees, sobbing, then reached up to Stella's bare feet and gently held onto her toes with the tips of his fingers, then rested his forehead against her bare feet. I heard footsteps coming down the hall and turned to see Mrs Pearce rushing towards the bedroom. I closed the door to and held my hand up to stop her in her tracks.

"Stay where you are, Mrs Pearce, just stay where you are."

She did as I asked and remained motionless a few feet from the front door. I turned back to Linney, who had not moved. I walked towards him, and he looked up at me; the pain and sadness in his eyes made it almost unbearable to look back into them. When he spoke, his voice was desolate and hollow.

"Leave me with her, Ellington. Go get me a knife so I can cut her down, son . . ." I nodded my head slowly, went next door and brought back the only sharp kitchen knife I possessed. I held it by the blade and handed it down to him. He reached up and took it out of my hand, then got to his feet.

"I want to be alone with her for a moment. Give me a few minutes, then you best go call for the police and an ambulance, Mr Ellington."

He turned back to Stella, and I watched as he touched the hem of her skirt with the back of his hand, then began to weep again. I turned my back just as he hooked his arm around her waist and began to cut into the cord above her head.

I walked out to the phone box, did as Linney said, and waited a few minutes before calling for both the police and an ambulance. As I got back to my digs, Mrs Pearce stood in the street and took my hand, squeezing it in her own. The unspoken sentiment in her simple gesture bolstered me as I returned upstairs.

When I got back to my bedroom, the door had been closed again and I felt the foreboding sensation that had struck me earlier. I gently pushed at the door and let it swing open slowly. Inside, I found Earl Linney hanging by his belt from almost the exact same spot that Stella's lifeless body had been suspended from a short time earlier. He had cut her down, closed her eyes, then carefully laid her on the floor. Her hands were placed across her chest, and in one of them she held the cloth toy rabbit that she'd cherished so dearly. Earl had taken off his coat and shoes and then placed them neatly at her feet. It was a simple gesture that told me that the alderman had made a terrible sacrifice and chosen to depart this world and join Stella on her journey to a better place. There she would finally hear for the first time the rustle of a summer breeze through the trees, the carefree laughter of children at play and the whispering words from a gentle guardian telling her that he would love her forever.

EPILOGUE

IT DIDN'T TAKE LONG before Detective Inspector Fletcher was breathing down my neck for answers. This time I gave him what he needed to know, and all of it the truth. There was little point in digging a bigger hole for myself by keeping him in the dark, so I told him exactly how I'd gotten myself involved in the search for Stella and that I believed that her disappearance was tied in to the murders of Clarence Mayfield, Jocelyn Charles, Virginia Landry and Carnell. After I had finished spilling my guts, I spent another two days in the slammer while Fletcher checked out my story.

My only consolation at being incarcerated again was the knowledge that Mickey Warren was in a cell two doors down from me. After being grilled for the better part of seventy-two hours, Warren cracked and confessed to his involvement in everything from murder and extortion to the procuring of woman for sex, admitting to playing his part with Papa Anansi in the slaying of all four of the victims.

The Blanchard estate had burnt to the ground, and the charred remains of both Terrence Blanchard and Papa were found among the ashes and rubble. Their charcoaled bodies were so badly incinerated that it was practically impossible to tell how exactly they had died, and that suited me fine.

Both Cut Man Perry and Elrod Haddon disappeared: the word on the street was that the pair of them packed up all that they could fit into a suitcase and then both boarded some ship or other and set sail for sunnier climes. They wouldn't be missed.

367

Alice Linney was arrested and charged with her involvement in the conspiracy to kidnap and subsequent kidnapping of Stella Hopkins. I heard that when the Bristol and Avon police turned up to slap the cuffs on her, she started to scream the place down and had to be removed from her home in a straightjacket. Unable to be questioned, the police had a doctor examine her and she was diagnosed as delusional and mentally unsound, and in an apt twist of fate was transferred to Stoke Park psychiatric hospital, the same place that Stella's mother, Victoria, had been sent to.

I was released without charge and told to keep my nose clean, and in an unexpected token of DI Fletcher's appreciation was given a lift back to St Pauls in a panda car. I returned back to my digs to the smell of fresh paint and found that in the short time I had been locked up, Gabe, my aunt Pearl and Mrs Pearce had let themselves in and made the place look as fresh as a daisy. A new bedroom door had been fitted and venetian blinds were now where the old curtains and rail had been. But I knew that no matter how much cosmetic rejigging had been done to the place, the tragic presences of both Stella and Earl would continue to linger within its walls.

I walked into my lounge and sitting on the lid of my Dansette record player was a note that had been left for me, handwritten in black ink in a copperplate style. I picked it up and read the simple message.

Dear Mr Ellington,

I hope you didn't mind me coming into your home and helping your family spruce the place up. I have to say, it needed it. I know we have not seen eye to eye since you first arrived, but I think that people sometimes come together for the strangest reasons, as I believe we have. Getting old and being alone is not easy, so

knowing that you are close by is a comforting feeling. I hope that in
the future you will think of me as somebody who is more than just
a neighbour, and as you have insisted that I should address you in
the future in a less formal manner, I trust that you will oblige in
doing the same to me, as friends should.

My sincerest best wishes,
Marjorie Pearce

After I'd finished reading the note, I grabbed my coat and took
a short walk in the afternoon winter sunshine to the Star and
Garter pub. I ordered myself a pint of Dragon Stout and sat
at the very same table where Earl Linney had first introduced
himself to me those few short weeks ago. I thought of our
meeting and how so much had changed since then. I reached
for my glass, took a long draught of my beer and kept drinking
for the rest of the day in the hope I could forget the past,
which for me seemed only ever to bring sadness and pain.

In my heart, though, I had always known the excesses of
drink only let you forget for a fleeting moment. Once it wears
off, you're left with the hard fact that all bad memories never
go away; they just hide out of sight in the backs of our minds,
then return to gnaw at your conscience when you least expect
them to. My mama had once told me that 'tears are the words
that the heart cannot express', and she had been right.

During the following weeks I attended the funerals of
Virginia Landry, Earl Linney, Stella Hopkins and my dear
friend Carnell Harris. I'd shed my fair share of tears at each
one of their interments and now chose to spend my time alone
in my digs, struggling to sleep at night.

★

A week after we had buried Carnell, Vic unexpectedly called on me. It was just after seven in the evening when he rapped on my door and strolled down my hall in a good mood, wearing a big smile on his face, a new bespoke Moss Brothers' grey tweed suit and a pair of spit-shine black leather brogues. In one hand was a bottle of Mount Gay rum and in his other a Fine Fare paper carrier bag. He walked into the kitchen, put the bag and bottle onto the table, then turned to me and opened his jacket to show off a flash pure-white cotton shirt and navy-blue silk tie.

"Well, whaddaya think?"

"You're looking sharp, brother, real sharp."

I stared down at myself and wondered what my relation would think of me. I was dressed in the same clothes I'd been wearing for the last two days, and was unshaven and tired. I sat at the table as Vic cracked open the rum and gulped back a couple of mouthfuls. He handed the bottle to me and I took a sip, then set the booze in front of the two of us. My cousin put both his hands on the table and tapped out a beat in front of me, smiling, his excitement barely contained.

"What's with you . . . You gotta date?"

"No . . . not tonight, JT, I got someting hotter than that going down, my man!"

"Yeah . . . and what's that?"

"I gotta bidness proposition and you included in it!"

"Oh no, no way, Vic . . . You ain't dragging me into your bootlegging and knocked-off white-goods rackets. I'll find me some honest work, if you don't mind?"

I sat back in my chair as I looked at him. His face clearly showed he was hurt by my comments.

"I ain't talkin' 'bout no bootlegging bullshit . . . I'm going legit! Now listen up, you smartass."

He sat down in front of me and opened his arms like a dodgy politician about to make a speech that nobody wanted to hear.

"I got myself this new direction I'm going in . . . boxing promotion! Now befo' you git on your high horse, start shootin' me down in flames, I want you to hear me out. I got Cut Man's old office: I ain't using it, ain't stupid enough to either! Now it's a little ripe in there at the minute an' I need to git the piss and puke scrubbed outta the shagpile, but I got to thinkin' it would make a great place fo' you to keep your ting going."

"Ting . . . what damn 'ting' are you going on 'bout?"

"You know! You checking tings out fo' folks, sniffing 'bout in other people's dirty linen, all that shit! You is perfect fo' it, brother, git it in that thick head o' yours, you're the real McCoy now . . . a proper shamus. Think 'bout it, you don't have be tellin' the world what you be doin' fo' a livin', just git yourself a brass plate put up outside a the front door o' the gym. I can see it now: 'Joseph T. Ellington, Enquiry Agent'. Now that's got real sweet ring to it, ain't no mistake."

He nodded to himself and took another shot of rum from the bottle, then reached into the carrier bag that he'd brought with him. He pulled out the teak box that he normally kept for me and which had once been the home of my police service revolver. He slid it over to me and smiled.

"I thought you'd best have this back. I been hangin' onto it fo' way too long now."

I looked down at it for a moment, then wiped the dust from the lid. I flicked up the two brass catches and opened it. Inside was the money that Earl Linney had given to me and the notebook that I had taken from Clarence Mayfield's place after finding him dead. I stacked them on top of each other and placed them next to me on the table, then reached into the box and took out a small black leather-bound Bible. I opened it up and thumbed through the pages until I came to where I had put a small black and white photograph. I lifted it carefully out and stared down at it.

The snapshot had been taken about three years ago. In it I was sitting outside of my house in an old wicker chair that had belonged to my mama. I held a glass of mango juice in my hand and both my wife, Ellie, and daughter, Amelia, were sitting at my feet smiling for the camera. The photograph had been taken by Vic when he'd made his last visit to us. It had been a Sunday, and my girls and I had just got back from the morning service at our local church. That afternoon I remember we ate salt fish and rice 'n' peas and we laughed at the jokes Vic had told us until our faces hurt. We drank rum punch until the sun fell out of the sky and my child fell asleep in her mother's arms. I stroked the faces of Ellie and my beautiful little girl with the tip of my finger. In my wife's hand was the Bible I now kept the photograph in. I returned it to the page where it now lived and closed it. I looked over at Vic and smiled.

"Thanks, brother."

I rose out of my chair and put my hand on my cousin's shoulder.

"If you don't mind, I'm gonna take a nap. I'm beat. We'll talk 'bout that bidness proposition of yours another time, yeah?"

"That sounds real good to me. Look, I'm gonna sit and finish a touch more o' this rum, perhaps put one o' your Ray Charles LPs on; I'll keep the sound turned down real low, don't you worry, I won't disturb ya. I'll see ya in a while."

I lay on my bed and took the photograph out of the Bible and put it under my pillow. I then placed the open book on my bedside to keep the unwelcome spirit of the duppy away, just as my mama had done for me when I was a small boy. I pulled the blanket over my body and curled myself up tight into a ball, then closed my eyes and slowly let my mind travel back to a time when I knew true love. I slowly embraced sleep, then once again felt the warmth of the sun on my face, the tender touch of two hands holding onto mine, and the waves roll over my feet as my girls walked me along an endless, beautiful golden shore towards the place that we called home.

ACKNOWLEDGEMENTS

THE ORIGINS OF *Heartman* and my detective Joseph Tremaine Ellington can be traced back to a single day back in the autumn of 2003. I was sitting in the Abbey Bar on Decatur Street in the French Quarter in New Orleans drinking an ice-cold, long-necked bottle of Dixie beer and listening to the blues singer Brownie McGhee, who was being piped through an old sound system from the corner of the dimly lit drinking den. Outside a storm had just broken and the rain was bouncing off of the hot pavement, causing steam to rise up in the street; everywhere smelt of a humid damp and it felt as if I'd been transported back to the "Deep South" of a hundred years previous.

On the table in front of me sat a battered copy of *The Neon Rain* by the wonderful American crime writer James Lee Burke. It was a book that always seemed to make it into my suitcase on my travels (it still does) and I must have read it a good dozen times, along with the other Burke books that featured his Cajun detective, Dave Robicheaux. For some time I'd struggled to find other writers that drew me in as Burke did. Yes, I had other literary heroes – Raymond Chandler, Ross Macdonald and Walter Mosley, to name but a few – but there was something about Burke's writing style that kept calling me back to him, as all good writers do. The books were not just about crime or those who fought it, but bigger things: family, friendship and issues of integrity and honour. They were so much more than just crime novels. And so, unable to find that kind of book, I decided to have a go at writing one myself . . . Ten years later, *Heartman* was finally a reality and had found itself a wonderful home with my publishers, Black & White.

The journey of a book from first words to completed manuscript and hopeful publication can be a long one, and *Heartman*'s has not been an exception to that rule. Luck plays a part and I have been lucky. There are many people who have played a big part in seeing the book you hold in your hands become the finished article it is today.

Part of my luck was to meet my literary agent, Philip Patterson of Marjacq Scripts. Phil took a chance on *Heartman* and has stood solidly behind it ever since. 'Mr P', as I like to refer to him, has suffered my constant emails of enquiry and has been through the lows of the rejection letters during the submission process and the ultimate high of finally brokering the deal with my publishing house. Always grumpy, but always right, his belief in me as a writer and in the material never wavered and I will be eternally grateful to him. Thanks must also go to the wonderful Marjacq Scripts team, Luke Speed, Isabella Floris and Guy Herbert, each of whom have played a very special part in bringing *Heartman* to fruition.

Thanks also to my miracle worker editor, Karyn Millar, and the brilliant team at Black & White Publishing, Alison McBride, Campbell Brown and Janne Moller, each of who had the same vision for *Heartman* as I did and ran with it wholeheartedly. Cheers, guys.

Special thanks to some great writers, the wonderful Mari Hannah and Anne Zouroudi, who both held my hand through good and bad times throughout the submission process. Thanks also to Damien G. Walter of *The Guardian* and Emlyn

Rees, who first picked up on *Heartman* and pointed me in the right direction. I'm indebted, you are both gentlemen of the first order, and the beers are at the bar.

Gratitude and love also to the fantastic Julie P. Noble for affording me her time and wit for those first read-throughs: you are a real rock and sounding board. A special shout of thanks to all the creative-writing students at Leicester University who critiqued my early work, and to Steve Jackman and June Watson of the Salmon Free House here in Leicester for inviting me to become their first Writer in Residence and for brewing the great 'Ellington's Ale'.

I tip my cap towards my old boss and dear friend, William Cheetham Fletcher. You may be in the book in name only, but your influence, guidance and wisdom will be with me forever.

Thank you to my family, sister Sally and to my parents, Ann and Pat, who have believed in their son these past forty-nine years and continue to do so, despite not really believing that being a writer is a "proper job".

Lastly, to my partner, Jen, whose love and care knows no bounds and who told me things would work out during the dark times ... Guess what, they did. I could not have done it without you and my two little princesses, Enya and Neve, who keep their daddy young and on his toes. We make a great team.